A Strong and
Sudden Thaw

A Strong and Sudden Thaw

R. W. Day

Lethe Press
Maple Shade, NJ

This Lethe Press edition published 2009 by Lethe Press, 118 Heritage Avenue, Maple Shade, NJ 08052.

Printed in the United States of America
Book Design by Toby Johnson
Cover art by Anne Cain

ISBN 1-59021-063-8   978-1-59021-063-5

Library of Congress Cataloging-in-Publication Data

Day, R. W. (Rebecca W.), 1962-
  A strong and sudden thaw / R.W. Day.
    p. cm.
  Originally published: Colton, Calif.: Iris Print, c2006.
  ISBN 1-59021-063-8
  1. Young gay men--Fiction. 2. Dragons--Fiction. I. Title.
  PS3604.A987S77 2008
  813'.6--dc22
                            2008045506

A Strong and Sudden Thaw

Chapter 1

There's an old scenic view about halfway up the mountain, alongside where the old highway runs. The signs are fading, of course, and the pavement's cracked and ruined, invaded years ago by roots of the scrub pines reclaiming what men stole from them back in the Before. There used to be a fence, a low barrier of iron-grey metal put up by the old people, but it's gone now too. My Mam always told me not to lean on that fence, and she was right, because one day late last summer, after a torrential rain that left us all knee-deep in cold black muck, that twisted metal fence went right over the edge. Just following after our whole world, I guess, plummeting over the edge into the abyss. Or at least that's what Grandmam says, and she ought to know, as she remembers the Before times. She tells stories that make the old world sound like spun sugar candy you get at the Harvest Fair. Rich and sweet, but destined to crumble away at the first hard rain.

But to me, the land is still sweet and the old scenic view a touch of heaven. I can't imagine how those old people in their metal wagons could have ever seen anything so fair as those far distant accordion-pleated ridges littered with the skeletons of trees, stark and bleached, reaching silently skyward in a useless appeal to the heavens, the patchwork of fields and red-roofed farmhouses, and soft clouds like the wool of our flock blending with the smoke from the chimneys to rise on the thermals.

This fall day, there was hawks riding the thermals, too, swooping lower now and again to spy out a mouse or ground squirrel. That time of year, game's hard to find, for hawks or for humans. But as I watched, the big one—the male—stopped, and I could see him hanging there, waiting and watching. Then he descended, spiraling down into the valley while his mate screamed in triumph.

Heavy wings beating the air, the male rose again, and I could see he had prey in his talons. Grandmam says it used to be that you couldn't even see into the next valley over because the air was so heavy with smoke and such from the machines. I can't fathom that. The air's always been clear, and mostly so cold and sharp it cuts you when you breathe, but I wouldn't have it any other way, as in those old times I wouldn't have been able to see the hawks in the valley like I do.

As I watched the birds take their prey off to their young, a shadow rippled over them and across the valley. I looked up, and above the hawks, so far distant in the sky that they seemed as toys, I saw the dragons. Still alive—so the posse had failed. Pa had figured they would.

Those dragons. There's a mating pair like with the hawks, or at least that's what we think. Jerzy Dodd, our hired man, claims there's three, maybe four, but Master Burke the School says he's wrong as dragons are territorial, not pack animals, and if there were three, the two would turn on the third and kill it. Unless the third was a baby. We figure there will be babies. That's one truth you can't ignore, male and female together eventually leads to babies, as true for dragonkind as humankind.

We're not sure where they came from, but Jerzy was the first to see them up in the high hills while he was tending our sheep. He'd gone behind a tree to—well, you can figure out what he was doing—heard a frantic panicked bleating and come running to find four sheep, one clutched in each cruel talon, winging their way upward to the top of Pine Bluff Ridge.

Of course nobody'd believed him. Pa figured he was making up tales to cover his own irresponsibility, and that the four sheep had really been taken by wolves or fallen into a crevasse and lost. But about two weeks later, the dragons lifted young Lorna Massie straight out of her playpen in the yard of her very own house. Lorna's mam had been hanging out the wash, had gone in for some extra clothespins and come out right in time to see the dragon, bigger than the Massies' whole house, scooping little Lorna up. She flung a pickaxe at the beast, and a scale had fallen off.

Well, everybody believed then. Jane Massie was a no-nonsense sort of woman, not the type for flights of fancy, and besides, there was that scale, green-gold and leathery, on display down at the school plain as the nose on your face. Lorna was gone, the scale was there. Added up pretty neat, folks thought. And then there were other sightings—for a while it seemed that you weren't somebody in our town if you hadn't seen the dragons.

Got to the point where folks was keeping their children so close that you'd think it was dead winter, not the middle of a fairly mild Indian summer. Still, you couldn't blame them. Bigger folk could spot the dragons and take cover, but the children hadn't a chance. I think that's where the old stories about virgins come from. In the olden days, anybody old enough to get out of the way was likely married off already. It was the young ones that got picked off.

So Sheriff Fletcher got a band of men together, and formed a posse to kill the dragons. About a week back they set off up the mountain, all grim and determined. My Pa and I watched them go, standing near the burying ground with Burke the Digger.

"Doomed to fail," Pa said, shaking his head as the line of men trudged by. Sheriff Fletcher had deputized Mister Zack Tyree to lead the group made up of three claim farmers from the south part of the county that I didn't know; Curtis Henslow, who kept chickens; and Mayor Casteel's do-nothing nephew Elmer.

"Elmer Casteel gets within fifty yards of a dragon, he'll shit himself. Tyree's the only one can hit the broad side of a barn, and he's got but one arm." The Digger spat sideways. "Should'a taken you, Brock. Hell, even young Davey here could handle himself better'n that bunch."

"Didn't ask me," Pa had said, and that was true. It was also true that my Pa was the best hunter in the valley, and everybody knew it. We always had meat on our table, even in the darkest winter, and he could track darn near anything that walked. Grandmam used to say it was a mercy the Ice had come, because if Pa had had to live in Before, he'd have been lost. So I wondered why he wasn't invited to join the dragon hunters—made no sense at all.

On the way back up the hill to our place that day, Pa had opined that, with the exception of Mister Zack, who'd likely been the sheriff's choice, the posse had been selected to give Elmer Casteel a chance to cover himself in glory so he could win a rich wife and maybe get out of Mayor Casteel's hair and quit asking for money all the time. Now, seeing the dragons still flying high above me, I wondered if the mayor had managed to solve his problem in a more permanent way. Money don't do you much good from inside a dragon's belly.

The dragons circled a few more times, then headed south. I pulled my jacket tight, wishing it would be truly warm, like in the stories Grandma told about Before. But it wasn't, and wasn't ever like to be in my lifetime. Those old days was a tale whose end had been told.

Dusk was already coming on by the time I was in sight of home. Our cabin sat atop a middling sized hill, and all the lands around it sloping down to the creek and a good ways beyond were Anderson lands, and had been since before the Ice. The sheep were back from the summer pastures now, and I could hear the sounds of the bells that marked them as ours. Jerzy was herding them into the barn, an unsettled cluster of dingy white bodies bleating and baaing as I passed.

The sheep were Mam's. She managed the flock and paid Jerzy's keep and the shearers in the spring from profits she got off the wool, which she sold in bulk to Perkin Weaver and sent to the cities in trade. I hate sheep. My sisters love them. All three of them adopt a new lamb each spring as their own special pet. Not me. Sheep are stupid—I've seen a flock of sheep follow their bellwether into a gully in a storm. The whole flock would have drowned if I hadn't been there to help Jerzy drive them out. Pa says I'm like him in that—he don't like sheep much either, though he likes the money they bring into the house. He says sheep and people are alike, mostly. I don't know that I agree, but he says I just haven't lived long enough yet.

"Boy, is your Mam mad at you, David," Jerzy called after me. "Says you and Benny C was supposed to be wintering in the herbs today. Benny C had to do it alone and he ain't shut up about it all afternoon!"

His sing-song voice faded away as I trudged the last few steps towards the cabin. He was right; I'd forgot completely. The herbs could have waited a day, though, or Ruby could have helped Benny C—it weren't like bringing herbs into the greenhouse was man's work. I'd have to sweet talk Mam, court her with the brace of rabbits I'd snared. Steeling myself for an argument, I noticed a strange horse tied up to our barn fence. Company. There weren't any way Mam would berate me in front of company. Sighing with relief, I swung the rabbits over my shoulder and pushed opened the door.

Smoking oil lamps blazed everywhere and the long table was set out with Grandmam's old china dishes over a plain white cloth. Grandmam says our cabin would have been called tiny back in the old days, but I can't fathom that. It's got a large common room where we do our living, then back behind are two goodly bedrooms, one for Mam and Pa, and one for Grandmam. A ladder leads to a loft above the common room where there are two more rooms, one for boys, and one for girls.

Because our place was built in the Before, there's a bathroom indoors too, but it don't work proper no more. We wash up in the tub, hauling water from the fire, but for our other needs, it's the outhouse in back. Grandmam says our place was originally a vacation cabin for Pa's family. I'm not sure what that means, really. She says it's like a house you only lived in sometimes, but I don't understand that—if you don't take care of your place year round, it'll fall to pieces pretty fast. I guess things was different then.

While Grandmam tended to the fire, Mam was working at the big black cook-stove, sending Delia and Ruby scurrying around like chickens with their heads cut off, fetching and toting and setting out food. Benny C was nowhere to be found, probably hiding in the barn pretending to do chores, sulking about me. Pa was seated at the table talking to the guest—Mister Zack Tyree, his sleeve pinned up at the elbow to hide where he'd lost his arm. So the posse was back, then.

"David, where have you been?" Mam spun around from the fire and almost struck Delia with her wood stirring spoon.

I held out the rabbits in mute apology. She shook her head and sighed. "Lord, you're your father's son. Take those skinny little coneys out to the larder and mind you hang them high, you hear?"

She weren't mad, then. That's what she always said when I come home, as though after hunting more than half my life, I'd forget to hang meat out of reach of scavengers. If she'd been mad, she'd have just taken the rabbits herself. I went out to the lean-to that served as our larder and strung up the rabbits. I'd skin them later and we'd have rabbit stew tomorrow.

Coming back into the warmth of the cabin I caught the smell of something roasting in the oven: mutton, I thought. When I said I hated sheep, I should have said I love them...served with new potatoes and fresh mint. The aroma was mouth-watering, and I was suddenly starved.

Mam lifted the speckled roaster from the oven. "Can I help?"

"Oh, just stay out of my hair." Mam shook her head. "Go on and sit with your Pa and help make Mister Zack feel at home."

Mister Zack was talking as I slid onto the bench next to Pa. "...and I'd not have credited it, Brock, if I'd not seen it with my own eyes. Big as houses and covered in scales."

Pa shook his head. "And you say your rifle didn't penetrate the hide?"

Now, that surprised me. Mister Zack Tyree was what Mam called a proper gentleman. He had a huge spread of land to the south of town and a house that would've held three of ours, which had been in his family since a hundred years before the Ice or more. His rifle was dead-on accurate and gorgeous to boot, all inlaid with fancy silver.

"Do you mean your silver rifle, Mister Zack?" I asked.

"Yes sir, David, that's exactly what I mean." Mister Zack leaned back in my Pa's chair, stretching his one full arm and his half arm behind him. "I got off three rounds point blank and you'd have thought my bullets were cast out of rubber, not lead." He leaned forward and grinned sort of wicked-like. "That fool Casteel had one of those new army guns and the bloody thing jammed six ways to Sunday."

Pa nodded. "The more moving parts you get on something, the more things go wrong. Like I've told you, Zack, in these times we're best off using older guns with simple actions, things we can fix ourselves without factories and trained gunsmiths."

I'd gone to school with Elmer Casteel—he'd been a few years ahead, but we'd read the same lessons sometimes as he wasn't the brightest wick in the lamp. "What did Elmer do then, Mister Zack?" I asked, curious.

Mam was setting steaming dishes of food around us and from the corner of my eye I saw Benny C slip in from outside. He sidled up to me and poked me hard in the back, but I ignored him, so he went off towards the fire to warm himself.

"When his gun jammed—and I might add that the dragons had not even deigned to notice our presence to that point—Elmer, brave scion of the Mayor's line that he is, threw that expensive firearm into the air and flew like a bat out of hell down the side of the mountain. He tripped on a root, twisted his ankle, and sliced up his lip."

Couldn't have happened to a better man. "Good."

"David!" Mam's hand reached out and cuffed the side of my ear, but not hard enough to hurt.

"Sorry, Mam." Though I weren't, not in the least. I turned back to Mister Zack, who looked for all the world like he agreed with me. "Is Elmer okay?"

"Not to hear him tell it. He made two of those claim farmers carry him in a litter all the way back to town, and he went straight to the healers. Was a bit put out when he discovered they were both upriver delivering a baby."

Mam was herding the younger ones to the table, settling Delia and Ruby on their bench. They squeezed together to make room for Benny C, who'd normally have sat by me, but Pa was there since Mister Zack had taken his chair. The baby was missing.

"Where's Almond?"

"She's down with a sore throat and fever," Mam replied, spooning out rich helpings of roast and potatoes onto the china plates. "And speaking of healers, you can take her down the hill to be looked over tomorrow."

It weren't a request, so although I'd planned to go check the traps in the morning, I just nodded and waited for the plates to be filled. Mister Zack and Pa had stopped talking, too, and Mister Zack was eyeing the food hungrily.

"May-Marie, that smells divine. Beef pot roast? I haven't had roast beef in a dog's age." I remembered that Mister Zack, being a widower, would be mostly left to his own devices when it come to meals.

Mam smiled and the compliment lit up her face brighter than the oil lamp hanging down over the table. My mam was a beautiful woman once, or so Grandmam says. I think she's still beautiful, with her thick honey hair and green eyes, but she's tired all the time and her face looks all washed out and grey from all the work she does. "And you won't be having it yet tonight, I'm afraid, Zack. It's mutton—I'm culling some of the rams before the true cold settles in."

"Well, whatever it is, it looks and smells delicious. And it's food I didn't have to cook, so I'm thankful for it." Mister Zack tucked his napkin onto his lap.

"Zack, we'd be honored if you'd give the blessing."

We all settled to quiet then as Mister Zack cleared his throat. Better him than me—I hated giving the blessing, especially when we had guests. Speaking out loud, talking to folks more than one at a time weren't something I was particularly fond of, and hadn't been since I was back at school and had made a complete fool of myself during the Fall Recitations every single year. Plus, I wasn't half sure there was anyone or anything listening to our blessing anyways. Not that I could say that to Mam, though.

"Thou who hast brought us safe through the rigors of the Ice and hast seen us to prosperity in this new time, look favorably upon Your children here assembled. Bless us with warmth and food and health. In the name of God. Amen."

"Amen," we all echoed, then for a while the only sounds was the unfamiliar chinking of silver on china. It was an odd sound—our everyday plates were wooden, carved by Pa. I expected Mister Zack Tyree ate off china plates every day of his life, and Mam would have been shamed to offer him dinner on ugly wood trenchers.

Though I tried not to stare as that'd get me sent to the barn for the rest of the meal, I watched Mister Zack from the corner of my eye. I'd never seen him eat before, but had often wondered how he managed it with one arm. It was a sight to see—he alternated fork and knife so deftly you'd have thought he was a whole man.

"So, Zack," Pa set his fork down. "You never did tell me how you managed to run those dragons to ground. Must have been a wonderment of tracking. No offense to you, but I didn't think you had those sorts of skills."

Everybody's eyes were on the guest, and I was glad Pa had brought the talk around to the dragons again, and I could see the younger ones were as well. They'd been shielded from a lot of the talk, but were curious about the beasts, as was natural.

Mister Zack laughed. "No offense taken, Brock. I'm a fair shot, but I couldn't track an elephant if it was fifty feet ahead of me with a sign tied to his ass-end. No, we ran across a small flock of goats—Brant McNally's, I think it was—completely untended, and Casteel came up with the idea of herding them out into open ground and waiting. Worked like a charm—that boy's got a devious mind."

"That seems awful cruel to those goats. They weren't doing nothing to warrant such treatment." My sister Ruby had a soft place in her heart for animals—all animals, probably even dragons. I really hoped Ruby married a town man, because if she had to survive on a farm doing her own butchering, she'd starve.

"Ruby!" Mam glared down on her like icicles. Children were mostly seen and not heard at the table, or else they weren't seen nor heard and ended up eating cold leftovers in the corner.

"No, May-Marie, it's a fair statement." Mister Zack turned to Ruby. "Don't fret, Miss Ruby. Those goats were old. Likely it was their year to be butchered in any case, and they went quick and for a good cause."

"Didn't work, though," Pa observed.

"Oh, it worked, all right. The dragons came; we just didn't have any weapon that would do the job." Mister Zack helped himself to seconds. "I tell you, Brock, I don't know what it's going to take to kill those things. They're gigantic and damn near armor plated."

"Giants." Grandmam had kept close to the fire as was her custom, not joining us at table. "There were giants in the earth in those days."

Mam gave her a sharp look, then turned to me. "David, take your grandmam a plate of vegetables."

I picked out the tenderest of the potatoes and carrots and put them in a small bowl. Grandmam took it, but made no attempt to eat, just sat staring into the fire, clutching onto the bowl for dear life.

"...will have to wait till spring now, I'm afraid," Mister Zack was saying as I got back to the table. "No point taking chances with the weather."

Pa was scowling. "Another five months of those damn things making off with the best of our flocks and driving the game away. We never had dragons in these parts before the Ice, damn its frosted soul."

"Brock, please, language—" Mam started to say, but Grandmam interrupted.

"Frost giants. It's Fimbulvetr; it's the cold before the end. Three ages of ice, then fire-giants will meet the frost-giants, Fenris Wolf will be released and the World Tree will be cut down." She looked fretful, holding her plate close to her as though one of those frost giants was lurking behind her to snatch it away.

"Fire giants would be a blessing right about now," Pa said mildly, looking across the table at Mam, who rose and led Grandmam away to her bedroom. "Sorry about my mother-in-law, Zack. She's getting on in years."

"No need to apologize." Mister Zack dismissed it with a wave of his one hand. "She's the only person left in this area who remembers Before. I think she's entitled to a little eccentricity. Though I admit to being curious as to what she's talking about."

"It's from her Bestamor, her own Grandmam. She was Danish and used to tell Gramdmam stories about them. Legends about their gods," I replied, staring down at the remnants of my plate. I loved listening to those stories, had begged over and over to hear about Loki and Thor and the rest when I was a young child. In school we'd learned the myths of the Greeks, but I'd never taken to those stories quite the same as to Grandmam's. Those old Danish people knew a thing or two about cold. No half-clothed nymphs and satyrs in Odin's hall.

"Ah." Mister Zack nodded, then got up from the table.

Pa stood up too. "David, I'll see Mister Zack to the road, then join you in the barn for night chores."

Ruby and Delia started in clearing the supper. Benny C would take a plate out to Jerzy, then he and the girls would get on with their school work. I was mighty glad those days were past for me. The only part of school I'd liked was the reading, and I could still borrow books from the school's meager lending library to my heart's content. Of course, I'd read them all ten times over before I'd ever left the schoolhouse, but at least now I wasn't expected to recite on them, I could just read for the joy of it.

Full dark had fallen, and a bitter wind sprung up from the west, carrying away the sounds of Pa and Mister Zack talking as they walked towards the Old Road. Our barn lay nestled into a fold of the hill, partially protected from the wind and rain and snow. Pa had built it, and it was solid and cozy, a home for the sheep during the cold months, and for Pa's horse Lightning and a small flock of chickens. Jerzy had a room in the back of it with his own hearth. I wouldn't have minded a place like that for myself someday, when I was grown. Mam spoke at times of building me a house when I married, but I didn't like that sort of talk much and would always turn the color of winter beets when she'd go on about it.

Marriage meant girls, and girls were trouble, and boring trouble at that. All clothes and cooking and begging to walk out with you, then when you finally gave in and went, they'd nothing at all useful to say. Joey Matthias said it didn't matter none, as girls weren't there to be talked to, and he'd go on about full breasts and tiny little waists and how fine they were, but I couldn't fathom it at all. And now Joey was getting married to some claim farmer's daughter not two years after we'd left school. No, that weren't for me.

I started in on my evening chores slowly, banking the barn fires so the animals would stay warm and safe, blanketing Lightning, and securing all the heavy wooden shutters. It was important work, especially this time of year when a freak storm could burst upon us at any time and the animals could freeze if the fire was left unmade. And if not made well, the fire could get out of hand and the barn and stock could burn.

Behind me, Pa came in and started pitching hay into the troughs. The larders were full now as harvest was behind us, and the scent of the hay mixed up with the stale sweat of the animals to tickle my nose. It was a home smell, a comfort smell like the roast mutton had been, and having Pa beside me, even though, as was his wont, he didn't speak at all, that was comfort too. Going off to a house of my own, with or without a wife, would mean an end to this. It would be change.

Oh, the seasons changed, with winter coming hard on fall, and then spring fighting tooth and nail for a toehold come April, but those shifts were temporary, and one chilly fall night was the same as any other, be it last year or the year before going back to before I was born. My leaving so that it would be Benny C who'd come out here every night and work beside Pa, that was for keeps. And what was happening to Grandmam; that was for keeps as well.

Pa must have somehow sensed my thoughts, for he stopped working and started stroking Lightning's brown flank. "David, when you take Almond down to Healer Findlay tomorrow, you might ask her if she could ride up and have a look at your grandmam."

I nodded. The chickens settled into their roosts and the sheep called softly to each other. I wondered, did they talk? Did the old ewes tell the young lambs stories about sheep gods and ram heroes?

"May-Marie won't say anything, not to you, not even to me, but she's worried. Sarah's over one hundred years old, it's natural for her to be declining, but it might be there's something we could do to make her comfortable."

As she's dying. I heard his unfinished thought. Grandmam's body had been frail for long as I could remember, but till recently her mind had been ever clear, and her wit would stab into you like sharpened steel. I closed my eyes and tried to picture our cabin without her in it; her chair empty and the fire tended by Delia or Almond. No. That was a change I couldn't conceive.

"Pa—"

He shook his head. "Just talk to the healer, David. That's all you can do. People die. It's a fact of life, whether we like it or not. Your Grandmam's had more years than most. Be thankful for that."

He gave Lightning a precious lump of store-sugar and murmured soft words to her that I couldn't make out, then left me alone to finish my work.

Chapter 2

Because Almond weren't yet five and feeling poorly, Pa gave me leave to take her down the mountain on Lightning. Lightning, poor mare, is the most ill-named horse in three counties. Mam says she ought to be called Wishful Thinking or Hope Springs Eternal, but though she's slow, she's a good and patient friend. So not in a dash of lightning, but slowly and carefully, she picked her way over the broken pavement of the Old Road leading to town.

I walked ahead leading the reins while Almond bobbed in the saddle, clinging lightly to the pommel in her fever. We'd been lucky in our family and Burke the Digger hadn't yet had to carve a stone with the name 'Anderson.'. But Almond's black hair hung lank over her thin face, and she was quiet the whole way down to the town of Moline. I was more than a little bit fearful for her.

To call Moline a town is, I'm afraid, more than a shade misleading. Compared to what I've been told of the big towns and cities, it's little more than a village; just a town square, an old highway that turns into Main Street as it passes through, and a couple of cross streets. The square holds the school, which also serves as a town hall, for it's the largest and best constructed building left standing. There's a church and a tiny post office nearby, Perkin Weaver's workshop and a few other storefronts where tradespeople conduct their business, a general store, and at the far south end of Main Street, the healer's house.

I mounted Lightning just shy of where Main Street begins in earnest, not wanting to walk into town like a man unfit to sit a horse. Almond leaned back against me, so sweet and trusting, and forgetting my disbelief of the night before, I said a quick prayer for her. It was cold as is fitting for October, but not so cold as to make riding unpleasant, and the touch of the wind on my face was gentle enough. A month or so forward, it would be biting, and nobody in their right mind would have any inch of their skin exposed to the elements.

The healer's house was built of rose colored bricks, a small, snug building, one compact story with dormers above, set slightly apart from the daily life of the town to give some privacy to those who come for treatment. I helped Almond from Lightning's broad back and knocked at the door. Healer Findlay had delivered all us children; she'd nursed us through childhood illnesses and had set the bones in my leg when I'd fallen down a cliff and the bones in my arm when I'd tumbled from Lightning learning to ride. She'd have Almond fixed up right as rain, I knew it.

The door opened, but it weren't a grizzled haired woman who stood framed in the open door. It was a man; a young man not much older than I, dressed in neat but threadbare clothing, and I recollected that Healer Findlay had taken an assistant.

"Hello, I'm Callan Landers. Did you need some help?" His voice was light, almost musical, but something in it reminded me of my Pa's the night before, reassuring and calm. This Callan Landers couldn't be more the opposite of Pa, though. Where my pa was short, burly, and strongly built, the healer was tall—taller than me, even, and I was taller than anyone in my family. Tall and slender, what Grandmam would have described as a 'long drink of water.' His hair reminded me of sunlight and shadow dancing over a field of wheat, dark in places, light in others, and his eyes were the almost invisible blue of the spring sky.

I felt awkward and clumsy as I smiled back at him. "My sister's sick. I was hoping we could see Healer Findlay?"

He knelt down so he was eye-level to Almond, who looked at him with the first spark of interest she'd shown since we left the cabin—she almost never saw strangers. "So you're not feeling well? Why don't you bring your brother into the house where it's warm?"

She nodded and grabbed hold of my hand, pulling me into the entrance hall.

"Healer Findlay's upriver, a good day's ride away. I only got back to town late last night myself," the young healer was saying as he brought us through the inner door to the exam room. "I'd be happy to have a look at your sister, though, and see what I can do."

"That'd be awful good of you. I'm David Anderson."

"Hello, David. I think I've seen you around town before. And this is?" He looked down at Almond, who had suddenly gone shy, clutching my hand and hiding her face against my trousers.

"Almond, quit that." I tried to pry her off me. "This is Almond, and I don't know what's come over her, Healer Landers, she's not normally shy about speaking up. Mam worries that when she starts school she's going to be forever writing lines and kept after for talking out of turn."

"She's ill and in a strange place with a strange person. It's not surprising she's a bit shy." He knelt again. "Almond. That's a lovely name. Did you know it's the name of a tree?"

Almond looked up, eyes big, and shook her head.

"Well, it is—a great big tree with white blossoms. Would you like to see a picture?"

She nodded again and let go my hand. Healer Landers turned to a long bookshelf that stretched almost the whole length of the room and pulled a thick volume from its place. I made out the words 'trees' and 'North America' on the cover before he flipped it open and his nimble fingers turned the pages to a color picture of a tall tree covered in white flowers.

"That's an almond tree from back in old springtime," he explained. Almond took the book, and Healer Landers swiftly plucked her off the floor and set her up high on a table, where she continued to stare at the book. It was the only book she'd ever held, as our school texts were too precious to be trusted to so small a child.

"I don't reckon we have those round here."

The healer had put a stethoscope around his neck and was warming the loose end in his hands. "No, not any more, Mr. Anderson."

"Mr. Anderson's my Pa. I'm David, Healer." I held out my hand and he took it.

"Callan. Stupid to be so formal, as I doubt I'm much older than you." His hand was cool to the touch and clean, and I felt ashamed of my square cut nails which never seemed to rid themselves of traces of dirt. He had a gentleman's hands, like Mister Zack. I turned his name over in my head, but I couldn't say it, couldn't treat such a person as though I was equal to him.

"I'm seventeen." Then I flushed, my mam's training too ingrained; I couldn't lie, not even about my age. "Or will be, come April."

"Twenty-three last month." He'd slid the stethoscope up under Almond's shirt. "Take a deep breath, sweetie." He moved the instrument around on her back and chest, and I wondered what those hands would feel like on my bare skin. I'd never had such a thought before; it troubled me, so I turned away and looked at the long row of books. I'd not seen so many books in all my life—not even the schoolhouse held so many. Some of the titles had unfamiliar healer words, diagnosis and treatment of disease and anatomy, but others sounded like story books. I wondered if Healer Landers had read them all.

20   R. W. Day

"There's been pneumonia around, but her lungs sound fine. Good." He put the stethoscope down and turned back to Almond. "What seems to be the matter, sweetie?"

"My thwoat." Tears were welling up in her eyes in a manner that I knew very well was done a-purpose. She'd charm the skin off a snake, Almond would. I started forward, to berate her for making a fuss, but he caught my eye and shook his head ever so slightly.

"Well, let's have a look, shall we? Stick out your tongue."

Almond clammed up tight and shook her head.

"Mam's told her not to stick out her tongue at people," I explained. "She's not wanting to be rude to you."

He laughed. You hear about folks having a musical laugh. Till then, I'd thought that was just fancy talk, but Healer Landers' laugh was like a low peal of bells from the old church tower. "Your mother's right, and you should normally never put your tongue out at someone, but I can't see what's amiss with your throat if your mouth's all closed up tight as a drum." He paused and thought for a moment. "How about I stick out my tongue at you first, Miss Almond? Then you'd have to get me back, or it wouldn't be fair."

She considered that for a moment, then nodded. Soon enough her mouth was open and he was pressing her tongue out of the way with a piece of polished wood, peering down her throat.

"This would be so much easier with artificial lighting," he sighed. "But it looks like she's got a slight inflammation."

"Mam's had her gargle with salt water, given her willow bark tea for fever."

"That's good—she should keep doing that, and I'll give her some horehound candies to keep the throat moist." He sounded angry. Almond was looking at the tree book again, turning the pages almost reverently.

"What's the matter?"

He went to a bin and started filling a paper poke with the speckled brown candies. "It's just so infuriating. Look at this." The healer set down the sack and pulled a large red book down from the shelf, thumbed through it, then pointed to tiny words on the yellowing page. "I'm almost positive she has a bacterial infection, probably streptococcal. This book tells exactly how to treat it, but it's useless. In the old days, we could have given her a pill or a shot that would have cleared it almost instantly. Now," he sighed. "Now we know what's wrong. We know what to do about it, but mostly can't do a damn thing to fix it."

There weren't much I could say to that, so I just nodded.

"I mean, Healer Findlay's upriver at the Benson farm right now. They've had a baby that's not quite right—it's not able to eat. That baby's going to die because we can't do a simple surgery that in your great-grandfather's day would have been routine. It happens every day, David, and sometimes I just get so incredibly tired of it all."

He was leaning against the desk, not looking at me, and I could sense that he wasn't truly talking to me so much as to himself. Truthfully, I didn't give a lot of thought to what we'd lost from Before—life was what it was, what it had always been, but I could feel the frustration coming off him in waves. Hesitating, but drawn to make some gesture of comfort, I reached out my hand and rested it on his shoulder, and he relaxed.

"I'm sorry. I've just met you, and here I am going off on you like that. Forgive me?" He turned to face me, but my hand lingered on his shoulder. It felt right that it should.

"Nothing to forgive." A loud pounding noise shook the small house.

"What the...?" Before the healer had time to go towards the door, it burst open and Elmer Casteel stumped into the room.

"I need a healer. Now." Elmer's gravely voice sounded like a growling animal.

Healer Landers stepped forward, deftly positioning himself between Elmer and my sister. "I'm with someone right now, but if you'd like to have a seat in the waiting room, I'll be with you as soon as I'm done."

"I've waited all goddamn night!" He seemed to fill up the room, soaking up all the peace of the place like a big old foul rag soaking up water in the byre.

The healer was outward calm, but I could see tiny tremors in his hands. Elmer Casteel could have snapped him like a twig. "I've been here, doors open, since just after dawn. It's going on midafternoon—if it was such an emergency, you should have come in earlier. Now, I'm afraid, you're just going to have to wait."

That didn't sit well. Elmer'd likely been hungover from drinking rotgut whiskey with his buddies half the night. Nobody ever saw him out before noon, injured or not. "I've been maimed protecting this town from a monster, and I'm entitled to treatment when I say!"

I stepped out from the shadowed corner. "Didn't know running like a scared rabbit was protecting the town, Elmer. Guess you learn something new every day."

He rounded on me, but I knew he wouldn't dare hit me, not out of respect for the healer's house, but because I was as big as him, the coward. "That's a goddamn lie. Who's been spreading that shit around?"

"Mister Zack Tyree was up to the house for dinner last night. He told us you threw your fancy gun away like garbage and went tearing off down the hill, tripped yourself up. Now, unless you're saying Mister Zack was lying..."

He went pale. There weren't no way he would accuse Mister Zack of being a liar, not in front of witnesses. One-armed or not, Mister Zack would pound Elmer into pieces. In our world, a man's word was all he had. We didn't have lawyers and contracts nor even much in the way of law enforcement beyond a sheriff, so your word was bond, and calling someone a liar was an almost unpardonable insult.

"Well, it don't matter how I got hurt," he mumbled. "I'm bleeding and I need a goddamn healer."

"That busted lip don't look half so bad as the one I gave you about four years ago when you was picking on Benny C in the schoolyard, Elmer. Now go on and sit down in the waiting room till Healer Landers is done with my sister. And you watch your foul mouth in front of her." I wasn't scared of Elmer Casteel and he knew it.

"You ain't heard the last of this, Anderson," he said, but he went, though not into the waiting room; out onto the street, judging by the slamming of the doors.

"He's probably gone off to find more liquor," I warned. "I expect he'll be back."

"Thank you for stepping in. I'm not much for physical confrontations in general."

"Didn't think you were." Suddenly it mattered that he not think me a common street brawler. "Nor am I, when it comes to that. But you can't back down from a bully like Elmer or he'll never let up on you."

"I know. I'd have managed him if I'd had to, but I'm glad you were here." He smiled, really smiled for the first time, and it went straight through me. "Though I'm sorry your sister had to hear all that."

Almond had spent the entire ruckus with Elmer just paging through the tree book, off in her own world. "She didn't pay it no mind at all. She surely loves your book."

The healer looked down at Almond, her nose riveted in a picture of a tree with green leafy branches sweeping gracefully to the ground as though it was living rain. "She can't read yet, can she?"

"No, sir. She'll start to school in the spring. The school don't have any books like that one, though." My eyes drank in the long shelf of books again. "Nor near so many as you have here. Are all these yours?"

"Oh, no. About half of the medical texts belong to Jeannie—sorry, I mean Healer Findlay. Some are mine, though. I brought them with me when I came here. Would you like to borrow one?"

Books are rare. Most families don't own more than a Bible, and quite a few not even that. When the Ice come on so sudden and the cold looked to last forever, folks panicked and burned darn near anything that would burn, books included. That Healer Landers, no, that Callan—I forced myself to think the name—would lend a book to a grubby boy who was a virtual stranger, well, that set me back, and he could see it in my face.

"I mean it. I can tell about people, whether they're book people or not. And you are. I trust you. Go on, take one." His slender hand traced enticingly over the spines of the books. All older than Grandmam, likely. It would be worth a fortune in the cities, this collection.

"I wouldn't know what to take." I moved closer to him, examining the row of titles and authors. The nearness of his body was comforting, like a warming pan in my bed of a cold night and yet disquieting somehow at the same time. I recognized one of the authors' names. "Mark Twain."

"Oh yes. Huckleberry Finn. That's wonderful. Have you read anything by Twain before?"

I nodded. "The school's got a copy of Tom Sawyer that I must've read twenty times. Is this sort of the same?"

He pulled down the book, a tan colored hardback with a picture of two boys, one black, one white, on a raft. "It's got some of the same characters, but it's a much richer story, far more a 'grown-up' book. I think you'll like it."

Our hands touched briefly as he handed me the volume. He looked me straight in the eye and I was lost in a dazzle of blue. I could feel my heart pounding in my ribcage as though I'd run a hard mile. "Thanks," I said, and looked down, suddenly shy.

"I'm happy to do it—maybe we can talk about it, when you're done." He turned away and began washing his hands in one of two basins set out on the table, not looking at me anymore, as though he was somehow embarrassed too. "Not too many people around here are interested in books."

"Kind of hard to be interested in something you ain't g...don't have." I never bothered much with proper speech, not even in the schoolroom, though I knew it right enough. Grandmam hated how we talked, so with her I forced the patterns and rhythms of the country down so she could pretend that the world hadn't never changed and her kin weren't ignorant hillbillies. It mattered with her. And for some reason, it mattered now, with Callan.

"That's true enough. I was raised surrounded by books, so I forget things are different here."

I wanted to ask about his childhood, would have loved to sit down with a hot mug of chicory or sassafras tea and listen to that voice for hours, but Almond was waiting, and I was pretty sure Callan had work to do. For that matter, so did I.

"How much do we owe you for Almond?"

There was a homemade bead abacus on the table, but Callan didn't seem to need it. "Are you paying in trade or cash?"

"Either one, whichever you prefer." Though it was still being issued by the government, cash money was rare. Most folks did their business in trade, but Mam got cash money for the wool she sold to the cities and Pa and I for the furs we trapped in winter, so we usually had coin.

"Five dollars cash, then, please. So few people have money, and I think we've about reached our limit of dried meat for this year." He made a face, and as I counted out the worn coins, I had a thought.

"I don't imagine Healer Findlay's much good in the kitchen."

"Neither of us are what you'd call chefs, but we make do." He touched Almond on the head and she looked up, startled, as though she'd been in another world. "You can look at the book again next time you come, Miss Almond. Or I have a nice one with flowers you might like."

"Thank you, Healer," she said, and her little arms came round and gave him a hug. He responded, kissing the top of her head.

"Come to dinner, then." I weren't a sick child, didn't need comforting like Almond, so why in the name of all heavens did I suddenly want to trade places with my baby sister? "My Mam's a wonderful cook, and besides, Pa wanted me to see if you'd come up and have a look at my Grandmam. She's doing poorly." I knew Pa had his mind set on Healer Findlay, but I wanted Callan. Wanted him to meet my family, to see my home as I'd seen his.

He lifted Almond off the table and set her on the floor. "All right. It will have to be tomorrow though, as I can't leave town with Healer Findlay gone."

"Right," I agreed. "Elmer Casteel might get a hangnail or something."

He laughed again, and so did I, and so did Almond, though she had no idea what she was laughing over. "It was nice to meet you, David."

"Yeah. Nice to know you, too. Callan." I said the name slowly, like we said 'amen' at the end of the blessing, and I held the sound of it on my tongue, wanting to keep the memory of the word locked there. He walked us to the front door and I could feel him, watching me ride away.

The schoolyard was chock full of children out for their afternoon recess, so I waved to Benny C, who was standing against a wall with his friends, trying to look tough. I didn't see Delia or Ruby, but a passel of girls was clumped together by the well, so I figured they was there somewhere. Almond made noises like she wanted to get down and play, but I kept her firm in front of me, wrapped in her coat and sucking on one of the horehound candies Callan had given her.

"No, Almond. You'll go to school in the spring, and then you can play on the yard." It was near time for the school year to end, just another week or two, and then the cold would keep the young ones indoors till spring. Grandmam says the school year used to run September to June and the summer was free. Before she started to get so forgetful, she'd tell stories of long lazy days chasing through the woods wearing hardly nothing at all, splashing in the creeks and swimming in something called a swimming pool, a type of false pond with clean, clear water.

Nowadays, the water never gets warm enough in these parts that you'd willingly dunk yourself in it, so I didn't know how to swim, nor did anyone I knew, but Grandmam made it sound like heaven, floating weightless in warm water with the sun beating down on you. Nowhere to go, nothing to do but rest. I couldn't conceive of it. There was always chores, always work to be done.

I wondered if Callan knew how to swim—he'd said he grew up surrounded by books, and that probably meant somewhere to the south of us, so it could be. As Lightning meandered down Main Street, I took Huckleberry Finn from inside my coat and looked at the two boys on the raft. What would that be like, two friends floating down the river into who knew what sort of adventure? If I hadn't had Almond in front of me, I'd have started reading right then.

"David!" It was Benny C, hurrying down from the schoolyard. "I almost forgot— Ma said for you to stop at the General, the R&A man's supposed to be in town with some new sort of wheat seed. She wants you to get some."

The Department of Reintroduction and Agriculture's forever trying to improve on the wheat and corn strains, make them more fit for the new climate, but it don't really seem to have worked yet. They get something that grows fine in a lab, but out here, where you can't predict the weather two days in a row, and where even in dead summer, a freak storm's likely to drop snow without warning, it's another story. But they keep trying, and so do we, as I'm fond of wheat bread when I can get it.

Haig's General Store is on the opposite end of Main from the healer's house, the last shop but one before you take the road back up the hill to our place. Only the tiny cottage where Taylor Mills attempts to eke out a living as an artist and jeweler stands beyond it. I expect he'd do much better over in Richmond or in the Southlands—we've not much extra money for fancy things, nor for the portraits he makes, though I've heard they're mighty fine. But he was born in these parts, so I suppose that's why he sticks it out. Home means something to most of us.

The General is a squared up log house that's been built on over the years as trade has flourished. There's a livery stable to the rear and a long fence in front of the storefront that I tied Lightning to, then deposited Almond in a corner of the porch and wrapped her up in both our coats, though the sun had come out and it wasn't too awfully cold for October.

"Is there pictures in your book, David?" she asked.

There were. I weren't happy about giving it up to her—having it near made me feel like I was still back at the office listening to Callan talk, but it would keep her quiet and still, so I handed it to her, warning her to take care of it.

The store was crowded with people, with the R&A man set up at the little table Mister Haig saved for the purpose. He must've just finished his talk, and was taking questions. All I wanted was to get my seed and get out—I'm not much of a farmer;

neither's Pa, really. But most of the crowd was claim farmers, always eager for any advantage they could get, for they had to produce enough crop to sell in order to keep title to their land.

A few of the men, friends of Pa's, spoke my name and touched their hats as I worked my way to the front, and I spoke back in turn. I had been out of school for almost two years now, doing a man's turn at our place for longer, but with these men I felt like a child, and expected I'd still a boy to them even when my hair had gone all grey.

"My question," a thin voice cut through the crowd, "is what's the R&A going to do about those dragons?"

I recognized the speaker as one of the claim farmers, though I couldn't put name to face. Immediately as he spoke you could feel the chill spread through the room, like when the pond iced over and everything froze, waiting.

"Dragons?" From where I stood, I could see the R&A man—he'd been talking quietly to Mark Bevins, a slight young farmer just starting out who'd been a year ahead of me at school, but when he heard the word 'dragons' he shut up right quick and his face turned pasty white. "I don't know what on earth you're talking about. There are no such things as dragons."

That got a reaction. You could hear rumbling about the scale on display down at the schoolhouse, and one of the claim farmers must have gone out with the posse, as he was shouting about how big they were up close. Joe Haig, who owned the store, came out from behind the counter kind of like he was ready to protect the R&A man if things went sour.

"No dragons? Tell that to little Lorna Massie, you pompous ass!" The shouting was growing louder.

The man was sweating, little beads of moisture clinging to his bushy moustache and sliding down his jowls. "I'm quite sure you're mistaken. What you're imagining to be a dragon is likely just a large turkey vulture or buzzard."

I snorted at that. It'd be some turkey vulture with a wingspan as wide as a house. "Well, I know vultures and I've seen these things, Mister, and they're not vultures."

There were murmurs of agreement, but the man looked at me, eyes narrowing as though to reproach me for speaking up in this adult company. Then he smiled, taking in my shabby country clothes. "Sounds like someone's been reading too many fairy tales in the schoolhouse."

Elmer Casteel would've hit him. But you don't get anywhere with people if you allow them to rile you up. I smiled back. "So you're saying the R&A don't know nothing about these dragons? They're not some new species you're trying to establish?" For they did that, too; bred and relocated game and farm animals, supposedly for our benefit.

He sighed impatiently. "Even assuming such creatures existed, which I assure you they do not, why would your government introduce deadly predators into a fragile ecosystem like this one? No. Now please, if you would like your wheat samples, please form an orderly line, and I'll be glad to dispense them. No more talk of dragons. Next it will be werewolves and vampires, I suppose." He chuckled, but the crowd was mutinously quiet as they formed a line.

As I was in no hurry I hung back, wandering out onto the porch to check on Almond who was happily telling herself a story from the pictures in Callan's book. A quick moving figure caught my eye and I looked up to see the healer himself, head down and wrapped in an oversized greatcoat, hurrying towards Taylor Mills' shop. I started to call out to him, but he was so clearly moving with a purpose that I kept my peace, wondering what purpose it could be that would send a young man I would swear had not two nickels of his own to rub together hurrying to that particular place.

Chapter 3

Mam's not one for lying abed in the morning, and when she's awake, we're all awake, so the sun had barely peeked over the eastern ridges before I was out in the barn, helping Jerzy with the morning chores. The byres and stables could use a good mucking out, but I hoped he'd do that on his own. It was shaping up to be a fine day, possibly one of the last fine days we'd have before the cold began to set in in earnest. Too fine a day for breathing dung and dust.

Lightning was gone from her stall, so Pa must have gone off early as was his wont this time of year. Some days he'd go down into town, others he'd ride over to Staunton for supplies we couldn't get locally, taking some of the furs to trade. Sometimes he'd take me with him, but I was glad today weren't one of those times. Callan was coming. To see Grandmam, I reminded myself, but it wasn't just the possibility of his helping her that was putting a spring in my step and a song on my lips.

Even Jerzy noticed it. "What's got you so happy?"

I just smiled at him, patted the nearest ewe on her woolly head and went in to breakfast, which was sausage and eggs, another reason to be joyful. I pulled out Huckleberry Finn and started reading, hoping to get a good start on the story before Callan came up the hill.

Of course, if you've got younger sisters, you can't do anything in peace. "David's got a book!" Delia's screech would peel the paint from walls. "Mam! David's got a book!"

"Shut up, Delia," I muttered, trying to keep my place.

"Where'd you come by that, David? Did you stop by the lending library yesterday?" The tone of Mam's voice said pretty clear that I'd better not have left Almond sick in the cold while I lingered over books.

"No, Mam. The book belongs to the healer's assistant, Callan Landers. He lent it to me."

She made an odd sort of noise, but didn't say nothing, just turned back to frying up sausage. Almond was sitting cross-legged near the fire, face all sticky from the candies, but she was clearly feeling better. "He's nice, Mama. He showed me a twee what's got my name."

"In a book," I explained. "He was real good with Almond. I told him what a fine cook you were, invited him up for dinner. Hope that's all right with you."

She smiled and began humming as she worked. Mam just loves to hear her cooking praised. "Of course, Son. Though we're just having those rabbits you brought in stewed with some vegetables and herbs."

That sounded a darn sight better than endless hunks of dried meat. As nobody said nothing about further chores, I kept on reading as Benny C and the girls went on down the hill to school, staying with the story till Mam finally realized I was sitting around the house on a perfectly fine day.

"David Anderson, put that book up and get outside. You know perfectly well that your Pa wanted you to walk the traplines this morning."

I was just thinking on whether I could walk the traplines with a book in my hand when Mam reached out and plucked it up from the table. "And I'll keep this safe. You don't want to give Healer Landers his book back with mud stains or worse."

I'd just been getting interested in the story, becoming acquainted with this slightly different, far more complicated Huck Finn and Tom Sawyer, so the normal feeling of freedom I'd have got from being outside on a blissful mid-morning was tainted some. Pa had taken the gun with him, but I didn't care. I had my hunting knife, my pride and joy.

The handle is antler, taken from the very first deer I ever killed. Deer are rare here now and getting rarer, and in truth, I'm glad of it. I don't mind shooting rabbits or squirrel or other small creatures, but I'll never forget the eyes of that deer staring back at me through the forest as I got it in my sights—it was as though it knew it was doomed. The venison was rich meat, but bought at a terrible high price. I made the knife handle to remember that.

The blade was Pa's when he was a boy and it's what they call Damascus work, beautiful ripply waves of metal in patterns like Jack Frost makes on the windows in winter. And it was strong; stronger than you could imagine. That knife could cut through fur and flesh and even bone near as easy as a table knife going through one of Mam's soft cheeses. I'd made a sheath for it with the help of Joe Haig's hired man

Philip, who was handy with leather, and I carried it with me most times, though Mam hated to see it strapped to my belt—she said it was barbaric. I suppose she was probably right, but it was handy to have it so close, and she knew good and well I'd never use it on a human being.

There were some parts of trapping that weren't much to my taste, but it was a fine walk and the weather couldn't have been better for October, warm enough to only need a midweight coat, my knit cap, and light gloves to protect my hands. On any ordinary day I'd have been long gone, but that morning I kept up what Grandmam used to call prevaricating and procrastinating, coming up with excuse after excuse as to why I couldn't set out.

The third time I went back into the house on some made-up errand, Mam put down her handwork and sighed in utter exasperation. "David, so help me, if you come back through that door one more time, I'm pulling the latch and you can sleep in the barn tonight. If your healer shows up while you're gone, I'm sure I'm capable of making him feel at home."

My healer. I liked the sound of that, thinking of Callan Landers as 'my healer.' I gave my Mam a kiss on the top of her head, and she grabbed hold of my hand, startled. I'm not much for physical affection most times, but the joy of the day that spread in front of me made it seem natural somehow.

I shouldered my small pack, which contained rope and bait and such things as I would need for my work, and started down the old gravel trail from the house to where I would pick up what was left of the Old Road. It went two directions, up towards our traplines and down to Moline, but when I got to the turn-off I sat down against the trunk of an old tree. It's not in my nature to shirk a job, but my mind was racing from one place to another, from Huck and Tom to Callan, to Elmer Casteel and the dragons and the R&A man, and I figured a few minutes pause wouldn't make no never mind. I closed my eyes, just for a moment to clear my mind.

"Isn't it a bit cold to be sleeping outside?"

My eyes flew open and I scrambled to my feet, arms and legs all a-kilter. His smile was like an invitation to a harvest feast. "Healer Landers, I'm..."

"Callan. Please. My friends call me by my name." Friends. I'd had some friends at school, certainly, though in the years since we'd left the schoolroom I'd seen little enough of them. The daily burden of living took too much to allow for idle pastimes. And really, they'd been more in the way of acquaintances than friends. A friend, a true friend who'd listen to me, who I could trust with all the secrets of my heart was something I'd not ever expected to find. Pa said my wife would be such a one, but I couldn't imagine baring my inner self to some silly girl.

"All right. Callan. I'm glad you found the place." He was carrying a healer's bag and wearing the same greatcoat I'd seen him in when he'd gone into Taylor Mills' place.

It was a fine coat; it looked to be store-made, which was rare in these days, for it was far too thin for our winters. I hoped he'd a proper coat set aside. And some better gloves, as the ones he wore were indoor gloves, knitted to the knuckle only, leaving the tips of his fingers exposed.

Some host I was, letting my guest stand in the cold. "I have to go walk my Pa's traplines, but I can take you up to the house first." But I didn't want to leave him sitting in my house listening to Mam go on and on while I tramped over the hills alone. I caught his eye then looked away. "Or you could come with me. If you'd like."

"I'd like that very much. I don't get out of town often, and I want to know your places. You can tell a lot about a person by seeing the places that nourish him." The sky seemed to reflect in his eyes, which for the life of me I couldn't seem to meet, just glance sideways at.

He left his bag stowed near the tree and we went along in silence for a ways. I watched him out of the corner of my eye. Those blue eyes were questing around, taking in the spiky pines and the scrub as though he'd never seen the like and it was all some rare treat. We crested the ridge and the lower valley opened up through the bare trees.

"Marvelous," he breathed.

"Guess it's different, then. Where you come from, I mean?" We stopped so he could take in the view. I'd seen it probably half a thousand times or more, but he was right, it was marvelous and it never failed to lift my heart. Places that nourish, he'd said. Yes. He had the right of it.

"Oh, very." He'd stuck his hands in his pockets and huddled deep into the coat. "It's flatter, for one thing."

"And warmer, I'm guessing. Trade gloves with me, why don't you?" I stripped the woolen gloves from my hands and held them out.

Of course he shook his head, refusing. "I'm okay." But he weren't.

"Really, I'm more than warm enough, and I'll be working up a sweat with the traps and you're just watching. Come on."

Reluctantly, he complied, and I slid the fingerless gloves onto my hands, feeling the warmth of his body trapped in the light wool that expanded to fit my larger hands. Callan had worn these and the heat of his hands fired them. Thinking on that stirred me through to the soles of my feet.

We started down the ridge into the woods again. "These are warm," he said, holding out his gloved hands. "Thank you, David."

"Mam makes good gloves and her wool's the best in the state. She won't let it be over-washed, so the oil stays in, keeps you warm and dry. These," I wiggled my fingers, "are fine for indoors, but not for outside round here, save for summer. You should've let me pay you for Almond with gloves."

"Maybe I can pay your mother to knit me some. How's your sister doing, by the way?"

"Much better—and she's all full of tales about the wonderful healer and his book of twees."

Now it seemed like Callan blushed a bit, the tips of his ears going red, though that could have been from cold. He needed a hat, too. "She's sweet. I never had any brothers or sisters."

"You can have some of mine," I muttered. "Starting with Benny C; he snores like a rusty saw going through a green log."

"I meant to ask you yesterday about the names in your family. I mean, Almond? It's a lovely name, but not usual."

I slowed our pace some, making it easier to draw breath to talk. "Well, the way my Pa tells it, he and Mam had an agreement that they'd take it in turns to name their children. Mam would name the girls and Pa was to name the boys, so I'm David, after Pa's older brother who died when he was young. Then there was almost four years between me and the next one, and he turned out a boy. Mam was worried there wouldn't be any girls, so Pa said she could name the new one."

"Benny C?"

"His proper name's Bennett Cerf Anderson, after a funny book she remembered from when she was a tiny girl. Bennett Cerf's Book of something or other."

Callan laughed so hard he had to lean against a nearby tree to support himself. "Oh, God, I'm sorry, David, I don't mean to laugh at your brother. I'm just imagining how it would have been if your mother'd grown up with Dr. Seuss books. Green Eggs and Ham Anderson."

I didn't get it, but I smiled anyway, wishing he'd never stop laughing. "It's all right. You should have heard my Pa. He swore Mam wouldn't be naming any of the rest of us after that, so we got Ruby and then Delia. Then Almond came along, and Mam asked if Grandmam could name her."

We started down the path, which wasn't really much more than an animal trail. The traps started just down the way a bit, and I was half-listening for the sounds of animals caught, hoping for once that they'd be empty as I wasn't sure how Callan, a healer by trade and clearly by calling, would take to seeing suffering creatures.

"Almond's the perfect name for her, I think. I've heard your grandmother remembers Before—I suppose she had a fondness for almonds."

"I think so. Her full name's Almond Joy Anderson, so I figure it's a happy memory to her."

He grinned, an utterly wicked grin, as though he knew something more than me. Which likely he did, as I'm hardly schooled at all, really. "A sweet memory, I'm guessing. Thank you for sharing that. Like I said, I never had much family, just my mother and me."

"Where's your name come from? Callan's not a name I've heard before." Saying his name still came awkward to me, but I wanted to hear it spoke aloud. There's a Bible story I recall about the Hebrews and how they wouldn't say the name of God because it was so precious and holy to them. That hadn't never made sense to me, not till now.

"It's my mother's maiden name. She was Nancy Elizabeth Callan before she married my father, and she was the last of her family, so she wanted the name to continue."

We'd come up on the first trap and it was empty. I replenished the dried meat that served as bait, mounding the pine straw around the harsh metal. The traps were old, milled steel made, according to Pa, in a way we can't do no more, so we take proper care of them. The new traps the smiths make today aren't near so good.

Callan was watching, marking my movements close as though there'd be a test to follow. "What sort of animals do you catch normally?"

I stood up and shouldered the pack, ready to move on to the next spot. "Fur creatures, mostly. A lot of fox, some raccoon. Mink if we're real lucky, squirrel if we're not. And the rare timber wolf, though they're scarce as hen's teeth."

"And you sell the pelts?"

"Yes. Good money in fur, especially shipping them north. Hard to believe there's still people living up above the Ice Line, but they say there is."

Callan shivered. "This is as far north as I'm prepared to go."

I stopped, grabbed a-hold of his shoulders and swung him round, bringing him up short in front of me. Before he could make a word's protest, my cap was off my head and covering all that golden hair. The fingerless gloves allowed me to feel it, so sleek like the finest fabrics at the General, the ones the women bought for their Sunday best. It took all I had in me to pull my hands away and turn back down the path.

"David—"

I could tell he was going to argue, so I cut him off. "You were raised by your mam, then?"

He sighed, giving in. "Thank you. Yes. My father was quite a bit older than she, and he died when I was very young. I don't remember him."

"I can't fathom not knowing my pa. He's taught me just about everything I know." I heard the keening of an animal in pain just ahead of us. It sounded like a fox. Pa would be pleased, but I weren't, not today.

Then in the sudden silence, Callan heard it too, and his face went pale, making the blue eyes stand out even more than normal. We came up on the fox from behind, and sure enough, it was caught by the hind paw, cruel metal jaws biting into fur and bone. This was the part of the trapline I despised.

"You might not want to watch this," I cautioned.

"I eat meat. I wear fur and leather. It's right that I should see the price." But he leaned back against a tree, not coming close to study on it like he had the empty trap. I stripped off the borrowed gloves and thrust them in my pocket and took out the heavy leather ones that would protect me from bites.

"Shh, I know it hurts." I spoke low to the fox, forcing myself to forget Callan watching and think only on the injured animal. "It'll be over soon, over quick and then you can rest." I continued to babble nonsense like you'd talk to a baby. It was the tone that mattered with creatures, not the words so much. The fox kept still till the end, and then quick as a snake, in desperation he tried to strike at me, cunning teeth turned towards my outstretched hand, but I had him round the neck, and my knife was out. "I'm sorry." The knife flashed red across his throat and I stood back to let the animal finish its death throes in as much peace as I could manage.

There's more blood than you'd think in even a creature so small as the fox, and in the long moment it took for him to bleed out, I hated the necessity that forced me to kill. I dropped to my knees, breathing shallow. I'd been doing this almost all my life, and still it struck me hard each time.

"You did that well." I felt a hand on my back, and then Callan was helping me up, steadying me. "You gave it the best death you could manage."

"I know. It's funny, I don't mind butchering the farm animals—that's what they're there for, and I don't mind hunting; I lose as many as I take or more, they've got a fighting chance. But I hate these traps." The glove I'd held the knife with was spattered with blood, and I wiped it on the pine straw.

"I can tell you're good with animals, the way you soothed the fox, showed it respect. David, everything lives at the expense of other life. Maybe in the old days people could get by without taking life—they had other sources of food, but we don't."

He was right, and I knew it. Our growing season was short and chancy and meat made up the bulk of most folks' diets. There weren't no way to have meat without death. I sprung the fox's body from the trap and trussed it up to carry home. "I try to make it quick. That's why I don't use the gun. Pa can always get them dead to rights on the first shot, but I miss a lot if they move. I'm surer with the knife."

"The gun would be easier on you, it seems, but the knife is more merciful for the animals." There was approval in his eyes, and my heart swelled and the sun shone just a little brighter.

I reset the trap, and we continued down the ridge silently, finding the next two traps empty and then coming on a dead raccoon. I stroked the fur of the stiff little body. The memory of the fox lingered on in my mind; the way life just seemed to seize up and vanish, leaving behind an empty shell that had no connection to the living creature at all. "Have you ever seen a person die?" I asked as I cut a length of rope to tie the coon.

"Oh, yes." His words came with a sharp intake of breath.

"Of course, I'm sorry—you're a healer, naturally you'd have..." I let my voice trail off as I worked the raccoon free and strung it with the fox.

"No. Not a patient. It was..." I looked up, but his head was turned away, and all I could see was his throat working.

"Never mind. Sometimes I don't know when to shut my face." Hoisting up the fallen branch I'd strung the animals to and picking up my pack, I struggled to think of something to say that would turn the mood.

"No, it's all right," Callan said, calmer now. "It was my mother. I can't talk about it. It's still too soon." He took the pack from me. "Let me help you with this."

Still silent, with me cursing what Grandmam called my 'satiable curiosity, we started up the path to home. We'd just come back to the trap where the fox had been when Callan broke the uncomfortable silence. "But when I am ready to talk about it, I think quite likely it will be with you."

A piece of grit must've landed in my eye; I blinked back a tear. "Thanks. I've never. I mean, I've never seen a dead person—our family's been lucky, though I expect Grandmam won't last out the winter." That was the first time I'd spoken that sure truth aloud, and though I ached, it felt somehow right to admit it, like I was letting her go, just a tiny bit.

"She's had a good long life. I expect she'll be ready to go when it's time."

I thought about how Grandmam's eyes would unfocus when she talked of the past, how of late she only seemed happy in memories and stories, and I knew he was right. "I'll warrant you're right; her death will be a mercy to her, but it's the uncertainty of it that's got me all anxious."

We were within sight of the tree where Callan had left his bag. "Timor mortis conturbat me." His voice was tight. "The fear of death disturbs me," he explained, then shook his head and smiled. "Enough of this. It's a beautiful day—if you close your eyes, it could almost be spring. Race you to the tree!" He was off, pack slapping against his back, so I dropped my burden and followed. For someone who spent his life indoors with books, he was faster than I'd have wagered, and I had to work to catch up with him. But I did at last, grabbing hold of the tail of his coat and dragging him down into a soft bed of pine needles.

He dropped the pack and rolled, pulling me over atop him and I pinned him with a wrestling hold I'd learned in the schoolyard. "Got you," I breathed down on him, triumphant. His face was flushed from running, and I noticed, not for the first time, how fine his features were. My legs were wrapped around his and something strong and bright moved in the pit of my stomach and the planet seemed to tilt on its axis.

"Yes," he whispered, his eyes full of mystery. "I think you do." I held my breath, uncertain, waiting, and then he grinned wickedly and his legs surged upward, breaking my hold and forcing me off, till we both collapsed in the bed of fragrant pine. I looked at him all disheveled and undignified, hat off, hair sticking every which way, and the thoughts of death evaporated into the sunshine. The serious healer who I'd been afraid to name became just Callan, and it was like some new and wonderful seed had taken root deep within me.

"Wait here," I said, and jogged back down the trail for the game I'd abandoned. When I got back, he'd straightened himself up, brushing the dirt from his coat, making himself into the proper young healer again.

"I needed that," he confessed. "It gets old, being so serious all the time. I think you're good for me, David. I hope we can do this again."

I didn't trust myself to speak, so many thoughts and words tussled in my head, so I just smiled and started down the road towards the cabin. Finally, feeling like I had to say something, I latched onto what he'd said before. "Actually, you can tell it's not spring even with your eyes closed. In spring there'd be birdsong."

"True. I'd forgotten that you do still get some birds this far north. You'll have to show me, all right?"

A promise of a future. "Sure, I'd love that. We get a few cardinals, wrens, that sort of thing. And crows and ravens, but nobody wants to hear their ugly song."

"Before the Ice this area would have been thronging with songbirds in the spring and summer. Yet another thing we've lost." He sounded matter-of-fact, not sad nor frustrated as he had in town the past day.

"What do you think caused the Ice, anyways?" It was the burning question of our time. Every liquored-up home-grown philosophizer in town had a theory on it.

"I don't know. There was a lot of flux with the climate in the Twenty-First Century, though from what I've read, that tended towards a warming trend." He pulled my hat back down over his head. "Which this surely isn't, and of course the Ice wasn't gradual at all. There's some talk in the scientific community about a climate weapon, or so I've heard."

"A weather bomb? That's what Burke the Digger thinks. But wouldn't that be a stupid sort of weapon? How could you protect your own country?" I could see the smoke from our chimney topping the rise, and the smell of the rabbit stew was floating right along with it, making my mouth water.

"Well, there were a lot of rogue nations and terrorist states back then who might not have cared who else was hurt so long as their enemies suffered. I'm not sure that we'll ever truly know."

"Elmer Casteel says it was aliens from outer space. He says they need a cold planet so they sent the Ice to kill us all off so they can take over."

He snorted, then caught the scent of the food on the breeze. "If that's dinner, it smells delicious. Aliens. From Uranus, no doubt. Elmer Casteel should write science fiction stories."

"That would require that Elmer Casteel know how to write. Come on, race you to dinner." And my heart was dancing clean out of my chest as neck and neck, evenly matched, we careened onto the porch.

Chapter 4

I'd been right on the mark—Callan ate like he'd never seen food before. The trade goods healers is paid in is supposed to be of the best quality, but the truth is folks give what they can afford to go without, not necessarily what the work deserves, so I suspected Callan didn't see fresh meat too often.

It makes Mam happy to see a man with a healthy appetite, and I could tell from the moment Callan came into the cabin and spoke to her so respectful, like she was a proper town lady, that she liked him fine. She hustled him over to Pa's chair and fixed him a bowl, leaving me to fend for myself. But I didn't mind, it was an ease to my mind that Mam liked Callan.

He spoke kindly to Grandmam, too, treating her like a real person, and not as a curiosity, a thing to be marveled at that she'd lived so long the way some folks did. And Almond latched on to him like a tick on a dog, sitting in his lap while he was trying to eat.

"Almond," Mam finally said, exasperated. "Leave the healer alone and let him eat."

Considering he was well into his third helping, I'd have said Almond's presence weren't much of a hindrance, and Callan must have agreed, for he shook his head and laughed.

"No ma'am, she's fine. I was telling David before how lucky he is to have so many siblings."

I still didn't hold that having Benny C steal my covers every night and being forced to help Ruby and Delia with sums was luck, but then I'd never been an only child and I figured it was like they say, that the grass is always greener in someone else's field.

"So you're an only child, then, Healer Landers?"

"It's Callan, Mrs. Anderson, and yes, I am. My father died when I was very young, and Mother never remarried."

Mam pursed up her lips then went to the cupboard, took out a loaf of wheat bread from the last baking she'd done and cut a slice for Callan. Corn bread was commonplace, but wheat bread was a rare treat, and sharing it was a sure sign of Mam's high regard. He took it eager enough, but then immediately split it in two and gave a share to Almond.

"Your poor mother. Bringing up a boy with no man to guide him. I cannot imagine such a thing. Though she's clearly done a marvel of a job with you."

He smiled at her, and for a moment, with the crumbly bread spilling over his face, he looked no more than my own age. "Well, she had help. I was raised surrounded by childless adults who spoiled me terribly, which is probably why I always wanted a brother to play with."

"Only children have it so difficult, I think. I feared for a while that David would be an only child, but then we were blessed with Benny C."

"Cursed," I muttered under my breath, but not low enough, as Mam said, "David," in that warning tone that was as close to reprimanding me in front of a stranger as she'd get.

Figuring I'd best get back on Mam's good side if I wanted the freedom to visit the town and see Callan again, I started clearing the dishes, taking them to the sink which was already filled with water from the well and set in to cleaning them.

"You're not from around these parts, are you, Healer?" I noted that Mam didn't use his name, but then I didn't expect her to. Mam has a strong sense of folks' places in the world, and a healer was someone with education and valuable skills and deserved, to her way of thinking, the respect of formality.

"No, ma'am. I'm from Florida originally."

"I've been there." Grandmam had been sitting by the fire as was her custom in the afternoons, so quiet that I'd almost forgot she was there and that she was the true cause for Callan's visit. Though she'd acknowledged his greeting when he came in, until this moment she'd not paid Callan any mind at all.

"Mrs. Beatty?" He eased himself out from under Almond and pulled one of the kitchen benches near the fire to sit beside Grandmam.

"I remember Florida," she said, staring into the fire. "My mother and father took me to Disney World when I was twelve and it was so beautiful, such a magical place. Warm, even in January, and covered with palm trees that looked as though they were made of plastic, but they weren't, they were real. Is it still there?" She looked up at him, fretful. "Seems like nothing's there anymore."

He reached out and took her hand, stroking her wrist, and then feeling for a pulse. "There are still palm trees if you go far enough south, though not so much where I lived. And Disney World's still there, though it's all in ruins now. The state government took it over and fenced it off behind a giant wall, so as to keep people out. For safety's sake. One of my mother's friends took me to see it and I stood there and touched that wall and imagined what was behind it." He released her hand. "It must have been a wonderful place in its day."

"Yes, a magical place, especially for children. All forgotten now." In the deepest winter, the snow covers absolutely everything and the world is empty and desolate. That's how Grandmam's voice sounded, and it made me want to take her in my arms, though I wasn't child enough to think I could make anything right for her.

"Not forgotten," Callan assured her. "You remember, and you've told your children and grandchildren, and they'll remember. It won't always be like this. We'll rebuild."

"It's always going to be cold, though, isn't it? Always so horribly cold." Though to me it seemed a fine warm day, she shivered, and I was struck by how tiny she was. When I was young, Grandmam had towered over me, and even though I was tall as her before I was eleven or so, she'd always seemed larger than life. But now she was shrunken, drawn in on herself. Callan glanced over at me, so I took up a quilt that Mam had been repairing and wrapped it around Grandmam's shoulders.

She patted my hand, and I looked down at her hand, tiny and translucent and spotted with age. Someday Mam's hands would be like that. And so would mine. And Callan's. I shivered, too, as though winter had come on in earnest.

"I'd like to listen to your heart and lungs, if it's all right with you."

"It'll make my children happy, though it doesn't require a degree from Harvard Medical School to know a woman over one hundred years old is likely to die, Doctor."

Callan sighed, and the winter that had crept into the cabin shadowed his face. "It's just Healer, I'm afraid, Ma'am. But I'll do the best I can." He rummaged in his bag, and the shadow cleared. "I'd completely forgotten I'd brought this."

Almond had been leaning on the table, listless as though she were on the edge of sleep, but she saw the bright green book emerge from the bag and she jumped up like a rabbit started by a fox. "Twees!"

Callan laughed and handed it to her. Mam looked like she wanted to protest— Almond's still young and not too careful—but she held her tongue and Almond took the book as though it was solid gold and went off to a chair near a window, talking to the pages as though she could read a story there.

"You're good for my granddaughter, young man."

"She's a bright, sweet little girl. I like her." Callan was warming the stethoscope between his hands the way he had for Almond.

"And she likes you. As does my grandson, I think." I had gone back to the dishes and I knew this wasn't meant for my ears. Grandmam had got horribly hard of hearing and had no sense of how her voice carried. But Callan knew. He glanced my way, caught my eye and smiled. I smiled back and ducked my hands down in the wash water, pretending to concentrate on the stew pot.

"I hope so. I've never met anyone quite like him—he's remarkable." He hadn't bothered to lower his voice and I felt a warm flush of pleasure at his approval. I'd been called many things by grown folks—dependable, reliable, solid. Never remarkable.

"Mind your work, David," Mam warned. She never liked any of us getting so much praise, save for Almond, so I turned back to the frigid dishwater and pretended not to hear.

"Though he's certainly his father's son and manages the hunting and farming just fine, he's got a good mind that's being wasted in this life. Almond's the same way. Smart as a whip and curious. She'll not be content to marry some farmer or hunter and spend her life knitting and stewing rabbits."

I shot Mam a look, and her jaw was set firmly as her knitting needles flew. I'd never heard Mam and Grandmam at odds before, had never thought about how they was mother and child and would disagree and row just like Mam and I did. Though they must have, many times.

"I'm going to take Jerzy some of that rabbit stew you don't appreciate, Mother," she said, stomping out of the cabin.

Grandmam sighed. "She just doesn't understand. I love May-Marie for who she is. I want her to love her children for who they are, not try to force them into some sort of ill-fitting mold. Is that wrong?"

"No," Callan assured her. "It's never wrong to want people to find their own paths. Now sit still for a moment and take deep breaths."

I watched him listen to her heart and to her breathing, and his expression grew serious, and I thought he could have been a real doctor, likely would have been had he lived Before, and it seemed so unfair that by being a healer he could touch that world, like he'd touched that wall down in Florida, but he could never see into it, nor be a part of it. Not ever.

"Your lungs sound clear, no trace of congestion, though your heartbeat is off. Have you experienced any chest pain?"

"Sometimes." I'd not known that. I wondered if my parents had.

"Now?" he asked sharply, and she nodded. Before I could dry off my hands and get to her side, Callan had his bag open and was slipping something into her mouth. "Thought so. Hold her hand, David."

I grabbed a-hold of her and she squeezed back, pouring all her pain into a grip that was surprisingly strong. "I'm here, Grandmam."

Callan was talking quietly, calming Grandmam like I had the fox, just a running river of words to flow over her while whatever he'd given had time to take effect. "Yes, it's still warm in Florida, mostly. You can walk on the beach in the summer and feel the sun on your back and the sand on your bare feet. And where I lived there's people from all over the world, well, their descendants anyway, people who were studying there and got trapped when the Ice came. And we've got some trade along the Gulf Coast, with Louisiana and Texas and even down into Mexico, so we get hot peppers and Mexican corn and chocolate."

"Chocolate!" she gasped. "Oh, I miss chocolate, hot cocoa on a frosty morning, so sweet with sugar...bitter else..."

"Shh. Don't talk, just breathe easy. David, please go get your mother."

I ran from the cabin, thankful that Almond was so lost in her book and the others were still at the schoolhouse. Mam was in the barn, not doing anything of note; just watching her sheep as they milled around the food trough.

"Grandmam's in a bad way—Callan says you should come."

"Is it her heart?" She was halfway across the yard to the cabin and I had to struggle to keep up with her, though my legs were longer and I spent my days ranging the hills while she stayed mostly to home.

"You knew? I'm almost seventeen, Mam, you can tell me things."

She stopped short of the door. "A parent wants to protect their child from pain— you'll understand that someday. It don't make a difference if that child is six or sixteen, or sixty, I expect."

Callan had moved Grandma back to her room and had lit all the lamps so the dingy corners of the windowless room were bright as day. "She wanted it light," he said, with apology, knowing, I suppose, that oil was dear.

Mam sat down on the edge of the bed and was stroking Grandmam's thinning hair. "Is she all right?"

"Yes, now. She's had a mild heart attack, I think. I gave her foxglove and the pain has eased. But I don't think this is the first one she's had."

"No. They've been coming fairly regular." Mam glanced at me, then away. "David, she didn't want anyone to know, not even your Pa. You really weren't being left out."

"It would be good if she could sleep," Callan said.

"I'll make some chamomile tea. That always calms her down." Mam went back to the stove and I could hear the banging of pans.

"My box," Grandmam said, reaching weakly toward her bed table.

Callan nodded to me. "Give her what she wants."

I took the tattered cloth-covered box that held Grandmam's treasures and memories and set it beside her. She felt inside it then took out a faded picture. "Wanted you to see this." She handed it up to Callan, and I moved close to him to have a look. He leaned back heavy against me, and I could feel how tired he was.

The picture was one I'd not seen before. It showed a family group all in faded color, a man and a woman and several children dressed in summer clothes from Before. Such a marvel that they could stand outside with arms bare to the shoulder, that the feel of air on skin should be a caress, not a bite.

"In the center. The youngest girl." Grandmam wheezed.

"She looks like Almond." And she did, long shiny dark hair, upturned nose and eyes that weren't facing the camera where they should be, but were looking for something else, something different and beyond what the rest of her kin could see.

"My mother."

Mam returned with a cup of steaming tea, Callan took it and added a drop or two of some unknown liquid and helped Grandmam to sip.

She made a face at the bitter liquid, but swallowed obediently. "I used to think the past, my grandmother's world was all in black and white like the old pictures and films showed it," she said, sipping again. "But I was wrong. The past wasn't grey. The past was all color, blazes of trees in warm October sunshine, the blue water of the pool on a summer day and all the girls in their bathing suits, skin so brown from the sun. It's the future that's grey. All grey and ugly." Her eyes closed.

"She's asleep now, and probably will be for at least six hours," Callan said, and he and I slipped from the room, leaving Mam behind to trim down the lamps and settle Grandmam. He collapsed onto one of the table benches and sunk his head onto his hands so the wheat-gold hair fell forward to obscure his face.

"Are you all right?" I remembered how after a hard hunt when Pa'd tramped for hours through the woods with his heavy gun and then with his kill strapped to his back, Mam would sometimes massage his shoulders. I suspected Callan's normal days didn't involve walking long traplines, seeing animals die, racing and wrestling and tending sick old ladies all before the sun began to sink. Without asking, for when you ask, sometimes the answer is no, I began to knead his shoulders.

Callan groaned, and I stopped immediately. "No, please don't stop," he said. "It's good."

Even through the shirt I could feel the tension, huge knots turning his slender shoulders inside out. My hands, large and clumsy, could not sew a button or hold a pencil with any great skill, but this they could do. Though it would have been easier without the layers of cloth between us. "If you loosen your collar, I can get under your shirt."

He froze for a moment. "No, probably not a good idea." His words sounded odd, sort of choked and strangled, and I relaxed my grip as he sat up. "That was marvelous, David—if you ever decide to give up country life you could make a fortune in the city as a masseur."

Mam came out of the back bedroom. "Well, one down, one to go. Almond, it's time for your nap. Almond?"

She was curled up in the chair with the book clutched to her chest, half-asleep already. She woke quick enough when Mam pulled the book away.

"No, I want twees!"

Callan chuckled. "She can keep it for a while if she—"

"No," Mam said. "Almond, you must give Healer Landers his book back."

I could see my baby sister was working her way up to a powerful pout. "Want twees, want twees, want twees!"

"She's almost five, way too old to be taking on like this," I said in apology.

"She's probably still a bit ill." Callan knelt in front of Almond and gently pulled the book out of her hands. "How about if I put you down for your nap? I'll tell you a story, maybe sing a song for you, okay?"

She nodded and slipped her arms around his neck. I pointed him up the ladder to the loft and awkwardly, carrying his unfamiliar burden, he ascended. We could hear the low sounds of Callan's voice, the same voice he'd used with Grandmam, and then Almond's reply, fussy but calming.

"That young man is going to make a wonderful father someday." Mam had taken up her knitting again. "He's far more patient with Almond than you ever are."

"He don't have to live with her pouts and her spells every single day. And she can say 'trees' perfectly well, Mam. You spoil her."

"She's my last baby." Her needles, carved wooden spikes that Pa had made, flickered in and out of the creamy wool. "You'll understand someday. And speaking of that, your Pa ran into Burke the School in town last week and they spoke about you and Luanna."

Callan was singing to Almond now, a soft true voice lifted in words I couldn't understand, foreign words. My own singing voice was something I was proud of now that it had settled. It was lower than Callan's, and I wondered how we'd sound together. "What about Luanna Burke?" But I knew, and Mam knew I knew.

"Oh, for the love of heaven, David, we've talked about this before. It's a good match. She's an attractive, strong young woman with a good settlement and a father who's somebody in this community. You couldn't do better if you tried."

"I don't love her." But I knew what she'd say to that. Love may have mattered in Grandmam's day, but no longer. Health, wealth, especially land wealth, and family, that was what made a match. I had the land, she had the family. The whole town would have looked on our joining as the most natural thing in the world. The whole town save for me.

"You'll come to love her in time. It's the nature of men and women. A man leaves his mother and cleaves to his wife and they become one flesh, as Scripture says."

It wouldn't have done me any good to argue with her, and besides, Callan was coming back down the ladder, and Mam never argued in company.

"She asleep?" Mam asked, looking up from her knitting to smile at him.

"Yes. And I should be going—I've left Healer Findlay alone long enough."

Mam gave him her hand. "I can't tell you what it's meant having you here today. You've been a blessing."

He fetched a vial of liquid from his bag. "Give your mother this when she feels pain. No more than two drops, and if that doesn't clear it, you send David or one of the children down to fetch me. Any time, night or day."

"How much do we owe you, Healer Landers?"

"Nothing. You fed me a splendid meal and I had a wonderful morning with David; that's more than payment enough."

Mam protested, but he held firm. "You want to pay me, allow David to come into town and visit on occasion. If he wants, I mean."

"Course I do, but that's not pay." I looked down at the pile of yarn and half-done gloves, then rummaged in the pockets of my coat. "Here," I handed him my gloves and hat which he had given back when we come in the door. "Take these."

He seemed startled, like he weren't used to getting gifts. "I can't deprive you—the cold weather's coming on and you're outside much more than I."

"Mam knits at lightning speed; I'll have me another pair and a new hat before the sun sets if she turns her mind to it." Mam was beaming with pride. For someone who don't like her children to hear good reports of themselves, she surely basked in praise of her own self. "It's all right, ain't it, Mam? You should see what he's got. Useless city gloves, all thin and fingerless."

"Of course, it's the least we can do. You've done wonders for my mother. And for Almond."

Callan was bundling up in his greatcoat, pulling on the hat and gloves, stroking the soft wool felted by a year's hard use. They were too big for him, but they'd do him better than what he had.

"I'll walk you partway down the path."

"If you like," he said. I tried to catch his eye and smile, to assure him that I did like, very much, but he was avoiding my eyes as he had in the office the day before.

The sun was fast falling away over the horizon and the wind had picked up, shaking the trees lightly. I thrust my bare hands into my pockets. "Should be light long enough to get you back down to town." Benny C and the girls should be coming up home any time now, and I had evening chores wanted doing or I'd have gladly walked him clear down to Moline.

He didn't make a reply and we walked in silence for a while. "So you're promised in marriage?" he asked in sort of an off-hand voice.

"No, I most certainly am not. That's my Mam's wishful thinking." The tree where I'd met Callan earlier that day was just ahead of us, marking the spot where the road to town began its winding journey down to town. "I get tired of her treating me like a child sometimes, not even telling me about Grandmam's illness."

It seemed that there were many things in my life I hadn't known, secrets my parents had kept from me. I wondered if this was what it was like for everyone, growing up to find out how little you knew and that the grown-up world was a mess of confusion and half-truths.

We'd reached the tree. "I suppose they had their reasons. I wasn't ever sheltered from anything as a child, and I can see some benefit of growing up free of adult worries as you have. Be thankful for your family, David."

"I am." And I was, even for Benny C. "And for you, too. This has been the best day ever, even with the bad parts."

"Have you had a chance to start Huckleberry Finn?" Callan asked.

"Only just—I like it fine so far, but I've a long way to go."

"I envy you the journey. There's nothing like reading a book for the first time, not knowing where it's going to take you, what's coming next."

Like friendship, I thought, but didn't say it, for I didn't want to sound stupid. "I'll come down when I finish, and we can talk about it, like you said."

"I'd like that."

Neither of us wanted to say goodbye, and I could feel the awkwardness, the sense that there should be some ritual or action to mark the end of this day and the beginning of...of whatever it was we'd begun. Tension slid in between us and the silence stretched near to discomfort.

"Your hat's crooked," I said finally, grabbing at whatever I could, and I took hold and straightened it, allowing my fingers to tangle a bit in the silky hair and touch his smooth cheeks. He was holding his breath, and I realized that so was I.

For an endless moment we stood like that till the sounds of distant voices curving their way up the hill broke the spell and I lowered my hands.

"Thanks," he whispered. I watched him go until he vanished around a corner, out of sight, but still before me in memory.

Chapter 5

That night I dreamt of Callan. We was wrestling again as we had that day in the pine straw, bodies rubbing and rolling atop each other. And I can't recall exactly what happened, but it became one of those dreams that take physical form, as the dreams of men sometimes do. I'd heard in the schoolyard that such things were normal and it happened to every man when he was young; it was part of what you did when you hadn't a wife. And perhaps it was normal, as they'd said, but it didn't seem to me to be normal to be dreaming such thoughts about your friends, so I woke up shaking and sick.

Benny C took one look at me all pale and weak and hollered for Mam, who made me gargle with salt water for fear I'd caught Almond's illness, then set Benny C to doing my chores. That didn't please him, till I reminded him that it meant a day away from school. Benny C was a wonder with the sheep, but didn't have much use for learning beyond what he needed to count the lambs each spring and figure Mam's profit on the wool. It struck me funny that the one of us named for a book should have the least use for reading.

I'd stowed Callan's copy of Huckleberry Finn under my side of the mattress, and as soon as Benny C had lit out to make a start on feeding the stock, I took it out and lost myself in the story of Huck, who had left Tom behind and gone adventuring on the Mississippi River with the escaped slave, Jim. Just as with Tom Sawyer, I found the rhythms and patterns of Twain's writing familiar and home-like, though Jim's speech was a fair challenge at times.

I knew about slavery, of course, as I had studied some history in school, but I had paid it little mind at the time, for it seemed an ancient atrocity, as far distant from me as the doings of ancient kings. But here it was, in black and white, as they say: a man who was less than a man in the eyes of the law, and for Huck to be helping him was breaking that law.

It disturbed Huck to be doing so, as it would have disturbed me. I had been raised to respect what law we had, and to assume that the legislators and governors and mayors my parents and the other adults selected would make wise choices. It seemed that had not been true in Mark Twain's day, and I wondered if maybe what the preachers said was true—that the Ice and all its burdens had made us better people than Before. The reading of the book passed the time for me till well past noon, when Mam stuck her head up the loft to check on me.

"You still sickening, David? Should I send for the healer?"

I came within a hare's whisker of saying yes, knowing that Healer Findlay would not ride so far on a case that wasn't an emergency, that it would be Callan who would come and lay his cool hands on my brow and slide his instruments over my chest and back. My body grew warm even thinking on it, and Mam must have seen my flushed face, for she came all the way up the stairs as she hadn't in years, not since Benny C was small, and sat by my bed.

"You're feverish, I think." Her voice held worry—I was seldom sick, not even as a young child.

"I'm all right. No need to trouble the healer." Flashes from the dream still strayed across my mind, and I knew I couldn't face Callan right then even if my life depended on it.

She looked skeptical, but held her peace, her face drawn, hands fretting at her skirts, and I remembered she had more than me to worry over. "How's Grandmam?"

"Better today, but she's stayed a-bed. It eases my mind that we've something to give her for the bad spells now. It's just been so hard—" She stopped mid-sentence, remembering, I suppose, who she was speaking to. A child.

"That's good, Mam, I'm glad the healer was able to help her." I wanted her to say Callan's name, wanted to hear it spoken aloud as though that would bring him closer to me.

"He's a nice young man, Healer Landers is. The sort of friend you should be making, a town man with a future in the community. I imagine he'll be married before the summer's out—after all, one day, probably not so far off, he'll be the healer. Quite a catch."

I thought about Callan with some unnamed girl, that dazzling smile turned on her, those eyes...no. "He ain't a fish, Mam."

"As good as. I'm just glad we have that understanding with Burke the School about Luanna, for an educated man like that would be a mighty temptation for him."

"I am not marrying Luanna Burke!"

She patted my hand the way you would a small child who didn't want to eat his vegetables. "I'll send Benny C up with some food for you, David. You get some rest, you hear?"

I tried to read some after that, but my heart wasn't in it. They'd make me marry her. Oh, the vows had to be made freely, and I could refuse. But to do such a thing would not only humiliate Luanna, who was a decent enough girl, but bring disgrace on my family as well. If I was still in these parts by my eighteenth year, there would be a house raising on the land that Pa had promised to me, and before I'd have a chance to blink twice, I'd be carrying Luanna over the threshold.

The thought of doing with her what a man did with his wife drew a long shudder from me. I'd never yet found a girl who sparked me like that. And now, with the dream of the previous night still lingering like long twilight in my mind, I wondered if I ever would. Could be there was something wrong with me, some part of me that was broken so I didn't think of girls the right way, and I sure couldn't figure out what to do about it.

"Pa says you're malingering." Benny C had appeared on the ladder with a bowl of soup balanced in his hand.

"Big word for a small fry," I snapped, but he knew I didn't mean nothing by it. I took the soup eagerly, for it had been a long time since dinner.

"David." He sounded serious, which weren't at all typical for Benny C. "Can I talk to you?"

I nodded, my mouth full of rich mutton broth.

"How do you know if you're in love?"

I spat the broth out. "Did Mam send you up here to talk to me about Luanna? Cause if she did—"

"Luanna? Luanna Burke? Who'd be in love with that horse-faced, buck toothed... ugh. No, I'm talking about Daisy Bailes." Benny C took after Mam, with near red hair and green eyes which looked all glazy-glassy now.

"Daisy Bailes—you mean that skinny little blonde girl with the freckles? She's seven years old, Benny C!"

"She's almost thirteen. You think time stopped because you ain't at school no more? She's thirteen and she's got these curves, David, and this smile that just grabs hold of you. I can't stop thinking on her."

"You're thirteen. You don't even know what love is." When I was thirteen, I'd cared about the games we played in the yard and books and learning about the woods with Pa. Neither girls nor love had been a part of my world then. Weren't yet, truth be told.

He'd sat down on the stool we threw our clothes over at night. "And I suppose you do? You ain't never even walked out with a girl so far's I know. Should've known better than to ask you for advice." He looked like he was going to cry.

"I'm sorry, Benny C. Tell me about Daisy, then." Though Benny C could be a horrible pain, it didn't do me harm to listen to him go on about the wondrous charms of Daisy Bailes, who still stuck in my mind as a skinny seven-year-old. He talked, and I ate and half-listened, making occasional murmurs and noises to let him think I was paying attention.

'...just love the sound of her name, you know. Though I can hardly bring myself to speak it—it's almost like, what's that word where you disrespect the Lord, like that. And the other day they was making us practice recite and she was my partner, and I swear to God, I got lost in her eyes. It was like I couldn't breathe and I felt all tight... you know." He looked embarrassed. "Down there."

I did know, and nodded, not meeting his eye, though I supposed as a big brother I should have given him comfort and assurance that such a thing was normal.

"So do you think I'm in love?" he asked as I handed him back the empty bowl.

"Certainly sounds like it. But you behave yourself with her, you hear? You're too young to be thinking of doing anything untoward, if you know what I mean."

He took my meaning, for we'd grown up around farm animals, and reproduction wasn't any mystery. Love, yes. Love was a mystery. But the process by which one generation begat the next was well-known. He scrambled down the ladder, beaming with joy that he'd been able to talk about his sweetheart for twenty minutes almost uninterrupted, and I had to smile.

Who'd have figured, Benny C in love? Unable to speak her name but longing to hear it, thinking on her day and night. And then, heart sinking, I recalled the way Callan's hair had felt between my fingers, the weight of my body over his and how I longed to hear his name. How I'd stroked the thin fingerless gloves, knowing they'd covered his hands.

No. It couldn't be—I couldn't be falling in love with Callan, with a man. But I clutched the book, the book he had held and read and loved, tight to my chest and lost myself in the memory of blue eyes.

Had Callan been a girl healer, there would have been nothing simpler than for me to go to my folks and tell them of my feelings. They'd probably have to pay Burke the

School some sort of settlement over Luanna, but they'd be thrilled and proud to have the healer as their daughter-in-law, and it would have been a match.

But he weren't a girl, and my parents would be horrified beyond words to learn of my desires. And so would Callan. And so was I, if truth be told. Such things were not done, though I'd heard they were common Before, part of the decadence of civilization. Then, yes. But not now. I couldn't tell Callan, nor ever let him see how I felt, for to do so would be to end our friendship for certain.

So I buried myself in the story of Huck and Jim, and in the endless round of chores; there's always work to do on a farm, particularly with winter coming. I did some hunting on the days that Pa stayed close to home, taking the rifle out and coming back with rabbit or squirrel to be stewed, or dried and salted to last us through the winter. I had to walk the traplines a time or two as well, but I did it swiftly, forcing myself not to mark each spot where we had lingered.

Because the school year was grinding to a halt, my evenings were spent helping the younger ones prepare for Fall Recitations. It was Benny C's year to do the Declaration of Independence, and I sat at the table, drinking in the last of Huckleberry Finn while my brother stammered out words he had no comprehension of at all.

"I ain't never going to learn this," he moaned.

"Just think what a lummox you'll look, messing up the Declaration in front of Daisy Bailes," Ruby teased, and Benny C, who'd obviously forgot that his lady love would be listening, turned white as snow.

"Leave him be, Ruby," I warned. "Come on, you'll get it. Let's start from the list of grievances; that's where you seem to lose track."

He clutched the edge of the table and started again, and I sank back into the pages of the book. I'd read it all, from the first word to the last, even the parts after the story ended that seemed to be just people talking about the story—like a school recitation, but wrote down. I'd liked it. Not in the way I liked Tom Sawyer or some of the other books I'd read at school—those had been just plain fun. This one made me think; I'd had to work at it some.

"And for the support of this Declaration, with a firm...re...reliance on the protection of divine Providence, we mutually pledge to each other our Lives, our Fortunes and our sacred Honor!" Benny C concluded triumphantly. "I done it!"

I thought he'd left out about three of the grievances against the king, but he was happy, and Mam was beaming proudly at him from where she sat knitting me a hat to replace the one I'd given Callan. I closed the book and put it aside carefully. "Good work, Benny C. Let's go bring in some firewood."

Benny C followed me out into the mid-October night. The air was biting; the first real cold we'd had. Halfway to the barn, I stopped and faced my brother. "I need a favor. Can you go round by the Healer's place tomorrow at lunch and give a message to Healer Landers?"

"Burke don't like us to go off the school grounds." *So it's going to cost you,* I finished silently.

"Burke won't never know, but if it'll ease your mind, I'll..." I wracked my mind for worst possible chore I could imagine. "I'll scrub out the sheep byre with Jerzy this Saturday; you can have the whole day to do what you want, maybe even go into town and see Daisy." I'd regret that when I was knee deep in cold muck, but this was important to me.

"You're on. What's the message?"

I told him, made him repeat it seven times because Benny C had a memory like a sieve and he was likely to get confused and end up telling Callan he was imposing taxes without consent or some other bit of the Declaration, but in the end he had it down.

If all went well, tomorrow Benny C would come home with a message for me, and the next day I'd see Callan again. True that I couldn't ever tell him how I felt, but I could see him, be his friend, spend time with him talking about books and about life, learning his ways—my guilty, secret pleasure.

The morning dragged on like the days leading to Christmas. Mam had given her consent that I could spend the afternoon in town, returning the healer's book and doing some marketing for her; Callan had sent a message, garbled horribly by Benny C, that either invited me to visit or told me that I should keep a standing army and quarter troops in his house. I'd be glad when the recitations were past and Benny C's mind was back to fixating on Daisy.

I did my chores without thinking, stoking the fire for breakfast, working the pump to bring water for the day's cooking and washing up, even gathering in the eggs, a job normally reserved for Delia. My body needed activity, needed to be moving with purpose to conceal the secret that my mind was already in the town with Callan.

Not so much a secret as I'd reckoned. It wasn't near to noon when Mam, her hands immersed in a vat of grease, looked up to see me walk into the frame of the door. "Go on down to town, you're worth nothing to me mooning around here like a lovesick ewe."

"Thanks, Mam." I took up the book, wrapped carefully in a threadbare but clean linen towel and slid it inside my coat pocket.

"Say hello to Luanna for me," she said.

"I am not—" I started to protest, then stopped. Better she think me lovesick over Luanna Burke than that it was Callan who held my heart. I just smiled back, and sprinted down the path.

It was a good forty minutes walk from our cabin to the outskirts of town, but I made it in much less, scrambling down the hillside heedless of rock falls, dodging from one cracked paving stone to the next; falling some, but always right back up on my feet. Then the trees cleared out some where the town people'd been harvesting them for timber and firewood, and I could see smoke from chimneys and the streets laid out.

It wouldn't do to come into town running as though I was being chased by the dragons; it'd stir up a fuss, and besides, I wanted time to compose myself before I saw Callan. I ain't much good at dissembling. Pa'd taught me that a man should be honest and truthful, and while I surely had my faults, lying wasn't one of them. The few times I'd tried to speak false as a child, my face had given it away, and it didn't seem like to me that I'd got any better at it.

But not speaking a truth weren't the same as telling a lie. If somebody were to take it in his head to ask me if I loved Callan Landers, that would be one thing; but that would be as likely as me being asked how I'd enjoyed my trip to the moon, so I should be safe...if I could only keep my thoughts from showing when we was together.

Walking up the street to the healer's, I thought on everything but Callan, forced myself to note the houses and shops I'd seen so often I barely noticed them, studied the brick and logs and timbers crafted by the machines of the Old People or hewn by the axes of my Pa's time. The school, the oldest building in the town, with its crumbling brick and odd spire; the little jail cells in their stone block building, empty now as usual.

Callan's house, though of course it was really Healer Findlay's house, was one of the oldest ones, with an old porch swing that had been repaired over the years so that the slats were all different kinds of wood. Despite the cold, Callan was sitting out on it; his hands, clumsy in my old gloves, holding a book.

"David!" He jumped up when he caught sight of me, and my resolve to school my expression into something unreadable crumbled like the brick of the school. I grinned back and sprinted up to the porch.

"Bit cold to be reading outside, I'd think." I noticed he was trembling. "And where's your hat?"

His feet—clad, I was relieved to see, in good solid boots—scuffed against the wooden porch looking for all the world like Delia when she'd been caught out playing in Mam's sewing box. "I...well, one of the claim farmers came in with his little girl yesterday, and honestly, David, they didn't have anything—they're losing the claim, being forced into tenancy. And the little girl had bronchitis that looked to be turning into pneumonia and she hadn't a hat and her coat was barely as thick as your shirt; she shouldn't have even left her farm, so I..."

I sighed, but weren't surprised, really. I'd seen him share the wheat bread with Almond, and how willingly he'd given his precious book to me when I was a stranger—it was just his way. "I understand. I'll get Mam to make you another—she's already outfitted us all for the winter."

"Thank you. You make me feel like family."

I couldn't love Callan like a man would love a woman; it would never be allowed and I had no notion of how such a thing could even be. But it might be that I could love him like a brother. A brother I chose, not one I'd got landed with by God or Nature and my Mam and Pa. "I'd like it fine if you'd think of yourself as family." I glanced up at him swiftly, uncertain if he'd meant his words as I meant mine. But I need have no worries, for he was grinning widely.

"If being family means hats and gloves and rabbit stew and spending time with you, then count me in."

Pleased and a bit embarrassed, I looked down at the floor, studying the dirt patterns his boots had left. "Thanks. Bit cold out here for you, though."

"I was waiting for you—let's go in." He led me into the waiting room, then down the hall and into a room I'd never been before. It was a sitting room, all proper carpets and furniture stuffed thick with padding, not flat and hard like the benches and chairs my Pa had made for our cabin. This was Callan's world. I wondered if it could be ever mine.

He sat down on a broad piece of padded furniture and gestured for me to come. "This sofa's springs are about shot, but it's better than being outside."

Though it creaked like a tree lashed by strong wind, it seemed mighty fine to me, soft and comfortable like what I'd always imagined a feather-tick mattress to be. There were pictures on the wall, the sort of thing that Taylor Mills painted; scenes of flower-covered fields the likes of which we would never see again, and pictures of men and women in fancy dress clothes. "You must have thought my place a sorry sight compared to this."

"Oh, no. Your house is a home. This may have nice things, but it's a lonely, cold room. It's people that make a place alive." He'd taken some trouble with his hair, looked like he'd had it trimmed up so it lay nice against his head. My fingers strayed up on their own, wanting to touch.

No. I stroked the soft surface of the sofa cover instead. "I guess these are Healer Findlay's things?"

"Yes. This is all left from her grandmother before the Ice. There's a kitchen and dining room in the back of the house, then two bedrooms upstairs."

I wanted to see Callan's bedroom, to be able to make pictures in my mind of him in his own place. "Could you show me? I'd like to see..." What was it he'd said? "The place that nourishes you."

"Meager nourishment in that room, but I'll show you if you like. It's little better than a garret and I'll warn you, the stove doesn't work."

He led me back to the hall and up a set of narrow stairs. "Jeannie's room is the larger, and it's got a fireplace." He gestured to a closed door. "And here's mine."

The door opened onto a room that was less than half the size of the loft bedroom I shared with Benny C, room enough for only a narrow bed, a small chest, and a stove. "It's cold as hell in here."

"Told you. I have good blankets and use hot bricks before bed. I manage." I wondered what he wore to bed, hoped he had warm bedclothes at least. It would be warm enough in that bed if there were two, sharing the heat of the covers. Our eyes met, and I felt the breath catch in my chest.

"Callan, I..." I didn't know what I was going to say, but the desire to speak a truth that shouldn't never be spoken fell on me.

"Funny, you know. In the old days they'd say 'hot as hell.' We say cold. I suppose it's because most of us don't have any real experience of heat anymore; heaven's warm, hell is more of what we have here. Of course, Dante saw parts of Hell as cold, so it's an old, old concept." He led me back down the stairs, saving me from ruining everything with my hasty words.

"Dante?" I watched the back of him as we descended the stairs; he had on store-bought trousers of light blue and a flannel shirt that was likely big enough for him and me together. I supposed some fat townsman had paid for his medicine with his old clothes. Callan should have fine things, things that were his, I thought, filled with a wild fierceness, and I remembered what my Mam had said about protecting the ones we love from pain.

"Dante Alighieri was an Italian who lived a very long time ago, wrote about a journey through heaven, purgatory and hell." We'd gone into the kitchen and he was putting a kettle on the hot stove and taking out two mugs. "I've got sassafras or chamomile or some nasty healing teas. Or...wait a minute!" Callan dashed out of the room and I heard footsteps drumming a rhythm on the stairs.

He returned with a small jar of dark brown powder, about the shade of good loam. "Cocoa! The last of what I brought with me. There's enough for you and for me, and you can take what's left home to your grandmother."

We didn't get import goods much in Moline. "You can't waste it on me," I protested.

"Giving it to you isn't waste at all." He measured out some of the cocoa into a pan and added white store sugar and milk from a bottle on a shelf. "Anyway, Dante wrote about nine circles of hell, each worse than the other with areas reserved for different sorts of sinners. The worst of them were icy levels."

The preacher at Mam's church sometimes spoke of hell and the punishment of the wicked, but he never got too detailed. "Do you believe in hell?" Most folks were religious after a fashion. Some were true believers and kept to Bible ways, though our family weren't like that. Pa had no use for what he called 'godly foolishness' and wouldn't take time from his hunting and trapping to go to church, and lately I'd been of the same mind.

"Only the hell on earth we create for ourselves," Callan said shortly, not looking up from the brown liquid that was giving off the most wonderful smell imaginable. "Same with heaven. No devils, just people, and we're more than capable of being evil on our own without having some supernatural agent to blame for it." He smiled sort of like he'd swallowed bitter medicine and was trying to hide it. "I hope that doesn't shock you. I know most people around here believe."

"It don't shock me. Sometimes I believe in God, sometimes I don't. I'm still sorting it all out, I guess. Wouldn't recommend you say such things to my Mam though."

"Oh, I wouldn't. Like I said, I know most people believe. Before the Ice, religion had declined quite a bit, but disaster tends to send people looking for comfort and explanation." He poured the cocoa into two chipped mugs and handed one over to me. "Okay, tell me what you think."

It was the sweetest thing I'd ever tasted. "It's like..." I struggled to find words to describe this wondrous drink. "Like in the mythology book at the school where the gods drink nectar. That's what this is like."

"My mother used to say that hot cocoa was liquid love. She'd make it when I was sick or hurt or discouraged, and things would always look up after that."

"You really shouldn't be wasting it on me—can't imagine that you'll get more anytime soon." But I was glad he'd shared it with me. It felt personal somehow, made me feel more a part of Callan's life before he'd come to Moline.

"You can get it in the cities, but it's awfully expensive. I'd been holding on to that for a while; I think it's time I let it go." He looked away. "And I can think of no better use than to share it with you."

We took our drinks back to the fancy parlor and sat quiet for a while. "So, could I read that Dante book?" I asked. Reading about wicked people being punished in hell would be something my Mam would approve of for certain.

Callan sighed. "Wait here." He went into the exam room and emerged with a book bound in leather and half-charred, swollen and buckled with water damage. "I'm afraid I can't really lend you this one. Not sure you'd get much use from it if I did."

I stroked the cover, which was rife with mold. "Did this happen in the Great Fires?"

"No, far more recent than that." I waited for him to explain, but he didn't, just kept looking at that book as though it had some secret meaning for him. A gust of wind rattled the window. "So did you like Huckleberry Finn?"

"I liked it fine," I told him, and, losing all hesitance and shyness, I began to talk about Huck and Tom and Jim and what it must have been like, rafting on the great river.

Callan just listened, mostly, beaming as though I'd paid him the highest praise, adding the odd comment or prodding me to explain myself.

"But what I don't understand," I said, "is what's at the end of the book. There's a long piece of writing talking about the use of one word, 'nigger.'"

"That's what's called criticism on the book. Before, there was a lot of sensitivity to that particular word. Some black people really objected to seeing or hearing it, so its use in the book was controversial."

"But it's just a name!" I protested. "Elmer and his gang used to call me every name from cry-baby to...to things I wouldn't repeat, and it didn't hurt me none—I just learned how to hit harder."

Callan drained the last of his cocoa, leaving a brown moustache on his upper lip. His tongue came out and cleared it and my stomach turned flips. "Okay, but think about how some city people call the people here rednecks or bubbas. How does that make you feel?"

I thought about that. Every summer we had the circuit judge through with his staff, and weren't shy about expressing their scorn for us, for our town and ways. Even in the court itself they'd called some of the defendants those names. "The circuit judge calls us that—don't really bother me too much, as we are bubbas, at least to him. No learning to speak of, most of us, anyways."

"But not everybody. And it's not formal education that matters. Look at you, David. You've just spent half an hour talking about a book, about ideas. That's not the behavior of a redneck or hillbilly."

That was true. "And it's not just me. There's more than a few here with real educations. Mister Zack Tyree was schooled in Charlottesville at the old University, and Taylor Mills was sent away for schooling somewheres."

You'd have thought the window'd blown in and the cold of the outside had swept through the room from the way Callan's back stiffened and his face grew grim. "Do you know Taylor Mills?"

"Not to speak to, but I know who he is." Then I remembered Callan, bundled in his coat, slipping into Taylor Mills' shop. "But you know him, don't you? I saw you the other day, going into his place."

He took a deep breath. "Yes. We talk sometimes. I haven't met too many people with education, or who care about books here, and he's incredibly smart. His parents had money, and they sent him to New Orleans to be educated."

"So you've that in common, both coming from the southlands?" Jealousy started to prickle my spine. Taylor Mills was older, older than Callan even, and he'd traveled and studied while I'd spent my life in one spot. He was a far more fitting friend for Callan than I could ever hope to be.

"I suppose." He turned to look at me, and his eyes were troubled. "Listen, David. Stay away from Taylor, all right? He's...he's difficult."

"Sure, whatever you say." He seemed so troubled that I felt obliged to change the subject. "Could I borrow another book?"

It was like watching one of the lamps flare up—he came alive and led me into the exam room while he studied on what to give me. "Something lighter, I think...No, that's not right..." He sighed in exasperation. "I wish I had more to choose from. Wait, I know." He pulled down a paper-bound volume with two men on horses dressed up like knights from the history books.

"Ivanhoe," I read. The book was scorched a bit on the edges, though not so bad as the Dante one had been. "Callan, this is falling to pieces. Are you sure you want me to—"

"I've read it a hundred times. Take it. Even if it falls apart completely, it's better that someone else knows the story than that I keep it on a shelf. It's like I said earlier; it's time I let things go."

He handed me the book and our hands touched as they had with Huckleberry Finn, and time stopped. I didn't attempt to take the book, and he didn't pull away. When I was in school, Master Burke had large cards with pictures of the Seven Wonders of the World, and he'd hold them up and tell us about them, and one was what he called 'the inscrutable Sphinx'. At that moment there was something inscrutable on Callan's face—the same mysterious thing I'd seen when we were wrestling, or when I put the hat on his head.

"Thanks," I finally said, and then, without pause, without time to think, I pulled him into a rough hug, the kind I'd seen my Pa give his brother Jake when I was small. But never did Pa and Uncle Jake's bodies fit so well together, nor did Uncle Jake ever give a half sob and shudder as Callan did, nor turn away whispering goodbye as I left, not sure if I had done right or wrong.

Chapter 6

As the end of fall eased into winter, we'd struck up a pattern. I would borrow a book, read it in two or three days, then go into town to see Callan armed with some errand for Mam, who thought I was using the visits to call on Luanna. What would happen when she learned the truth was something I didn't let myself think on. Callan and I would talk in the sitting room, or in the kitchen over cups of sassafras tea, as the remaining cocoa had been mixed with some white sugar and sent up home for Grandmam.

Oh, she'd been mighty thrilled to have it, even mixed with goat's milk instead of the cow's milk she'd had in her childhood. Mam was pleased, too, and filled with praise for Callan as the rare sort of healer who knew that the spirit of a person could be weary and wounded as well as their body.

So we drank our tea, cupping hands around the mugs to drink in the warmth of the liquid outside us as well as inside, for it was turning cold in earnest now; true winter was coming. I dreaded the day when I'd wake up and find the world gone all white and frozen, for that would be the end of my visits with Callan till the spring thaw. Dreams and memories would have to last me through the cold. Those dreams hadn't gone away, and I woke up most mornings still gripped in memories of Callan. Benny C had begun to complain that I was keeping him awake with my thrashing, and I was thankful that I'd never been one for talking in my sleep.

It had come round to mid-October and I'd brought back Lord of the Flies, which I'd finished in under a day. I didn't understand all of it, and it disturbed me greatly to read, as the doings of the boys on the island reminded me of stories I'd heard about the early days just after the Ice when people forgot their humanity and fell upon one another like wolves. I said as much to Callan.

"I think that's what the book is about. How close we all are to barbarism. Scratch the surface of a civilized man, and there's a savage underneath."

"I guess. I can't fathom it, though, the way those boys acted. And they was educated folk?"

"Finest products of their culture, but left to their own devices, they turned into a mob. Individual people are fine, but groups and mobs can turn ugly at a moment's notice. They feed each other's fears." There was something off about Callan's mood that day; he seemed to be hungering for something. Mam would have asked him if he was ill.

"You okay?"

"Yes. I'd just forgotten...It's nearly winter. You won't be able to visit much more, will you?"

"No. Even if I thought I could make it down the hill, Mam wouldn't never allow it. There's stories about folks freezing to death being outside only half an hour in a hard storm, and storms can come up without warning." For a while, the only noise was the regular ticking of Healer Findlay's wind-up grandfather clock. "I'll miss..." To say I'd miss him would sound wrong, girlish. "I'll miss our talks."

"So will I. I'll have to give you a whole stack of books to take back today, just in case the weather sets in earlier than we expect."

"That'd be nice." I fingered the edge of Lord of the Flies, which, like about half of Callan's books, had burned patches or water damage. "It's awful generous of you, books being so rare."

"You don't have any at your house, do you?"

"Don't think so. The school books are loaned, never saw a Bible growing up. All the stories we ever heard was told aloud."

"And that's the problem with the way things are today. Nothing's written anymore. Words that are written exist outside the minds and imaginations of the writers. Spoken words are ephemeral." He looked at me sort of sideways and must have realized I didn't understand. "They vanish, like mist when the sun breaks through."

I liked that about Callan, how he never dumbed down his speech for me, just made sure he explained himself clear. I was learning more from being his friend than I'd got out of eight years of Burke the School. "Well, Grandmam told us the same stories the exact same way every night for years. I could speak those tales in my sleep word for word as she'd given them to us."

"Oral tradition's an old way of transmitting information, sure, and in traditional cultures where bards and storytellers begin training in early childhood, it can be fairly accurate. But our culture isn't like that." It was cold near beyond the strength of the parlor stove to combat, so we were sitting fairly close together, though with the layers of clothing we were wearing it weren't too intimate.

"Maybe it's becoming that way, though?"

"I sincerely hope not. When the libraries burned, people gave their lives to try to keep our civilization from being lost, you know. I'd hate for that to have been in vain."

I hadn't known that, though I knew about the burning of the libraries—we'd had it at school. "They died for books?" I surely loved to read, but couldn't for the life of me imagine throwing myself in the path of an desperate mob of freezing people to save books.

"Yes. Some were killed quickly by gunshot; others burned with their books. It was brutal." He stared at his hands. "Or so they say."

"That's..." I didn't want to say stupid, for it seemed that something in this was not ancient history to Callan. "Foolish," I finally concluded.

"I suppose the world would consider it so, especially today. But it wasn't so much the books themselves as the ideas they represented." He reached down to the table in front of us and picked up Huckleberry Finn. "I've been re-reading this since you brought it back. Huck and Jim are like old friends to me, and this might be one of the few copies left—I would hope I'd have the strength to speak up if it was endangered, David." He was very serious, and so sad, like what we was talking of was far more than a flight of fancy. "Though likely I wouldn't. I'd probably just let it burn and save my own cowardly skin."

I didn't want to see what was like to be our last day together for a time swallowed up in bitterness, so I slid closer, for comfort's sake. "You ain't a coward. You come all the way up here from Florida on your own; that takes a heap more courage than I'd ever have."

"It's not courage when you have no choice. I couldn't go home, not after..." He gave that small sigh again that I'd come to learn meant we was treading on thin ice. "I thought I had an uncle up in Charlottesville. I got there to find he'd died, so I started back down south. I got as far as Moline when my money ran out, and Healer Findlay was gracious enough to take me on. That's not courage. It's desperation." I sidled up even closer such that our legs were lying in a line each against the other.

He didn't move away and I could feel his breathing, quick and shallow, and I leaned my head on his shoulder. Callan sighed, then relaxed a bit, just resting quiet-like, allowing me to linger there, so I turned my head and kissed him on the cheek. Nothing untoward—just a simple kiss like I'd have kissed Mam or Grandmam, or even Pa. Brothers and friends kissed, after all. I'd read it in books; remembered how in Scripture Judas had kissed Jesus, though that weren't an example I'd want to hold to.

His cheek was a bit rough, not stubbly like Pa's, but still the face of a man, not a boy. He stiffened up immediately and turned to look me in the eye. "David, there's something...I'm not sure how to say this..." I could see him fighting for words, something I understood only too well, for words never came easy to me the way they seemed to for Callan.

"You can tell me, whatever it is."

He was turning his hands over and over in his lap, restless, the way Mam did when she was stewing on something. "I think you should know that—"

A sharp noise in the hall sent me scrambling away from Callan like I'd been burned, and we both looked up. Sometimes there'd be folk come for healing while I was there and Callan would have to leave, though most days Healer Findlay was around somewheres. Callan had been a mite worried that he was shirking his responsibilities, but she'd reassured him that she'd managed fine on her own for years and he was, as she put it, entitled to a life. But today she'd gone downriver, leaving us alone.

"Damn it all to bloody hell," he swore, the first curse words I think I'd heard him say. "Later, I promise. No more waiting."

The door burst open, and the cold of the outside rode in on the coattails of Taylor Mills, who stood staring down at me like I was a bug he'd found on the bottom of his boot.

"Hope I'm not interrupting anything?" He arched his narrow brows, and though he was a handsome enough man, with clear grey eyes and hair like an autumn sunset, I didn't like the way he looked at us, like he'd discovered an egg that had been left rotting in the hayloft.

"Yes. You are, actually." Callan's reply was clipped, and he stood up. "Is there something I can do for you?"

Mills looked from me to Callan then back again. "Aren't you going to introduce me to your...friend?"

Callan looked as if he'd like to refuse, but reluctantly nodded to me. "David Anderson, this is Taylor Mills. Taylor, this is David Anderson."

I'd known him by sight of course. And surely he'd known me; though he'd only been back in town a bit over a year, Moline wasn't so large that you'd not know your neighbors.

"Brock Anderson's boy. Of course, of course. I've heard a great deal about you." He'd moved further into the room and was very close to Callan now. "Hear that you're quite the little intellectual." I didn't need no fancy education to read the scorn in his voice.

"I said, was there something I could help you with, Taylor?" Callan broke through my reply before I even had thought it out. Takes me near to forever to put my thoughts into words sometimes.

"Well, I was thinking we could work on that problem I've been having. You did say today would be convenient, as I recall?"

Callan glanced at me and sighed. "If you wouldn't mind, David? I know I'd promised you books, but—"

I stood up. "I expect the weather'll hold another week or so. I'll be down to watch the school recitations, in any case."

"Mmm." Taylor Mills was studying a painting on the wall; I wondered if it was his own work. "So sorry you have to go, David. Maybe we can meet again sometime, talk about those books you seem to like so much."

Callan was leading me down the narrow hall to the door, and Mills was right behind us, acting like he didn't want to miss anything we might say to one another. We stepped outside and Callan pulled the door shut behind us right in Taylor Mills' face.

"I'm so sorry about that. He's..." He run his hands through his hair.

"You'd said he's difficult—I'd say you was right." It was midafternoon, the sun at its highest, and the wind had died some. "I could stay round town for a while, if you think you might be finished before school lets out?" I'd promised Mam I'd walk the girls up the hill, as Benny C had asked to stay over at a friend's house for the night.

"Shouldn't be more than an hour." He glanced over his shoulder at the closed door. "Fifteen minutes more like, but better give us an hour."

I started down the steps and Callan went back through the door. Then I stopped, because Taylor Mills' voice came through loud and clear. "And just what the hell was that about? I thought today was ours?"

"I wasn't expecting David to finish the book so quickly." Callan's reply was muffled.

Mills' laugh sounded like it was forced from his body. "Not surprised about that—I doubt that ignorant bubba can even read without following his finger across the page."

My heart sank, and I remembered our talk about Huck and Jim and the word 'nigger.' I'd been wrong. It hurt like a mortal wound.

"Shut up!" Now Callan was shouting. "You're not fit to say his name!" I'd never heard his voice raised, not once, and now it was raised in defense of me; I longed to linger near the door. But Mam's teachings about eavesdropping were pretty clear, and in any case, they must have moved down the hall, as I couldn't make out nothing else.

It weren't too cold at the moment; some townfolk was out, weathering their houses and small gardens, doing a bit of trade. I figured I could kill an hour at the General easy, looking at the goods, or talking to Mister Haig or Philip. Might be some word from Washington on those dragons the R&A said didn't exist that I could take home to Pa.

There was a fair crowd at the General; a few women doing marketing, and men standing back by the counter chewing the fat with Mister Haig. Just as when I'd come for the seed, they greeted me warmly and asked after my Pa and Mam. Mam had asked me to pick up a few notions for her sewing, so I had Mister Haig pack them up and put them down to our account.

"Hear any more about the dragons?" I asked the group of men. They sort of exchanged shifty glances and wouldn't meet my eye.

Then Mister Haig said, "Mayor's asked us not to talk to the women and children about it, David. Sort of afraid it'll create a panic."

"I'm near on seventeen," I protested, but from behind me I heard, "That's still a child, little boy. Stay away from man's doings."

It was Elmer Casteel, loaded down with bottles of white, creamy liquid. The Casteels kept cows, the only farmer round these parts who did, and they jacked the price of the milk and beef so high that most folks could have more easily drunk liquid gold. We could afford it, but Pa'd always refused to pay the prices, saying goat's milk was good enough for his family.

But that cow's milk would be just perfect in what remained of Grandmam's cocoa. I'd had it that way with Callan and compared with what we'd made at home, it weren't at all the same. I'd saved some money of my own; not a lot, but had surely enough put by for a pint of milk.

"How much for a pint of that?" I ignored his jibes at me; every man there knew Elmer Casteel for who he was and knew me too.

"Five dollars gold," he said, smirking.

"Elmer, that's twice what you charge anyone else," Mister Haig said sharply. "You give David a decent price or you can peddle your cow piss on the street."

He grumbled low so's we could pretend not to hear it and lowered his price to three dollars. I could've dickered a bit, maybe brought it down to two and a half, but it wasn't worth it. "Done, now give me the milk."

"Give me the money," he countered, and I realized I'd walked out of Callan's sitting room so flustered that I'd left my bag behind.

"I left my bag at the healer's place. I'm good for it."

He shook his head. "No money, no milk. I'm done here, got to walk right by there to get to my uncle's place, so you can fetch it. If you really got any money, that is."

I ground my teeth together, but agreed. Elmer settled up with Mister Haig, leaving all the bottles save one, which he handed off to me. "You c'n carry that."

"Taxes your muscles something awful, don't it, Elmer?" I started back down Main Street and he trailed behind me as if he didn't want none of his gang to know he was with me. Suited me fine, as the last thing I felt like was making small talk with Elmer Casteel.

The place was closed up, but I knew the door was never locked during daylight hours. I'd hoped that maybe Callan would be done with whatever problem Taylor had and would be waiting for me, but as I entered the house, I saw the door to the exam room was shut tight like it was in use, so I figured I'd slip back to the parlor, get my bag, and pay Elmer, no one the wiser that I'd ever been there.

The parlor door wasn't latched, so I pushed it open. It was a good door with hinges well oiled so that it opened smooth and silent, giving no warning that I was there. The room was as we'd left it, down to the mugs of tea we'd shared sitting on the table. The sofa was unoccupied and so were both overstuffed chairs, but Callan was leaning against the far wall, shirt loosened to expose a smooth, flat chest, trousers down to his ankles. His eyes were closed, but his face wore an expression I'd never before seen: a look of pure bliss. And on his knees before him, moving rhythmically back and forth, mouth where one man's mouth shouldn't never be on another man, was Taylor Mills.

The bottle slid to the ground and shattered, sending milk spilling across the wood floor. Callan's eyes opened and he saw me, and for a moment I saw the fox, caught in the trap and knowing I was its death.

"Oh God no, David..." He shoved Taylor away, violently forcing him back so he slipped in the puddle left by the milk, and scrambled backwards away from both of us. Then footsteps and Elmer's voice, "Damn, Anderson, you clumsy lunkhead! You're payin' for that!"

Taylor was up and trying to get past me, but Elmer was in the door, and he took one look at him and at Callan, who was still near mother-naked, and started hollering bloody murder. All the while I was frozen in place like a snow statue on a January day.

Taylor was gone and Elmer, too, raising the alarm, and still I kept on staring, not understanding, not wanting to be understanding what I had seen, for to think on it was making my head swim and my stomach turn into knots. Callan hadn't moved neither, was just staring at me, waiting for something to cut through the silence.

Shouting from the outside, new voices—men's voices—broke the spell, and Callan pulled up his trousers, covering that which I had tried not to see. But of course, I had seen, and now my dreams would have fact behind them. Hopeless dreams, and now I knew it. Though it seemed Callan shared my secret sin, it was Taylor Mills he wanted. Not me.

I tried to speak his name, but the words weren't working, and I heard the sharp retort of footsteps on the porch and voices raised in anger while the room began to spin, and I tasted the tea in my mouth like foul medicine, and I was falling. Falling into a pit with no end, because Callan wasn't ever going to be there to catch me.

I woke with the taste of bile in my mouth and a softness under me that weren't my own mattress. Eyes open, I saw sunlight streaming in through a curtained window and the chaos of a destroyed room. I was in the healer's parlor, and I was alone. Why was I... It came back in a flood, the picture of Callan and Taylor, horrible and yet fascinating, the milk bottle that still lay in pieces on the ground, and Elmer's squeals. Like a pig who'd won a prize.

The table'd been upended, and I picked up Callan's copy of Twain's book and slid it in my pocket so it wouldn't get hurt, then I went out onto the porch. Sheriff Fletcher was talking quietly to a group of three men. The only one I recognized right off was Mister Zack Tyree, but they all looked pleased to see me. "David, you're all right!"

"Yessir," I replied to the sheriff, but I was craning my neck around to see any sign of Callan. "Can I ask-"

"Hold on one moment, please, son." The sheriff turned back to the men. "I'd say he'd have gone south, so Zack, take your people that way. He's on foot, but I doubt he knows the game trails, so stay with the old roads."

Mister Zack nodded grimly and led the other men away, then the sheriff turned back to me. "Terrible thing this is, David. I'm sorry you had to be a part of it."

I didn't care about that. "Who are they looking for?" I couldn't imagine that Callan would have run.

"Taylor Mills. He hotfooted it out of town with young Casteel just behind him. About two miles behind him by now, I'd say. But don't worry, we'll bring him in."

I wasn't worrying over Taylor Mills; he'd run off and left Callan to face the law. For all I cared he could freeze to death on the hills and good riddance to bad rubbish. "Where's Callan?"

Sheriff Fletcher put his hand on my shoulder. I'd never noticed it before, but he and I were of a height now. "He's over at the jail, David. I know this is hard for you—I'd heard he was your friend."

"He is my friend," I said. And it was true. It had hurt me bad, seeing Callan with Taylor, knowing he didn't care for me as I did for him, and more than that, that the trust and honesty I thought we'd had between us was all a sham. But he was still my friend. And I had to see him.

"You go on home, you hear? I sent your sisters up the hill with Haig's Phil, and I'm sure your parents are expecting you."

I nodded, and started up the street, but at the first cross road I turned, heading toward the jail. It was a rare thing—a building from the Before still used for its original purpose, though I found it hard to imagine that Moline had ever had enough crime to fill the four cells. Nowadays it was mostly liquored up farmers, sleeping it off where they weren't liable to get into fights or fall into the creek and drown.

The jail office was set smack in the front of the building, and Deputy Aaron Wells was sitting at a desk, feet up. I knew Aaron; he was a decent man who'd been a year ahead of Elmer Casteel at school.

"Afternoon, Deputy." It didn't do no harm to give folks the proper respect due their titles when you was asking for something. "I'd like to see Callan Landers, please."

"Oh, David, I don't think your Pa would like that."

"He ain't here. And I'm seventeen." For the first time since I was ten years old, I'd knowingly bent the truth. Seventeen still weren't of age, but it was close enough for most things in our town.

I could see him considering the matter. "Sheriff wouldn't like it either. But I can't see how it would hurt, so go on. But you got twenty minutes tops."

I thanked him and walked down the bare corridor to the cells. It was colder inside than out, likely because the only heat in the whole building came from a brazier in the office and the walls were crumbling concrete block. The cells themselves were barred and dingy, with neither lamps nor candles nor windows, the only light streaming in through a window at the end of the corridor. There was no furnishings save a chamber pot on the floor and a hard bench built into the outside wall. Callan lay on the bench facing away from me with a thin blanket pulled over him. "Callan?"

He didn't turn. "Go away, David. You shouldn't be here."

"I ain't going nowhere till I know you're all right."

"I'm fine." His voice sounded hoarse, as though he'd been screaming.

"Then get up and show me." I didn't pay no mind to proper speech nor manners. There weren't any cause for pretense between us, not no more.

He pushed the blanket back and sat up. The light was just good enough for me to see his lip was split and one of his blue eyes was ringed with purple bruising.

"Who done that?" I couldn't credit that Sheriff Fletcher would have ever struck a man without cause.

He gave a haggard smile. "You were fainting; I tried to help you. They seemed to think I was resisting arrest. It's okay, just bruises." But he groaned low as he stood, and favored his left side strongly as he walked over to the bars where I waited.

"David, I'm so sorry you had to see that. I never wanted—"
I didn't wait for him to finish. "Why on God's frozen earth didn't you tell me? Couldn't you trust me, Callan?"

He backed away from the rage I couldn't control. "It's not that! I wanted to tell you. I started to, today before...before Taylor...showed up. But there just aren't any words for it that aren't ugly." Sinking back onto the bench, he lowered his head into his hands. "There used to be, though. For the ancient Greeks it was the highest expression of love. Even in the Bible, young David loved Jonathan with a love surpassing the love of women."

"Never heard that in Sunday school," I said softly.

"No, don't suppose you did. But you're right—I should have told you."

"What happens now?" In the back of my mind, I knew that there were laws about this sort of thing, but I had no idea how they worked. The law was something I'd no experience of beyond watching the circuit judge each summer like Grandmam said they'd watched the circus freak show in her day.

"Well, I don't know much about Virginia legal procedure, but in Florida there'd be a Grand Jury hearing where witnesses would testify, and then they'd decide if there's enough evidence to try us. Well, me, as they tell me Taylor's not been found." I'm shamed to say the bitterness in his voice at his love's betrayal lightened my heart. And then what he'd said penetrated the fog that still surrounded me.

"Witnesses?" I breathed out, relieved. "Callan, you're saved. Elmer Casteel's a bald faced liar and every man in this town knows it. Ain't nobody going to believe a thing he says, not over your word. Why, if he said the sun was up at noon, folks would run outside to check."

Even in the half-light I could see the pity in his eyes, in the set of his mouth. "David. There's another witness, well spoken and reliable, a young man with a reputation for honesty. He'll be believed."

No. Oh, no. I couldn't. I didn't know I'd spoken aloud till he replied. "You have to. Listen, don't worry. There's not likely going to be much consequence to it all."

The shadows had been lengthening and I knew my time was short—Aaron would want me gone before the sheriff returned. But I had to know. "What do you mean, not much consequence? What could happen to you?"

"Well, you have to understand that the law against...what I've done passed not long after the Ice came, when people were afraid, and fear makes people do crazy things. Religious people thought God was punishing us for certain types of behavior, so they worked with others who were justifiably concerned over the decline in population and—"

"Callan, just tell me."

"It's a worst case scenario, and highly unlikely—I've only ever heard of it being applied in cases of corruption of a child, or rape—but in most states, the maximum penalty for sodomy is death."

I gripped the bars, afraid for a moment I was going to repeat my shameful fainting spell of before. "Death?" I whispered. "For that?"

"No. I told you not to worry about it. Most likely it'll be banishment from the town or maybe physical punishment." In the old days they'd locked criminals away for years and years. We couldn't do that—didn't have the extra men to guard them nor the provisions to keep those who did no work. So petty crimes were punished with beatings, and serious ones with hanging. He pulled the blanket around him, and I wondered if the shivers were down to cold or fear.

I couldn't do much about the fear, but I could help with the cold some. "It's cold as hell in here, and you ain't got a coat or even an outdoor shirt. I'm giving you my coat." I started to strip it off. I could hear voices from down the corridor. The sheriff was back.

"I should protest and say no, but it's going to be freezing in here tonight, and I'm grateful for it." He seemed formal, like things had changed between us, and I wondered if they would ever be the same.

"Can I ask you something?" He said nothing, just looked up at me. "It seemed like...I mean, before Elmer commenced to screeching and everything went sour, that you were taking pleasure in...in what Mills was doing?" I tried to imagine what that would feel like, though it weren't Taylor Mills' mouth I longed for.

"Oh, yes. I suppose. Though it certainly wasn't worth what I've lost."

"What do you think you've lost?"

"My freedom, for one thing. My job, most likely, and the respect I'd started to earn in this town. Probably my home. And your friendship; that hurts most of all." The words cracked like melting ice.

"I'm here, ain't I?" My limbs felt heavy, the weight of gravity pulling me down.

"I rather thought you were here to get answers to your questions and say goodbye." He'd come back towards the bars, still limping.

The sheriff was shouting at Aaron and his voice echoed clear into the cell. "I'm here because I want to help you, Callan."

The milk jar had smashed on the floor of the parlor, fragile, precious glass fragmenting and falling into pieces. That was Callan then; he shattered, collapsing against the bars, head down so I couldn't tell if he was crying or just breathing harshly. Our hands touched, lightly at first and then with crushing force, as I poured all my unspoken feelings into my grip.

I heard my own name being called and I thrust the coat through the bars.

He'd pulled himself together enough to smile at me. "The sheriff might not like you giving me this."

"He won't never know. Pa says Sheriff Fletcher's a decent man but couldn't detect dog doo if he stomped on it."

"Not exactly Sherlock Holmes then?" He'd slipped the coat on—it was too big, but that was all to the good.

"Who's that?"

"He's in a book. I'll..." I could tell he was going to offer to lend it to me, then stopped himself. Everything had changed. The door to the cell area slammed open.

The book—I'd almost forgot. "Check the pocket."

He felt into the front pocket and took out Huckleberry Finn. "Thought you might like to spend some time with a couple of old friends." I smiled, and he returned it, and I figured maybe things weren't the same, but they were right enough to work with.

Chapter 7

Sheriff Fletcher had a few choice words to say to Aaron about letting the prime witness in to visit the suspect. "Especially since they're friends, you dunderhead! Bet you didn't even pat him down for weapons!"

Aaron hung his head, and so did I, figuring I'd earned the dressing-down I was about going to get. The sheriff shook his head in disgust. "He could've snuck Landers a gun!"

"Aw, Sheriff, I would'a seen a gun."

"You wouldn't see your nose if you was staring in a mirror. Get on home. I'll take over here." Aaron hightailed it out the door, leaving Sheriff Fletcher looking at me. He stroked his beard and I thought on how it hid his expression, made it hard to know what he was thinking, and wondered if that was one reason men grew beards. I ain't got any whiskers to speak of yet. I wondered if Callan shaved regular. I supposed he must—he was twenty-three, after all.

"David. What am I supposed to do with you?" He sounded genuinely confused.

"Is there a rule that says prisoners don't get visitors?"

"No, son, of course not. But I know your father wouldn't have wanted you to see that young man. And you know it, too."

True enough. Neither Pa nor Mam would have countenanced me seeing Callan again. But it didn't matter. "With respect, Sheriff Fletcher, and I do respect you and my Pa both, I have to follow my conscience; it wouldn't be right to just abandon a friend."

He sighed. "You're your daddy's boy, David. Guess I'll leave him to deal with you. Go on with you."

I started to go, wanting to make it up the hill before sunset, then turned back. If anybody knew the truth of what was to happen to Callan, it ought to be the sheriff.

"Can I ask, what happens now?"

He'd sat down at his desk and had taken out a book from the drawer, a law book, I figured. "To tell you the truth, I'd rather none of this ever come to light. Though I don't condone this sort of...behavior, I don't much care what folk get up to behind their closed doors." He opened the book, carefully turning the pages. "According to the law, there's a hearing before a Grand Jury. Probably happen day after tomorrow, as we need to get this done before the weather sets in. Then I figure a trial."

We had trials once a year, in August, when the circuit judges came through. Surely they weren't planning on keeping Callan locked up through the winter? "In August at the Circuit?"

"No, we'll send for a special judge from Richmond. Should all be over and done within a week, if we're lucky and the snow don't fall."

"Of course, I guess everything depends on what the Grand Jury finds, right?"

"Suppose so." He drew the lamp closer to his book. "Better you should ask your Pa about that—he's on the Grand Jury for this term."

I hurried out of the jail and back up the old road to home, moving quickly, pushing my body hard so that I shouldn't have time to think, but it didn't work. Of course I'd known Pa was taking a turn on the Grand Jury. I remembered when he'd been appointed at the August Circuit, and how proud I'd been because mostly it was town folk called to serve. But now he'd have to sit judgment on Callan, and he'd have to listen to me...No. I couldn't say the things I saw in front of a group of strangers, and certainly not my own Pa. Callan was my friend, and the second worst thing in Pa's eyes was betraying a friend. But the very worst was telling lies. It seemed I was trapped.

Dusk had fallen before I got home, a sudden dusk that come on as I was rounding the bend to the tree where I'd met Callan the day we'd walked the traplines. I stopped there, wrapping myself up in the memory of what his eyes had looked like when I'd pinned him to the ground under this very tree, then went inside to face my folks.

Mam was sitting at the table with one lamp burning in front of her and her hands was still. Mam is always busy. From the moment she rises up till she goes down at night, her hands are moving; cooking, sewing, knitting, spinning, cleaning. But tonight she was just sitting. And the girls was nowhere to be seen, though it was just past supper and they ought to be at the table doing their lessons. Grandmam was up, sitting in her accustomed place by the fire.

"Sorry I'm late," I mumbled. "There was some trouble in town."

"I know. Your Pa's been called out to help in the search for Taylor Mills."

I pulled on a spare coat that hung on the pegs by the door, hoping that Mam wouldn't ask about my good one.

"Where are you going, David?"

I couldn't face her questions nor her sympathy, not yet. "Chores want doing."

She stood up. "I think we need to talk about this. Sit down." When I didn't move, she put her hands on her hips. "David Anderson, you're not too big to put over my knee if it comes to that. Now you sit yourself down right now."

I sat, and she put a plate with some cold meat and goat cheese and the last of the wheat loaf on it in front of me. I ate without thinking, but I must have been hungry, as the plate was clean in no time flat. With my mouth still full of cheese, I muttered, "You want to talk, so talk."

She put her hand on my shoulder. "Oh, sweetheart, you don't have to be all manly and tough with your own mam. It's not every day a boy comes to find out someone he thought was a friend is involved in the worst sort of sin. I imagine you're awful confused right now, and feeling mighty betrayed."

She was right on that, though not for the reasons she supposed. I kept my mouth shut, but her sympathy was making my stomach clench.

"We were all taken in by him; it's like they say in scripture, evil and corruption can wear a pleasant face—"

"He ain't evil! Nor corrupt, neither! You don't know what you're talking about." I pushed back from the table, knocking the bench to the ground. "And if this makes Callan evil, then—" I stopped. I'd been going to say, 'so am I,' thinking that if she knew her own son had 'unnatural' desires, she'd have to accept it. But I could hear Callan's words echoing in my mind. In the eyes of the law, I was still a child, and corruption of a child, that would get the death penalty. "Then I guess evil ain't so bad!"

Grandmam stirred in her seat and looked up at us. "What's David gone and done, May-Marie?"

"Not David, Mama. That healer that was here a while back."

"Oh, yes. He sent me cocoa." Grandmam stared into the fire. "Such a nice young man. What's he done, then?"

Mam flushed. "He's...David and Mayor Casteel's nephew caught him. With another man."

Grandmam turned slightly to face us and giggled like a girl. "Got an eyeful, did you David? They should've locked the doors, I'd say."

"Mother!" Mam's face was like fire. "David shouldn't never have seen such a thing!"

"I expect he's seen men's 'things' before today, child. All he has to do is look down." Grandmam was livelier than I'd seen her in months.

"That's not—" she sputtered. "That's not the point, and you know it. It's immoral for two men to lie together. It goes against the Scripture and the law!"

I remembered Huck Finn, floating with Jim down the Mississippi, contemplating the law that allowed for one man to own another. "If there was a law against you and Pa loving each other, would that make you stop, Mam?"

"How dare you!" I'd never seen my Mam so furious. Mostly she was like a squall storm: quick to rise, quick to die down. This time, something I said had dug deep. "Don't you dare liken what those two perverts get up to with the love between you father and me!"

"For all you know, Callan might feel just the same about Taylor Mills as you do about Pa!" It tore me up to admit that, as Mills weren't near worthy of him, but I was hoping I could bring her to see reason.

"I won't suffer to hear that young man's name mentioned in this house again!" She stormed over to the stove and commenced stirring a pot of something.

"Then I won't stay in this house!" I slammed the door behind me and stood in the frigid night air, breathing in cold so sharp it bit into me, but welcoming each pain in my chest as I drew breath. It was better than the pain of remembering what had happened.

The barn was warmer than the outside by a long ways. The body heat of the stock and the barn fires already burning for the night kept the chill at bay. Jerzy was back in his lean-to, and I was glad of it, not wanting to make talk with him. Not now. It had all gone so fast, from the moment I pushed open the parlor door to seeing Callan at the jail to the fight with Mam; there had been no time to sort it all out. I settled against a pile of feed bags and pulled a worn horse blanket around my shoulders.

I'm not much for reflection and deep thinking. Life don't allow me a lot of time to sit and philosophize, and till recently, I'd never had much worth philosophizing over anyways. I read books, sure, but they was pure enjoyment, an escape into a world different from my own. It took Callan to show me that books could be more than that. He opened up a world to me where educated folk talked about ideas and dreams. And he showed me, through no intention nor fault of his own, some truths about myself as well.

I ain't normal. I made myself say that in my mind, to name it as a truth. I'd never liked girls the way I was supposed to, and now I knew why. It had taken Callan's presence in my life to wake that part of myself, but I couldn't never let on, not to him, not to nobody. The town would blame him for corrupting me, and I figured he'd blame himself as well, and that I couldn't have. But knowing he was the same as me, that I weren't alone in this fearsome strangeness, that was a mighty comfort.

The barn door creaked open and I looked up to see Ruby standing with a big mess of quilts in her arms. "Thought maybe you'd be needing these."

Pride warred with the desire for warmth, and lost. "Thanks, Ruby."

"Mam and Grandmam are rowing something awful. Woke Almond and made her cry." Ruby, so often a tease and a thorn in my side, seemed weighed down and sober. "Figure your friend must've done something terrible. Did he kill a man?"

I almost laughed thinking how unlikely that would be. "No, nothing like that. You're too young to understand."

She scowled down at me in the half-light. "That's what Mam said too. I'll ask Benny C when he comes home. He'll tell."

He would, too. He and Ruby were closest in age of all of us, barely a year apart, and Benny C couldn't resist carrying a tale. He'd tell Ruby and probably Delia as well, but not the whole truth, for he'd not know that. Just half-truths and rumors, making Callan look like a cross between the Frost Giants out of Grandmam's stories and Satan himself. It was better that she have it from me. "He fell in love, that's what he done."

"Ooo!" Ruby squealed. "With another man's wife? Is he locked in 'dultrous passion?"

"What in the name of all that's warm are you talking about?" 'Dultrous passion. I shook my head.

"Benny C's girl Daisy has a book—it's her mam's, but she's been reading it and telling us the story at recess. There's this young, beautiful woman and she's married to this old man with a whole lot of money and—"

I cut her off, as she'd have gone on for an hour or more over it. "No, he's not in love with another man's wife. It's...he's in love with another man."

She was quiet for a minute, thinking on it. "How's that even work? Where would they get their babies?"

I'd been like that as a child, not imagining any purpose for two people to come together in sexual congress save for making life. She'd learn. "Not every couple in love has babies, Ruby. Mister Zack and his wife never had none, and they was married for upwards of ten years till she died."

I could see she was still trying to work it all out. "Mam was screaming that your friend's a sodomite, and Preacher's talked about how God destroyed their city. I can't see God doing that just 'cause two men fell in love." She thought I was holding out on her, not telling the whole truth.

"God's ways can be something of a mystery." It was Pa. He was holding a lamp, and the dancing light reflected in his dark eyes. "Go on inside, Ruby."

"I was bringing David his blankets," she said stubbornly.

"That was good of you, daughter. Say goodnight to your brother now."

She gave me a swift hug. Pa held the door open for her and watched her run back to the cabin. Then he closed the door, set the lamp on a stand, and came over to set on a bench nearby. The sheep made gentle bleating noises as he walked by, greeting him.

"It's going to be powerful cold out here tonight, son."

I turned away from him. "Not so cold as it is in that jail cell."

"We caught up with Taylor Mills just outside of town. He was holed up in the ruins of the foundry."

I didn't say nothing—didn't much care about Taylor Mills.

"He tried to fight some, but it weren't no use."

Still I sat, knees pulled up close to my chest, just waiting.

"That's my spare coat you're wearing, ain't it?"

I nodded.

"Gave the other to the Landers boy, I suppose." My head whipped around. "Come on, David, I've been your Pa for going on seventeen years now. I know a thing or two about you."

"They didn't even let him get his coat before they took him, Pa, and the blanket in that cell wouldn't have done for a donkey."

"Get your fight down, I ain't criticizing you none. I 'spect you'll get the coat back and I'm proud of you for caring for your friend."

He sank down off the bench to sit beside me. "My land, this floor's cold. Makes me long for a nip of whiskey."

"Do you think Callan's evil? Mam said—"

"Your Mam and I don't see eye to eye on matters of faith, David, you know that." One of the yearling lambs had broke away from the huddled mess of sheep and had come over to Pa, who reached out and nuzzled it. "No, I don't think he's evil. But he's misguided to say the least, and no matter how this all comes out, this ain't a friendship that you can continue."

"You always said a man ought to be loyal to his friends, now you're saying I should abandon Callan at the first sign of trouble?"

"This ain't just a 'sign of trouble'—it's a felony, and if your Mam turns out to be right, a mortal sin. I don't want him corrupting you, or having anyone in town thinking that he has."

"I don't care what everyone in town thinks."

"I know you don't, and mostly I'm glad of it. You make me proud most times, son. And I know you'll make me proud tomorrow as well."

Tomorrow? Even in the dim light, he must have sensed my question.

"The Grand Jury's convening at nine o'clock down at the school."

I hugged myself tighter. "Pa, I can't! Ain't there any way you can get me out of it?"

"I've heard tell how you was all over town today claiming the rights of a man; at the General, in the jail, and I'm not saying a word against that because you've done a man's work for more than a year and I'd say that entitles you. But you can't be a man and a child both. A child might be excused from testifying, seeing as we've got Elmer as witness, too; but a man will do his duty." His voice was mild, but I could hear the steel in it. "David, I don't know the healer boy very well, but until this incident I've heard naught but good about him. I don't think he'd want you to become a liar or a coward on his behalf."

The lamb had moved over to me, cool black nose pushing against my shoulder. Its wool was soft and thick and warm, and I clung to it as Almond did her stuffed dolly. Pa was waiting for an answer. "I'll do what's right, Pa."

He stood, brushing bits of straw and wool from his trousers. "I never doubted that, son. I'm just sorry you have to be involved in such a thing. Growing up's hard enough as it is—I'd have done anything to spare you this."

But sparing me this would have meant sparing me Callan and our friendship, and that I could never wish for. "I know, Pa. I know."

I trailed behind Pa all the way down the hill the next morning, not speaking till we reached the school. We entered through the double doors and went straight into the main room, which was empty save for Healer Findlay and Sheriff Fletcher. "Where's all the kids?" I asked. I hadn't gone back into the cabin and had figured the girls had gone off to school as normal.

"Burke's called a holiday," Pa answered.

"Some holiday. Celebrating the crucifixion of Callan Landers and Taylor Mills." Healer Findlay never pulled her punches, and I liked her for that. The Healer was ordinarily the most energetic woman I'd ever seen, just bursting with life. Today, though, she looked world weary and older than I'd ever seen her, grizzled hair caught up in a sloppy bun and with what I was sure was the tracks of tears on her face.

"Jeannie, hush. The law's the law." The sheriff had been arranging things at a long table, and the room had been done over, with most of the student desks moved back against the wall and a long table sitting near the teacher's podium with five chairs behind it. A lone stool stood a few feet away, and on the table was a book of laws and a Bible. The courtroom setup was familiar to me, as this was where the Circuit met, but then there'd have been rows of seats and benches for the spectators.

"That doesn't mean I have to like it. The law is an ass, as a wise man once said." Then she saw me standing behind my Pa and her expression softened. "Hello, David."

I nodded, but didn't speak. I'd thought it through all night and all the way down the hillside, and I knew what I had to do. It only remained to be seen if I had it in me to do it.

The door opened behind us and Burke the School and Curtis Henslow come in, talking quietly, then Elmer with his uncle the mayor, and an older man about Healer Findlay's age who I'd seen around town of late but did not know.

Mayor Casteel greeted everybody like he was hosting a campaign shindig, pumping hands and clapping backs. "Dirty business," he kept saying over and over. "Dirty, dirty business."

"Mayor," Sheriff Fletcher said with thinly disguised distaste. "You didn't have to come."

"Just supporting my nephew, and of course letting the public know that I'm standing up for what's right and seeing justice done, Bill." Mayor Casteel was a great beefy bull of a man, fitting for one who raised cattle, I suppose, and he dwarfed the sheriff, who was long and rangy like Callan.

"Well, Grand Jury proceedings is closed to the public, and that means you as well. And what're you doing here?" he said to Mister Henslow.

Healer Findlay spoke up. "He's here for me, Bill. Curtis is our alternate, remember, and I'm sorry, but I've got to recuse myself from hearing this case. I've become very fond of Callan over the past year and I couldn't be impartial, not even if I wanted to. Which I don't."

"I should do the same, with my boy as one of the witnesses." Pa glanced back at me.

"Now Brock, I don't think that's necessary. There's nobody thinks you'll be anything but fair. And besides, there's only one alternate." That was from the man I didn't know, and there were murmurs of agreement from the rest.

Finally, Sheriff Fletcher escorted the mayor out and the group assembled around the table. Pa and the unknown man were opposite each other on the ends, with Burke and Henslow in the next seats in, leaving a space at the center for the sheriff. "You're welcome to stay, Jeannie. I know it's irregular, but you're on the Jury, after all."

She smiled and took a seat near the back. "Most obliged, Bill."

The unknown man looked a bit unhappy with that, but held his tongue. Sheriff Fletcher sighed. "Guess its time to bring in the accused, then." He vanished into Master Burke's office then came out leading Taylor Mills, who was shackled with old iron chains, and then Callan. I sought out his face, but he was looking down, refusing to meet anyone's eyes. I was glad to see he weren't chained, just handcuffed, and he moved better than the night before, though he seemed bone-weary.

Then the sheriff turned to Elmer and me. "You two will wait in the hall unless you're actually testifying. David, your pa's requested you go last, so go on out there. Elmer, put your hand on the Bible and swear your oath."

I could hear Elmer's words, promising—falsely, no doubt—to tell the truth, the whole truth, and nothing but the truth, as I left the room. There was a bench outside,

A Strong and Sudden Thaw   81

and I sat on it, waiting. The door remained open and nobody told me to close it, so I didn't, hoping I could hear some of what Elmer said.

I snuck a look around the corner into the room. They was all staring at Elmer, save for Healer Findlay, who seemed to be looking at Callan (who was still looking at the floor). Then almost as if she'd heard me, she gave me a sharp glance and shook her head, so I returned to my bench.

I couldn't make out much of what Elmer said, save for one time when he said something about 'Solemnites,' which had the Grand Jurors laughing fit to beat all. It weren't long before Healer Findlay came out, red-faced and burning with anger.

"They're ready for you, David," she snapped.

"What did Elmer say?" I couldn't imagine that he'd have said much that could condemn Callan, as he'd come in late and missed what I had seen.

"I'm not able to say till you've given your own testimony," she said, then, glancing into the schoolroom, added, "but that Elmer Casteel is a piece of work."

She returned to her seat and I walked up the aisle to the front, passing Taylor Mills, who was clanking his chains idly as if he was acting a ghost in a school play, and Callan, who tensed his shoulders when I walked by. I wanted more than anything to reach out and touch him, to let him know he weren't alone, but the five stern faces waiting for me drew me on, and I put my hand on the Bible and said my words.

"Please state your name for the Grand Jury," the sheriff said.

I cleared my throat. Sitting here like this was too much akin to school recitations to be of comfort. "David Everett Anderson."

"And your age?"

"Sixteen."

The sheriff looked over at Curtis Henslow, who was scribing notes on a sheet of paper. They'd just recently started up making paper in bulk again, and it was used mainly for things such as this—records and legal papers and the like. "Let it be noted in the record that David, being a minor, is testifying with the advice and consent of his father, Brock Anderson, here present." Then back to me. "And your occupation?"

"Farmer."

"And David, do you know the defendants in this case?"

"Yessir. That's Taylor Mills yonder, and that's Callan Landers." At the sound of his name, Callan finally looked up to me, and in the light from the hanging lamps I could see that the black eye had bloomed with horrible bruises, and there was a cut on the side of his face that I'd missed in the dark cell. But his eyes were still bright and blue and he looked glad to see me despite it all.

"Fine, fine." The sheriff took up a paper and passed it to Burke the School. "I'm going to have Master Burke read parts of this indictment so you're clear what we're doing here, David. You just ask if you don't understand something"

Burke began as he had begun everything he'd read through my years at the school, by pulling his glasses from his shirt pocket and putting them on. Eye glasses was rare and expensive. Most folk who were short-sighted just did without, but not Master Burke, who had money and wanted folks to know it.

"To wit: To the Circuit Court of Virginia holden at Moline, Virginia for the transaction of criminal business; the Grand Jury of Moline, Virginia, on behalf of the Commonwealth of Virginia on the sixteenth day of October in the ninety-first year following the coming of the Ice, on oath complains that Taylor Mills, thirty-two, and Callan Landers, twenty-three, of Moline, Virginia did in the presence of witnesses commit vile acts of sodomy and perversion in violation of Virginia Code Section 18.2-361..." Burke looked up. "I won't read the code language unless you want to hear it, David."

I shook my head. I didn't want to hear none of it; it didn't matter a whit to me what the law said. I'd been raised to respect the law, but I'd weighed that respect against my love for Callan, and it weren't no contest at all.

"And further, that the aforesaid Taylor Mills did feloniously flee in the face of justice, and the aforesaid Callan Landers did resist the rightful arrest of his person..."

"He did not!" I jumped off the stool, but Pa shot me a look, so I sat back down while the horrible words washed over me. Callan was looking paler by the minute, and I wished Healer Findlay or someone who cared for him could go to his side. They wouldn't even let him sit on the same row as Taylor, as though they was afraid they'd commence to sodomizing right there in the schoolroom.

Finally Burke put down the paper and asked me if I understood the charges and I realized they were doing this because I was a child. Probably because of Elmer and his 'solemnites,' they figured I didn't have any idea of the meaning of the charge. Truth be told, they was mostly right, but I surely didn't want to delay this with any more explaining. "Yes. I understand."

Satisfied, the sheriff began to question me. "Tell us what happened, David."

"I got up round dawn like normal, helped Jerzy with the sheep and then come in for breakfast—"

They were murmuring to each other, and Sheriff Fletcher held up his hand. "No, sorry. I meant what happened in town. The Grand Jury doesn't care what you eat with your porridge. Just the part that relates to the charges."

Though the fire in the big black stove hadn't been built up and a cold wind was coming down the northern ridges in full force that day, it was getting mighty warm in that room. I could feel sweat trickling down my back as though it was July. "I went into town to return a book I'd borrowed from Callan. While we was talking, Taylor Mills come in and wanted something, I assumed he was in need of healing."

The unknown man looked up. "Were you in the habit of visiting Mister Landers?"

"Yes." He had eyes that set me to thinking of the Ice, frigid, barren. Ugly. He stared down at me and I didn't look away. "He's my friend. And I know everybody else up there but you, sir, so would you mind giving me your name?" That would be insolence coming from a child, but my pa'd named me a man, and a man deserved to know who he was speaking to.

"My name's Hennessy, David. Please continue."

Hennessy. It weren't a family name from these parts. "Anyways, I went on down to the General and run into Elmer Casteel selling his milk, and I figured my Grandmam would appreciate some real cow's milk like she had as a girl, as she's ailing, so I bought some. Only my money was back at the Healer's house." I took a deep breath. Now it was time to do what I'd set my heart and mind to.

"So I went back there and Elmer followed me. He stayed outside while I went in." I wanted it clearly understood that Elmer hadn't seen nothing much—couldn't have, as he'd been standing in the street almost the whole time.

"And then what happened?"

The sweat turned from a trickle to a stream, and I could feel my palms growing damp as I clenched my fists together. But I kept my mouth closed tight.

"David?" Sheriff Fletcher said my name gently, like I'd speak to a wild creature. "It's hard to say these things, I understand that, but you must tell the Grand Jury what you saw."

Hennessy's ice eyes were drilling into me, but I turned to look at Callan and kept silent.

The sheriff turned to my pa. "Is he scared or just being stubborn?"

Pa shrugged. "He's stubborn. And loyal. Son, we talked about this. You got to say what you saw. The truth ain't ever something to cover up."

"Not all truths need be spoken, Brock Anderson." That was Healer Findlay, and she was smiling at me.

"You're out of order, Jeannie." Sheriff Fletcher stood up. "David, I'm giving you one more chance to speak, and if you don't..." His voice trailed off, leaving me no doubt that whatever he would have followed with would be mighty unpleasant.

"You make that boy of yours behave, so help me, or I will!" Mister Hennessy stood up, too, and he looked ready for a fight. Pa didn't even raise his voice nor leave his seat, but the look in his eyes must've been something dreadful, for Hennessy sat down straight off.

"David, you said you'd do what's right," Pa persisted, with the other men at the table nodding in agreement.

"I am doing what's right," I replied, forcing the trembling in my limbs to still. "And Sheriff, I'll willingly take whatever consequences come of it."

I couldn't tell what Callan was thinking, whether he was proud of me or angry, but there was no doubt that the members of the Jury weren't too pleased. But I'd done it. Elmer couldn't have seen anything that would condemn Callan; I wouldn't speak what I'd seen. Without evidence, they couldn't possibly bring in a true bill. Callan was free.

Chapter 8

They poked and prodded and protested, but in the end Sheriff Fletcher put down his papers. "We might as well just go into deliberations."

"Can't we make him talk?" Hennessy seemed most agitated of all, even more than Pa, who had his mouth drawn tight and his arms folded against his chest. He seemed outwardly angry, but something in his eyes put me in mind of the day I'd killed my first deer, how proud he'd been then.

The sheriff fumbled in the book of law for a moment. "No, a Grand Jury hasn't got the power to compel a witness to testify, nor to punish him for refusal." He set the book down and looked straight at me. "But the Circuit Judge surely does, and don't expect him to be patient with you if you keep this up. Those jail cells are awful cold this time of year. If you don't believe me, you can ask them." He jerked his head towards Callan and Taylor Mills.

But I had no fear of that. There would be no Circuit Judge nor any trial. Oh, I supposed that they could send for a judge to deal with Taylor's flight, but I knew they wouldn't bother for something as trivial as that.

"Jeannie, you want to sit in on the deliberations?"

"No, Bill. I've seen enough farce for one day. I'll wait with David, if that's all right."

As the Sheriff took Callan and Taylor Mills back to Burke's office to wait, she led me out to the bench again, and this time the door closed soundly behind us, leaving no possibility that I could overhear. Still, I figured it shouldn't take long. "Can't imagine they'll have much to deliberate on. They got no evidence."

"Oh, there was evidence a-plenty, David. To hear Elmer tell it, he witnessed such acts of unspeakable perversion as to strike him dumb."

"What the...I told you, Elmer weren't even there! And if he was struck dumb, it was the first time in his miserable life that he shut his hole."

"Oh, he claims he saved you from a fate worse than death. Why, without him there, he says you'd have been solemnized." She snorted.

"Well, he's lying. Don't tell me you think they'll believe him?" How could they? Nobody trusted Elmer. He'd made his reputation at five years old lying about hard candies he'd stole from the General. It was only his family's influence that kept him out of jail himself.

Healer Findlay's hair had come loose from its bun and framed her angular face, softening it. "I don't know. I'd like to think they won't, but this is an issue that clouds reason and blinds folk to the truth." She was quiet for a minute, then said, "I'm not sure I really want to know the answer to this, but would your testimony have helped or harmed Callan?"

"Harmed him." It would have been nails in a coffin, telling what I'd seen.

"Then I believe that you did the right thing, though if it comes to a trial, you'll have to tell it. He'll understand."

"It won't come to that." I clung to hope, but a hard lump was growing in the pit of my stomach.

"Oh, that reminds me." She slipped off to the entry hall and returned with my coat over her arm. "That was a noble and decent gesture, giving Callan your coat. It got very cold last night, and I'm not sure how he would have managed. He's still not used to our climate, poor love."

"He can keep it if need be." Pa had said nothing more about it, and Mam, who might have been expected to raise a fuss, hadn't noticed.

"No, it's all right. I took him blankets and his own coat. And even if they return a true bill, I'm going to ask Bill to turn him over to my custody. The jail isn't set up for long term confinement."

I put my ear against the stout oak door, trying to hear, but there was nothing but a muffled rumble. "I wish I could hear what they was saying!"

She looked me over, then wrinkled up her face in thought. "Well, you know, David, I don't see that you have need for two coats. If I was you, I'd hang one of them up. In the coat room."

The coat room. It was more like a passageway, really, starting in the old school kitchen and running along the side wall to the front of the classroom. It was dank and musty and smelled of sweat left behind by over a hundred years of children, but it opened out near enough to the front that I should be able to hear anything said by the men at the table.

"Yes, ma'am. I think I'll just do that." I made my way into the dark old closet and sat cross-legged near the door. I had no illusions that Pa would approve of what I was doing, and for a moment, as I first heard my own name spoken, I considered going back to wait with Healer Findlay. Listening into matters that weren't my business was wrong and I knew it. But knowing that Elmer'd lied so badly, I couldn't wait to hear the outcome like one of our sheep just standing around waiting for the shearing.

"...no question that Elmer's lying, at least in my mind." That was Henslow, I thought, recognizing his thin, reedy voice.

"Doesn't matter. We have to go by the evidence we have, and we can't prove he lied. Brock, your boy is clearly covering up for his friend." Hennessy, I thought. "If Landers and Mills hadn't been doing anything wrong, David would have been willing to tell it."

"We can't assume anything from his silence—the law's clear on that." Sheriff Fletcher sounded troubled.

"Sheriff, I know the law, but I also know common sense. Those two were engaging in sodomy, and I've no doubt of that. I say we vote now."

There was some low murmuring I couldn't make out after that, then my Pa spoke up. "How about that we bring back a true bill on Mills, but not Landers? He's young, was probably influenced or coerced."

"You have no proof of that!"

"Mister Hennessy, you have no proof beyond the dubious word of Elmer Casteel that they were engaged in anything illegal to start with." That was Henslow again. Sounded like he and Pa were for letting Callan off, Hennessy for bringing charges. That left the sheriff and Master Burke as unknowns.

"I can accept that there was some degree of influence, but really, Callan Landers is twenty three, not thirteen. He's not a child to be allowed to evade responsibility for his actions." Master Burke had always been big on responsibility; it's about the only thing he had in common with Pa.

"I'm not saying he's not responsible, Jeroboam," Pa said. "Just that there might be... what's the word, extenuating circumstances. How about a lesser charge, then? Indecent exposure or something."

"That's not an option. We can only consider what we've got before us," the sheriff explained.

"Then let's consider this," Mr. Henslow said in a slow voice. "Jeannie Findlay ain't going to live forever. She's already slowing down; young Landers has been doing about half her traveling for the last six months. I don't know about y'all, but I don't cotton to the idea of doing without a healer."

They all got quiet then. "Curtis, you know we can't take that into account."

"Not officially, no."

Long minutes stretched out, then I heard the screech of a chair pushed back and footsteps pacing the floor. "Sounds like we're all agreed on a true bill for Mills, and Curtis and Brock support letting Landers go and Mister Hennessy and Burke say otherwise."

"So that leaves you, Sheriff." Hennessy's voice was oily and thick, and it occurred to me that nobody'd called him by his first name, that even the sheriff, second in authority only to the mayor, had called him 'mister.' Who was he? "I must point out that it's somewhat illogical to charge one and not the other in a case like this. Really, Mills could hardly have been sodomizing himself."

"I guess I've got to agree." Sheriff Fletcher sounded reluctant, like a man forced to face something he'd rather run from, and I knew my gesture had been for nothing. I'd held faith that these men, so much older and wiser than I, would see what I'd seen so clearly and do what was right. Cold came over me, like ashes of a dead fire on a winter day. I reckoned I'd better be with Healer Findlay when they came out to get us, so I slipped out of the closet.

She must've seen on my face what the outcome was because she slid her arm around my waist and gave me a hug. "You tried, David. You did as much as any friend could expect. More, really."

I didn't have time to reply, as Burke was opening the door. I saw that Callan and Taylor Mills had already been brought back in, and they were standing side by side in front of the table. The sheriff cleared his throat, and, looking down at the papers in front of him, began to read.

"Taylor Mills, Callan Landers, you are hereby informed that on a vote of four to one, this Grand Jury has brought back a True Bill of Indictment in the aforementioned matter. You are to be tried at the earliest convenience by a judge of the Virginia Circuit here in this place, and until that time will be held in confinement in the Moline town jail."

I couldn't see Callan's face, but his shoulders was tight and his head bent, like he was fighting back tears. I was thinking furiously, four to one? It had been three to two when I left the coat closet. Who had changed their mind so quickly? I glanced over at Pa, and he looked back at me, and I knew it must have been him, unable to cast his vote from anything other than the obvious truth. I couldn't hardly fault him for following his lights; I'd done the same, after all, but it hurt nonetheless.

"Sheriff, I'd like to request that you parole Callan Landers to my custody. I'll see that he stays put and shows up for his trial." Healer Findlay had come up front, facing the Grand Jury.

Before the sheriff had a chance to even open his mouth to answer her, Hennessy jumped in. "The Grand Jury isn't going to allow—"

"It's not a matter for the Grand Jury. The sheriff of this town has sole authority over the granting of bail in absence of a judge." I wouldn't have wanted to be Hennessy, staring down Healer Findlay in a rage; sure enough, he backed down.

"All right, Jeannie, on your word. And a cash surety of ten dollars gold." He turned back to Callan. "Do you have that, young man? I don't want Healer Findlay paying your bail for you."

"Yes, sir. I do." That was the first I'd heard from him all day.

"Then bail's granted. You're confined to your house until the trial, to have no contact with anyone save myself or Healer Findlay." He glared at me. "Is that clear?"

Callan nodded.

"As a matter of curiosity, what about me?" Taylor Mills asked mildly, as though the whole proceeding was somehow beneath his notice.

"You got anyone willing to stand surety for you?" the sheriff snapped. "Thought not, and anyway, you're a flight risk. I'm afraid you'll just have to stay in jail. Don't worry, I'll set a decent fire and pile on blankets. We've already sent for the judge; trial should be within the week."

They'd already sent for the judge? The hearing was all a sham, then; a story with the ending already written? Pa's head whipped around at that, but Sheriff Fletcher silenced him with a look, and then he was moving forward to unfasten Callan's handcuffs.

I pushed my way through the school desks to Callan. "You okay?"

"I believe the sheriff said he wasn't to have contact with anyone, young man. I expect that includes you." Master Burke was halfway to his office, but he'd always seemed to have eyes in the back of his head. Must be a teacher thing.

"He ain't paid his gold yet, Master Burke, so in my book he's still in sheriff's custody. Anyways, I ain't hurting anything, just talking."

"He hasn't paid his gold yet, David." Burke said, sighing, but he disappeared into his office without further argument.

"I'm better than I should be, thanks to you and your coat." Healer Findlay had her hand resting light on his arm and I longed to do the same, but I knew that wouldn't be tolerated. Callan smiled at me, a shadow of his real smile, but more than enough to warm me. "David, you shouldn't have refused to testify. I appreciate it more than I can ever say, but you mustn't ever put yourself at risk for me."

"It didn't help anyhow." I glared up at Hennessy, who must've just noticed me talking to Callan, for he was staring down at me with an expression like he'd trod in something nasty.

"Anderson, I'm beginning to wonder if we should have brought in three indictments today, not two," he drawled in a tone that could've been in fun, but could just as likely be deadly serious.

Pa didn't take it as any joke. "You threatening my boy, Hennessy?" His voice was real calm, but it was the calm before a mighty storm, and the annoyance and upset I'd felt over his voting against Callan disappeared. I was mighty proud of my Pa. This Hennessy was clearly somebody in town, but he didn't care. "I wouldn't take kindly to that. Might just hold spreading lies and vicious rumors about my son against a person."

Everyone had gone deathly still. Even the wind had stopped battering at the windows. The sheriff moved away from Healer Findlay and towards Pa. "Nobody's saying anything against David, Brock. Are they, Mister Hennessy?"

Mister Hennessy shook his head tightly, and I could see he was afraid of Pa. Good.

"Right. I'd say we're done here. Thank you all for your service; expect we'll see you back here for the trial in a few days."

Pa came up to me. "Say goodbye to your friend, son. We've got a long road ahead of us."

"I'll see you soon." I tried to sound reassuring, like Mam talking to Almond. "It'll be over quick and we can get back to normal."

"Pretty quick, considering the judge is already on the road." So he'd caught the meaning of that as well. "I hope you're right."

Pa was waiting by the door. "David."

"Promise me something?" Callan's voice dropped to a whisper.

I never gave my word on a promise till I'd heard it spoke. "What?"

"When it comes to the trial, you tell the truth, no matter what you think it'll cost me. You heard that man Hennessy, I don't want any hint of this mess to touch you. If it weren't for Taylor, I'd just plead guilty and be done with it."

"Don't you dare do that!" I knew in my heart that the evidence wasn't strong enough for an impartial judge to find him guilty. Not without my story.

"David!" Pa was losing patience, and Healer Findlay wrapped a coat around Callan's shoulders.

"We've got to go, David," she said, then started up the aisle, leaving me and Callan alone, though still in front of the watchful eyes of Hennessy and the sheriff.

"Take care," I said, and as I walked by him, I let my fingers graze his, just the lightest of touches, but he caught hold of them and squeezed lightly.

"I will. And you as well." Then we was apart again, him going towards Healer Findlay, me to Pa, and I wondered if he'd noticed that I'd never given my word to his promise.

Pa was walking awful slow up the road considering how infernal the wind had become, so I weren't surprised when he stopped at the corner of Front Street which led to the jail and sheriff's office. I'd expected some sort of dressing-down before we got up the hill. But that wasn't what he had in mind. "David, I need to have words with Bill Fletcher. You can go on ahead."

"I'd rather go with you, if it's all the same."

"Suit yourself." He shrugged. "If there's one thing I learned today it's that you've a mind of your own."

He waited like he was expecting an apology of some sort, but I surely wasn't going to apologize for doing what I believed to be the right thing, so I followed him up the street. Our slow pace had allowed Sheriff Fletcher to be back to his office ahead of us, and he was just coming out of the area where the cells were when we pushed open the door.

"Was expecting I'd see you again today, Brock." The sheriff sank down in his chair. "Have a seat."

"No, don't think I will, Bill, if it's all the same to you."

Sheriff Fletcher eased his boot-clad feet up on top of his desk. "Suit yourself."

I chuckled, thinking how the sheriff was talking to Pa as Pa had talked to me, but got myself in hand pretty quick, as I had no wish to be sent outside into the cold to wait.

"Suppose you want to know about the judge being sent for already." It weren't really a question, so Pa didn't answer. The sheriff took a small flask out of his desk. "Drink? It's supposed to be whiskey, but I think it's some of Casteel's cow's piss gone off."

Pa took a long swig. "Be mortal glad if they ever get the breweries back to running right."

"Ain't that the truth?" The expression on the sheriff's face as he swallowed made me wonder why grown folk bothered with alcohol. It surely didn't seem to taste very good. "I didn't have a choice about sending for the judge. Hennessy insisted, and I wasn't in any position to argue. The evidence seemed pretty damn convincing. I know Elmer lies like a fancy Turkey carpet, but figured David's testimony," he lifted the flask to salute me, "would nail it."

"I don't like being played for a fool nor used, Bill. Not by you, certainly not by Hennessy."

I had to know. "Who is he, Pa? Everybody seemed to treat him like he was something special."

Pa's jaw was set. "He's from the government. A goddamn bureaucrat."

"From the R&A. Don't know much more than that, except he came in with papers that forced him down our throats, put him on the Grand Jury and the Grange and the School Board and every other group or committee or division in town." The sheriff passed Pa the flask again, but he waved it away.

"Now wouldn't it have looked just jim-dandy if the Circuit Judge had ridden into town in three days' time to find he had no prisoners to try? What if we'd voted not to indict?"

A violent gust of wind rattled the door. "There wasn't any real possibility of that and you know it. And for the record, I don't like being bulldozed and used any better than you do." He took another drink. "My God, I hate this business sometimes."

Pa didn't seem too pleased by the answer he'd got, but at least he'd got an answer. "Well, we'd best be heading up home. Either David or I will be bringing the young ones to school till the end of term on account of the weather—we'll check back to see when the trial's scheduled."

Sheriff Fletcher got up to walk us to the door. "David, you got a pass today on account of we didn't have any real means of forcing you to speak, but I meant what I said back at the school. The judge will expect you to testify. And I don't want him going back to Richmond telling all the important government men there that the whole town of Moline's not able to make one sixteen-year-old boy behave."

"I'll speak to him. He'll do his duty, Bill," Pa assured him, but I didn't say a word. I wasn't sure what I was going to do come the day of the trial. Pa wanted me to speak, Sheriff Fletcher wanted me to speak, even Callan wanted me to speak, but I weren't responsible to any of them, just to my own conscience. And that was saying, clear as a bell, that just as Huck had defied a bad law to free Jim, I should do whatever it took to save Callan.

It took the Circuit Judge just two more days to make the journey from Richmond. Pa said he must have grown wings to make it so quick, as almost the moment we got home, the skies opened up, and frozen rain and sleet pelted the cabin, and it didn't stop for over twenty-four hours. That came close to being the longest day of my life.

Mam didn't say a word about our fight, but I could tell by the set of her mouth that she weren't about to forgive me anytime soon. Pa told her of the events of the day, and she just shook her head and said, "Oh, David," in the voice she used when I'd done something truly awful, but that was the end of it.

School was out of session that day because of the Grand Jury hearing, and the next day Mam kept the young ones home for fear the rain would ripen into snow and strand them in town. So I listened to Delia recite her lessons and did chores and played checkers with Benny C, and did anything I could to keep my mind occupied and away from thoughts of Callan and the trial. And that was Wednesday.

Thursday the rain had fallen off to a miserable drizzle, and although the slopes of the hills were like to be turning to mudslides, Mam sent me down to town with Benny C and the girls. I stopped by the sheriff's office, but there was no news, then walked slowly by the healer's house, once, twice, then three times, in hopes that I might see sign of Callan or that Healer Findlay might catch sight of me and come out with news. But the curtains was drawn and the door remained shut tight, though I stayed till the rain had soaked me down to my long woolen underwear.

I did business for Mam while in town, speaking to some of the women who took in her wool for spinning, and visiting Perkin Weaver in his workshop, where I spent a long dry hour listening to him go on about the new patterns he was trying and the lichen dyes he thought he could use to get new colors. I passed the General, where I saw through the window that Elmer Casteel was selling his milk again, and almost, almost I went through that door, but I knew that would end badly, with more broken bottles and maybe broken bones, and me in the cell opposite Taylor Mills.

So I pulled my sodden coat around me, and went to wait at the school till I could walk my siblings home. Sheriff Fletcher was waiting there for me. The judge and his people had come, and the trial was set for nine the next morning. By noon, it should all be over.

"Oyez, oyez! The Circuit Court of the Town of Moline is now in session. The Honorable Judge Prescott Wilder presiding. All rise for His Honor, the judge!" The sheriff was done up in his blue wool uniform, something we didn't see much, and he looked mighty uncomfortable, tugging at the stiff collar and holding his breath against popping a button.

The judge, splendid and terrifying in flowing robes, gestured for us to sit, and took up some papers and began to study them, muttering under his breath. We tended to get the same judges again and again for the summer circuit, but this one was a stranger, a black man with a stern face and gravelly voice that sent chills down my spine when I was introduced to him as witness. Like as not, Sheriff Fletcher had told him of my obstinacy before the Grand Jury, and I could see him naming me delinquent and trouble-maker in his mind. Well, we would see.

Master Burke had outdone himself; the classroom was utterly transformed with the teacher's desk elevated on a stand, a witness chair, and tables for the accused and the prosecution. It might have been a picture from one of our Civics texts, with the flags of the state and the nation bracketing the scene. Every chair and bench in the town must have been brung in for the spectacle, with rows packed full of people all wrapped in their warmest, for despite the old stove going at full blast and the crush of the crowd, it was powerful cold and the rain was still falling.

I was sitting in the first row, in a seat set aside for me. Pa was somewhere to the back, and Mam had flat refused to come down the hill, using as excuse that she was needed home with Almond and Grandmam. I was glad she weren't there, no matter which way the snow blew.

"Hello, David." Healer Findlay sat down beside me. Like the schoolroom, she was utterly transformed, with her hair slicked back, wearing a ladies' long suit of fine store-bought cloth. I forgot sometimes, seeing her all my life riding the hills in men's clothes doing her work, that she comes from money and quality.

"Is Callan all right?" I should've greeted her proper, but the thought of him, of seeing him again, filled me up so full I hadn't room for social graces.

"Well, he's scared, though he won't admit it. But he's holding up. Oh, and he asked me to make sure you were all right, and to give you this." She fumbled in her reticule and took out a book, which I slid into my coat pocket without looking at it, though the hard rectangular feel of it brought Callan to mind even more clearly.

The judge put down his papers and rapped his gavel sharply twice, bringing the hall to order. "Sheriff, bring in the accused."

Like moths drawn to a lantern's flame, the crowd craned their necks towards the back of the room, following Sheriff Fletcher as he strode grim as death to bring forth the prisoners. Mills looked gaunt and filthy, a far cry from the dandified gent who had insulted me, but I had no thought of him. Callan walked beside him, head held straight ahead, looking neither to the left nor to the right. He seemed thinner, and the hair was the faded wheat of autumn now, not bright summer, though I was grateful to see the bruises on his face had faded. But he, along with Taylor Mills, was shackled. I started out of my seat, blood boiling at the sight of it, only to be pulled down by Healer Findlay.

"It's the law," she cautioned. "And if that's the most indignity that he faces today, we should count ourselves lucky."

As a witness for the prosecution, I was behind that side's table, and Callan was standing diagonally from me, so I could study him during the reading of the indictment, memorizing every line of his high cheekbones, the straight nose and slender neck. He flinched when the sheriff read his name, and again when the charge was proclaimed, but other than that he did not waver.

The sheriff's stream of words died out and the judge looked down over the teacher's desk to the two of them. "Do you understand the charges as they've been presented to you?"

As one, they gave their assent.

"And how do you plead?"

Taylor Mills went first. "Not guilty."

Callan hesitated, but then he also said, "Not guilty." I noted that the two of them never looked upon each other—neither one ever turned his eyes to seek the other as I'd have thought lovers would do. But perhaps that was deliberate, to be more pleasing to the judge.

"It is within my purview as judge to declare that these two cases shall be treated as one for the purposes of conducting a speedy trial." He looked out over the crowd. "And let me make it clear that this matter touches on abhorrent and repugnant matters of a nature highly inappropriate for children. I will have order in this courtroom, or the room will be cleared."

As a group, the courtroom seemed to sit up straighter, hanging on the edge of their collective seats like a pack of wild dogs, waiting for raw meat.

"Proceed." Judge Wilder nodded to Sheriff Fletcher, who rose and looked straight at me.

"The Commonwealth calls David Everett Anderson to the stand."

I said my words on the Bible as I had at the Grand Jury hearing, gave my name and age and occupation, not seeing the crowds, not seeing Pa out there trusting that this time I'd do right as he knew it, seeing only Callan, who'd finally met my eyes. He was empty, resigned. Waiting for me to speak the words that would mark him as abnormal and evil for all the town to hear and know, for it to be set down in a written record; and as he'd taught me, what was written endures.

"All right, David, please tell the court what happened to you on Monday, October 15." There was an edge to the sheriff's voice as we stepped off onto this now-familiar road.

I took one last look at Callan, trying my level best to let him see reassurance and support, to tell him silently that he weren't alone; then I turned to face the judge. "Your Honor, with all respect—"

"Wait!" Callan was out of his seat. "I want to change my plea."

Chapter 9

A murmur rippled through the courtroom, and Judge Wilder slammed his gavel down so hard it's a wonder the desk didn't split like a log being chopped for firewood.

What in the name of warmth was Callan doing? I tried to catch his eye again, shaking my head, doing everything I could to silently communicate that he should sit down and let me do what I had to do. It was all right. I'd worked it all out in my head. If I kept silent, they'd likely throw me in jail for contempt; well, I could survive that—Taylor Mills had. That judge weren't going to stay around Moline through the winter, so he'd have to let me go before the true cold hit, which could happen at any time. Without me, they were left with only Elmer as witness, and I couldn't see that he would make much impression on a judge not swayed by the Casteel name. I was the only real witness, or so I figured.

I'd figured wrong. There was two more witnesses: Taylor Mills and Callan.

"Are you saying you wish to plead guilty?" The judge sounded pleased as punch at the prospect.

"Yes."

"And you are fully aware of the range of possible penalties for this offense?"

"Yes, sir." I saw Healer Findlay get up and go to the large bay window, looking out at the freezing rain. She held her handkerchief up to her face, and I wished for the first time in my life that I was a girl and could have cried openly without shame.

"What the hell are you doing?" Taylor Mills jerked at Callan's sleeve, handsome face boiling over with rage. "We talked about this, how can you do this to me after—" And then he followed Callan's line of sight, which had turned from the judge to the witness stand where I sat. "You deceitful, traitorous little slut—"

The gavel rapped again. "Mister Mills, if you do not be quiet you will be removed from this courtroom." Turning back to Callan, the judge continued. "Are you also willing to testify against your co-defendant, should he continue in his plea of not guilty?"

This time the answer was barely heard even at the front of the courtroom. But Taylor Mills had heard it, and his face went to stone.

Judge Wilder turned to Taylor Mills. "In light of this development, do you wish to alter your plea at this time?" The judge leaned forward and spoke low, but I could hear him clear enough. "I strongly encourage you to do so, and not waste this court's time on a foregone conclusion."

"Since you put it that way, Your Honor, and seeing as I've been stabbed in the back by someone I trusted—" Mills' voice dripped with venom. "Yes, I'll change my plea."

"Good." Then, realizing that I was still sitting beside him in the witness chair, the judge smiled at me. "Thank you for coming forward to do your civic duty, young man. You are excused." He paused and looked at me with what appeared to be genuine concern. "I'm personally very sorry you had to be drawn into this sordid affair. Part of the role of the law is to protect young people from being traumatized by such sordid affairs."

"I'm not traumatized," I started to object, but Sheriff Fletcher was hurrying me back to my seat as the judge turned to face the crowd.

"This crime touches on the public morality of your town. The perpetrators constitute a potential threat to the children of Moline by act and example. So before passing sentence, I will entertain any testimony that might have influence on the severity of the sentence."

Healer Findlay was already in front of the bench, handkerchief away. "Your Honor, if it please the court, I am Jeanne Findlay and I have the privilege to be the town healer and Callan Landers' employer."

"Findlay. Any relation to Roland Findlay?" the judge asked.

"Yes, sir. He's my younger brother." That was promising. I didn't know much about the doings of city folk, but I did know that it was mostly a matter of friendships and marriage connections, which was partly why my Mam was so desperate to have me tie the knot with Luanna Burke.

"Splendid lawyer, Roland Findlay. He's argued before me many times. I believe the General Assembly's considering him for the next vacant judgeship."

"So I'm told," Healer Findlay answered, just like she was making small talk at a barbecue, and I wanted to scream at her to get on with it. "In any case, when I say I have the privilege of working with Callan Landers, I mean that word in its fullest sense. He is without doubt the most gifted healer I have ever seen. His knowledge rivals that of the old time doctors, and he has a touch with patients that cannot be taught." She looked over at Callan, who was flushing a bit.

"I can say without exaggeration that his services to this town are valued beyond measure, and for the town of Moline to lose him would be a mighty blow. He's made a mistake, yes, and I'm not excusing it, but I'm asking you to take into consideration that he's had a stellar reputation until now. Please do not sacrifice the future of the town and of this exemplary young man for one admittedly serious lapse of judgment."

She sat down and the judge seemed to be chewing over her words, but before he could reply, another voice spoke up from near the back—Mister Hennessy.

"I'm afraid I can't agree. This isn't just a temporary lapse of judgment. These men have engaged in behavior Holy Scripture describe as vile evil—"

Judge Wilder interrupted. "Now, John, you know the law can't base its findings on scripture; that's unconstitutional." The judge knew Hennessy. Knew him well enough to call him by his first name. That couldn't be good.

"That's likely to change after the next Congressional session, Judge, but for now I'll leave the religious argument, though this is a godly town which wouldn't want a sinner treating its children."

"Then I'd better resign," Healer Findlay snapped. "I'm a sinner, and so are you, along with everybody here who isn't Jesus Christ himself!"

The judge raised his gavel, but she bowed slightly and stepped back, and Mister Hennessy went on as though she hadn't even spoken.

"So I'll approach it from a medical angle. In Richmond we have books which prove that the medical professionals of Before, who had far greater knowledge and wisdom than any small town healer, viewed homosexual behavior as a mental illness. These men are not only felons, they're insane. They must be punished for their crime to the fullest extent of the law so that the people of this community are protected. That's why the Grand Jury voted to indict, and we expect you to do your duty." He sat down amidst a scattering of applause.

Healer Findlay weren't about to let that go unchallenged. "Your Honor, Mister Hennessy is wrong. That medical opinion was altered in the last part of the twentieth century to reflect a more enlightened view—"

Hennessy was up again, cutting her off. "At a time when godless radicals had control of the professions—"

And this time the gavel came down. "Any further outbursts from either of you and I will have you both removed!" He gathered up a sheaf of papers and glared out over the crowd. "Any further comments?" he asked, in a voice that clearly said there'd better not be.

But Pa stepped forward. "Sir, my name is Brock Anderson. That's my boy David you had in your witness stand there and I sat on the Grand Jury. I ain't a healer nor a government man nor anything else of consequence, just a farmer and hunter. But I got to tell you that Healer Landers has done wonders for my wife's Mam, both in fixing her ills and in lifting her spirits. He's been good to my little girl too, and to my boy. Though I can't condone what he done, he's young."

"He's twenty-three, Mister Anderson. That's well above the age of legal adulthood."

Pa scratched his beard. "There's twenty-three and then there's twenty-three, if you know what I mean. He's young, and Taylor Mills ain't, and in my opinion, Healer Landers is as much a victim as he is a criminal here. I ain't got no proof of that, as I was reminded during the Grand Jury hearing, but it's my honest belief, and I'd be much obliged if you'd consider that when making your decision."

He started to sit down, then paused. "Oh yes, and Mister Hennessy was wrong. The Grand Jury voted to indict at his insistence. I let myself be swayed against my own better judgment and that pains me something fierce. To...what was it Hennessy said? To punish them, particularly Callan Landers, to the fullest extent of the law wouldn't be justice. It would be flat out wrong." There was applause for Pa, too; louder than for Hennessy, I thought.

"Fine. I'm ready to pass judgment now." He turned to face Callan and Taylor Mills. I couldn't see his face from where I was sitting, though I craned my neck and wiggled in my seat like a four year old at a long church meeting.

"Taylor Mills, Callan Landers, you are guilty by your own admission of the crime of sodomy. Before passing sentence, I would like to say for the record that I find this crime to be beyond the pale of civilized behavior and utterly disgusting. My first instinct is to follow the recommendation of Agent Hennessy and apply the full penalty of the law in this case."

You could have heard snow falling to the ground, it was so still. "However, my faith teaches justice tempered with mercy. Therefore at noon today, you will each be taken to the place of punishment for the town of Moline, there to be stripped to the waist, branded as befits your crime and given twenty stout strokes of the lash by the Commonwealth's Executioner. From thence you will be driven from this town with only the clothes on your back to make your way in the world as best you may. And may God have mercy on your souls."

"NO!" My chair crashed backwards as I jumped to my feet, and the gavel struck down again and again.

"Hush, David," Healer Findlay said, holding me back with surprising strength, her eyes steady on the judge. "Wait."

"If I might be allowed to continue." Judge Wilder narrowed his eyes at me. "In view of the eloquence of Healer Jeanne Findlay and Mister Brock Anderson, and the willingness of Callan Landers to plead guilty and thus save the town of Moline the time and expense of a trial, I am inclined to be lenient. In light of his youth and value to the community, I hereby commute his sentence to branding and five lashes, plus a fine of thirty dollars gold and a period of probation, the details of which shall be determined by myself and the sheriff and mayor of Moline."

The gavel slammed down one final time. "Court is adjourned."

The room erupted in a stream of talk and confusion as the crowd began to clear. Taylor Mills had collapsed with his head on his arms and Callan was whispering urgently to him, but Mills didn't seem to be responding. I waited with Healer Findlay while the room slowly emptied, my head aching something fierce.

Then Callan stood up and came away from Taylor, looked over to Healer Findlay, and nodded. She propelled me towards him, not that I needed much encouragement, as it was all I had been able to do to keep from going to him long before. I did look around for Pa, but he was no longer in the courtroom, and neither was Mister Hennessy, nor the Judge nor the sheriff.

"Not much time," he said, before I could even manage a word about the trial or my testimony or his plea, or the horrible punishment. I'd seen men lashed before; it was common enough for petty crime, as was branding. We didn't have the paper records they'd kept Before, so whenever someone committed a crime, it was marked on his body for a living record of the offense. "I don't have thirty dollars gold," he said to Healer Findlay. "The ten I used for bail was all I have. Can you...?"

She nodded. "Of course. Consider it a bonus—God knows you deserve one."

"No, I'll pay you back." He bit his bottom lip, worrying at it. "If you don't mind, could you go fetch the money now—I want this over and done with today."

She hurried off, leaving us alone. This time I spoke first. "Why did you do that? I had it all worked out."

"No. I know what you were going to do, and it wouldn't have worked. They'd have forced you to testify or held you in contempt and put you in jail, then relied on Elmer like at the hearing. There wasn't any way this wasn't going to end in conviction." He glanced around, then lowered his voice. "I need you to do something for me, David."

"Yes, anything." No matter what it was, I owed him. He'd done what he did to protect me; my throat grew tight even thinking of it.

"In my room, under the bed, there's a bundle with clothes and provisions and about five dollars gold. I want you to run and fetch it, and when this is all done and they drive Taylor away, I need you to find him and make sure he gets it. It's his only chance."

"All right."

"I know it's asking a lot of you—you'll be breaking the law and violating the judge's order—but I need to believe that I haven't condemned Taylor to death with what I've done today. Can you understand that?"

Oh yes. I could understand loving like that, where nothing mattered but the welfare of the one you loved. "Yes. I'll see he gets it. But this, this sentence! Are you..."

"Don't worry about that. I'll manage to get through it somehow. People survive worse than this all the time."

Pa and the sheriff were standing at the door, looking my way. "After they...later...I'll come and see you; got to return your book, after all." Though I hadn't even opened it yet, it was a link to Callan, an excuse to come round and see him.

"Keep it through the winter, David. I don't think you should be seen with me after today. And I don't want you to come to the square at noon."

"I can't let you face that alone!" That would be cowardice of the worst kind, to run out on a friend when things are darkest. Taylor Mills had run off on Callan, leaving him to face the law on his own; I wouldn't never do that.

Now silent tears was running down his cheeks, and it looked as though he was coming undone; that disturbed me more than anything I'd seen so far. "Promise me, I don't want you to see..." He gasped and gave a half-shudder, pulling his composure around him like that old greatcoat of his. "I've brought enough harm to you."

"Why not let me decide that? If we was reversed and it was me being lashed and branded in front of half the town, could you run off and leave me?"

"No. No, I couldn't." He sighed and moved like he was trying to run his hand through his hair, but the cuffs and shackles prevented it. Out of the corner of my eye I could see Sheriff Fletcher coming towards us. "I expect the sheriff's going to take us back to the jail till it's time. I'll...I'll see you later, then." He didn't remind me about the bundle for Taylor, trusting that I'd do as I said. I wanted to be worthy of his trust.

I stared at him, not knowing how to say goodbye. When I saw him again, it seemed to me like things would be different somehow; either he would be changed or me, or maybe both of us, and what I had started when I opened that door and dropped the milk bottle would have come full force. "Callan."

"David." He smiled warmly, fear and sorrow pushed aside. "Thank you for what you've done through all this—nobody could ask for a better friend." He looked like he was going to say more, but Sheriff Fletcher took him by the arm. He looked back just once, smiling slightly, then disappeared through the door.

Whether by accident or a-purpose, Healer Findlay had left her house unlocked and I found the parcel without trouble. The rain had slacked off, but the air still held moisture and frigidity that assured me that there'd likely be snow before the day was out.

I wandered around the streets of town, knowing that Pa was somewhere, probably looking for me. I didn't want to see him, though I was proud to be his son. He'd not hesitated to stand up to Mister Hennessy nor to the judge even though I knew he didn't have any sympathy for what Callan had done. But seeing him now, he'd want to talk, and I just couldn't face it, couldn't face him.

Most folks were at home, probably having an early lunch so they could come out and view the spectacle. I hated public punishment; the few times I'd been whupped at school, it had been the eyes of my classmates on me that had stung worse than the paddling. Pa said it was to discourage others from committing the same crime, but it seemed to me that what Callan had done weren't like thieving, which almost any man could see himself taking to if the need is great enough. Only certain men were drawn to that. Like Taylor Mills. Or Callan. Or me.

It was too cold to loiter in the streets like a summer layabout, so I ended up back at the empty school on one of the benches, taking the book from my pocket. Crime and Punishment. I wondered if he'd chose it a-purpose, then opened and began to read.

I hadn't got more than a few pages in before I realized the crowd was gathering outside the school. Moline was too small for a proper town hall, so the school served that purpose, and the schoolyard doubled as the place of punishment, save for the rare occasion when there was a hanging to be done. Then it was a tree along the creek that served, for to have a hanging tree in a schoolyard would be a chancy thing. But for floggings and such, it was the playground where we'd spent our recesses climbing the decrepit equipment left over from Before.

Among that was two upright metal poles capped with a ring. Grandmam said they was for a game played with a rubber ball on a rope hung from the ring, but in our day, they was used for a darker purpose. I knew what would happen. Callan would be stripped to the waist and his cuffs chained to the ring, then he'd be branded somewhere on his body. I hoped not his face. Oh, dear God, not his face.

I closed the book. It weren't in me to concentrate on a made-up tale when such things were happening here in my real world. If this was a book, I'd be able to stop it. My plan would have worked, or at the last minute there would be a pardon, or I would fight off Judge Wilder's men and carry Callan off to safety. That was what happened in the romance stories—the hero saved the girl from the villain. But I was no hero, nor Callan anything like those pale helpless heroines. And Judge Wilder and Sheriff Fletcher weren't villains, not really. They was just doing their jobs, doing right as they saw it, same as me.

Healer Findlay stuck her head in the schoolhouse door, bringing an icy gust of wind with her. "Here you are. Just thought you'd want to know they're doing Callan first, then Taylor. Bill Fletcher's just brought them out."

I got up and slid the book back into my pocket, and pulled on my gloves, as I saw there was flakes of snow on her head and shoulders.

She came all the way in and shut the door behind her, cutting off the howling wind. "And where do you think you're going? I know for a fact that he doesn't want you out there. Go around to my place and wait; I'll bring him home when it's over."

I shook my head. "I been through this with Callan, and I'll go through it with you if I have to. I ain't going nowhere save for out in that square."

She pursed her lips, but I could tell she weren't truly angry. "Well, David Anderson. You came out of your mother's womb ass-backwards and you've done everything your own way ever since, so far be it from me to try to convince you. I've got to go." She grimaced bitterly. "The presence of a healer during physical punishment is required by law—isn't that considerate of them?"

I followed her out. The snow was falling hard and fast, big thick flakes swirling around me, already turning the ground white. "Healer, Taylor Mills ain't going to make it, not in this, is he?"

"No. Not unless someone takes him supplies and warm clothes. Then maybe he'd have a chance." She had stopped walking and was looking at me sideways.

"Let's hope somebody does that, then," I remarked, trying to sound like Pa when he was being casual.

"That somebody would be breaking the law, you know."

"I heard it said just a few days back that the law is an ass."

She chuckled. "So it is. I guess somebody should know they're taking Taylor out by the western road, then."

She slipped away to the front of the gathering crowd. I searched out the crowd, found Pa standing to the back with the Digger, sharing a pipe. Tobacco's fairly expensive, though it used to be a big money crop in this state. But one of the ways Digger got paid was in the leftover tobacco of those he laid to rest, so he usually had some stowed away. The smoke rose up through the snow, which was slacking off some, as though God wanted to look down and watch the spectacle.

I suppose it was because I was a witness in all this, but people moved out of the way for me, leaving me a place down near the front where I could see real well. I couldn't see Taylor Mills yet, but Callan was at the front of the crowd surrounded by the Judge and Sheriff Fletcher and Healer Findlay and another man I didn't know who must have been the Commonwealth's Executioner come over from Richmond with Judge Wilder. Nearby, there was a roaring fire in a big rusted brazier and sticking out from it was the end of a branding iron, almost exactly like the one we used on the sheep.

The sheriff was talking to Callan, who was nodding in response, then they uncuffed his hands and stripped off his shirts, baring his chest to the frigid air. Then the cuffs was back on his wrists and lifted up to be chained to the pole, forcing him to face away from the crowd, which was a small mercy. If there was any mercy to be found in this.

The crowd was larger than I'd hoped, and they was all looking eagerly up to where Callan was shivering. I'd seen him bare just once before, that horrible day when my action had started all this, but then I hadn't had time to really look at the smooth lines of his body, or how his skin was totally unblemished. No scars nor burns nor any of the other marks that befall most of us who grow up in farm country. He was perfect and smooth and beautiful.

Healer Findlay went around to face him and she put something in his mouth—probably a leather strap, I thought. Mister Zack Tyree had told me about how he'd bit on a leather strap to keep from screaming when they dug the bullet out of his arm back when he'd been in his hunting accident as a boy. Then she stepped back as the Commonwealth's Executioner come forward with the iron in his hand. He looked to Healer Findlay, who pointed to Callan's left, and as the iron come down on Callan's left shoulder, he screamed—oh, God, it went straight through me like a knife—spasmed and strained to get away, then sagged unconscious, held up by the chained cuffs.

The crowd was all full of murmurs and cries, and I could smell the acrid smell of burning human flesh. It was a stink I would never forget, even if I should live as long as Grandmam.

Healer Findlay was having some sort of row with the Judge. I couldn't hear the meat of it, but I could see on her face the moment she lost. She waved something under Callan's nose, reviving him, then helped him to stand and replaced the piece of leather.

The executioner had put the iron back in the fire and was testing the whip. It was a fine whip, braided leather and a full nine feet long, and every time he cracked it, the watching crowd gasped, like he was doing tricks at the Harvest Fair. And every time the thing cracked, Callan flinched.

"Get on with it, you sadistic bastard!" This time I heard Healer Findlay plain as day. Judge Wilder looked displeased, but he nodded, and it began.

I'd never thought it could take so long to count to five. The leather strap lasted through the first two strokes, then fell to the ground as Callan groaned aloud, where it rested in the snow along with the spatters of blood that was flying back from each stroke of the lash, turning the ground crimson.

He screamed on the fourth stroke, and on the fifth, I'm shamed to say I closed my eyes and stoppered my ears with my hands like a child. Then it was over and they were letting him down into Healer Findlay's arms as I forced my way around to the back of the poles.

Despite the cold and the snow which had started back up again, sweat matted Callan's hair and his face was pale, white as the ground that supported him as he lay on his side, shivering. "Oh good, David. I'm glad you're here after all," Healer Findlay said. "I have to stay out here while they do Taylor; can you take Callan into the school and stay with him there till I come? There's a pallet prepared down near the stove."

I nodded, having no desire to see anything further. The most I'd ever witnessed before had been two lashes given for petty larceny. Five was bad enough, I didn't know how Taylor Mills would survive twenty. "How can I carry him without..." I gestured at his back.

"I can walk," Callan said, so I helped him up by his right arm and slowly got him into the school. The fire from the stove was dying a bit, so I built it up then, sat down, not sure what to say nor do at such a time. I'd been right. It was all changed.

A scream from outside told me they'd moved on to Taylor. Callan bit back a sob. "Oh well, better than burning sand, I guess," he said finally, as though he couldn't bear the silence, punctuated with the screams of the man he'd loved.

"Burning sand?"

"That's the fate of sodomites, in Dante's hell." He was laying out on his right side, facing away from me. The brand was oozing blood, the flesh around the wound charred and ruined. I thought about the sound of his screams and the iron scent of blood on the snow, and I cried, silently, so as not to disturb his rest.

Chapter 10

That night winter set in with a vengeance, and as I sat in our cabin, reading by the dim light of the lamp, I couldn't help thinking about the two men on the road that night: Judge Wilder with his escort and their fancy tents and government issue gear on the well-traveled road to Richmond, and Taylor Mills, alone, with only what Callan could spare him, heading west into who knew what sort of danger.

I'd caught up with him easily enough, on account of his injuries. Healer Findlay had been allowed to treat them and give him what she could for the pain, and then he'd been taken to the edge of town and cast out. Only the Judge's men, Mister Hennessy, and a few others went along; most townfolk were already holed up in their houses against the snow, and the countryfolk were on their way back up the hills. Besides, I think we was a little ashamed, sending a man to his death in such a way. A hangman's noose would've been quicker. And kinder.

Mills had taken the parcel without hesitation. "Surprised you'd bother sticking your neck out for me," he said in a raspy sort of voice, quite different from how he'd sneered at me at the healer's house. "With me out of the way, it gives you clear sailing, doesn't it? Kind of makes me wonder whether you two had this planned all along."

I didn't like the way his mind was moving. "You can believe whatever you like, but Callan would never do that. He's never...never done anything...wrong...to me." The snow was falling heavier and I needed to be moving on, and so did he.

"Now, isn't he just the soul of restraint? So fucking noble. And if Taylor gets sacrificed in the bargain, well, that's just too damn bad. Taylor doesn't matter, Callan doesn't matter. All that matters is that poor David won't be inconvenienced. Give me a fucking break."

"There's a shepherd's cottage up the path about an hour's walk to the west. It's got a fireplace and a good stout roof. I'd stop there for the night if I was you."

I'd hurried away, thinking that he had less chance than a flame in hell, but I'd done what I'd promised and could look on Callan with a clean conscience. It was dark by the time I got back home, but nobody made nothing of it; Mam just set a plate of food down for me without a word, and I slid back into the patterns of my life.

School was still in session for another week, though the days was shortened up on account of the weather. I walked Benny C and Ruby and Delia down each day then came straight back up the hill, then Pa fetched them home. Neither Mam nor Pa told me not to see Callan, but then, they didn't need to, because Healer Findlay had already done it on the day of the trial.

"Part of his probation is that he's not to have any contact with you, David," she'd explained while treating Taylor Mills, cleaning out his wounds while I tried not to look. "Not till you're a legal adult, at any rate." She'd stared at me sharply. "And don't you even think about violating that restriction. If he breaks parole, the full sentence will be reinstated, and..." She gestured to what used to be Taylor Mills' back, and I'd agreed readily enough.

So I stayed away from that end of town altogether, and on the night of the school recitations, though I knew Callan was there, sitting to the back with Healer Findlay, I didn't turn around nor acknowledge him. But I felt his presence the way I was aware of my own arms, and I didn't hear one word of the recitations, because my mind was walking the traplines on a warm fall day.

October bled into November with one day pretty much like the others; chores following on chores, doing sums with the girls so they wouldn't lose what they'd learned that year, talking with Grandmam and listening to her stories, and reading Callan's book a few precious pages at a time. On days when the weather broke, I'd go hunting with Pa, then work with Mam to salt down meat to last us through the coldest months. She was still cold to me; I hoped it didn't take her so long to thaw as it would the world outside, which was like to stay frozen till March at the earliest.

Only it didn't. Come the second week in November, a hard rain blew in from down south, and it brought behind it a warm front that melted the icicles and turned the frozen ground to mud. It wouldn't likely last more than three days, but it was a blessed reprieve from the cabin fever that had already begun to set in. Early morning on the second warm day, I asked Mam if I could go over to the Ridges for the day, just to get shut of the house.

"I don't know, David. This weather can't last—I don't want you caught out that far from home."

"I'd say it's good for another day, Mam. I don't feel any change in the wind."

"Let him go, May-Marie," Grandmam said. "A man needs to get out and breathe free air while he can."

Mam stared at me, sizing me up and down, and it seemed like some of the ice between us melted. "Go on, then. Take a satchel and collect some tree-lichen if you happen on it. Perkin has a bee in his bonnet about trying for a better purple on the next batch of wool."

So I packed my bag with warm gear and necessities in case Mam was right and I was wrong and I got caught out. In this world, you're prepared or you're dead.

The Ridges are to the southwest of our land; they stand between us and the old Western Highway, the road that Taylor Mills had taken when he was forced out of town. It's rough country; rock slides and fallen trees and hidden ravines make for treacherous passage at the best of times. In true winter it's impassable from the ice, and in the spring the mud makes it just as bad. But it's far and away the most beautiful stretch of land I've ever seen. When the mist hangs over the ridges in the morning, the entire world turns the blue of flame, and your troubles sort of hang on the air, then vanish as the fog lifts. It's my favorite place in all the world, and I'd hoped to show it to Callan one day.

I struck out off-road, collecting some lichens for Mam, but mostly just letting the warmth of the southern wind and the sun thaw me out some. I'd got about half a bag of mosses and lichens gathered up, and was near to a grassy rise that had good sitting-sized rocks, thinking it would be a fine time to see what Mam had packed for me for a midmorning breakfast, when I heard a sound. A coughing-like sound, and human for sure.

I moved cautiously towards the sound, using all the wiles Pa had taught me for taking prey unawares, as I didn't really want company. As I peered through the dead branches of a beech tree, I saw a slender man sitting on a rock, wheat-gold head buried in his hands. My heart clenched. It was Callan. And he was crying.

I cleared my throat and stepped into the clearing. He looked up, and for a moment I caught his eyes unguarded, and it was the strangest thing, like words in the air between us. Then the mask came up and he stood so that we was facing each other on opposite ends of the clearing. "David. I...I should go. We're not supposed to be seen together."

I started forward, hands out and open as I'd approach a wild thing. "Ain't nobody going to see us up here. I've missed you."

"I've missed you too. What are you doing up here?"

"Mostly just getting out of the house. And gathering lichens for dyes." I held up my pack.

Callan relaxed a bit, sitting back down on the rock, but I kept my distance. What would have been familiar and a comfort but three weeks ago was now awkward and passing strange.

"What are you doing up here, anyway?" Then I realized what it must be. "You're looking for signs of Taylor Mills, ain't you?"

He nodded.

"I wouldn't worry about him none. He seemed in good enough shape, and I got him your packet and directions to the shepherd's hut. There's a map to shelters painted on the wall there that will take you clean down into North Carolina. I expect he's sitting in a bar somewheres around Raleigh, drinking up whiskey and missing you something terrible." That last was hard to say, but I wanted Callan to know he could talk free to me about it, that I was fine with what he was.

"No." He looked off down the ridge then back to his hands. "He's dead, down in that ravine. I caught sight of his boots, but hadn't the stomach for a closer look, I'm afraid."

Scrambling down the rocky hill into the ravine, I saw the boots before I saw the man. "Mister Mills?" I said, stupidly, as though he'd lay down weeks ago to take a nap and was somehow just resting. So I held my breath and moved closer, looking past the boots and trouser-clad legs to the body and face.

I remembered telling Callan how I'd never seen a dead person before. I hadn't expected my first one to be like this. My stomach churned, and I forced myself to think 'animal' and 'body'—not the living, breathing Taylor Mills as I'd known him.

"I'm coming down," Callan called out. "It's stupid to be so cowardly."

"Stay where you are!" I said, and moved so I was between the top of the ridge and Taylor's body. Three weeks of weather and worse, and Callan had loved him. No. I clambered back out of the ravine.

"David, I've seen bodies before. It's all right."

"Not like this you ain't. Trust me. Remember him like you seen him last."

He laughed but there weren't no mirth in it. "The last time I saw him was just before they took me out to the square, when he cursed me and said he hated me."

"Then remember happier times. I got to admit, I didn't much care for him." I had to be honest, though it was wrong to speak ill of the dead. "But I know he mattered to you." I reached out and clasped his shoulder. "I'm sorry."

For a moment he relaxed, closing his eyes. "I'm just sorry you never saw him as I knew him at first—he was incredibly intelligent and witty, and he could charm the skin off a snake. I'd never known anyone quite like him."

I didn't know what to say. I hadn't never lost anyone I cared for, and the words that wanted to come out of me seemed cheap and false, so I just nodded.

"We had a fight, that last day when you...when we were arrested."

"I heard some of it when I was leaving your place." I remembered Mills' voice, all full of contempt for me, and Callan, strong in my defense.

He thrust his hands, wearing my gloves, I noted, into his pocket of his greatcoat. "He accused me of..." Eyes flickered over me, then back down to the ground. "Of something. And I denied it, so he called me a liar and hit me."

For a moment I was glad, mortal glad, that Taylor Mills was dead. "He struck you?"

"Yes. It had never happened before, and he was quite sorry. What you walked in on, that was him, 'making amends.'" More bitter laughter. "I expect it would have been better if we'd just had a fistfight—nobody'd have cared at all about that. Fighting is normal."

A shadow darkened the clearing, and I glanced up to see the dragons winging their way south.

Callan smiled. "But then, what's normal in a world with dragons? Should we hide or something?"

I shook my head. "No, they ain't hunting. If they was hunting, they'd be circling over the same places." I looked back down the ravine, wondering if maybe the dragons had got Taylor. But no, they'd have taken him off. That would have been better all ways round. "I guess we ought to bury him," I said.

"I don't have a shovel or any tools."

I didn't neither, but it seemed wrong to leave him lie there. "There's a cliff face about twenty yards on up the path. If you was to gather some large rocks and chuck them down the ravine, I could pile them over him. Raise a—" I didn't know the word.

"Cairn. Yes, that would work. But let me come down and help."

"No." I'd do whatever need be to make sure Callan didn't lay eyes on what the weather and the wild had left of the man he'd loved. "It's better this way, we divide up the work and nobody has to climb up and down the ravine more than once."

I could see he knew the real reason I didn't want him down there, but he let me have my way, and we set to work. It takes a powerful lot of rocks to cover a man, but in the end, where Taylor Mills had been was a grey mound of granite stones that should allow him to rest in peace. More peace than Callan had, I thought.

When I laid the last rock in place, I called up, "You want that I should say some words over him?"

"He didn't believe. It wouldn't mean anything to him." And I didn't believe most times myself, but I said a few quiet words anyway, just to lay him to rest, then climbed out of the cool ravine into the sun.

It was still a glorious day, and only just past noon, for we'd worked quick. Callan stretched his arms out.

"You okay?"

"Yes. That was more physical work than I'm used to doing, and I'm still recovering from...you know."

"How's your back?" I remembered five long gashes, each deeper than the one before.

"Mostly healed. I've got scars, but that's to be expected."

I rummaged in my bag and handed him some jerked meat, then laid out goat cheese and a skin of water. We ate for a while in comfortable silence, then he picked up his own bag. "I should be heading back. Thank you for helping with Taylor."

"Do you have to go?" It was almost warm enough, especially after the hard work of raising the cairn, that I could've taken my coat off. We wouldn't see the likes of this weather for months, and I might not have the chance to be with Callan alone again for years.

"I should. I'm breaking the law just by being near you." But his voice was soft, like he was hungering for something, and the bag fell down to the ground.

"Ain't nobody going to know. We can have today, and just forget about the whole damn mess." I liked that we were near enough of a height that our eyes met so easy. "I can't never take away what's happened to you, though Lord knows I would if I could, but I can give you a day that's just ours. Yours."

You hear tell about people 'warring within themselves' but I'd never seen it for true till then. I could see him weighing the word he'd given to the Judge against my offer, and though he knew what the right thing was and so did I, I was heart-glad when he looked up and nodded.

The whole glorious day stretched in front of us unbroken like the roads of Before, leading off to wherever we wanted to go. "All right. It's your day—what do you want to do with it?"

He didn't have to give it a moment's thought. "You're going to think this sounds silly, but what I'd really like to do more than just about anything is play."

"Not sure what you mean."

"I told you how I didn't have brothers or playmates my own age to speak of. I see the boys on the playground here, running races and playing ball and wrestling—I've never done any of that, really. Just by myself, which isn't the same thing at all."

No, it wouldn't be, I thought, remembering long Saturday afternoons with Benny C, teaching him how to kick the ball Pa'd made us from leather scraps, and all those games of football on the play-yard. "All right, then. We'll play." I emptied out the sack that had held Mam's lichens, stuffed it with pine straw, then tied it shut with rope. It weren't much of a ball, but it would do.

"That there's your goal," I said, pointing to a pair of trees at the far end of the clearing. "And here's mine."

And we was off. We had to stop and refill the ball twice, as it was bleeding pinestraw with every kick, but that was no bother to me, not when I was watching guilt and responsibility and pain fall from Callan's shoulders like rain rolling off a tin roof as we ran and kicked and tackled.

I was the stronger, but he was the quicker, diving to the ground to stop my ball from reaching his goal, using his long legs to advantage as we ran, his lithe body slipping easily through the trees. I showed him the ropes I'd tied to the high branches, and he grabbed hold without hesitation and flew out into the afternoon sun, laughing for true, with no trace of bitterness; all masks cast aside.

I forgot myself, forgot about the trial and its outcome, and the events I'd set in motion. I forgot, or at least put aside, the unanswered, hopeless love I had for Callan, and we were just friends for those few hours—two boys doing what boys had done since Cain and Abel run the first foot race, back when time began.

And because I forgot who I was and what I was, I neglected to mark the passing of time and the subtle signs of shifting winds that Pa had drilled into me since I was old enough to be out by myself. I forgot myself in childhood, where the weather's a grownup's concern and someone else is always there to worry over when it's time to come home. That's the only excuse I can make for my failure to notice the storm.

It wasn't till the sun was sinking behind the western mountains that I stopped, leaning against a tree and breathing hard, and realized with dismay that the temperature had plummeted and icy droplets of rain was mixing with the sweat on my brow. Callan had collapsed on the ground, and he must have felt it as I did, because when he looked up, the boy was gone, and it was the man who was looking up at me.

"We've gone on too long."

I nodded somberly. The rapidly-cooling air was heavy with moisture, and though I might possibly make it home across the ridge, there wasn't no way that Callan could descend those rocky, mudslicked hills to town with clouds over the moon, and rain or worse pouring down on him.

"I'd best be going, then." He pulled himself up, wincing a little.

"You'd never make it down safe; likely end up lying in a ravine with your neck broke." Like Taylor Mills, I didn't say, but we both heard it anyhow. "We'll have to stay at the shepherd's shelter."

I could see he wanted to argue with me, but couldn't, not with the wind starting to whip up from the north and the rain hanging on the edge of sleet. I led the way through the woods to the shepherd's place, and he followed, not speaking, as our words would've been blown off by the wind anyway.

The shepherd's shelter is a cabin of sorts. It must have been much like my own home long ago, but where our place had been cared for and repaired and lived in, this one was left to rot after the Ice. It got used in the summer when the flocks was ranging the fields; that's how it took its name. I'd stayed there along with Jerzy, and so had Elmer Casteel, and just about any other man or boy who kept animals. We all pitched in to keep it maintained well enough that it would keep out the worst of the rain and the wind, and it had a stone fireplace with a chimney that still drew fairly well—with that and the blankets in my pack, we'd make it through the night.

The sun had vanished by the time we came upon the cabin. Dark logs blended into the dark woods around it, and a door that was half off its hinges squealed open as I pushed against it and we ducked in out of the rain.

"We'll have to fix that door, come spring," I commented. I could barely make out the edges of the room, but I knew the fireplace was dead opposite the door. "Let's get a fire going."

There was wood kept inside, near the hearth, well seasoned and dry, and I laid the fire while Callan watched, then took out my flint and steel. Matches are rare and expensive, and most folks just keep something burning in their homes most of the time, so they don't ever have to worry about starting a new fire. Callan watched me fumble with the curved piece of steel, slamming it again and again against the flint while sparks flew up and I cursed a blue streak. "Don't tell nobody how awful I am at this."

I could feel his smile even in the dark. "Your secret's safe with me."

Finally the fire flared up, and we moved close to it, for the shadows of the rest of the cabin were unsettling. "I wonder what it would be like to have false light, like they had Before."

"It's amazing. It floods all the corners of the room, makes night into day." I looked up from where I'd been laying out my bedroll near the fire, surprised. "There are demonstration projects down south using water and wind to create electricity. We'll get it back, David. Maybe not in our lifetimes, but by your children's day, we'll have electricity, and telephones and the like."

It didn't seem likely I'd have children, but I didn't say nothing of that, thinking how fine it would be to turn a switch and have light, or hot water that you didn't have to fetch in and simmer for hours on a stove. Of course, at that moment, I'd have been grateful even for the stove and the pan to cook the water in. "I don't have much food left. Just the rest of the cheese."

"It's enough." We ate the cheese and drunk rainwater I caught in a battered tin cup while the rain beat down on the roof, leaking through in places, but not, I was pleased to see, near the fireplace. The chimney wasn't drawing so well as it had the last summer and the cabin was rapidly filling with smoke, turning the clear air to haze.

Callan stood up and went to stand near the door, looking out at the night. "It's turned to sleet, I think."

"Figured it would. Hope Healer Findlay's not too worried about you."

He sort of sagged against the door frame. "I expect she'd find it a mercy if I died up here. I'm so goddamn useless now. Can't treat children, can't look upon men unclothed. And then about half of our patients won't let me see them anyway; they'd wait for Jeannie, even if they were bleeding to death. I sometimes think she's only keeping me around for pity's sake. Or to make sure she gets her thirty dollars' worth."

"That's not true. And the town will come around—they'll forget in time." I recalled how he'd been, filled up with a love for his work, questioning and learning all the time. Now it was like he'd been hollowed out and filled up with bitter herbs.

"It's such a chore to even get up in the morning, to eat, to drink. Almost more bother than it's worth." The dark had somehow freed him to speak his mind, and I sat by the fire, feeding it tinder and listening. "There just isn't any point. Everything I wanted is all in ruins, and to top it all, I've lost the only person that could have ever meant—" He broke off, as though suddenly reminded that he weren't alone.

"He wasn't good enough for you," I said. I'd put a piece of unseasoned pine on the fire and the sap made the flames flare up. "You could do better."

He nodded, then turned back to face the sleet. "Go on to sleep, David."

"You can't stay up all night—it's going to be freezing." I had an old quilt for under us and two blankets for the top, including one Grandmam had saved from Before that had some kind of special stuff in it that kept a body real warm. "Two sleep warmer than one."

"I don't think that's such a good idea—I doubt your father or the sheriff would approve."

"They wouldn't approve of you freezing to death, neither. Come on, I'm not a-feared for my virtue." I shed my boots and coat and slipped down under the covers far from the fire, leaving the warmest part for Callan. He slid between the blankets and pulled as far away from me as he could get without actually climbing into the fireplace.

"I ain't going to bite you." But he stayed away, and I was a little thankful, for the nearness of his body, the smell of it, the heat from it, was moving in my blood something fierce, and if we touched, he would surely know my secret.

The fire popped and crackled, the rain and sleet thrummed on the roof, and we was both breathing regular like we was asleep, but neither of us was. I chanced a look at him in the firelight and he was flat on his back, looking up at the ceiling, eyes open.

"David, are you awake?"

"Yes."

There was a silence so long that I thought maybe he'd found sleep after all. Then in a quiet, hesitating voice, he continued. "I told you that I fought with Taylor on the day we were arrested, that he accused me of something."

It weren't really a question, and he didn't seem to want an answer, so I gave none. "What I didn't tell you was what he accused me of was being in love with you."

I caught my breath and froze, and it seemed like the world froze, too, for I couldn't hear the rain nor the fire nor the scratching of the trees against the cabin. No sound save the pounding of my heart in my chest, and Callan's voice.

"And I need you to know, because the silence is eating me alive—I need you to know that he was right."

Chapter 11

He was right. Before I could even think what to say, Callan pressed on, as though driven to say what was in him all in a haste or not at all.

"I don't expect you to be anything but disgusted with me; I certainly know that nothing could ever come of it, and telling you is likely the death-knell of what's left of our friendship, but the thought that I was deceiving you was..." He paused like he was searching for the right word.

"Callan?"

"Yes?" The fear in him hung on the air like the smoke filling the cabin.

"When did you know? I mean, was it all of a sudden, or did it come on you gradual-like?"

"When did I know what, that I loved you?"

I turned onto my side and propped myself up on one elbow, watching him. "No, that you liked men. I mean, was it something you figured out gradual, or did it hit you all at once?"

"I've always known, I think. I can't remember a time when I wasn't aware that I was...different. Then as I got older, I came to understand what the difference was. So it was gradual, I guess."

In a great rush, I forced it out. "It was all at once for me. I just looked at you that day on the trapline and I knew that I wanted...wanted something I didn't have words for. I don't know if it's men I like or if it's just you—don't care really." And I leaned over to where he lay still on his back, looking stunned as a deer trapped by a lantern, and kissed him, awkwardly, on the lips.

I hadn't never kissed anyone like that before. I hadn't expected the dry brush of lips, the rough stubble against my cheek that answered the question of whether he shaved or not, nor ever dreamed that such a simple thing would leave me so completely undone. Caught off-guard, he reacted on instinct, hands coming up to tangle in my hair, pulling me down, down into a tangled swirl of lips and teeth and tongues and oh, how had I never known what this could be?

"No." He broke it off and scrambled backwards, knocking one of the logs loose from the woodpile so that it clattered away across the wooden floor. "We can't...I can't... If I start, I won't be able to stop, I know it." His eyes were heavy lidded, face flushed.

"I don't want you to stop. Please, don't stop."

"We have to—for your sake and for mine." But I could see the 'no' might be on his lips, but weren't in his heart or body.

"Come lie back down. It's not fit for man nor beast." I patted the quilt beside me.

"I'm so weak," he said as he slid back under the covers, facing me as we huddled close. His arms went around me, and he buried his face in my hair, and I could hear him whispering harshly, almost angrily, "Because of the cold, that's all, just because of the cold. I'm so sorry." His breath felt warm in my hair.

"You've got nothing to apologize for—I kissed you."

"I know it isn't really what you want. Lots of boys have crushes on older boys or men; it doesn't mean anything."

Even through the layers of clothing, I could feel the hard planes and angles of his body. "I know the difference. And I'm not a child—I know what I want."

His breath caught. As his arms tightened, I wriggled closer, tangling my legs in his. He pulled the top blankets over our heads—something I normally didn't much care for, being all enclosed like that, but it felt right with Callan. Like being truly safe for the first time in my life. "I kind of figured you'd want the same thing," I added, muffling the words in the hollow of his shoulder blade where his shirt had come loose. His skin was soft and warm and I would have given a year of my life for us to be bare, skin against skin.

"More than there are words for the telling," he said, and kissed me again, just the lightest brush of lips on lips.

"I know when we leave here tomorrow it ain't like we can go back to Moline and set up housekeeping, or even see each other, maybe not for a long time. I don't like it one bit, but I know what the world is. Just let's give each other what we can."

His arms tightened, one hand slipping up under my shirt, exploring my back. I remembered a day so long ago when I'd watched him with Almond, thinking on what it would feel like to have those hands on my body. Now I knew. It felt like heaven.

"I'm not sure, David." But I could tell, hearing the words beneath the words, that he was sure. And so was I. I stopped his mouth with my own, and finally he quit fighting me (Or was it himself?) and kissed me back. His tongue was deft and eager and his body molded itself against me, exactly as I'd dreamed it would. My heart was caught all up in my throat; I was so a-feared I'd do something wrong now that the moment was here. The ghost of Taylor Mills hung between us for a moment, then I pushed it away. It was me Callan loved, me he wanted.

My hand passed between our bodies, fumbling all awkward with the buttons of Callan's trousers while his breath came ragged, in fits and starts. He groaned into my mouth when I closed around him and a fire flared up in me, knowing that I was doing this, that I'd broken through that infuriating calm. It was odd and yet wonderful, touching another man, stroking that velvet-hard length as he shuddered out his release saying my name, not as a shout, but soft, a whispered prayer.

"Sorry," he gasped out after. "I couldn't last, not after two months of wanting."

The need to feel his body against mine was overpowering—the layers of clothing, a blessing in the cold, had become a burden. I started to pull at his shirt, using my hands as he had on me, tracing up the small of his back until my fingers met the first of the gashes left by the whip.

He seized up, then wriggled a little, dislodging my hands. "Shh. Patience," he murmured and then slipped out of my arms and down into the depths of the bedroll. Oh, God, he was kissing me in places I'd never dreamed a mouth could go till I'd seen it with...I wouldn't say the name, not even in thoughts—even through my trousers it was beyond anything I could have imagined. And then his fingers, nimble healer's hands, deftly unbuttoned the placket of my trousers, teasing with agonizing slowness till his mouth, sweet heaven, his mouth enveloped me with a radiant warmth that couldn't ever end, drawing waves of pleasure out of my whole body.

I collapsed like the granite on the face of the mountain last summer, crumbling into glorious dust, and all the tension of the past weeks dissolved as Callan wrapped himself around me once again and I slept.

I came out of a wondrous dream to find it real; I was truly in Callan's arms. Dawn was breaking, and the weather had let up enough for the sun to be casting just the smallest bit of light through the boarded-up windows. We'd have to be moving soon; Pa would have figured I'd find a safe place to hole up, but they'd be fretting back home, and I didn't want to cause them worry. On a day such as this, the whole world should be as full of peace and contentment as me.

"Are you awake?" he asked, as he had the night before. When he told me he loved me. The words still played over and over in my mind like Almond singing the same line to her nursery song. He loved me. I realized then that I'd not said it to him.

I love you. I tried the words out, tasted how they'd feel. I'd said them to Mam and Pa and Grandmam, and Almond. But that was different love, so this would be a first time. Another first time. "I love you, Callan."

He kissed my hair. "I wish we could stay right here forever."

"We'd starve. And probably freeze. Not sure which would get us first, though."

His laugh was music and he rolled me onto my back and kissed me again. "It would almost be worth it." His kisses trailed down my neck and I sighed and stroked that silken hair; not a stolen touch seemingly by accident, but mine by right.

"I expect we got a bit of time yet. I want..." I thought about it, then chuckled. "I guess I don't know what I want, I mean the hows and whats of it."

"I think I've got that part covered." He slid atop me, covering my body full length with his own. My hands came up under his shirt, and he iced up again when I touched the scars.

"Do they hurt?"

He shook his head. "No. They're...ugly. I hate them."

"I hate that they did such a thing to you, but I can't hate any part of you." My fingers traced up and down his back, learning every part of him, smooth and scarred alike, and he stilled and let me, though his breathing was a-flutter like birds' wings. Then we were moving against each other while we kissed, and the tension stretched between us taut as rope.

Callan broke the kiss and groaned aloud, and the sound struck me deep in the vitals; I didn't care how cold it was, we was shedding clothes, frantic to touch and be touched.

And then I heard my name. Not cried out by Callan in passion or pleading, but raised in the distance by a more familiar and unwelcome voice. My Pa.

"No, not yet!" But Callan was off me and pulling his clothes around him, lifting one of the blankets to set it on the opposite side of the room. There was more voices than Pa's; I could hear other men calling my name. Pa wouldn't condemn Callan for not freezing to death to save my reputation, but others might not be so reasonable.

"'Spect he's in the cabin, Brock. Boy has a head on his shoulders." I thought that was Mister Zack Tyree. Callan's eyes met mine across the room.

"I do love you, David. I won't ever forget this."

I didn't trust myself to speak. It wouldn't do for Pa and the men to find me all unmanned by tears, so I simply nodded, and the door opened.

It weren't pretty, what happened after that, but it weren't too horrible either. Pa and Mister Zack and Sheriff Fletcher had come out searching for me and Callan both, and they'd half-expected to find us together. Callan was brilliant, apologizing for breaking his parole, convincing them all that I'd found him lost on the Ridges and had saved his life. Sheriff Fletcher kept looking at the two beds like he weren't buying it, but he kept his peace.

"Couldn't hardly expect either of you to sleep outside," he said. But he took Callan back to town straight off, not even giving me time to say goodbye. Mister Zack come back to our house, where Mam thanked him for aiding in the search by making him hotcakes with the last of the wheat flour, served up with real sugar syrup. I got cold meat left from last night's dinner. The thaw, such as it had been, was over.

So the winter come back, and this time it stayed. Grandmam says that Before, folks used to choose to come up here during winter. They'd pay cash money to stay in cabins like ours for a few days or a week, going out in the snow to play and walk and ski. There even used to be a ski resort nearby, Grandmam says, though it's all a ruin now and nobody skis no more. When the snow comes, so does the wind and the ice, and nobody in sound mind would go out for more than ten or twenty minutes, let alone plummet down a mountain faster than a horse can run.

So we stay home mostly, tending the sheep and the greenhouses beside the barn, and work on repairing tools and gear and all the sorts of things that keep a farm running during the growing times. And we play games. Mam doesn't approve of cards, but Pa's a fair hand at poker, so he and Benny C and me and Grandmam when she's up to it will get up a game. And there's checkers and chess, played with pieces Pa carved for Mam when they was first married.

Trouble was, every time I dealt out a hand of cards or set out the pawns in their row on the board, I imagined myself playing with Callan, wondering if he was any good. I figured as well as he mastered his expressions, he'd be able to bluff his way through any hand he held, so he'd take me at poker; probably at chess too, for I could see him being able to do what Pa said you needed to do to be good—think three moves ahead. I couldn't do that. I looked at the chess board and I saw how I might move, but not what my opponent might do in response and certainly nothing beyond that. So I lost, most times, unless I was playing Ruby.

What I hated most about winter, and what caused folks to sicken or even turn violent, was the lack of privacy. It was easier for the town folk, who could at least go visiting with some assurance that they'd make their destination without a storm blowing up in the meantime. I wished sometimes that we was like the Casteels, who had a town house and also a farm, and left their hired folk at the farm during the winter. There just weren't anywhere to go to get away from the family, and as much as I loved them, I weren't a child no more and needed time to myself.

Benny C and I worked it out so we each got an hour alone in the bedroom each afternoon. I spent mine thinking of Callan. I suspected Benny C was doing the same thing as me, save his mind was likely on Daisy Bailes. If I'd not had that hour's outlet, I can't fathom what my nights would have been like, for the dreams was bad enough as it was, with my mind and body flooded with images of Callan's face as my hand had sought him, and the way his body had felt atop me. It seemed impossible that Mam especially couldn't figure what ailed me, but Mam was still cold to me, and in truth, her mind and heart was elsewhere most of that winter.

For Grandmam was sinking fast, sickening beyond what we'd seen before. The medicine Callan give her worked to quell her bad spells, but her mind was wandering back through paths of her girlhood; about half the days she didn't know nobody save Mam.

We took it in turns, me and Benny C and Ruby, to sit with Grandmam some each day, just being with her so Mam could get some rest or tend to Almond, and it was during one of my spells sitting with her that she started to tell the stories.

Grandmam had always been a fine one for stories. She spun tall tales of her girlhood that I couldn't hardly believe, though she swore they was true: flying in a machine clear to California in a matter of hours; being able to talk to folk around the world without waiting the months for the post riders to come through; going to see stories acted out on screen bigger than life, even things that could never be, not even in those days, like battles in outer space and such like. We'd loved those tales, as they brought her world—the world of Before—nearer to us.

But she'd also tell us yarns that were in no part true, the stories of the gods of her Danish ancestors. About Odin and how he'd hung on the World Tree seeking wisdom; and his grand hall of five hundred forty doors, Valhalla, where the warriors would live after death. Ruby always liked the Valkyries who chose the slain on the field of battle, and for Benny C, it was the story of beautiful Balder, slain by mistletoe. Oh, she knew other stories, from other lands—Greek myths and Russian stories and stories from the island of Britain about King Arthur and his knights, but it was the Danish tales that she always seemed to come back to. And that winter, at least with me, it was almost always the story of Fafnir.

I don't think a day went by in December that I didn't hear the tale of the dwarf Fafnir, transformed into a dragon and set to guard the most incredible hoard of treasure ever known in the world of men. And of Siegfried Volsung, the hero who slew the dragon and then went on to glory and death. But sometimes in her story, Fafnir had been a giant first, not a dwarf, and sometimes it seemed like she was muddling it all up with scripture and it was David and Goliath, and on those days she'd look at me so odd, like she didn't even know me.

The dragons hadn't been idle while Callan had been going through his ordeal and I'd been coming to recognize my terrible and wonderful difference. They'd been raiding the stock of the claim farmers through the fall, taking sheep and goats and even the occasional mule or donkey. And Mister Zack Tyree had lost two of his fine horses, killed but not carried off. So Grandmam's meandering mind thinking that them dragons was like Goliath of Holy Writ, with me being David, was a mite unsettling. I weren't the sort of man that dragon-slayers was made of, nor did I think a slingshot would do aught to those dragons save get them more riled up.

But I always smiled at Grandmam when she told the tale, and asked her for more, so that she perked right up and told it, going on about Siegfried and his fair Brunhilde till she drifted off to sleep by the fire.

So I heard tales, and I read, finishing Crime and Punishment in mid-January and wanting so much to talk about it with Callan, but instead I talked to the sheep, just to be able to talk about it. And I walked up to the tree where I'd wrestled Callan to the ground every day the weather would allow, just to touch it and recall better times.

It was on one of those trips that I saw the package, wrapped in oilcloth, hanging from the tree out of reach of what animals might still be about. I didn't dare linger long enough by the tree to open whatever it was; though I had no inch of skin exposed save for my eyes, the wind was biting and giving me a blinding headache as it swirled the powdery snow around my legs. Exposed skin in such weather would take frostbite in no time at all, so I made my way back to the barn where I sat among the restless and warm bodies of the sheep and unwrapped the folds of the bag.

It was a book, one I'd last seen being pulled out of Almond's hands by Callan so's he could take it on home. Trees of North America. He'd gifted it to Almond, writing her name on the cover in plain block letters. Neither Mam nor Pa said a word when the book appeared at Almond's bedside in the morning, though they must've known where it come from. Everybody loved Almond and wasn't none of us who would deny her.

And in that book was a piece of old paper, almost as valuable as the book itself. The new paper didn't have the fine quality of the older stuff; it was thick and stank of the mill, and you could see the fibers all rough and ugly in its surface. Not this, it was creamy and smooth with a pearly tone to it that seemed to blend with the brown ink that had been used to write upon it.

It was from Callan; a note, the first written word I'd seen in his hand, save for the carefully printed 'Almond Anderson' on the fly-leaf of the trees book. This weren't done careful at all—it looked more like it had been dashed off quick so that nobody'd catch him writing it. And he'd had to take a mighty risk bringing it and the book up the hill; he must've come on one of the warmer days, but even so, you never know when the weather will turn against you. So I valued it beyond gold and kept it in my pocket, folded, reading it again and again.

David,

   I thought your sister might enjoy her 'twees' book to get through the cold season. Bet she'd learn her letters without half trying if you used this.

   Hope you are enjoying *Crime & Punishment*—it's not one of my all-time favorites, but I thought it fit the occasion on which I gave it to you. I hope we get a chance to talk about it sometime.

   And since it may be a long while before you can borrow another book, I found this poem for you which seems to fit things. It's by Shakespeare.

> 'Let me confess that we two must be twain,
> Although our undivided loves are one:
> So shall those blots that do with me remain,
> Without thy help, by me be borne alone.
> In our two loves there is but one respect,
> Though in our lives a separable spite,
> Which though it alter not love's sole effect,
> Yet doth it steal sweet hours from love's delight.
> I may not evermore acknowledge thee,
> Lest my bewailed guilt should do thee shame,
> Nor thou with public kindness honour me,
> Unless thou take that honour from thy name:
> But do not so, I love thee in such sort,
> As thou being mine, mine is thy good report.'

Missing you.

Yours,
Callan

I read it through three times before I understood that this weren't a love poem, as most folk would think of such a thing. It was a more like a farewell; and as I read it again and again, lining the fancy words in my mind till I had it by heart, it drove me near to crazy, wondering what sort of frozen hell he was going through in the town.

Chapter 12

Sheep must be some of the dumbest creatures ever created, but after five months crowded into a stinking barn, I had to feel sorry for them. They'd lost weight, and their wool was matted and dull, though Jerzy spent long hours with them, talking to them and grooming them and playing with the yearlings as best he could manage in the cramped barn. Jerzy would've been welcome in the house during winter, but he seemed to prefer the company of sheep to people. After what had happened to Callan and Taylor Mills, I'd come to agree with Pa that there weren't much difference between people and sheep, so I never pressed him to come inside when I took him his meals.

It was drawing on April when we'd had a run of ten full days without snow, and the mercury in the old thermometer had begun to slide up the scale—not too far, but enough to let us know that winter was finally playing itself out. The sheep wasn't the only ones to be feeling the pinch of winter—we was all strung-out weary and thin and weak. Usually, even in winter, Pa managed to bring in fresh game on occasion, but this year pickings had been slim, and one day Pa'd come back from the traplines cussing a blue streak, as some creature had made off with not only the animal he'd trapped, but had pulled the iron trap right out of the ground, taking it as well.

"Those dragons, I'll bet!" Benny C thought it powerful exciting that we had dragons. "Bet they don't have dragons in Richmond," he'd boasted, as though it were something the Commonwealth government there would want—the State House, the big museum to Before, and their very own dragons.

"'Spect you're right," Pa had said, looking so down in the mouth that Mam had given him leave to slaughter one of the older ewes so we could have fresh meat for a time.

So when the tenth day come and it was fairly certain the storms had passed for another year, Pa picked up his long rifle, put together a pack and went off to hunt. I'd have asked to go with him, but I was hoping Mam would need some supplies in town, where I might at least hear word of Callan. That note, particularly the poem, had me spooked, as it sounded as though he was shutting the door on anything further between us. And while I wouldn't never do anything that would put him at risk, the probation wouldn't last forever, and I'd be of age in a year's time. I needed to speak with him; we'd had no time at the shepherd's cabin.

"Need anything from town?" I asked Mam as the door closed behind Pa. She looked up at me with narrow eyes.

"No. You stay away from town till I say, David. Too many...distractions in town for a boy your age." She had little clay pots all over the kitchen table, sorting seeds into each to get a start on the growing season. The greenhouse kept the perennials alive through the winter, but lots of things had to be started fresh each spring. I knew I was maybe a week away from having all my time taken up by work, so this might be my only chance to get away.

But asking a second time did no good with my Mam. All it did was set her more against whatever I wanted, so I held my tongue and paced to the window and back. Ruby and Delia had taken their dolls out to the greenhouse to play, Benny C was up in our room, and Almond was plucking at Mam's skirts, bored to distraction. Like me.

"David, why don't you and Jerzy and Benny C drive the sheep up into the north pasture today? It's a bit early, but I think it'll be all right."

Our north pasture sat on a treeless hilltop maybe a two hours' walk from the cabin. It weren't going into town to see Callan, but it sure beat pacing the floors of home waiting for the sun to set so I could sleep, only to get up and do it all over again. "All right."

She cleared a place on the table and set to making us a sack lunch of the ever-present dried meat and cheese, and for treat, a few withered apples she'd been holding back. Almond saw the apples and lunged for them.

"Take your sister, why don't you? The girls don't want to play with her, and she's just getting underfoot here."

I wanted to protest that it hadn't mattered none that I never wanted to play with Benny C when we was young, she'd made me anyways, but I figured having Almond along weren't a burden, and might even be a blessing. She had a gift for making days seem a bit warmer, though she could be ornery as cuss. "Can we take Lightning, then?

Almond's not going to be able to walk all the way there and back, and she's getting too big to carry."

"Am not," she sputtered, and as Mam looked away from her, she stuck out her tongue at me. Something she'd learned from Callan. I stuck mine out right back at her.

"I suppose that poor horse needs to get out in the sunshine as much as any of you. Yes, go on with you, take her."

It seemed to take Jerzy next to forever to round those sheep up. They'd not been out of the barn for so long, I'd swear they forgot what the sky looked like, and I knew how they felt. I was so eager to put the cabin behind me that I had Lightning saddled and ready to go in no time, and Almond was prancing around the yard playing horsey, complete with loud neighs and whinnies that made me and Benny C laugh out loud.

Finally we was ready, and with Almond and Benny C on Lightning leading the way, and me and Jerzy driving the flock, we started upland, to what I'd come to think on as Callan's tree, then instead of turning off into the woods or down towards the town, we moved up onto the higher country. There weren't so many trees up this way; the winter wind was brutal here, and though the whole hilltop had once been a forest, now it was more like a meadow. Grasses had come up some, not enough to tangle in my legs, but more than enough to give the sheep some nourishment, and we had to be pushing on them constantly to keep them from stopping right where they were and feeding.

So the two hours stretched to almost three, but none of us minded, as the sun had come out in full and was warming us through our jackets. The trillium was starting to show itself, and as we passed a ruined cabin, the sight of the bright green shoots of a few daffodils lifted my spirits mightily. The only thing that could have made that day any better were if Callan was with me, but I had hopes of seeing him soon, so I whistled a bit as we topped the rise to our north pasture.

The sheep scattered immediately to their placid grazing, and Jerzy went off to sun himself, contemplating whatever it was that went on in his head. Almond slid off Lightning into my arms, then run off right quick for the sunning rock, a large flat boulder smack in the middle of the field. I smiled, seeing as she'd tucked the Trees book in amongst her jacket and was now settling in to tell herself stories. Callan had been right—she was halfway to learning her letters, and I figured she'd do right well at school when it started up later that month.

"Better check the fences," I told Benny C, and he cantered off on the long circuit of the pasture. The fences were split logs, and tended to fall in winter. This year was no exception, as he told me when he come back around.

"There's a whole section down over the rise, and the back gate's hinges are twisted something awful—they need to come off and be hammered flat."

Benny C weren't strong enough to lift the split logs back into place, so after giving him my knife to pry up the hinges, I started down the slope to set the fence to rights. There's nothing like hard work in the warm sun to drive just about everything else out of your mind, so for an hour or so, it was just me, the fence rails, and an occasional curious sheep I had to send packing.

So I can say for excuse, and a sorry one it is, that I didn't hear Benny C's cries when they started up because I was heaving logs and humming to myself. And then I heard him, but figured he was playing. For all he's trying to be a grown-up man in love, Benny C's a fine one for pretend games, so at first I figured he was a cowboy and the sheep was Indians attacking him. But a cowboy wouldn't be screaming for me by name, nor calling out Almond's name neither, in a tone that turned my blood to ice when I paused to truly listen. There was trouble for sure.

"I'm coming!" I shouted, and I ran flat out, or as best I could after a long winter doing nothing more taxing than chopping firewood and lifting chess pieces. I topped the rise, panting with the effort of it, and my stomach clenched tight as I saw the dragon.

It was circling, drawing lazy spirals in the sky that grew tighter and tighter as it honed in on its prey—not any of the sheep, not even the horse, but on Almond, laying on her rock, lost in her own world of green forests and flowers where Benny C's warnings couldn't even be heard.

"Almond!" But I was too far away. The sheep were panicking, scattering across the field, and they was loud, so loud with their anxious bleating. Why didn't she look up to see? "ALMOND!" I set in to running, but the dragon was circling lower now.

"Goddamn you! Take the sheep! Take the horse! Take me!" I waved my arms in the air, trying to get it to see me. "Here I am, here!" But it was like it had eyes only for the tiny girl on the big flat rock, laid out like a snack on a platter.

Benny C had mounted Lightning and was trying to get the horse to charge at the dragon, but she was too scared and Benny C couldn't control her. Still, he was closer than me. Jerzy was trying to get control of the sheep—he weren't no use at all. I cupped my hands to my mouth to holler at Benny C to get to Almond, but he was already off Lightning and moving, flying through the grasses, pushing past the sheep with my knife in his hand. I ran, too, still shouting, and finally she sat up, and let out a horrible, high-pitched shriek as the beast overflew her so close that she was forced back down onto the rock.

It was toying with her, like our old barn cat had played with mice before it would pounce, and there weren't nothing I could do, even could I reach her in time. "Almond, get off the rock! Get down flat!" Though I knew she heard me, she froze like a rabbit, with her dark hair hanging down like a curtain in front of her face, as a child playing peekaboo thinks if it can't see you, then you can't see her either. But the dragon's eye was turned right on her.

The thing hung in the sky, a sort of sickly green, with what seemed to be a snake's belly and a scaly back. The wings weren't feathered, and looked to be the only vulnerable places on the thing other than the flat red eyes. "The wings!" I shouted to Benny C, who was almost within reach of Almond. "Slash at the wings!"

Then the dragon plummeted to the ground like a stone, talons outstretched. Almond screamed as the thing grabbed ahold of her, then before it could take off, Benny C leapt at it, slamming my knife into the armored scales on its side. The steel blade might have been paper for all the good it did.

"NO! The wings!"

The dragon knocked him back hard with its tail, but he got up again, blood running down his face, and as the beast flexed its muscles to rise, he stabbed my knife into the leathery wing and pulled down hard, tearing the flesh clear to the bone. The dragon shrieked, let loose of Almond, who crumbled to the ground, and made its way off.

Though I hoped Benny C had hurt it bad, I spared no further thought nor time for the monster. Almond's belly was a mess of blood where the talons had bit into her, and she'd gone unconscious; a small mercy. Benny C was crying, the tears blending with the blood on his face. "David, I'm sorry, I'm so sorry..."

Callan! I cried out silently, wanting more than anything to have him beside me. He'd know what to do. He could save her. But Almond was lying there bleeding into the ground, and Benny C needed me to be strong. "No time for that! Get on Lightning and get down to Moline and fetch the healer. I'll take Almond on home." I could see her chest moving slightly—the only sign she was alive. Her face was white, so white, like a sheet or a ghost or snow.

"You ride faster than me," he protested, but I was already on the ground beside Almond, trying to staunch the bleeding and not to see the gaping holes the thing had left in her.

"You can't carry her, not all the way home. Now go on, get!"

He was gone, and I lifted her up, thanking God (for at that moment I believed in God with a hunger beyond reason) that it was downhill all the way.

"What should I do?" Jerzy was crying; he loved Almond, like we all did.

"Stay here, in case they come back for the sheep," I answered, turning tail and running down the trail fast as my burden would allow. Though what good he'd do if they come back, I surely didn't know.

I held her belly against me, trying to put pressure on the wound as I ran, but the blood was seeping out too fast, soaking into my shirt, and every time I breathed in, I could smell the iron-stink of it. Limbs aching, legs cramping, arms weary; the run up the hill at the pasture had exhausted my winter-depleted muscles, but I couldn't stop—it would mean her death if I did. I'd considered taking her down to Moline on the horse, but if both Callan and Healer Findlay were off with patients, which was often the case, it would mean Almond would be without any help at all. At least at home, there was Mam, who had some small knowledge of doctoring. And if the worst happened, though I could hardly conceive it, I wanted her in her home with her Mam and Grandmam and brothers and sisters.

No! I forced my mind to think, to work, to focus on anything save the pain in my side and the pounding of my heart and the limp body of my sister in my arms. I remembered the R&A man, denying the dragons' very existence. Damn him, damn them all to frozen hell! I wondered what Callan's Dante would have done to government men.

Almond stirred a bit as we neared Callan's tree, and best as I could considering I had no breath in me, I made soothing sounds. I'd made the two hour journey in less than one, I realized, as the comforting sight of smoke from our chimney reached me. She come awake then and started in screaming, and there was no soothing her.

Mam heard us coming, and had the door open before I stumbled in, gasping, "Clear the table!"

Clay pots, dirt and seeds went crashing to the corners of the room as Mam's arm swept the table clean and I lay Almond down, her poor piteous body contorting in pain. Grandmam started up, then collapsed back in her chair, clutching at her chest.

"Ruby, get Grandmam her medicine!" Mam snapped, and grabbed a handful of towels from the stove and started packing them down on the wound, trying to keep Almond still. "David, what in the name of God done this?"

"Dragons...one of the dragons, Mam, it just attacked her out of nowhere. I sent Benny C for the healer."

Speak the name of the devil, I thought as I caught the muffled sound of hoofbeats and saw a figure at the door. It was Callan, and I felt lighter, easier in my mind than I'd been since I first looked on Almond's hideous wound. Our eyes met for the first time since that cold November morning when Sheriff Fletcher had led him away, but only for the briefest moment, then he was shedding his coat and opening his bag, getting straight to business.

"Healer Findlay's gone up to the Barnes farm; I know you'd prefer—"

"Just save my baby." Mam's voice was screwed tight, and she seemed small, shrunken like Grandmam, so I put my arm around her and she rested back against me as if I was Pa while we watched Callan work. It was so hard to be a grown-up and bear her up when all I wanted was to fall into her lap and howl at my horrible failure to protect my baby sister. But I managed it; I guess that's what it means to be a grown-up. Managing.

Almond's screams had faded to whimpers, and Callan gave her some medicine right off which seemed to calm her, but his face, as he pulled the towels away, had gone as pale as Almond's. "Mrs. Anderson, I need you to boil some water, and do you have any alcohol?"

Mam handed over Pa's bottle of whiskey and was already at the stove, shoving logs into the oven to heat the surface, and I wished I had a job to do, something to take my attention away from the sodden red towels.

Callan was shaking his head. "I've never seen the like. The claws must be huge."

"It grabbed hold of her and then let her go. Can you help her?" I stepped closer and looked down at Almond. Her breathing was shallow, and her skin was going grey, and Callan was cleaning the wounds with the alcohol.

"I'll do my best. Get me some clean cloths—cotton, not wool." Mam fetched him what he asked, then went back to where Grandmam rested near the fire, and they was holding hands. Ruby and Delia sat together on the hearth holding hands, too, absolutely still as precious time slipped away. The only break in the terrible silence was the crackling of the fire, Almond's occasional whimper and Callan's voice, mumbling to himself under his breath. I couldn't make out what he was saying, but it didn't sound good.

The door flew open and Healer Findlay burst in. "Your note said it was an emergency, so I—Oh, sweet Jesus!"

They exchanged looks, and Callan shook his head slowly. Healer Findlay felt for Almond's pulse, and they whispered together for a few moments. Then she put on a false voice, like the one she'd used to calm me when I'd broke my arm back when I was seven. "Let's see what we've got here. Good, you've cleaned the wounds. The smaller ones aren't a problem, but..." Her voice trailed off, the falseness seeping away like Almond's blood had done. So much blood. "This one here." She pointed towards Almond's lower belly. "That's—"

"I know. She'd need surgery to even have a chance, and that's assuming infection doesn't set in..."

"What's happening to my baby girl?"

Callan stayed close by Almond, but Healer Findlay come over and took Mam by the arm. "Looks like the puncture's torn her bowel in a couple of places. There's a procedure for fixing that, but it's not something we can safely do here. And I've never even seen it done."

"I have," Callan said quietly. "But in a sterile room, with a trained medic."

Mam grabbed at his sleeve. "Could you do it?"

"No." Then he paused. "Well, maybe. But not here, and there's not time to get her to town, and even there's not ideal." He'd stopped tending to Almond, and was just waiting. We was all just waiting.

"So what do we do?" I'd never heard Mam so beyond herself. What a day for Pa to go hunting—I'd have given anything to have him walk through that door.

Callan was looking not at Mam, but at Healer Findlay, who closed her eyes so all you could see was wet tears staining her aging cheeks. "We keep her comfortable and let her die in her own mother's arms, May-Marie."

Mam gasped and collapsed against the healer; Callan swore aloud, a foul word I'd not suspected he even knew, and spun out of the cabin, slamming the door back so hard it rattled the windows. Leaving Mam to Healer Findlay, I followed.

He'd found the axe I'd been using to chop wood the day before and was slamming it into piece after piece of cut log, splitting the wood into splintering bits of kindling. I could still hear Mam crying in the cabin. I'd never heard her cry before.

I took up the spare axe from where it hung on its peg and set to working alongside him, saying nothing till we'd made a fair sized pile, and Callan buried his axe in the log he'd been using as support.

"You're pretty good at that," I said. "Better'n I'd have thought." It was an odd conversation to be having, with Almond dying twenty feet behind us, but there weren't anything I could say about that, nothing that wouldn't open a gate within me that I weren't sure I could close. And I remembered how Pa was, how he showed such calm all the time, never getting riled up, no matter what. I guess maybe this was how he did it, by putting his mind elsewhere.

"Part of my probation is having to chop firewood for half the town. I wasn't near so skilful when I started out—nearly cut my foot off a couple of times, but I learned." He stripped down to his shirt sleeves and I watched the muscles in his arms flex as he moved. "I like it. Gives me something to do when...when I can't do anything real about something. Like this." He picked up the axe again, and started in on the wood, but talking this time, timing his words with his blows. "If I had proper training, if we had the equipment and supplies they have in the city, your sister...Almond might—" He turned away and set the axe down gently.

"I wish Pa was here." Dusk was coming on—it was still early spring and the daylight hours was short. I stuck my head in the barn. Benny C was grooming Lightning, not with any serious intent, just bringing the brush up and down automatically. Dried blood crusted his hair and forehead. "You ought to get that looked to," I said, but he shook his head.

"Suit yourself. Why don't you go up the trail and see if Pa's on the trapline? He ought to be here."

He dropped the brush to the ground, and I hadn't the heart to remind him to put it in his place. "David, I tried. You know I tried, don't you?" His voice cracked like a boy going through the change, though he'd hit that already and gone beyond it.

"Course I know it," I said. And he had. So had I. And Callan, and Healer Findlay, and Mam, but it hadn't made no difference. I watched Benny C walk away, hands in his pocket, head down like he was trudging against a great wind.

"I should go," Callan said. "There's nothing more I can do here; Jeannie's the best one to help your Mam, and we're not supposed to be—"

"Don't. Please." I was trembling, and the axe I'd still been holding fell to the ground, my arms suddenly too weak to swing it.

"Please. That's the most erotic word in the English language, you know." Callan looked at me, not moving to go.

"Let's take the wood round back."

We gathered armfuls of the split logs to take to the woodshed. I watched Callan walk ahead of me, and my mind went where it shouldn't have been able to go on such a day, and I despised myself for it, but the minute we was alone in the dark woodshed, the logs was falling to the ground and our lips met. It wasn't a gentle loving kiss; not tender nor hesitant, but hungry and longing and hard, as though he could kiss away the last few hours, take away the memory of my failure and his own, and have Almond sitting by the fire reading her book like it should be.

I kissed him back just as hard, and without words, I felt how it had been down in the town alone, chopping wood to take away the memory of what we'd done, not from shame nor regret, but because the wanting of it was eating him alive.

I pushed him back against the woodpile, and we broke apart, gasping. "Oh, God, what am I doing? My sister...how can I want...?"

"We're human and alive. It's not an uncommon reaction in the face of death. But we can't, you know that, don't you?" I knew he wanted it as much as me—it's hard to hide such things—but he was right.

So I pulled away and nodded, miserable with wanting and grief. "It hurts so bad, Callan. I've never lost nobody, and Almond, she's special."

"Yes. She is." He started to pick up the wood we'd spilled and stack it neat, one piece at a time. "When my mother...died, it was like my world was ending. For a long time afterwards, I resented every day for being a day she wasn't alive. It took me a long time to realize what I was really feeling was anger at myself. I was alive and she was dead, and that wasn't how it was supposed to be."

"This is my fault, though. If I'd kept her closer to me, been faster, she might... things might be different. Can you fathom that?" But how could he? Callan was strong. Not like me.

"Oh, David. I can understand, better than you might think." He put down the wood and blinked a couple of times, as though thinking something through. "I want to tell you—"

A shriek, muffled only slightly by the logs of the cabin, rattled the walls of the lean-to. Callan's head bowed, as though he was praying, though I knew he didn't believe. I turned away from him reluctantly, knowing that with Pa gone, my place was with Mam.

She was sitting atop our kitchen table, something I'd never thought to see, hair mussed and falling down from its usual tidy bun, and Almond was clutched in her arms as she rocked back and forth, singing a wordless sort of tune. Grandmam had Delia on her lap, and Delia, so grown-up, now had her thumb in her mouth like a small child...like Almond. Ruby stood with Healer Findlay, eyes red but calm. Ruby had a head on her shoulders, that's what Mam always said. Ruby's like Pa. I'm...I'm just David. Almost a man, and men don't cry.

Chapter 13

In the summer, round about the time of the Harvest Fair, the school puts on what Master Burke calls tableaux, where the students act a scene from history or out of a book by just standing in place while he wanders around the scene, telling the story. If you'd looked in our cabin at that moment, you'd have thought we was in one of them tableaux. Nobody moved, nobody spoke; it was as Callan had said—the world was ending. Finally, Ruby burst into angry tears and was caught up in Healer Findlay's arms, and as if that was a signal for us to move, I started forward to Mam so that I could lead her away from Almond, the way I figured Pa would.

"Come on, Mam, come lie down." I weren't much good at giving comfort, but I put my hand on her rocking shoulder.

"I ain't leaving my baby girl. She needs me." And she clutched tighter at Almond's still body.

The door opened; Pa stepped over the threshold and I'd never been so glad to see him as I was at that moment. "What the Sam Hill is going on here? Benny C can't finish a thought to save his mortal soul, and there's a healer outside chopping our firewood, and—" He broke off midsentence as he saw Mam on the table with Almond.

"Brock, there's been an accident," Healer Findlay started to say, but Pa was already taking my place beside Mam, easing Almond from her arms. She clung to him and cried and cried, till finally he lifted her up in his arms and carried her into their bedroom, beckoning to Healer Findlay to follow.

Ruby'd calmed some, and had come up to the table to gaze down at her sister's body. "She ain't there anymore, is she, David?"

I looked at the silent body of the little girl who'd hardly been able to keep still for more than a minute unless she was asleep, who'd been forever full of questions and songs and stories. Her eyes were opened, dull and empty. I knew I should close them, but I couldn't bear to touch her like that. "No. She ain't. This is just sort of like a snail's shell. Or a snakeskin after the snake done moved on. Looks like our Almond, but it ain't."

Delia had left Grandmam's lap and ventured forward cautiously to look for herself. "So where's she at?"

I don't know, I cried out inside, but Delia was just eight, and she deserved a better answer than that. "She's...she's in a better place than this. A warm place with trees that stay green and leafy all year round and flowers that never, ever fade and die. And she's not alone, neither. She's got all our family that's gone before around her to care for her. And she won't never be cold again, nor go hungry, nor be sick or scared," I said.

Nor be joyful or laugh or learn to read, nor grow up and fall in love, nor be a Mam her own self or have important work like Healer Findlay. All that she would ever be was right there on that table. And what if this life was all we got, with hers ended like this? I felt the cabin walls closing in on me, needed to get out and breathe the air, wanted to swing that axe again with every stroke aimed not at the wood, but at the dragon, and at myself.

Pa come out of the back bedroom, ignoring me and the girls and Grandmam; he stroked Almond's hair, and closed her lifeless eyes, studying her while we waited. The cabin door creaked open, and Callan come in, bringing Benny C, eyes red, but his crying done.

Finally Pa looked up. "Jeanne Findlay says it was one of them dragons what done this?"

I nodded.

"Goddamn them," Pa said, and for the first time in my life, I could hear the anger in his voice, feel it tremble. "It's past time there was a reckoning. They'll answer for this, I swear it on her life!" Pa picked up his rifle that he'd leaned up against the door when he first come in.

"You can't be serious! You know you can't take on those dragons by yourself! The whole posse couldn't take them! Benny C stabbed my knife into the side of the one what done this to Almond and it just bounced off the side." I'd lost my sister, and as good as lost Callan—I couldn't lose my Pa, not now.

Pa looked at Benny C. "You did that, son?"

Benny C squirmed a bit, unsure if Pa was riled at him or not, so I answered for him. "Yes he did, Pa. And he stabbed it in the wing; that's what made it let Almond go."

"That was well done of you, Benny C. You make me proud. But it don't change the facts. I'm going down there, and I'll have satisfaction."

"Pa, you can't..."

Callan spoke softly; I'd forgotten he was there. "He's not after the dragons, David. It's the R&A. Mister Hennessy."

Pa nodded. "If the government would do its goddamn job, protect us as they ought, my baby girl would be alive. They're supposed to relocate creatures—well, they can relocate them dragons straight to hell."

"Pa, you can't go down to town and..." What was he intending to do, threaten Mister Hennessy? Shoot him? "You'll just get locked up in jail for disturbing the peace at best, or worst, the circuit judge'll be back round, and this time it'll be for murder! We need you here, not stuck in a cell."

I could see I wasn't reaching him, so I appealed to Callan. "You agree with me, right?"

"Actually, I think your father's got a point. I think the government has a lot to answer for." He glanced at Pa. "Though I'd recommend leaving the gun behind."

"Hmf. Would you, now?" But he put the gun down and surveyed Callan, as though seeing him for the first time. "I don't approve of the choices you've made, I got to admit, and don't want you round my boy more than can be helped. But I'm glad you was here to try to save my Almond. Jeannie told me how good a job you done—weren't your fault she died."

"Doesn't feel like that," he said, looking not at Pa nor at me, but down at Almond.

"No, it sure don't, not to any of us," Pa said, looking to me and Benny C in turn. He turned back to me. "Don't worry, I ain't spoiling for a fight, but I want some answers to a few questions, and I aim to get them." Then he pushed past me and we heard the sounds of Lightning, cantering off down the path.

"He's going to get himself killed." I considered following, but had no chance of catching him, and the young ones were staring after Pa like their world was ending. Which it was, I supposed.

"Arrested, more like." Callan picked up his bag. "I need to go. I really shouldn't be here in the first place.—"

The girls were going up to their room, and Benny C was sitting by Grandmam, staring into the fire. The cabin was full of people, and yet it had never felt so empty. "I'll walk you out," I said, wanting time to say goodbye to Callan proper.

We went out into the cooling afternoon. I'd have to go back up to the pasture, fetch home Jerzy, and probably the sheep as well. Couldn't hardly leave them there as dragon bait, and he hadn't the sense to bring them home on his own. Sometimes I thought he was lucky, being simple like that; there was always someone to tell him what to do and when to do it.

Callan was strapping his bag to the back of a horse I didn't recognize. "Yours?"

"No, I wish." He stroked the gleaming black mane. "He belongs to the post rider. He's staying over at the General and offered it to me for the trip up, and I figured it was faster than any of the nags Joe Haig keeps." It was a nice- looking beast, all sleek and muscular, like a post horse should be.

"That was nice of him." We was talking of nothing, making light chat as though my sister didn't lay on that table waiting for Mam and Grandmam to lay her out for burying. "Callan?"

He looked at me like he was wanting to take me in his arms, and I almost hoped he would, but at the same time was feared that such a thing would start what couldn't be stopped. "Yes?"

"Do you think the R&A brought the dragons here?" That hadn't been what I was going to say, but since Pa's angry words, the thought had been stewing in my mind.

"I don't know. They had to come from somewhere. I don't believe in fairy tales and magic; those beasts were bred or engineered somewhere by somebody. Seems logical that the government would at least know about it."

"But why would they set them loose on innocent people? That don't make sense."

"Maybe it was an accident; they got loose on their own, and now somebody in Washington's trying to cover it up. Or maybe it was deliberate. It does seem like this area's not well-liked."

I hadn't ever thought of that—I rarely gave thought to any part of our national government save for the R&A, and the army which marched through every two years or so, just making its presence known, according to Pa. "Why do you say that?"

"Well, most parts of the country have electrical demonstration projects, either hydroelectric or wind power. There's plenty of wind, bare hilltops that would be perfect for windmills, so why not here? Most places, even small villages, have an R&A agent assigned permanently to assist with planting and animal husbandry, that sort of thing. You...sorry, we haven't till just recently."

"I didn't know that." We'd always had agents come through several times a year, but Mister Hennessy was the first government man we'd ever had live here.

"No reason why you would; it's normal to you. Just stands out to me, as I'm not from here. It just seems like someone doesn't want Moline to thrive." Callan put his hand out to rest on my shoulder. "Don't worry about any of that. It'll sort itself out, and you've got real troubles to concern yourself with. I'm sorry about Almond, you know."

"I know." I felt all tight inside. "Glad it was you that come up to help. I've missed you something awful."

"I've missed you too." He swung onto the back of the horse. "I'll see you at the funeral, though we won't be able to really talk, I imagine."

I leaned against his leg and he stroked my hair for a moment. It weren't a sexual touch, nothing like that, just comfort, and I soaked it up. "Take care," I said, finally stepping back.

He rode away down the path, and I set my shoulders and turned back to the cabin.

Pa came back late that night, neither arrested nor with any visible marks of a fight, but he was in a foul temper, and after a brief check on Mam, who was sleeping fitfully under a draught of some kind from Healer Findlay, went straight to the barn to do chores. Of course, Benny C and I had already done them, but Pa did them again, and nobody said nothing. We all understood.

It had been a nightmare afternoon. Once Pa had gone, Mam come out of the back bedroom, face all grim and determined with Healer Findlay at her side, ready to prepare Almond for the bury-hole. Grandmam had risen up to try to help her, but collapsed right away, so Ruby'd taken her and Delia to bed, then come back to help.

I should be ashamed that my thirteen year old sister was able to stay by Mam, stripping the tattered rags of clothing from the little body and washing it with warm scented water while I, almost a man, fled to the yard at the first sight of pale flesh marred with blood almost black. But nobody said nothing to me, and I realized it was the difference between men's courage and women's. I had felt no fear for myself when I faced the dragon, but to face what the dragon had left of my baby sister, that was beyond my strength.

So I'd gone back to the pasture, borrowing Healer Findlay's horse. There's great comfort in being on horseback. You can feel the muscles of the animal working beneath your legs and thighs, the warmth of the beast flows into you, and you ain't a human person no more, but something different, apart, and I longed for the nothingness that comes when your mind detaches from your body and you're just riding without thought.

Though the afternoon was turning to evening and the sun's retreat left the world chill and barren, I worked up a sweat and managed to forget, if only for a brief hour, what had gone before. Forgot, that is, till I come up the rise to the pasture and the whole thing flooded back. As I'd figured, Jerzy was still sitting there, on the rock where Almond had been, with the sheep huddled around him. He started to ask after Almond, but my face must have told the story, as he crumbled into noisy tears, then abruptly thrust something into my hands.

It was Almond's book, and in the last of the light, I could see the dark stains of blood spattering the cover. I slipped it into my pocket; the weight of it sagged my jacket down, slapping against my leg as I rode back ahead of Jerzy and the sheep. And this time oblivion escaped me; each jarring blow of the book cried, 'Almond,' driving deeper and deeper into my chest till finally the tears came, and I clung to the horse like a child on his first pony, wanting to go back and erase this day.

We buried my baby sister two days later on a day without sun. The whole town turned out, from the mayor down to the claim farmers, none of whom had likely ever even heard the name Almond Anderson.

The Digger had come up to the farm and measured her for her box, and the likes of that coffin hadn't never been seen in Moline. The boards was old, machine milled hardwoods from Before, sanded smooth, stained dark with oil, and buffed till they gleamed. Mam had wrapped Almond's body in soft wool from our own sheep, woven into a worn white blanket that had comforted Almond in life, now cut into swaths and stitched together, swaddling her like the baby she was. Her head rested on a pillow Grandmam had fashioned, with clumsy stitches, as she could hardly see to wield the needle, but Almond was beyond caring and Grandmam, though she couldn't make the trip down the mountain, had wanted a part in the burying.

Of all of us, only Mam was a regular churchgoer, and then only in summer, and Pa was positively hostile at times and had refused to let us be sprinkled, reasoning we could make the choice for our own selves when we was grown, but Pastor Daniels was willing to do the ceremony anyway. He at least had met Almond. Most of the people crowding into the school hadn't never laid eyes on her, but they'd come to stare on her poor body like a freak in a Harvest Fair sideshow. I hated every one of them so fierce that my face burned with it.

"I am the resurrection and the life," Pastor Daniels began. I didn't pay heed to the words, just let the sound of them fall over me like snow, burying my feelings deep so that I might make it through this day without shaming myself before the town. I joined in at the psalm, knowing the words by heart from school recitations, and said 'amen' when I was supposed to, but it didn't mean nothing to me. I didn't care if the dead would rise incorruptible when the last trump sounded; my sister was dead and going into the ground right now.

When the final 'amen' sounded, the pallbearers come forward to carry her out to where the Digger's cart waited. We followed without speaking to the graveyard, which was about as far as you can go and still be in the town.

The lid to the coffin was resting near to the open hole. Grandmam says that in her day, coffins went down to the earth covered in flowers, but what flowers as we had were still buds, barely beginning to live. Earth, and only earth, would cover Almond.

It was the custom for folk who had known the dead to speak about them, to share a short tale or memory. I didn't figure the speaking would go on for long, most folk not knowing Almond from Adam, but then, I didn't count on her being practically a celebrity.

Joe Haig talked about selling her candy sticks, and Burke the School about how he'd looked forward to teaching her, and Perkin Weaver about how she'd played with the treadles on his loom when Mam had brought the wool down to him. Then Mayor Casteel started in on how she'd loved his milk, when I knew perfectly well Almond never drunk nothing but goat's milk her entire life. Pa sort of started forward at that, but Mam grabbed his arm, and he kept his peace through the seemingly unending parade of men and women. Healer Findlay spoke good words, comforting words, not to the crowd like the others had, but to Mam and Pa, and I took some comfort in hearing them.

Then a familiar wheat-gold head moved through the parted crowd. Callan come forward to take his place near the small box, looking down at her closed eyes, and closing his own while he said his bit. "I saw Almond Anderson three times in her life. Once when she came to my office, once at her house when her mother was gracious enough to offer me hospitality, and on the day she died, when I failed..." His voice broke off. "She was beautiful and happy and mischievous and intelligent. She loved books." He pulled a book from his jacket, and I recognized the bloodstained Trees of North America, which I'd returned to him through Healer Findlay. He laid it gently in the coffin, and that gesture, the giving up of something which I knew to Callan was precious beyond gold, moved me more than any words yet spoken.

After that nobody else come forward; it was the family's turn. The girls just said goodbye; neither Mam nor I could force words from our throats, just stroked her cold head, but Pa, ignoring the crowd completely, talked straight to his little girl, for what I figured was the last time.

"Almond, sweetie, I failed you. Fathers are supposed to keep the monsters away from their little girls, and I didn't do that. And I'm sorry, so goddamn sorry—" I saw Pastor Daniels sort of make a frown at the profanity, but he didn't dare to interrupt. "I swear to you, on your grave, that no other child will suffer—" Abruptly he stopped and turned to face the Digger, who waited impassively by the cart. "Nail it shut, God damn it. Just do it."

For a while, the only sound was the angry bite of the hammer against the wood of the box; slow, rhythmic, like church bells marking the passing of a soul. Then the pallbearers were lowering her down with ropes as the coffin creaked and shifted, and Mam screamed and crumbled to the ground, heedless of the eyes of the whole town on her. Pa and Healer Findlay pulled her up, holding her tight. I kept Delia close to me, turning her face into my shoulder. Scared as she was from seeing her sister laid in the ground, the sight of her Mam all undone was more than she could manage.

Then before Pastor Daniels could speak the final words, the committal words of ashes and dust, Mister Hennessy stepped up to the hole and looked out over the crowd. I was mightily gratified to see he had the remnants of a fine shiner around his right eye. Pa might not have been spoiling for a fight, but he'd found one, it seemed.

"Good people, Brock Anderson is right. This tragedy should never be repeated."

"Should'a said that when they took my Lorna!" That was Devlin Massie, and there was a murmur of agreement with him.

"I was not among you then," Hennessy went on, holding up his hand for silence. "I assure you that had I been present, steps would have been taken to assure your safety. The Department of Relocation and Agriculture—"

"Don't believe in dragons!" Joe Haig called out.

"Will be informed of this occurrence." He was smooth, I can say that much. The interruptions flowed around him like water passing around pebbles in a stream. "I will personally travel to the regional office of the R&A to consult with colleagues so that we might determine how best to proceed."

"Bring in the army!" That suggestion, from back among the claim farmers, was greeted with cheers.

"Yeah, I hear they got working grenade launchers down at Fort Eustis."

"There's nukes at Langley!"

"I hardly think the intervention of the army will be required—this is essentially a case of animal extermination. You don't need a thermonuclear warhead to take care of a pest."

"My Almond weren't killed by a fucking groundhog," Pa snarled. At that, Pastor Daniels did start to protest, but the air felt thick, like a lightning storm was coming, and I figured Mister Hennessy had better quit while he was ahead.

"I apologize for my poor choice of words, but really, do we want the army here? Do you want them eating your crops and confiscating your livestock for as long as it takes them to settle this problem? Let me work with the R&A, we'll find a way, I promise you. I will leave tonight, and together, we will solve this problem. Pastor, if you would?" He nodded, and Pastor Daniels delivered his invocation and the crowd started to disperse. slowly, though, and I reckoned it was a good thing that Moline hadn't got a tavern or inn, because if some of the men had an easy way to get themselves liquored up, there'd have been bloodshed for sure. Not what I wanted for my sister's legacy.

Some folk were coming up to pay their respects, though Pa had gone off to talk to Devlin Massie apart from the rest of us. I had my hand shook about half a hundred times and was mighty weary of it, and wanting to go home when I noticed Callan at the end of the line. Finally. Nobody could say nothing about him consoling the bereaved. I'd at least get to touch his hand.

But he didn't offer it; just kept his hands down in his pockets as he told me again how sorry he was.

"Thanks." Then, casting about for something to say, some reason to keep him near me, I went on. "Mister Massie was right, the government should've done something when Lorna got took. Don't suppose it was because the Massies are black, do you?"

He bit his bottom lip so the blood left it, then flooded back in as he spoke. I wanted to kiss him so bad I could taste it. "No, more likely because they're poor. And they did send the posse—remember, Elmer and his heroics?"

"But that's just local, not the Commonwealth or the R&A. Seems like those dragons might be hunting from other towns than Moline."

"That's a thought. I wonder if anyone's thought to send word and ask."

"I don't believe you boys are supposed to be talking." Mister Hennessy'd come round behind us, and I wondered how much he'd heard.

"I was just expressing my condolences, sir," Callan replied calmly.

"You've had ample time to do that, now move along." The man's expression was so severe that if he were to smile, his face would likely crack and shatter like a badly fired pot.

"Thank you, Callan," I said, and extended my hand so he'd have no choice but to take it or appear rude. He took it, fingers warm from being down in his pockets, and I held on to the touch as long as I could before Mister Hennessy's glare drove Callan away.

"You really should be a bit more particular about your choice of friends, David. You've a whole town full of people to choose from. Don't associate with the wrong sort."

I thought about Elmer and his gang of friends, drinking rotgut behind the General at all hours of the day, making trouble in the streets, then remembered Callan, reading, speaking quiet words of peace, loving me so sweetly, working to save Almond's life. "I won't, sir. Thank you."

Chapter 14

You wouldn't think it, but life goes on, even after you lose somebody. School started up like it always did round about that time, so every day, Benny C and the girls would make the trek down the hill, and every afternoon they'd come back, regular as clockwork. Mam cooked dinners and knitted and sewed and dealt with her flock, and Pa and I walked the traplines and hunted, and we all tended the crops, planting and weeding and watering just as if Almond weren't lying dead in the graveyard. It was funny how much we missed her, for while her presence hadn't been a help in the sense of sharing the work, her absence was a powerful burden.

We was all mighty cordial to one another, but there was walls up between us, and we all felt them. Pa was gone more than he needed to be and Mam, always busy, now refused to be still at all unless she was asleep. The girls turned to each other, playing quiet games, spending extra time on their schoolwork. Benny C, well, his injuries healed up nice, leaving only a tiny scar on his forehead which, had Almond not died in the getting of it, would have been his claim to fame in the town—he could have earned his place on the playground for the rest of his school days with a dragon fighting wound. But he never spoke of it.

He kept my knife though, and I hadn't the heart to take it from him. I'd watch him in the yard, playing games of knight and soldier, retreating into a childhood world of make believe. He even gave the knife a name, the way the old time folk named swords. He called it Gram, after the sword that Siegfried used to kill Fafnir in Grandmam's story.

Grandmam herself continued on as she had before, but she seemed not so much to weaken as to shrink, as though all it would take would be the passage of enough time, and she'd shrivel away to nothing. I often caught her staring at me like she wanted to tell me something, but she rarely spoke, not even to tell stories, not no more. Mam said that Grandmam wanted to die. I suspect she did. I did, more than once in those first days.

I missed Almond. I missed Callan, too. In a way, that was the worse of the two. Almond was gone for good with no hopes of ever coming back to us; Callan was an hour's walk down the mountain, and the knowledge of his nearness ate away at me, even in my dreams. I'd be walking and catch sight of him, just ahead of me, and I'd call out to him, but he'd keep walking. So I'd run after, but no matter how hard I ran, he was always just ahead of me, just beyond my reach. Then I'd wake up, heart pounding and sweat pouring from every inch of my body from my dream exertions.

Or other nights, it was that afternoon in the meadow again, but instead of Almond on the rock, it was Callan, and the dragons came and tore him to pieces while I watched, helpless. Those were the worst, sending me out of bed to huddle in the corner of our room so I wouldn't disturb Benny C with my shaking. Though judging by the words he cried out, he was having nightmares of his own about the dragons. I hoped that when Mister Hennessy brought back help and we got rid of those monsters once and for all, the nightmares would ease up, for him at least.

Pa commented at the table on the fifth night after the funeral that the infernal rain would slow Hennessy down, and Mam looked up at him as though she wanted to say something, but she bit back her words. Mam didn't think Mister Hennessy nor the government would be able to do aught about the dragons. She'd been down to town twice in that first week to talk to Pastor Daniels, who'd come to the conclusion that the dragons was God's judgment on Moline, an opinion that Mam had started to ape whenever the subject come up.

"Can't fight the will of the Lord," she said finally, and that brought me up short. Such talk was like rubbing a cat the wrong way: it made the hair on the back of my neck stand up.

"It ain't the will of the Lord that Lorna Massie or our Almond should be dead so young."

"We can't know His will, David. Might be He needed a particular angel in His heaven," she argued back, but Pa left the table directly after she spoke, and so did I. I couldn't stomach the thought of a god who'd kill a young girl for no reason. God, if he existed at all, had thousands on thousands of angels in his angelic choir—what'd he need our Almond for? The dragons was unnatural monsters for certain, but not from God. I was with Callan on that one; something or somebody had made those beasts and brung them here. And while we might not know God's purposes, those of men could surely be found out. But Mam wasn't about to listen to such talk.

For me, that week was a sort of revelation. I didn't belong in my own home no more. I weren't at school, and weren't needed to help on the farm, not really—Pa and Mam could manage fine without me, and while me and Pa saw eye to eye on most things, Mam was a different kettle of stew. The 'will of God' nonsense was bad enough, but she started in on my betrothal to Luanna Burke again before Almond was even cold in the ground, wanting me to marry her that summer, wanting to build us a house and give us sheep and a goat and maybe even buy a cow off of Mayor Casteel, and wouldn't it be nice to have a place of your own, she'd say.

And it would have been, but not with Luanna. A small cabin or house I could share with Callan, he doing his healing, me hunting and providing meat for our table and growing the grain that would make our bread. I was a fair hand at cooking when I had to be, and we'd manage fine without a woman. And we'd have nights together, in our own bed, where nobody could interrupt us nor tell us our heart's desires was evil or corrupt. But such thoughts were fantasy, as much as Benny C stalking giants and dragons in the barn with his magic sword. So discontent festered in me like an itch and I felt like my skin didn't fit no more. I took to flying off the handle at the least little thing, resenting every day because I didn't spend it with Callan, and of course, always at the back of my mind, my little sister's absence gnawed at me like rats on rope.

Until finally I'd had enough. I didn't care what the sheriff thought, nor my Pa nor Healer Findlay nor Mister Hennessy—I had to talk to Callan. I'd never put him at risk; the memory of his punishment never completely faded, nor did the sight of Taylor Mills laying dead in the ravine, but the rule was that I couldn't be near him, not that I couldn't talk to him at all. I would send a message through Benny C, as I had before. But not in spoken words—words that, as Callan said, fade away like the mist when the sun comes out. Besides, I couldn't trust Benny C to get a spoken message right; it would have to be in writing.

Had Almond lived, that might have been a wall that would have stopped me dead, for we had never had paper in the house, but Pa had bought a First Reader for Almond—sent clear to Atlanta, Georgia for it—so that at least one of his children would start school with a book of her own. It lay wrapped in a cloth in the cedar chest in Pa and Mam's room, and it had come with a real writing tablet with a pencil, not a slate like the rest of us had got by with. So that morning, with Pa gone on a two day hunt and Mam out feeding the stock, I stole into their room, holding my breath, and tore a piece from that tablet and scrawled a note to Callan.

It couldn't be personal—Benny C would have to deliver it, and he'd read it, as sure as ice is cold. So after a casual 'we're all getting on fine, hope you are well' I wrote on the one subject that I knew would be safe: the dragons. I asked if he'd heard any word of the dragons being seen in neighboring villages, Crawford to the north, or maybe Boone to the east, and whether there was word in town of Mister Hennessy's return. Just questions, questions he'd have to answer, maybe asking some of me so that I could write him back. It weren't the same as being together, but I would welcome his note like a starving dog welcomes meat.

"Wonder if you'd mind dropping this by the healer's house after school," I said to Benny C as he was setting off after Ruby and Delia.

"Where'd you come by paper?" He looked at me all suspicious, but he took the folded paper without hesitating.

"Ain't none of your business. All you got to do is take it to Callan. You've been holding on to my knife for over a week now, I'd say you owe me this much."

"Just drop it off?"

"And wait for an answer." Benny C grumbled a bit, but he pocketed the note and high-tailed it down the path. I fretted all day, worrying on how Callan would feel when he saw my note, and what he'd say.

Benny C was smart enough not to take the note out in front of Mam, and waited till we was in the barn together to hand it off. Pa had come home that day and there was fresh meat roasting in the oven and biscuits from a sourdough starter that he'd got from a claim farmer he'd done some butchering for, and we was hurrying the chores so as not to be late. The smell of the biscuits slid through the chinks in the cabin and turned the whole hilltop warm and welcoming.

"Thanks," I said, waiting for him to leave before I opened it. "I'll finish up here— you go on in to supper."

It was the same writing as the note he'd left with Almond's book back in the winter, but messier, like he'd either been in a hurry or else in some distress. I hoped it was the first.

Very good to hear from you—glad you and your family are managing, tho I know it can't be easy. In answer to yr questions, we have had men from Boone in town of late, but they've made no mention of dragons. There's been no word from Crawford at all, which is causing some worry. Coincidentally, I am traveling there, in fact, leaving tomorrow early with what medicine we can spare, as there's concern there might be illness.

I smiled at the thought of Callan, spelling out 'coincidentally' and shortening 'your'. He wrote like he talked, and longing for him, so fierce and sharp, swept over me so that I had to dig my fingers into a nearby hay bale, letting the stalks of hay cut into my hands to distract my mind. And waiting there, forcing my breaths to deepen and calm while hoarding the echo of his voice and the memory of his hands, I got an idea.

It had been a fine supper, with Mam trying her best to make things seem as they had been, though she'd still had to remind Delia to lay one place less at the table. I ate hearty, for if my plan worked, I might not get a decent meal for a day or so, then retired out to an old rocker on the porch. I chipped away at the bark of a thick pine stick with an old knife I'd found in the barn, waiting for the moment when the time would be right. Plotting and scheming was, I considered, an awful lot like hunting.

Pa came out of the house and leaned against the porch rail. "You've been mighty cross with your Mam of late, son."

So've you, I wanted to say. But I knew I weren't too big for him to lay out, and I'd figured this talk was likely long overdue, so I just nodded and kept on whittling and rocking.

"There comes a time when a young man outgrows his home, you know. There ain't nothing wrong with that, it's the way of the world. Man gets to be seventeen, eighteen, don't want to be tied to his Mam's apron strings no more, so he starts to cut them. Some turn wild, like Elmer Casteel and his crowd, causing trouble for it's own sake; some get married—"

"I ain't—"

"Hold your peace." I kept still, but rocked that old chair so hard it was like to fall to pieces. "Some get married, some light off to parts unknown. Point is, it's powerful hard on the mother, no matter which way it comes about. And particularly now, when your Mam's just lost one baby, well, it's a hard time."

"She's the one wants me married off!" I set down my halfhearted carving.

"She sees that as the safest way, the way to keep you near to home, living the kind of life she thinks will make you happy. And she'd like grandbabies—her arms are empty and aching now." He picked up my knife and the piece of wood, and started to work it his own self, roughing out a shape with quick, skillful cuts. "I don't see it, myself, leastwise not with Luanna, and I'm trying to make your mam see it, too, but it would help if you'd be a bit more patient with her."

"I'm going mad up here, Pa. Walking the same dang traplines every day, picking the same weeds out of the same fields and tending the same sheep, it's..."

"It's what adult life is mostly like," he said grimly, "And you'd best get used to it. Don't matter if you marry Luanna Burke or the Queen of Sheba or nobody at all, whether you live here on the farm or down in town or even in a palace on the dark side of the moon, one day's mostly like all the rest, and the ones that's different is mostly pain." He was a better carver than me—under his hands the ugly piece of wood was becoming a snake, twisting and wriggling like it was alive. "And even if you was to get your heart's desire," he put the knife aside and looked down at me, "you'd likely find it turns to boredom just like most other dreams made real."

I wondered what dreams he'd had that had gone sour. I knew nothing much about Pa's life before he'd married Mam. "I'd like to go off on a long hunt," I said, kind of casual-like, changing the subject. "Two days, maybe over the mountains north towards Crawford—there's been good hunting that way in the past." I knew Pa hadn't been into town for at least four days, and had hopes that he'd not have heard the rumors of illness in Crawford. He'd never let me go if he had.

Pa stood up and brushed pine shavings from his trousers. "Guess there's no harm in that. Might give you space to think on some of what I've said, figure out what it is you want. Your mam loves you, David. So do I, and we only want what's best for you."

"I know." Though I couldn't remember him saying the words before, I'd never had doubt of my family's love.

He handed me the carved snake. "Wants a bit of sanding and finish work, but it might make a child's toy."

"Mam would say it's the devil his own self," I said, looking at the little serpent. I'd always hated that old story—Eve got all the blame, or the serpent did, while Adam hid behind his stupid fig leaves and played dumb.

"Just a creature, neither good nor ill, son. And you might be a bit more tolerant of your mam's religion—it's giving her comfort."

I remembered him walking out on her talk of Almond as the newest baby angel, but kept quiet, my mind full of plans. I was going to Crawford in the morning, and so was Callan. We would be together again. I would see him, would be with him again where nobody could see us, just like we'd been up on the Ridges.

I played the scene as I imagined it, me coming upon Callan, the look in his eyes when he saw me and knew we was alone, and what would happen after, over and over in my head that night as I tried to sleep, and it kept the dreams away. Of course, the thought of it also pushed sleep away for most of the night, so when dawn came, I was plumb tired out, but determined to go on with my plan. A sleepless night wasn't going to bar my way to seeing the one I loved.

Mam packed me trail food and a travel pack, and Pa let me have the gun, which was good, as he'd expect me to bring back game, and the gun would make it quicker than laying traps or snares. I reclaimed my knife from Benny C—just for the trip, I assured him—and he looked at me funny. I realized he'd read the note and knew darn well that Callan Landers was on his way to Crawford, too. I waited for him to speak it, but he just pursed up his lips, looking for all the world like Mam in a snit, and turned away. Sometimes Benny C could be all right, he really could.

The weather was breezy but clear, though I expected rain before the day was out; there was rain most days in spring. I hurried along the north road, hoping I hadn't got ahead of Callan, and for once, my luck held. He'd stopped to adjust the pack on the second horse he was leading when I come upon him. His head was bent over the strap and he didn't see nor hear me, so I coughed to catch his attention.

He looked up right quick, and I saw fear in him, as was only natural being caught out alone on a road. Then he saw it was me, and for just an instant, his joy was unguarded and my heart leapt. "David? What are you—"

I dropped my pack and flew at him, kissing him like there was no end to it, hands in his hair, stroking his cheeks, pushing him up against the horse, which stood still and patient against the onslaught. After a moment's shock, he was kissing me back, and our bodies fit together just as they had in my memories. As one, we withdrew a bit, just looking at each other, no questions, no worries to mar the moment of contentment.

Then he came back to reality. "What are you doing here?"

"I'm going to Crawford, just like you. Figured we could go together." I couldn't tell how he was taking my being there. Oh, his body had reacted right enough, but his face was distant now. "If you like, I mean."

"It may not be safe," he warned. "I told you in the note, there's possibly sickness there."

"Then you shouldn't be going alone." I picked up my pack and took the reins of the spare horse. "Nobody in Moline will ever know. And I'm weary of missing you."

"I know how you feel." He considered it for a moment, but only the briefest of moments, before giving in to what he surely wanted as much as me. "If you can manage without a saddle, you can ride. Those packs can go behind us." We shuffled the load, then started up the road. It was a Before road, pavement split in spaces, but still in good enough order to take us where we needed to go. Parts of it was even wide enough for wagons, so we rode side by side, and for a while it was everything I'd dreamed it would be as we rode in a comfortable sort of silence.

"I didn't have much chance to speak to you at the funeral, nor at the house when... that day. How have you been? I mean, how was the winter for you?"

He was quiet for a while. "You mean apart from cutting enough firewood to stoke the flames of Before hell? Not great. I can hardly work—an awful lot of people still won't let me treat them, and of course I'm not allowed to treat anyone under eighteen nor young men up to thirty. And then there's been...well, I guess the best word for it is vandalism of Jeannie's house. Foul words painted on her fence, rotten food thrown at the door, that sort of thing."

I had a pretty good idea who'd be behind that. "They ain't touched you? You ain't been hurt, have you?" If Elmer Casteel or his gang laid a finger on Callan, I'd take it from their hides by inches.

"No. Not yet, anyway." His face was shuttered tight, like houses in winter.

I reached out across the gap between us, just barely able to stroke his thigh, not in desire or longing, but in friendship. "Callan, I wish I could do something, anything. Seeing you like this, treated like that..."

His fingers come over mine, icy cold. He ought to be wearing gloves—seemed like he hadn't got used to our climate, though to me, the day was fine and warm. It was too hard to keep the contact across the moving horses, so I let my hand fall away. "I know you'd help if you could. And I think I could take it all, the names and the abuse and even the loss of my work if I could just see you, but..."

"I know. But I'll be eighteen in a year, then everything will be different." But would it, really? People weren't likely to change.

We fell quiet again after that. I knew as well as he did that while we might not be risking his punishment once I was of age, and we could be friends and talk about books and such again, it wouldn't never be enough for us. I'd sipped from a fountain so sweet that no other water would ever sate me, and I knew that mere friendship would seem a pale substitute.

"You should know that I'm thinking of leaving town." I started to speak, but he silenced me. "I love you. I'll likely always love you, but being so near you and unable to...to act on my feelings is driving me out of my mind. Can you understand that?"

I didn't trust myself to words, so I nodded, hoping he'd see.

"Good. I don't want to, but if I can go somewhere else, start fresh—"

"I could come with you." Like Pa had said, young men leave home. He was expecting it; he'd make it right with Mam somehow.

"Just about anywhere we'd go we'd have the same problem. You won't find a lot of towns very welcoming to a pair of sodomites."

I hated that word, the condemnation and hatred behind it. An ugly word for something so fine and beautiful as what I felt for Callan. "Nobody'd have to know. We could pass as brothers, or just friends sharing a house."

"Anybody who saw us together for any length of time would know otherwise. I can't hide how I feel about you, and you..." He laughed, and it wasn't bitter, but a shadow of the musical laugh I'd loved. "You show every thought and emotion on your face, David. It's part of what I love about you—you could no more be dishonest than you could fly to the moon."

"I stole that piece of paper for the note," I said stubbornly. "And I lied to Pa about this trip. I can learn."

"No. I don't want you learning deception for me. This is better."

I wanted to get down off the horse and pull him into my arms and scream. How could it be better for us to be apart? But he was going on. "Don't worry about it right now; I still owe Jeannie money, and I wouldn't leave without making that right, so probably not till summer's end at the soonest. Most likely next spring."

"Great eighteenth birthday present for me," I said. "Please..." I bit the words off in my mouth. Begging Callan wouldn't work, and I didn't want him to give in to me against his will, anyways. "You said not many places would accept us? So some places would?"

"A few. Florida's not so bad as here—it's still illegal, but nobody enforces it unless there's a child involved. Parts of California, if you can get out there, just about anything goes. Washington DC, surprisingly, has a reputation for almost encouraging it. But of course, you have to have permission to even visit there unless you're in the government."

So there was hope. "Promise me you won't go off and leave me if we can figure out any other way?"

"I can't see you leaving these mountains, David, especially not for Florida—it's incredibly flat; you'd hate it. But yes, I promise. It's not like I don't want to be with you." He spurred his horse on a bit faster. "Let's forget it for now. I just wanted you to be prepared, in case things go that way."

I shoved the unpleasant thought of Callan's leaving to the back of my mind and increased my own horse's pace to match his. "So what makes you think there's disease in Crawford?"

"Well, they tell me travelers normally come over around this time, exchanging news and selling goods. And there've been none. No post either. The only explanation anybody can make of it is an illness might have struck."

"So they sent you?" Seemed a bit much to expect, sending an assistant healer alone into something so serious.

"I'm expendable, and you'll note, by the way, that Mayor Casteel doesn't have much concern about the virtue of the young men and boys of Crawford."

"Well, I'm here. I can fetch and tote for you, at the least."

"David, I appreciate the help, but you mustn't take any risks. If there's disease, you must promise to listen to me, do exactly what I say. We can't risk bringing it back with us."

There'd been a rumor about three years back that a dose of some type of pox had got free of a deteriorating government lab and wiped out a town down in North Carolina. I didn't know if that were true or not, but it was surely true that influenza had swept through Richmond when I was five and killed nearly half the city before they'd got it under control. Epidemic weren't nothing to take chances with. "Of course. You're the healer. I'm just...the man who loves you."

He smiled. "And that's more than enough for me, love. I think that's the turn off to Crawford, isn't it?" He pointed to a trail leading over a broken-down fence and upward into higher country. The trail was too narrow for us to ride side by side, so I let Callan pull ahead while I followed, watching the sun glint off his hair. Nothing, not

Almond's death, nor Callan's decision to leave, nor even the nagging fear of what we'd find waiting for us in Crawford could keep the song from my heart.

True spring had come to the mountains, and it was beautiful beyond what I could put to words; the greening of the trees, the flowers clustering in the sunny spots, and the sky so blue. Colors just seemed brighter somehow, sharper and more real, in this higher country than back home. Talk was hard going single file, so I started to sing—nothing much, just an old song my Grandmam had taught me. I have a fine and true voice, though it's bragging to say so, neither too low nor too high, and even with the jostling of the horse, I was able to keep on pitch.

Callan picked up on the chorus right quick and joined with me, creating harmony, his own voice lighter than mine and a bit higher, the same sweet voice that had sung Almond to sleep a lifetime ago. We sounded good together. If we could find a place for us, a safe place, I knew we could be happy.

The trail broadened out as we approached the town. I'd been to Crawford once with Pa when I was about Ruby's age; I remembered it as a busy town, a bit bigger than Moline, with a proper town hall and an inn with a tavern. Most folk there lived in the town proper, where we in Moline tended to be more spread out in the hills, probably because the lands around Crawford were rockier and less easy to farm.

The song died mid-note, and I pulled up level with Callan as we rode in dead silence. It was a fine spring day, for sure, and back in Moline, I knew there'd be all manner of coming and going, but here, all the houses we passed had shutters and doors tight closed. No man, no woman, no child nor horse nor goat nor chicken, not even a cat could be seen as we traveled down the length of the main street to the far end. There was no life in Crawford.

Chapter 15

We rode up and down the main street, then down two of the side streets, the silence broken only by the rustling of the wind and the nervous whinny of the horses. Callan held up his hand for us to stop in front of a red brick building with a familiar sign in front of it—the town's healer lived and worked in this place.

"Stay here," he said, and dismounted. Rummaging through his pack, he took out a cloth mask and tied it over his face. My heart was flopping like fish we took out of the creek in high summer. If all these folk was dead from some fearsome disease, surely that little scrap of cloth wouldn't do no good at all.

"Callan, don't." I started to slide down off my own horse, but he pulled the mask down and looked at me, stern-faced.

"David, you've got to let me do my job. I know what I'm doing, now stay put."

"But—"

"I mean it."

I stayed put endless minutes while Callan disappeared into the healer's house, then came out, shook his head and ran across the street to an old clapboard house with a sagging wooden porch. I could see him rattling the doorknob, but the door didn't budge. Locked. And with an old lock—the kind that takes a key, not latched with a string like our cabin. Callan searched the porch, then picked up a big urn, probably an antique from Before, and heaved it through the glass window.

The glass shattered into a million pieces. If there'd been anybody alive in Crawford, they'd have heard that for sure. He stood waiting at the window to see if somebody'd come, fists clenched and back tight, then he climbed carefully through the window and into the dark house.

He come out almost immediately, through the door this time, and pulled the mask off his face. "It's okay," he called. "Nobody's there. No people at all, no bodies either. I'm guessing the other houses are much the same."

Oh, I didn't like this. From the moment we'd realized something was wrong in the town, I'd assumed we'd find bodies; I'd been surprised I couldn't smell the decay. Finding them dead would have made sense. "Where are they, Callan?" My voice cracked like I was thirteen again.

He swung back up into his saddle. "I have no idea. The house still had furniture, personal items, that sort of thing—didn't look like they'd packed up and moved on. Let's search the rest of the town, see if there's anybody left here."

The rest of Crawford was pretty much like those first streets. Callan stopped to check a few more houses, finding no sign of life in any of them, neither human nor animal. At the end of the fourth side street, Callan pulled the reins up short, and I followed his gaze across the street. The house he was looking at had been small, probably one story—couldn't tell for certain, as it was an utter burnt-out ruin. And it weren't the only one. I pointed to three other houses on the same street, all consumed by fire.

Now, it ain't unknown for homes to burn. We heat by wood, and build with wood mostly, too, so it's a hazard you learn to live with. And in town, sometimes the fire will spread, jumping from roof to roof, taking two or three places together. But these four places weren't next to each other, nor across from each other, nor did they share any other thing I could see apart from being on the same street. It was like an epidemic, not of disease, but of fire.

"But just on this street," Callan said, mostly to himself. "What's special about this street?"

"Seems like an ordinary street to me." I followed the road with my eyes as it continued beyond where we was standing. "Looks like it heads off into the mountains."

"South." Callan whispered. "Towards Moline. Come on, let's check it out."

I took Pa's rifle, because you never did know, and followed him up to the nearest of the burnt-out houses. The roof had collapsed, but the brick walls, blackened with soot and smoke, stood like an old broken snail's shell. It weren't a home no more, just like Almond's poor body weren't a person when we laid her to rest. It had rained since the house went up, and the soggy timbers of the roof lay black and broken, covering what was left of the furnishings, and the smell was horrible. Rotting corpses would have been better than this, this acrid scent of ash and fear and hopelessness.

"Chimney fire that spread to the roof?" I asked. The place seemed to swallow up my words as they come from me.

Callan hunkered down by the fireplace. "No. The chimney's not especially burned, nor has the mortar in the bricks disintegrated. This fire started somewhere else."

Pa could have told us where, I reckoned. It was a sort of tracking, only instead of a living creature, it was the path of the flame we were trailing. I tried to think like he would have. "Roof's completely gone. If it didn't spark from the chimney, maybe lightning struck the roof?"

"It's a one story house surrounded by taller neighbors. There's nothing here that would draw lightning."

I made my way carefully around what was left of the little house. No one part of it looked any worse or better off than any other. "I ain't no expert, but I'm pretty sure this fire started on the roof then burned through. The windows is smashed, and there's not so much debris as you'd think a house of this size would hold." The sun was pouring in from where the roof used to be, casting odd shadows on the remnants of the walls.

"They had time to haul things out onto the street, toss them out the windows. Good thinking. I expect you're right, but if it wasn't a chimney fire, nor lightning, then what..."

The thought must've crossed both our minds at the same time for we met eyes as one. "I ain't seen sign that those dragons breathe fire, Callan. They didn't breathe fire at Almond, nor at any time I've seen them flying nor hunting, and I'd wager I've seen more of them than most anybody."

"But they must. In all the stories they do, and I'm beginning to think that's what all this is. A story that somebody's telling, using us as puppets."

A rippling shadow crossed over the sunlit floor and I looked up, expecting to see a dragon high overhead, but it was just a big old crow. It settled on a roof joist, let out a harsh caw, and set to preening its inky-blue feathers. There weren't nobody here to care what we did, so I caught Callan's hand. His fingers was like ice. "Come on, let's get out of here."

The whole place was spooking me awful bad, though I hid my fears as Callan insisted on checking the other burned houses, just to be sure. Each of them was almost the image of the others, with chimneys intact and roofs burnt away—walls, too, if they'd been wood. The last one, another brick cottage closest to town, was the worst of all.

"It's not rained on this," Callan said sharply, after feeling the dried out and charred timbers that blocked our way into the house. "When did it rain last?"

"Day before yesterday down home, but I don't know for sure here." But that had been a mighty storm that had blackened the sky for miles and miles. There weren't no way Crawford could have escaped it.

"Then this fire happened yesterday or the night before, then."

I started forward, clambering over the fallen timbers, but Callan called me back. "It could still be hot in there."

I went on, but took care where I stepped, grateful for my good boots that would guard my feet from any remaining embers. It didn't smell hot, nor feel more warm than any of the other houses, but unlike the others, it was crammed with debris: half a chair, what must have been a sofa like the one in Healer Findlay's house, and ghosts of cabinets with slagged pottery and melted silver. Nobody'd saved anything from this place. Whether it had been dragons or lightning or the hand of a mythical god, it had struck hard and fast.

Callan come in behind me and had gone back down a hall, or what would have been a hall had there been full walls. Like a little child away from his Mam, I wanted to follow him. My skin itched with the wrongness of this place. "There's nothing here," I called out to him. "Let's go."

In answer, he gave a strangled cry and came tearing down the hall, face set and pale. He pushed past me, stumbling over the timbers and out into the sunshine. I should have followed him; I wish with all my heart that I'd done so, had gone to his side and not down that hall. For lying between four burnt timbers that was all that was left of a bedstead was the blackened corpse of a child.

I stared down at it; not much bigger than Almond, I thought, though it was difficult to tell. Where Almond's body had looked like a wax doll, human in appearance, this child did not. But it had been, once. It had been someone's darling baby and pride and joy, sleeping in a big bed such as this in a room that, from what remained, looked larger than even Mam and Pa's room at home. There was a metal band melted around the blistered wrist, a bracelet of gold, though any stones had fallen and cracked in the heat. So it was a girl-child.

I heard a noise behind me and turned to see Callan in the door frame. He weren't looking at me, nor at the child's body, just staring into the space where a wall had once been. "This place isn't safe, you should come away."

He was likely right, but I couldn't leave her in a place like this. "I got to bury her. It ain't right that she don't have a proper grave."

Looking like he was struggling to hold down his gorge, he nodded. "Go ahead, I understand. I'm sorry, I...I can't help you, can't..."

"Why don't you meet me at the Inn in about half an hour? Ground's soft, won't take me long."

Callan left, mumbling thanks, and I went to the next house over, where I took a blanket, blessing whatever it was sent them running off without their household goods, and then I wrapped the body and carried it out of the ruined house. She was so light, like a feather, like nothing. We ain't much when we're dead—I was coming to find that out. I didn't know where the Crawford graveyard was, but figured she could rest just as easy in her own back yard, so I found a shovel and set to work.

It was closer to an hour by the time I finally put the last shovelful of dirt over the tiny body and tamped it down hard so no wild things would dig at her. She'd had enough indignity visited on her young self. Though I thought when I'd seen her that I'd never be hungry again, I was, for it had been harder work than I'd figured. I figured I'd set a meal for Callan and me from the trail food Mam packed, maybe at a table in the Inn, which wouldn't feel so much like breaking in as taking our meal in a private house.

Both horses was tied up to the post outside the Inn and had been fed and watered. Callan must have had the same thoughts of food I did, for he'd already set meat out, but he weren't eating it, just staring at it like it was poison. He'd found a bottle of something in the cupboards, too, and had poured a drink. I hadn't never seen him drink alcohol before, and couldn't imagine him like Elmer, all drunken and spoiling for a fight. He hadn't seen nor heard me come in, and I watched as he tossed back the drink in one gulp, then poured himself another and downed it too. He stared at the thick glass, turning it over and over in his hand, then without word or warning, threw it against the far wall where it smashed into pieces.

The world was upside down, so I tried to right it. "Should have played baseball with you, that day on the Ridges. You'd be a fair pitcher with that arm."

"I've played baseball. Once. I'm too short-sighted to hit the ball, and until I spent six months with an axe in my right hand, I couldn't throw at all." He handed me the bottle. "Put this somewhere, would you? I don't want to drink any more, if for no other reason than it tastes like horse piss."

"I ain't actually ever tried horse piss, maybe I should give it a go." But I set the bottle aside. "She's buried. A girl, probably not much older than Almond."

Callan's face was shut tight, eyes flat and lifeless as the corpse I'd just buried. He didn't answer me, so I kept talking, like you do when you've got a case of nerves.

"What I can't figure out is what on earth would make folks leave in such a blue streak that they'd abandon the body of their child? I can't imagine Pa nor Mam running off and leaving Almond to lay in the house alone like that."

"They surely loved her," I forged on. "She had a gold bracelet and a big old bed and..."

He walked over to where I'd put the bottle, and took a drink, making a sour face at the taste of it. "How pathetic a healer am I? Can't even look at a dead body. And to think, I used to want to be a real doctor. That's a joke."

I wanted to ask what lay behind it all, but he'd tell me when he was ready. What mattered was the hurt in him; that I couldn't stand, so I took that bottle out of his hand and poured its contents out on the floor. The innkeeper weren't likely to complain, but the smell of it sharpened the air and immediately made me wish I hadn't. "It was a hard sight. Made me sick to my stomach and I've spent all my life around animal bodies, helped with butchering and burned diseased carcasses, too. I don't know what's in your past that's got you turned inside out like this, and I don't need to know, but you got no cause to blame yourself nor to beat yourself up for leaving."

He let me lead him back to the table. "Now eat something, cause we got to think, and that ain't exactly my strong point. I need you."

His hand caught at mine as I was moving it away, and he pulled me to him. "And I need you, it seems. I never thought I'd need anyone, not like this. Want, yes. Love, oh, yes. I wanted to love and be loved, but to need someone, to be dependent on them and to know that the world is only right when they're in it, that was something I've never desired. It scares me." We were face to face; I could smell the whiskey on his breath, and his grip on my wrist was almost painfully tight. "It scares me how much I want you, how much I need you."

I didn't know what to say, was afraid anything I said would be wrong, so I leaned in and kissed him lightly on the mouth. I held back from passion, though my blood was running hot and I felt that wonderful tension coursing through my body. "Good thing I'm here, then, ain't...isn't it?" I finally said.

Still so close I could feel his heart beat, he said gently, "You don't ever have to do that...correct your speech, I mean. Not for me. I love the way you talk. Your speech is of these mountains, and it's part of who you are. Never be ashamed of it, David. It's you, and I love everything about you."

The kiss this time was passion, twisting and turning and giving and taking; kissing till I'd forgot time and place and knew only that Callan loved me and wanted me and needed me. He pulled away first, leaving me breathless atop of one of the tables with the taste of whiskey in my mouth.

"No, not like this, not here. Not yet." He sort of shook himself and his voice sounded angry. "We've got all night, and we've beds enough to choose from. This night is going to be as perfect for you as I can make it."

I shivered as his words struck me through to the bone. We'd have this day, and then that would be all we'd have for a year, or maybe forever if he really went away. I wanted it to be right, too—I could wait.

I drew the drapes open and flung up all the window sashes to ease the scent of the whiskey, then set him down and handed him food, and we both ate in the daylight.

"You're right," he said, changing the mood back to the task at hand. "It must have been something horrible to make them leave so quickly. The whole town emptied in less than a day—that's remarkable, David. Even when there's a war on and people are evacuating ahead of advancing armies, it seldom happens that quickly, and there are always stragglers, or people who refuse to go for one reason or another."

"Not here." I cut a piece of smoked sausage. "Someone or something made them go. Or..." I looked around the room, but like the rest of the town, there was no sign of fighting or struggle, no blood nor damage to any of the buildings, beyond the burned houses. "You don't think the dragons ate them all, do you?"

Callan took the sausage and our fingers touched. He was warmer than normal, possibly from the whiskey, and his hands was smooth, even after a long winter's labor. "No, I don't think two dragons could eat a whole town full of people without leaving a trace. There's something else we're missing. Let's go over to the town hall; maybe there's something there that will help us figure it out."

But there wouldn't be; the folk of Crawford hadn't any better way to keep written records than my own folk. The only records kept in writing were court papers, and they was always sent on to Richmond at the end of the court session. Still, I was glad of an excuse to leave the inn with its stink of whiskey and the ghosts of Callan's pain.

The town hall was about a half-dozen houses down, and I couldn't help looking in the windows of the places we passed, seeing pictures on walls and tall clocks still wound and ticking, chairs pushed aside as though whoever'd been sitting in them had just gone out to the kitchen and would be back directly. A child's toy, a red painted metal truck that must have surely been over a hundred years old, lay dropped on a porch, abandoned. I sought for Callan's hand, feeling unsettled and raw.

Callan stopped in front of the house next to the town hall, staring into its window and dropping my hand. "Now that's odd."

The glass was new; you could tell by the twisted swirls in it—old time glass was clear as, well, as glass. What we got now weren't near so well made, so I had to stop and look twice before I saw what Callan meant. The house was empty. There weren't a stick of furniture to be seen.

"Maybe it was empty to start," I suggested, but I knew that couldn't be true. The place was kept up, yard neat, porch swept clear of dust, even fresh paint on the shutters.

The door was unlocked and we found as we searched the place that it was mostly cleaned out. There was marks on the floors and walls where carpets had lay and pictures had hung, but apart from that and a few large furnishings like the bed and stove, you'd have thought nobody'd lived here in years. Our footsteps resounded like drum beats and when Callan spoke, his voice echoed up to the rafters of the abandoned house, making him sound like a preacher declaiming from Holy Writ.

"This person knew. He knew they were leaving in time to send off most of his things." He was opening kitchen cabinets, checking every shelf and drawer like they'd hold the answer to all our questions. "We have to find out who lived here."

But how do you figure out who lived in a house when there's nobody to ask and nothing writ down that would tell it? If you come into Moline and wanted to know who lived in a particular house, you'd ask the neighbors, or you might go to the sheriff, or over to the General. If a body walked into our cabin and dug around some, they'd come upon Mam and Pa's marriage papers that have their names on it. In most houses there'd be baptism records, or a copy of a land deed or a claim farm agreement, some few precious papers, or photographs with names recorded on the back—Mam had been to Richmond and had her picture made once, long ago when she was a girl, and some families, like the Casteels and Burkes, had portraits done every year.

But any papers or pictures in this house was gone, along with whoever had lived here. "Figure we might go ahead and search the town hall like you said. Might be deeds or maps or something there," I said to Callan, who was trying to lift the heavy mattress to see if anything was under it. I took hold of it and pulled it up so he could search.

"Umph." I strained to keep it from falling on him. "This is heavier than a straw tick."

"Feather bed," he said, stepping back so I could let it drop. "Quite nice one, too. Whoever he was, he had money." Then he smiled at me. "Have you ever slept on a feather mattress?"

I shook my head. Never anything like this, so thick, and both firm and soft at the same time.

"Tonight you will." Oh, that was a promise, and it was all I could do to turn away from that bed and continue to wander the empty house, looking for signs that surely didn't exist. We'd got mostly through it when I figured if we was staying in that house for the night, it might be good to lay in a fire while the sun still shone. The sky was clouding up mighty fast; rain was moving in from the west, and I surely didn't want to be stumbling around in an unfamiliar yard in the dark and damp looking for firewood.

So I brung in a stack of wood and started to lay a fire when I noticed a whole mess of something that weren't wood half burnt up in the grate. I was mighty sick of the smell and sight of char by then, but I fished it out, thinking it might be important. "Callan, what do you make of this?"

"It's a book." He took it reluctantly, as though the idea of a book destroyed was almost more than he could stomach, and carried it over to the table near the window. "Not a published book—it's some sort of log or journal." Now that we was in the light,

I could see he was right. The cover was flaking leather, twisted by the fire, and almost all the pages was gone, as though it had been thrown on the fire spine up.

"Can you make out anything?" I didn't see how he could; the pages crumbled into black dust at the lightest touch.

"No, it's a dead loss." He sighed. "Another dead end."

I took it from him and tried to flatten it down. "Looks like it's been branded." I didn't look at Callan when I said that, didn't want to remind him of what he carried on his shoulder.

"Oh, of course," he said, and took the book closer to the window, tracing what was left of the design with his fingers. "Not branded—stamped. Damn this stupid glass."

We went out onto the street. The rain was moving in fast, with gusts of wind whipping around the corners of the buildings, stirring up the grass. It weren't hardly lighter outside than it had been in the house, the sky had grown so dark, but it was enough for us to make out a circle with a bird, wings out, over top of two interlocking letters.

I'd seen it before, on every packet of seed we'd planted since I was old enough to dig a hole in dirt. "It's the seal of the R&A."

Chapter 16

Lightning flared in the sky to the distant west. The storm was bringing more than rain, and we had two horses to see to. Everything else would have to wait.

"I'll find a stable for the horses; there should be one behind the Inn," I said. "Why don't you go on ahead and check the Town Hall—I wouldn't know what I was looking for, anyways. I'll meet you back here when we're both done."

Thunder rumbled after the lightning, and I figured it was about seven miles away. Storms could move mighty fast this time of year. Callan glanced skyward. "All right, and I'll find us something for supper. Some sheets for the bed, too, if I can."

My face turned hot from thinking about that bed, and what we'd be doing in it, but the wind was rising and I could hear the horses behind us, getting restless. Animals can sense the weather's change better than humans, and if you could judge anything by the horses, we were in for a powerful big storm. They was pawing the ground and tossing their heads something fierce, though they calmed as I stroked and patted each of them in turn.

I led them behind the Inn where a well-built stable waited with stout doors and shuttered windows and abandoned feed spilling out of a trough. I found a discarded brush and gave each a swift currying, not so much for their looks, but to settle their agitation some, then I left them blanketed for the night and stepped out of the stable into the beginning of the storm. Rain was spitting down around me and the wind was gusting, blowing cold sprays of water every which way; I didn't know what time it was, but the darkening sky made it seem suppertime or later. Flashes of lightning had been jumping across the horizon the whole time I was with the horses, and judging by the distance between light and sound, I'd say the storm was within two or three miles of being on top of us.

Callan must have found some lanterns and candles, for as I come up on the R&A house, there was light behind the curtains. When I opened and shut the door, quick so the rain wouldn't blow in, the whole room was flooded with light and there was a warming fire going; a whole slew of pillows that Callan must have taken from half a dozen houses were lying in front of it, along with a glass and a bottle of something on the floor.

"Callan?" He came out of the kitchen carrying two plates piled high with food. His face lit up like one of the lanterns when he saw me, and I slung both our packs down beside the door as thunder rattled the windows. It was the funniest thing, but seeing him like that, making me food, fixing up a home for us, even if just for a night, gave me such a feeling of joy, far better in a way than the moment when Callan said he loved me. This was what I wanted for our future: just us together, making a life.

"Just in time. Come sit down."

I pulled off my boots, shed my jacket, and took one of the plates over to the fire, where we sank down onto the downy pillows. "Did you find anything helpful over at the town hall?"

His cheeks flushed red, like Delia caught sneaking food from Mam's larder. "I didn't ever get to the town hall. I spent the last hour hunting up all this." He pointed to the pillows and the food and all. "I guess I should have brought over some chairs, but this seemed nicer." He stretched out so his toes was nearly in the hearth, and I couldn't help noticing how fine and straight his long legs looked in the firelight.

"It's good." I'd never ate in a house save for at a table, but there weren't a reason in the world why Callan and I shouldn't do things our own way. He slid down, propping himself up on one elbow, and I did the same, facing him, with the plates of food between us. There was wheat bread, cut into slices, but browned somehow, with melted cheese between them.

"I did the best I could with the sandwiches," Callan said. "The bread is stale, and the cheese wouldn't melt right over the fire in that stove. No wonder he didn't have it sent on to wherever he went."

I bit into one of them, and it was warm and gooey and the best thing I'd ever tasted. "I think you done fine. I guess you wasn't fooling, back when you said you cooked okay."

Lightning flared outside the curtained windows and Callan rolled over onto his back, nibbling at one of the sandwiches. "My mother worked an outside job the entire time I was growing up, so I learned early on to make a few things. Cheese sandwiches aren't exactly gourmet cooking, but I'm glad you like them."

Propped up by the pillows, I leaned against him, eating and watching the fire, listening to it crack and pop, forgetting that we was in a strange man's house in an empty town. This was our house, at least for this one night.

"Oh, and I found this, too." He sat up and grabbed the bottle. It was dark glass the likes of which I'd never seen before, almost black, with a sort of metal cloth covering the top of it, which Callan peeled off as he spoke. "Down in the cellar at the Inn, and I'm betting nobody knew it was there. It predates the Ice for certain."

Under the metal-cloth there was some kind of cage, holding the stopper in place. "Is that whiskey?"

"No, champagne. Imported, I think, but it's hard to tell, as the label's so faded." He'd taken off the wire cage and was pointing the bottle back towards the door, working the stopper with his thumbs. "Almost there, hang on..." The stopper gave way and shot halfway across the length of the house with a pop like baby thunder, and I laughed aloud.

"That's like the pop gun Pa made for Benny C."

"Similar principle certainly, except there's considerably more force behind it," Callan agreed, handing me a glass of the fizzing liquid. "Try it. Everybody should have champagne at least once in their life."

I took a sip. It was odd, like drinking air; it tickled my nose and lips, and made me warm to my toes. "I like it. Ain't never had nothing like this, save maybe the sarsaparilla they sell at Harvest Fair."

"Champagne was the drink of choice from Before for celebrations. Anniversaries and..." He looked sideways at me, then down. "Weddings, that sort of thing."

"Don't you want none?"

"I'll taste some of yours. I think I've had enough alcohol for one day."

The rain was beating down on the roof hard now, drowning out the thunder, even. I put my sandwich down, thinking now was as good a time as any to get any unpleasantness behind us. "I know it ain't none of my business, but I was wondering..." He was still sitting up, looking down at his hands. "I ain't never seen you drink; you don't strike me as the type to look for answers in a bottle."

"I'm not, as a general rule. I've only been truly drunk one time in my life and I regretted it immensely."

"Well, earlier on, when you was...when you had that whiskey, I thought it was because of seeing that child's body, but now that I think on it, I got to ask if it was something I did."

"No, it wasn't you. I don't want you to think that for a moment." He slid back down into the cushions, turning to face me. "Come on down here, David," he said, and gently he turned me round so we was stacked like spoons. "This will be easier if I'm not looking at your face, okay?"

I nodded. Our bodies fit together like a glove to a hand, with his arm resting over me and his hips molding themselves to me in a way that was powerful distracting. A couple rain drops made their way down the chimney flue, and the fire hissed like an old barn cat.

"You were right the first time. It was seeing the body. It brought back memories that I've tried, really tried hard to push aside, but apparently that hasn't been successful. Do you remember once when we were talking about dead bodies, I told you I'd seen my mother's body?"

I nodded again, feeling my hair tickle his chin as I done it. When we'd had that talk, I'd never lost anyone; I hadn't never looked on one I'd loved dead and gone, and hadn't truly understood what it was like, but now I did. "She die in a fire?"

"Yes." His arms wrapped a little tighter, almost too tight, but it seemed like what he needed.

I turned in his embrace and begun to kiss his cheeks, licking up the traces of tears, lips light over fluttering eyelashes. "I'm sorry," I whispered into his ear, not sure if was apologizing for what had happened back then, or what happened today, or for asking about it and stirring up a past he'd rather leave buried.

"It's okay. There's a lot more to it, and I promise to tell you eventually, but can we let it go for now? I want tonight to be just about us, nothing of the past, not my mother or what happened in town, none of it's going to intrude."

I sat up and sipped at the glass of champagne, then handed it to him. He sipped too, and smiled, but it was a sad sort of smile. I sought about for something to please him. "Champagne is wine, right?"

"Yes. I don't know exactly how they make it, but it's a type of wine." He sipped again, then refilled the glass. The warm feeling was spreading through my body, and I could feel heat radiating from the fire, and from Callan. I stroked the back of his hand wrapped around the bottle, and he moved closer to me, snuggling against my side, contented-like. He was where he belonged. Nothing in the past could touch us here.

"You know, in the deep hills, where there ain't preachers nor much government save when the Circuit Judges ride, if two people share a meal and wine..." I glanced behind me to where the door to the bedroom stood open. "And a bed, they're married in the law." I think it must have been the champagne that gave me leave for such boldness, but Callan didn't seem to mind.

"Yes, that's the custom most places, but you've got it wrong, unfortunately—it's not just any two people. It's got to be a man and a woman." He let go the bottle and started to play with my fingers, stroking and touching ever so lightly, then walking them up my arm, over my shirt till he come to the shoulder, then across to my throat where my buttons was.

"I don't want a woman," I said, and the first button slid out of its hole under his touch, then the next and the next, till I felt cool air tickling my chest.

"Good," he whispered into my ear while his fingers worked their way down my chest. The rain hadn't slacked off any; it seemed like the entire storm had come to roost on top of this little house. I started to unfasten Callan's buttons as well, but my fingers were big and awkward and kept tripping over themselves till I swore in frustration.

He laughed and kissed me on the forehead, and sat up, pulling his shirt over his head in one swift movement. He had on an undershirt, a summer weight one without sleeves, and the muscles of his arms and his shoulders gleamed in the firelight. I caught a glimpse of the brand on the left one, but didn't let my eyes linger there. "I believe I promised you a feather bed?" he said.

I'd never known you could be eager and terrified at the same time, but oh, I surely was. Up on the Ridges, it had been awkward and fumbling and both of us uncertain, but it had been me taking the lead. Here he reminded me of how he'd been when he was healing: focused, confident, knowing what he wanted, when I didn't really know nothing.

The fear must have showed on my face even in the firelight, like everything always does. "And you know that the only thing we absolutely have to do in that feather bed is sleep, right? If all you want is what we did before, or even just to sleep together, that's fine. I don't want to push into anything you're not ready for."

"Feels stupid to be all on pins and needles, like some dumb girl on her...walking out for the first time."

Callan laid another log on the fire. It must have been well-seasoned, for it caught straight off, and the fire flared up. "It's not stupid. I'm scared to death."

"You're scared? What have you to be a-feared of?" But he was—I could see it in his eyes.

"I've never been with anyone who wasn't more experienced than I am. I'm afraid I'll mess it up for you, and I desperately want it be right. Because you're right, this is like a wedding night, David." So he'd caught what I'd started to say; he felt the same as me. It was like everything we'd done and been through had led us here, and what we did here would point us in the way we'd go on—it mattered. He was standing up by the fire, so I stood too, though my legs was shaking so bad it seemed like they'd collapse under me.

"I wish it could be, for real, I mean. I wouldn't never want to say vows with anybody but you." Thunder, distant now, rolled over us as the rain slacked, and Callan dug into his pocket for something.

"You know I'd marry you if we were allowed. What I said before, in the Inn, that was the truth. I do need you and love you in a way I've never loved anyone else."

"Taylor Mills—"

"Taylor was my friend, and yes, I slept with him, but I didn't love him and he certainly didn't love me. I'm sorry for what happened to him, and it was my fault." He held up his hand to stop up my protests. "I'll always regret that it ended like that, but it would have ended in any case, because once I came to know you, I couldn't be with anyone else." He pulled a small box out of his pocket. "Here." I caught a flash of gold as the box opened. "I always keep this with me—it was my father's wedding band; just about all I've got left of him aside from some books. I can't wear it—he was bigger than I, and I'm afraid it would fall off and be lost. But it ought to fit you just fine."

Then he slid the cool gold band onto my finger, and it was the finest thing I'd ever beheld in my life. Mam's wedding band was plain and tiny, and Grandmam's, though bigger, was still just a plain stretch of gold. But this was carved and chipped in a twisty pattern, and it felt heavier than any jewel I'd ever seen. "I...I can't keep this."

"I know. They'd see, and you'd never be able to explain. Tomorrow we go home and we'll have to deal with whatever's happened in this empty town and the dragons and the R&A. And if they figure out we've been here together, it's likely to get ugly. But just for tonight, to sort of make it more real, more right, to remind you that I really do love you, will you wear it?"

I didn't trust words, so I kissed him, pouring out all my love into the kiss till we was both breathless. "I think I'm not so nervous now."

"Good. To do this right, I'm supposed to carry you over the threshold, but I think you're going to have to forgive me for skipping that particular tradition."

The thought of Callan carrying me anywhere made me smile. He was strong, stronger than he looked, but I outweighed him by more than a few pounds. "I can walk," I said, suddenly shy again. "Callan, I don't mean to sound stupid or unschooled, but, beyond what we done on the Ridges, I ain't really sure what it is that two men can do together. I mean, the older boys at school told stories, but they also used to tell tales about seeing Bigfoot out on the Ridges on moonlit nights, so I ain't taking their word for nothing."

So he told me, and I guess I'd better keep my eyes peeled for Bigfoot next time I'm abroad in the night, as the school talk was mostly right. What he said made a deep gnawing pit in my stomach, but it also stirred me, and above all things I trusted Callan that he wouldn't lead me anywhere that weren't good and right.

So I followed him into the bedroom where he'd made up the bed with clean sheets and a comforter he'd got from somewhere, and more pillows, so that bed looked like a corner of heaven, just waiting for us. The wind was whipping around the outside walls, driving the rain into the windows, though I couldn't see it, for the curtains had been drawn. One large lamp sat burning on the floor, as the bed was the only piece of furniture left in the room. It didn't give much light, but I guessed we wouldn't need light for what we was going to do.

I stood on one side of the bed and Callan stood opposite, and I froze again, uncertain of what I should do. He slid off his undershirt and then commenced to unfastening his trouser buttons, and I watched his clothes fall away till he was bare and the smoky lamplight turned his skin to sweet honey.

I hadn't never seen him, nor any living man save myself like that, and oh, he was young and strong and fine, like the drawings and sculptures in the art history book that Master Burke wouldn't let the girls look on, for those old people made much of the male body. And looking on Callan, I understood those old Greeks and Romans, and couldn't for the life of me understand why anybody thought women the fair sex. I knew from the way he was smiling at me that he was waiting for me to take off my own clothing, but I was suddenly ashamed of my own body. Where Callan was slender as a creek-reed in summer, I was bulky, and the hair on my body was dark while his own was golden and near invisible. If this had been one of Grandmam's stories, then he'd be Baldur and I...well, likely some troll or wight.

"Don't be shy." He came over to me and helped me out of my shirt. "Your body is beautiful." And I believed him, seeing myself in his eyes. Somehow my trousers and underthings was around my ankles, and I stepped out of them and into his arms so we was skin to skin, chest to chest, thighs pressed against thighs; so good, so sweet, his hands run over my back and then down lower, sending chills up my spine while the rain's rhythm pounded on the roof.

Callan leaned me back onto that mattress and for a moment, I forgot the insistent need of my body and marveled at how it felt, descending into the feathers, like falling into warm air. But only for a moment, as Callan was over me, his desire pressing against my legs which opened and moved for him in a strange dance; not the dances of the Harvest Fair, all sweating and stomping and tossing your partner awkwardly around an old barn. No, this was most like the gentle tossing of the trees in the summer breeze, swaying and bending and giving and taking.

You'd have thought I wouldn't know the steps, but somehow I did mostly, moving on instinct to touch and caress and kiss, using my mouth on him clumsily, though he didn't seem to mind, judging by the sounds he was making and the way his hands tightened in my hair. Somehow I found myself knowing when to turn, when to lay quiet, when to breathe, and when to keep utterly still, as I knew it on the hunt. And when at the last moment I froze, all at once frightened and unsure, Callan was a marvel, making what should by rights be awkward into something right as the rain on the roof.

There was some pain, but he'd warned me of that, and soothed me through it, holding himself still till I adjusted to his presence within me, though I could feel him trembling as he held himself back. We was facing, and I was glad of it, for the look on his face when I nodded that he could break the spell and start to move will stay with me till the day I die.

It wasn't till then that I understood what it meant, in the marriage lines when it says two becoming one flesh. I'd loved what we'd done on the Ridges, but now, with this, Callan was part of me and I of him. My hands stroked his back and shoulders, urging him on, but he needed no such thing, letting go at last and driving me into the mattress till all I knew was his body and mine and the release that had to come or I'd surely die of it. Callan's hand come down between us and took a-hold of me, knowing just how I needed it, firm and strong, the way a woman likely never could have, and caring more for me than for his own pleasure.

It come over me from within and without, like nothing I'd ever dreamed, and my whole body shook and shuddered and clenched around him. "Oh sweet God, Callan!" I cried out, and as though the sound of my voice was a trigger on a rifle, I felt him seize up and spasm, and his face was pleasure and pain all wrapped together.

It was like a death, though without the sorrow; the death of the old David, and the birth of someone new, someone bound to Callan. Too soon, though, we slid apart, and lay side by side on that wonderful mattress. I felt as if I'd run the traplines three times without stopping, limbs heavy, body aching and sore a bit, but in a good way.

The rain was still coming down and the room had cooled; there weren't no fireplace in this room, and the part of my mind that was still working wondered why on earth the R&A man hadn't put his bed on an inside wall, but I couldn't rouse myself enough to get up and move it, nor to put on clothing against the spring chill. Callan got up to put out the lamps, then I felt the coverlet being pulled up over me, and I turned to take him in my arms.

"You're cold," I said.

"You ought to know by now that I'm never warm. In summer some, but mostly not even then."

"I'll make you warm." Benny C said I was like an oven—I was forever pushing him away in winter as he tried to suck the heat off me. I wrapped my legs around Callan's, and moved us around so that his head was resting against my shoulder while my hands stroked his back under the heavy covers. "Thank you. For..." I figured if I was going to do a thing, I ought to be able to speak it. "For making love to me. Guess I'm a solemnite now."

He giggled in fits and starts. "Oh my God, that idiot Elmer—I swear to you, David, there I was at the hearing, my life and freedom at stake, and all I wanted to do was collapse laughing. Yes, you're a solemnite, and I'm a solemnizer, and I wouldn't have it any other way." Then he turned serious. "And I should be thanking you. That was the most amazing, marvelous thing I've ever experienced."

His hands were stroking me too; it was like we couldn't stop touching, couldn't get enough of each other. I felt the strange weight of the ring on my finger. "You can't go away, not now. Not without me."

"No. I don't think I could. That was just me trying to be sensible; always a mistake." His right hand caught my left and touched the ring.

"I know I ain't near good enough for you, not your equal—" Callan pressed a slender finger to my mouth. "You have to stop that. You're every bit good enough for me; I'd say it's more the other way around. In every way save for formal education, you're more than my equal. You're good and strong and kind and generous. We complement each other."

I puzzled over that. "Well, you surely just complimented me, so I guess I—"

"No, that's not what I meant." That finger had left my mouth and traced down my jaw to my chest, and I felt my body stirring again. "Complement. To make up for each other's weaknesses. I meant that we belong together, are made for each other sort of like a lock and a key."

I gasped and fought to hold control of myself as his fingers, followed by his tongue, flickered over my nipple. "Well, it was mighty fine being the lock. Do you think I might take a turn at being the key sometime?"

This time the laughter was louder than the rain and he commenced in to tickling me till I was wriggling under him, begging him to stop, but not really wanting him to. I fought back, trying to find the places that was most sensitive, to learn Callan by heart like I'd learn a well-loved book, and we rolled on the bed till he was under me, with his legs wrapped around mine in a wrestle hold, and I could feel how much he wanted me. I looked down into his unshadowed eyes, as I had that day we'd wrestled on the traplines.

"How about right now?" he asked, and the world, which had been so badly wrong for so long, turned right.

Chapter 17

I came awake slowly, wrapped in Callan's arms. The rain had stopped, but the pre-dawn air had turned cool. Callan still slept, likely more used to sleeping late than me, so I just studied his face, at peace for a change, with a slight smile curling his lips. I wanted to touch him, but feared to wake him, for once Callan woke, everything would change. The world we'd built inside these walls the previous night couldn't last.

He stirred, and I could see his eyelids fluttering as he come out of deep sleep. "Good morning," I said, and kissed him.

"Mmm. Good, yes. Very, very good." His arms tightened round me.

"A body could get used to waking up like this." Like you was two parts of one person; like you was home.

"Wish we could."

But the sun was coming up, and I knew it was like one of those old tales where the magic vanishes at the stroke of midnight. "Do we have to go now?"

"Soon," he said. "But not yet." We had a few precious minutes, maybe so much as an hour to spend together, and you would think we would have used it in love-play, but we didn't. Oh, we touched, right enough. It was like we couldn't leave off touching each other. Arms wrapped around, trying to get so close that we would become each other, we talked, spinning dreams and making plans as boys will. And we was boys then, though Callan was three-and-twenty and desperately adult most times; for these moments, he was young as me. I was coming to know him, to know what pleased him, how he liked to be kissed hard and touched light, what would make him laugh, how to turn his mood bright when the dark overtook him.

Finally, though, I could see through the drawn curtains that it was growing late, and my stomach rumbled loud enough that Callan heard it. "It's time, David."

I held out my left hand and looked at the ring one final time, then slid it off my finger and gave it back.

"I'm going to hold it for you," he said. "And someday, though I don't know when or where, I'll give it back. But the thought behind it is always with you."

We kissed a bit then, quiet desperate kisses, then without speaking, we got up and dressed and left the bedroom, closing the door behind us. Callan laid out a quick breakfast of cold cheese sandwiches and some dried fruit he'd brought, which we ate standing, neither of us wanting to return to the pillows where the champagne bottle still sat in front of the banked fire.

"Guess we ought to check out the town hall," I said, bringing us back to the empty town and the burned-out houses.

"Yes," Callan said, his mouth full of sandwich. "I still think there must be some sort of record left, some note or warning or something as to why these people left their homes overnight."

I tidied up some, feeling foolish for doing it in an empty house that likely nobody'd ever step foot in again, but my Mam's teachings stayed with me. Then we walked to the town hall. Yesterday, I would have held Callan's hand, but I was making myself walk at a distance, untying the bonds between us a bit.

The Crawford town hall was a small brick building with a large room that I expect was used for the court session and four good sized offices. The sheriff's was marked with a star on the door, and the mayor's was likely the biggest. Those two was mostly cleaned out, or hadn't held much to start with. A third held a bunch of seed packets and instruction books from the R&A, and I figured it had belonged to the man whose house we had used. We searched that one from top to bottom, with Callan even taking the time to go through all the big manuals page by page, looking for notes and loose papers.

Finally he tossed about two hundred pages of "Evaluation of Seed Longevity in Temperature Extremes" onto the floor in disgust. "They can't publish or reprint real books because of the paper shortage, but every town can have a copy of this garbage?"

"There ain't nothing here." I supposed we might haul some of the seeds on home with us—weren't no sense letting them rot in an empty town—but we weren't no closer to knowing what had happened here than before.

Callan's mind must have been working on the same lines as mine, because he was gathering up seed packets into a pile. "Why don't you take a look at that last office while I see what we can salvage here?"

I didn't want to be away from him, not even for the briefest moment, not when we had what was like to be a full year apart ahead of us, but he was right—we didn't have much time. I could stay out another day on my own, and might have to, so as to take enough game to make Pa believe I'd been hunting the whole time, but Callan was expected back today—the town would be waiting to hear if there was epidemic.

The last office was the smallest, set against the back of the court room. There was a desk covered in dust, an old leather chair and a wooden trestle table, poorly made, with a barrel on one end and box on the other, and the box had lettering painted on it. One word: "Inbound." So this was where the post was sorted.

There was mail in the box. I didn't know if they just didn't take the time to sort it out before running, or if the post rider had come while they was leaving or after, but there was a stack of letters sitting in the box waiting to be sorted. I picked them up and started to look at each in turn, overcome with the thought that these folks, wherever they were, had written their relatives and friends in Crawford and might never hear back. I hoped wherever the Crawford folk had gone, they was safe.

Most of the letters were names which meant nothing to me, just ordinary folk living ordinary lives, and I figured their letters would be like such things are, full of births and deaths and troubles and triumphs. Not my business, and I had no wish to make it so by intruding into the privacy of these people more than I already had. But towards the bottom of the stack was a name I knew. Not on the address—it was to an S.R. Morgan, a name unknown to me. But the return address, clearly printed in a neat block hand, read "J.P. Hennessy, Moline, Virginia."

"Callan!"

He come running into the room, looking like he expected me to be in some trouble. "What's the matter?" I handed him the letter. He'd know better than I what it all meant.

"Morgan? Do we know any—" He broke off, seeing what I had seen. He skimmed it through quick one time, then looked up at me, chewing on his bottom lip, which I was coming to know meant something had him riled up.

"What is it?"

"Morgan must have been the owner of the house we stayed in. He was the R&A representative here, part of the Bureau of Special Projects, as apparently is Hennessy." He kept his eyes on the paper now, as though not wanting to meet my own. "Best if I just read the relevant part to you, I think.

Regarding the question in your previous report, I think it safe for you to proceed with the next stage. We've run into a bit of a snag here, as one of the Objects has gone rogue and attacked a young girl from one of the difficult families I mentioned in my last report. I had a visit from the father this evening, and though I think I put him off, he's not the sort to be palmed off with false promises.

So I'll be taking steps to neutralize that problem—the oldest son is consorting with a convicted felon and sodomite, so I'm planning on approaching things from that angle. That should distract the man from any further intervention in our affairs. The clearing of Moline should be underway by August as scheduled.

He stopped reading. The silence in the room stretched out between us as Callan looked down at the paper in his hand. "I don't understand. The Objects? Does he mean the dragons?"

"Yes. It seems that they've had some sort of means to control the dragons, but it's not working any longer. If I'm reading this correctly, they weren't supposed to attack Almond, or anyone in your family for that matter."

"Because my Pa's not the type to roll over and take it." If Mister Hennessy was in front of me, I'd have beat him into the ground, and when Pa found out, there'd be murder done. "But I reckon it was part of the plan to have them kill Lorna Massie and all those folks' goats and sheep and horses!"

"And burn out the town of Crawford. And empty Moline by the end of the summer."

This was stark raving mad. "We got to tell. We got to take that letter back to town and..." Where would you take such a thing as this? "And take it to the mayor," I said, but there weren't no conviction in my voice. Mayor Casteel wasn't like to go up against the R&A, not even to keep the town from being emptied like Crawford.

"What makes you think he doesn't already know?" Callan folded up the letter slow and careful, like he was trying not to do or say something he didn't want to face up to. "This makes no sense, David. If the government wants land, they don't have to go through all this rigmarole with dragons. They've got the right to condemn any property through eminent domain, and the army to back their actions up."

"Army comes in, starts moving people around by force, the word's going to get out. And besides, it's like you said about evacuating. There'll be folk who won't go, no matter what, who'd put up a fight to keep what's theirs. Like Mister Zack, or Nate Clemmons, who used to be mayor before Mister Casteel. His family's been on their land near as long as there's been land to be on. And—"

"Your father," Callan finished, looking sober. "David, you can't let on that you know anything about this." His voice sounded sharper than I think I'd ever heard it before. "You can't tell your father or the mayor or sheriff. And I know it's asking a lot, but if you can get your father to back off on the dragons, you'd better do it."

Back off? Back off from finding out why they'd killed my baby sister? Why they wanted us off our land? "Why would you ask such a thing? We got to find out what's going on! What do they want Moline for, Callan? This is about the most piss-poor farmland around, and any minerals here was tapped out years ago. They want something or they're protecting something, and it's too big for us to find out on our own, especially since we can't even…can't even hardly be together to work it out. My Pa can help. He's like a dog with a bone, Callan—once he sets himself to a task, he'll get it done come sundown or snowstorm."

"Because Hennessy is threatening you. 'Consorting with a convicted felon and sodomite'" he spoke from memory. "If your father stirs up trouble, I can almost guarantee you will find yourself up on charges and in a cell."

Oh, sweet Lord. "And you beside me."

"I doubt they'll even bother with a cell for me. I've corrupted you," he said, and I started to protest, but he cut me off. "No, this is planned out all too well, and there's too much we don't know. We can't fight it. Not openly."

It was going on noon. The horses was probably restless beyond measure, and I knew Callan at least had best be moving on, but to leave like this, with all our hope ground up into dust and Moline destined to end up empty and abandoned like Crawford was more than I could stomach. "So they win?"

He crossed the room in three steps and took me in his arms, and I held him tight, the sweet scent of his hair tickling my nose, feeling his breath in my ear when he spoke. "I don't know. I only know I love you, and nothing is worth bringing harm to you."

His arms were so strong around me, as though they alone could make me safe. I remembered how I'd wanted to protect him from the court—I could hardly fault him for wanting to do likewise for me, but it wasn't just me, it was the whole town, all of our lives and homes. "I can't let it lie, Callan. I just can't."

With his face buried in my hair, I felt more than heard his answer. "I knew that. I can't either, really. I've come to care about people in Moline; I can't let them be driven away like these people were."

He pulled apart from me and slipped the letter into his shirt pocket. "I'll show it to Jeannie. Next to you, I trust her more than anyone I know, and her brother's a lawyer in Richmond. She'll know what to do."

Relief flowed over me. Healer Findlay would take the letter, and all would be well. Such things should be in the hands of proper grown-ups, not left to Callan and me to manage.

The horses was chomping at the bit to get on the road, and, though it pained me to think I'd be leaving Callan, so was I. This place was cursed; standing on the empty street with the wind swirling around me, I felt it down to my bones. We'd brought some small blessing to it, coming together in love, but it was full of ghosts. As we passed the R&A house, Mister Morgan's place, Callan's hand squeezed mine.

"I don't know when we'll get to see each other again."

"I come into town fairly regular after the shearing, buying supplies at the General, bringing wool to the women who do Mam's spinning. Might be we can work something out." But I doubted it. The town was too full of folk eager to see Callan come to a bad end. The times we'd had together had been because he'd been able to get away from the town.

He knew it too. "I might be able to see you in passing, but we couldn't get free to talk, let alone anything more...more personal." The word brought me back to the feather bed and Callan's body moving over mine, and I let out a little sigh. It was going to be an endless summer.

"Maybe you can get away, up to the hills. I think Benny C would carry word for me."

"I don't know." He seemed doubtful. "We're heading into the busiest time of year for healers. All you clumsy farmers, cutting off your toes with scythes and dropping logs on your legs." He smiled at me to show he was joking, but there was truth in it. Muscles weak from a winter's inactivity strained mighty easy in the spring, and any way you wanted to look at it, farming and hunting was dangerous work. Might be that he couldn't get even an afternoon away.

"We'll manage," I said, more hopeful than I felt. We'd reached the outskirts of town, and I figured this to be as good a place as any to say goodbye, to send Callan off toward Moline with his news and his hidden letter, and me up into the higher country to take some game before heading home. "Guess this is goodbye, then."

"Not goodbye, love. I hate that word. English is an awful language in that way." He stroked my hair, lingering fingers tracing down my cheekbones. "The French say au revoir, which means 'till we meet again.' And there are other languages where the word for hello and goodbye are the same, so every parting has the hint of the next greeting."

"I like that, because I surely don't want to say goodbye to you, Callan." My voice broke, and some of the road dust must have got in my eye, so I turned away so he wouldn't think me weak. Arms cradled me from behind and I leaned back against him.

"To think just yesterday I was planning to leave town, to say goodbye to you forever. And now I'd sooner die—leaving you behind would be like leaving a part of myself. You're quite remarkable, David. You made me change my mind without uttering a word of argument."

"Never found it did no good to try and argue a body out of what he had his heart set on. I'm mighty glad..." Glad he'd changed his mind, glad we'd met and had the night, and glad I'd learned what my body was made for, but I didn't say none of that. "For everything."

He kissed the place where my neck meets my shoulders, and I shivered. "Hmm. I'd better stop, I think, before we get carried away."

"Too late," I muttered, and turned to him, so full of longing and desire and love, and I could feel him against me and knew it was the same for him. If it had been left to me, we'd have pulled a blanket down from the pack and spent the next hour together, despite the chill the rain had left behind.

But Callan was stronger than me, so first lips and then bodies separated slowly, and without a further word, he took the lead reins to the pack horse and mounted up. I watched him till he turned off and disappeared.

I stayed in the woods another full day and night, wandering slowly towards home. I made a few halfhearted attempts to take game, but it weren't no use, as all I saw was rabbits and squirrels, and them I could take close to home with no trouble. All the big game had made itself scarce, and more than once, flying high overhead, I saw the likely reason for that: the dragons, coasting on the thermals, hovering between Crawford and Moline, so that I was sure their lair must be found somewhere in this country. I made no attempt to find it, for what would be the point? I weren't Siegfried.

It seemed to me that there weren't no point in much of anything. I'd found my heart's desire, and it had been wonderful beyond measure, but it now was put up on a high shelf out of my reach, the way Mam used to put her needles up so Almond wouldn't swallow them, and I wondered if I was ever to be old enough to grasp it for myself. A year's time, at least. And then there was the dragons, tools of our own government. The memory of that burnt-up body and the stench of ruined houses kept coming back to me, except the body was Ruby or Delia or Benny C, and the house was my own home.

The morning of the second day, I reckoned enough time had passed for Callan to get home and give his news. I could turn up and nobody'd think it likely we'd been together, so I turned south in earnest, covering ground as quick as I could without running, and come midafternoon, I saw smoke rising up from where our cabin should be. My heart stopped for a moment, but then the smoke curled skyward in a tight swirling plume, and I knew it for chimney smoke, not a house fire.

But you'd have thought it was a house fire, or a late season blizzard, or some other disaster from the way everybody was all agitated at home. Mam greeted me by sweeping me up into an embrace such as she'd not done since before Callan's trial, and Pa was home, as were all the young ones, which weren't usual during the day at all.

"I was just about to go out looking for you, son," Pa said, looking grave. "C... someone from town had been over Crawford way and come back with word that the town's empty. We was feared you might've run into trouble."

And again, to my shame, I lied to Pa. "I never made it to Crawford, Pa. Game was so poor I stayed in the deep woods, hoping to find something worth taking." He was looking at me funny, so I babbled on, telling him how scarce the larger animals was, and describing the rabbits I'd seen. Funny how lying seems to loosen up your tongue.

"Well, no harm done." He glanced over at Mam, then back to me. "Come outside with me for a minute, David."

I followed him back out the cabin door. The cold front the rain had brung with it was just beginning to ease up; I hated when it switched from warm to cold and back again—you never got used to nothing. I wondered if this was how Callan always felt in our climate. Then I remembered how Pa had started to say his name and then stopped. Maybe there was something wrong. Maybe he knew what we'd done, that we'd been together, and just didn't want to say it in front of the young ones.

But no, that weren't it. "We're trying not to alarm the children without cause, but you ought to know that the dragons came back the night you left and burned out two houses on Elder Street. The Careys and those two bachelors who work for Casteel, Len and..." He sought for the name.

"Paul." I knew them—they was in Elmer's gang of thugs, probably some of the ones that had been causing Callan so much grief. I couldn't be sorry for them, though I ached for the Careys, a young couple with a new baby. John Carey had still been at school the year I started, and he was a decent man. "Anybody hurt?"

"No, thankfully. And Hennessy's back. The mayor's called a meeting tonight at the school; all the able bodied adults are to attend. Your Mam will be staying up here with your Grandmam—she's going downhill fast, David; you should spend some time with her while you can. But not tonight. Tonight I need you with me."

I don't remember ever in my life having Pa say he needed me, nor anybody if it come to that. I flushed all warm with pride. "Of course, I'll be there, Pa. You can count on me."

He put his hand on my shoulder. "I know it. I don't know what's coming, son. Some folk are already talking about picking up stakes and going wherever the Crawford folk went. A couple of the claim farm families have already left. The preacher's still going on about God's will, and I think he's going to recommend leaving."

"I ain't leaving my home." But I thought maybe Mam might want to for the sake of the young ones, specially if Pastor Daniels supported it.

"No, none of us is leaving. Your Grandmam can't travel, and my little girl's lying in that graveyard, and I won't have her abandoned and forgot. No power under heaven will move me off my land." He stared out over the hilltop, which had that spring green you only get after a hard rain; everything around us coming to life. Life fighting for life, soaking in every morsel of sunlight and warmth that we was fortunate enough to get. No, Pa wouldn't leave, not willingly. But I reckoned there was folk in Crawford had loved their land every bit as much as Pa, yet they'd gone, and if Callan and me was right, gone without fight nor fuss, gone without trace.

Chapter 18

Seemed like the only times we gathered as a community was for trouble and sorrow. Three times since fall had I seen the school so full of people—Callan's trial, Almond's funeral, and now this meeting. The days was still lengthening, so the sun had gone down by the time we come into town, just Pa and me. Benny C had wanted to come too, arguing that, as the only person who'd hurt one of the dragons, he'd need to tell his story. It seemed like Pa was leaning towards letting him go, till Mam put her foot down and said she'd already got one son acting above his age and wouldn't be having another, and that was the end of that.

We didn't speak much going down the mountain, and what we did say was mostly casual remarks on the weather and the way the plantings was coming in—nothing of consequence. My life, leastwise the things in my life that had meaning, wasn't nothing I could talk about with Pa. I understood what had driven Callan to seek out Taylor Mills—he at least would have understood what I was feeling and not condemned me for it.

The school was a blaze of light—it looked like they'd hauled in every torch and lantern in town to light the path and turn the dark building into daylight. A crowd of men—the Digger, Mister Zack, Joe Haig, and some others I didn't recognize—was waiting outside, smoking and chewing and looking grim, and Pa went over to join them. There was already people inside, but I didn't want to join them. The part of me that had common sense knew that nobody could tell by looking on me what I was, yet I couldn't help thinking that it had to show somehow, and that made me shy away from people.

"David." I heard my name from out of the darkness near the playground, and there weren't no mistaking whose voice it was. Callan. I knew he'd be there—he was the main witness to what had happened in Crawford, and I'd steeled myself to look on him and somehow not let my feelings show, but in the half-dark it didn't matter a whit.

"Callan." Checking that Pa was turned away from me, I sidled over to where he stood, leaning against a set of climbing bars. "You're okay. I was worried."

There weren't no moon and the torches didn't cast much light over here, so I couldn't make out his face, but I didn't have to. His hand come over to cover mine where I'd rested it on the bar. "I'm okay. I was worried about you, too."

I glanced back to the men. We didn't have much time. "Pa didn't say anything about the letter. I figured he'd know all about it—"

"There's a problem." Out of the darkness I heard Callan's name spoke by one of the men around Pa, and Callan paused, but it was just the Digger talking about Crawford. "We had another 'incident' at Jeannie's the night I came home."

So help me, before this was done, I was going to pound Elmer Casteel into the ground. "Damn that Elmer, Callan. Do you want me to take care of him?"

"It wasn't Elmer or any of his friends, not this time." Mayor Casteel and Mister Hennessy had come out of the schoolhouse and was surveying the yard as though looking for someone.

"How do you know?"

"Well, the insults were spelled correctly—that's one thing. And whoever it was ransacked my pack and stole the letter before I even had a chance to show it to Jeannie."

My heart sank. That was all we had proving that the R&A was involved. Without that letter and with me not supposed to even acknowledge I was there, it was Callan's word against Mister Hennessy's. "How did such a thing happen?"

"I'm so disgusted with myself. I should have known there might be trouble, but I was so tired. I got back into town and spent the next few hours being interrogated on what I saw in Crawford by the sheriff and Mister Hennessy, who had just come home himself, then there was the first fire. You know about the fires, right?"

"Yes, Pa told me."

"Two men were injured fighting the fire and Jeannie was downriver, so I had to treat them, and by the time it was all done, I was utterly exhausted, just dropped my bag in the exam room and collapsed on the sofa. They must have come into the house sometime after that. I didn't hear a thing."

"So nobody knows but us." This was bad. I'd been counting on Healer Findlay telling us what to do, but now...

"We're ready to begin," Mayor Casteel's voice boomed over the crowd and almost as if answering him, a little wind picked up from the creek. Callan shivered.

"I've heard some things about what this is all about, what's going to happen tonight—Hennessy came to see Jeannie today, and reading between the lines of what he said, it doesn't look good. You've got to promise me you'll just keep quiet through this, David. Don't let on that you've been to Crawford, that you know anything about the letter or have any suspicion that the government is involved. Just listen to what's said and–"

"David." Pa's voice was sharp, and Callan's hand slipped out of mine quick as lightning.

"Promise?" The lanterns was being carried into the schoolhouse, leaving us even more in the dark, but I didn't need to see his face to know how much in earnest he was.

"Yes." But I crossed my fingers. I wanted to give Callan peace of mind, but couldn't truly promise when I didn't know what was coming, and no promise on earth would stop me from looking out for him as best I could.

"David!" That was as near as Pa ever got to shouting.

"Go," he whispered, and I went, more to keep him out of trouble than for any other reason. I started into the schoolhouse, but Pa grabbed hold of my shoulder and spun me around, hard.

"Enough of this, David. I've told you to stay away from him, and by God, I mean it. I thought it was him pursuing you, but now I'm beginning to think it's been you all along. You give that young man some peace, do you hear me? If you don't care about your own reputation in this town, you might have a care for his. Every time you see him alone like that, he's at risk of ending up flogged out of town. Is that what you want for someone you claim to care about?"

"How can you even ask a question like that?" I pulled away from him and stomped off into the schoolhouse, as angry at myself for knowing he was right as I was at him for saying it.

The place was jam-packed, even more than at the trial. There was all sorts, from back hills folk craning their necks around as though they'd never seen such a marvel as our schoolhouse to Nate Clemmons, the former mayor I'd told Callan of. Mister Clemmons had a huge spread of land that spilled across the lines of three counties and a fine house in Richmond; he was the richest man I'd ever known. Sheriff Fletcher stood near the podium, and though he weren't in uniform as he'd been at the trial, he looked darn near as uncomfortable as if he had been. The mayor was still standing off near the back, talking real quiet to Mister Hennessy, and they was both watching the back door like a pair of hunting hawks.

When they saw me come in, the whispering stopped, but I ignored it and went on up near the front. Funny how people don't like to sit in the front much. Probably feared they'll get drafted into something unpleasant. I didn't sit, though, just stood off to the side waiting, watching the door. When Pa come in a few minutes after me, Mayor Casteel stopped whispering again and just stared at him, though I don't think Pa took no notice of it, but when Callan come in just as the sheriff was stepping up to the podium, the mayor and Mister Hennessy both smiled, and I was chilled through worse than being caught out in a January blizzard.

It never meant nothing good when a man like Mister Hennessy smiled to see you—I was scarce seventeen and I surely knew that. And Callan had been right: whatever was going on, the mayor knew darn well what it was. Pa took me by the arm and set me down so I couldn't see Callan no more. The sheriff finally cleared his throat and called out, "Let's get settled."

Nobody paid him a lick of attention, so Master Burke come out of the back office with his school bell and rung it like a crazy man, and everybody sat down and got silent. Takes a schoolmaster to quiet a schoolroom, I guess.

Not being one to take the back seat when he has the opportunity to lead, Mayor Casteel was bustling down the aisle faster than the bride in a shotgun wedding. "Thank you, thank you, Master Burke. Now settle down, everyone, don't want to have to make you write lines," he joked, looking nervous. "You know why we're all here. Our town is being terrorized by dragons. Oh, I know it's hard to believe, had a hard time accepting it myself, but we've all seen them, most of us have lost stock to them, and two of our young citizens have been taken to early graves, Lora Massie and Alma Anderson."

"Almond," I hissed, and none too quiet either. "And Lorna."

Pa let out a word to describe the mayor that would have made Mam say "Brock!" in that voice she used when she was real unhappy.

Mayor Casteel had kept on talking, though he glanced at Pa in a way that made me sure he'd heard. "And just two days ago, two of our families, including my own hired hands, Paul Cassovetti and Len Jennings, were burnt out of their homes."

I noticed the mayor didn't have any trouble remembering nor saying the names of his men, but Callan had asked me to sit tight through whatever happened, and pointing out the obvious fact that the mayor was an ass weren't reason enough to break my word.

"And recently, we have come to learn that our neighbors to the north in Crawford have apparently vanished."

That word must not have spread to everyone, for a rustle of whispers spread through the room, and more than a few people turned back to look at Callan, who was staring out the window into the dark.

"If you'd allow me, Your Honor, I can shed some light on what's happened to our neighbors." Mister Hennessy strode forward to the podium, and it struck me how ordinary he looked. In so many of Grandmam's stories, evil on the inside shows up on the outside, with the villains of the tales being either hideous to look upon, or else bright deceivers more beautiful than the angels, but Mister Hennessy was just a man. You'd see him on the street and not even turn around for a second look.

"As you know, I've been in Richmond until very recently, trying to get to the bottom of this tangle. And I do have news on that, which I will pass on to you, but to turn my attention to Crawford, I'm afraid you may have been unduly panicked due to a misunderstanding. The people of Crawford made the logical decision that to stay in an area plagued by dangerous animals was simply not worth the risk, and they asked the government, through the person of their R&A representative, to assist them with a mass relocation. Essentially, they exchanged their poor and rocky farmland in these dragon-plagued hills for rich land to the west. They are well on the way to their new homes, happy and healthy."

"But why didn't they leave word?" someone from the audience shouted out. "I heard they didn't leave any note or sign or nothing."

"That is untrue. They left a sign painted on the door of their town hall. I can only assume that the emissary from Moline," and he cast a scathing glance in Callan's direction, "suffers from some defect of vision, or else cannot read."

I was half out of my seat before I remembered I wasn't supposed to know anything about Crawford, and anyway, Pa had an iron grip on my arm, keeping me down. I'd bet if we went back to Crawford now, there'd be a nice sign, big as life, telling the whole story. There didn't seem to be any way that we could win this thing; not against an enemy that had all the power and money they could want. Healer Findlay was sitting in the front row facing the crowd along with the sheriff and mayor, and she looked like she'd smelled something foul, but kept quiet, too.

"Be that as it may, I want to assure you that no harm has befallen the citizens of Crawford. They made a decision for the good of their families, and I think it might be one we could learn from."

Now the whisper became an outright rumble, and Mister Clemmons, who had come down to the front to sit right across from Mayor Casteel, stood up. "Are you saying you believe we should run? Are you implying that the armed might of the United States government and the Commonwealth of Virginia are insufficient to handle two overgrown lizards?"

Mister Hennessy had the good sense to look embarrassed at that, and Pa was making satisfied noises next to me. "Damn good thing Nate Clemmons is home from Richmond for a change. He ain't likely to roll over and play dead for the pleasure of the R&A."

"No, no." Mister Hennessy was trying to be reassuring, but it come off like he was nervous. "Of course not, not yet. But as a last resort, if all else fails, isn't it reassuring to know that your government will take care of you?"

"A man takes care of himself," Pa said, loud enough to be heard this time, and I saw heads nodding in agreement. Callan was staring out of the window, leaning against the glass and looking utterly defeated. He'd said he knew what was coming, and seeing him like that was making a horrid empty pit open up in my belly.

"Of course, Brock, and that's what we intend to do. Before we even think of evacuating, we'll take all possible steps to deal with the threat these dragons pose. But we must think to the future, and to our children's welfare. We have an enemy that can fly, comes out of nowhere, and now has shown that it has the capability to burn us out of our homes. And even if we manage to kill these two, who's to say there aren't more of them out there? You cut off the head of the hydra and two more take its place."

Though most of us, me included, hadn't the least idea what a hydra was, there was agreement with that, and I could see plain as through glass that this town was divided, and there surely were plenty of people in this room who was ready to run. A few more burnt-out houses, a dead child like I'd buried in Crawford, and the balance would shift.

Mayor Casteel was back in front again, wiping his brow with his handkerchief, for it was mighty warm in there with the press of the bodies. "So as we consider our options, Mister Hennessy has been consulting with his colleagues in the Department of Relocation and Agriculture—"

"Do they believe in dragons now?" Joe Haig shouted, and all of us who'd been in the General that day when the seed man had made his denial murmured agreement.

"Allow me to answer that, if you would please, Mayor." Hennessy was slick, I'd give him that. I couldn't bring myself to look at him, so turned in my seat to watch Callan. There weren't any rule against looking. "You may not realize that field agents, the ones who come through here with seeds, are not given full briefings. Their jobs are quite simply to supply you with the best agricultural information and products to assist you with your crop. They are not privy to matters of relocation policy...er...matters of importance." Callan stiffened, hearing what I had heard, and I caught how quick Mister Hennessy talked over himself. He'd slipped, but it seemed nobody else in the crowd had caught it, for it passed uncommented, and he kept going. "Anything beyond the planting of crops is not their affair. I assure you, the Department knows very well that these things exist and are working to find a permanent solution."

Matters of relocation policy. But not relocation of the dragons. Of us.

"So," Mayor Casteel said, beaming as though he'd just won re-election, "I'd like to welcome to our meeting Mister George Delahaye."

Now everybody turned to face the back as a stranger emerged from the shadows near the classroom door and strode forward. If Mister Hennessy had a forgettable face, this man did not—I'll never forget that sight of him, not even if I live as long as Grandmam. His features was flat, like someone had bashed his face with a shovel. After he'd done shaking hands with the mayor and sheriff and greeting Mister Hennessy, he turned to face the crowd and I saw that his eyes were small and narrow. Not narrow like an oriental man, just narrow-mean, like a snake, looking up at you ready to strike. He was tall too, tall as me, but far more filled out—a young man, yet with not a trace of boyhood left in him, powerfully built, and dressed in clothes that hugged to his body and showed it off. I figured he'd done that deliberate to make an impression, and it was working, as I could hear some of the women's sighs of appreciation. His hair was longer than custom in our area, long enough to pull back in a leather band, blue-black where mine was more smoky charcoal, and straight. Severe. That was the word for this George Delahaye. He was a severe man.

As Mister Delahaye took his place at the front of the room, Mister Hennessy went on. "Mister Delahaye is a freelance agent of the government, currently on assignment to my own Bureau of Special Projects. He comes to us with impressive credentials and recommendations—he's worked in law enforcement with the Department of Investigation and since coming on board with R&A has been instrumental in several large scale animal incidents, including the troubles in Atlanta that you may have heard of."

Most of us, I expected, had heard stories of how the animals from the old Atlanta Zoo had run wild after the Ice, breeding up colonies of predators that had terrorized what was left of the city. But lions and tigers and bears wasn't dragons. I could kill a lion, and probably wouldn't need anything more than Pa's rifle to do it.

"Agent Delahaye will undertake an expedition to eliminate our problem. He has training and weapons that should make it possible for him to succeed in damaging or destroying the beasts where the best efforts of our town have failed." I wanted to point out that Benny C'd damaged that dragon just fine with my knife, that we didn't need this severe man with his iron eyes, but it wouldn't have made no difference at all. "His fee will be fully paid by the R & A and he's going to be working mostly alone, so none of our own will be put at risk or asked to take time away from home during this busy spring season. He's asked for the services of a healer, just in case of emergency, and of course we've readily agreed."

I looked at Healer Findlay, who was glaring at the mayor, and I wondered how she'd be able to make such a trek into the high country, then it struck me. Hennessy came to see Jeannie tonight, and it doesn't look good. They knew Callan had read the letter. He was a threat to them; not much of a threat, considering how low his standing in town had grown, but enough of one to warrant...what? Surely they wouldn't go so far as to...I turned back to look at Callan, who was still staring out the window as though he hadn't a care in the world, as though he weren't about to be sent up into the roughest country around with someone who looked like he'd as soon as kill a man as talk to him. I brought myself back to what Mayor Casteel was saying.

"...is an excellent tracker, and given what maps we have available, should be able to find the dragons' lair and make an end to them."

And make an end to Callan. I'd seen the way the mayor and Mister Hennessy had looked when Callan walked in, all smug and satisfied, like cats that had taken a bird, and now I knew why. I stood up, and when Pa tried to pull me down again, shook his arm off hard and stepped away. "Mister Mayor, nobody round here knows this country like I do, and I'll tell you those old maps ain't likely worth the paper they're printed on. I'll guide Mister Delahaye, if he'll have me."

Except for those times when we was intimate, I'd never seen Callan do anything nor say anything that wasn't planned and controlled, but now he turned away from the window, his face revealing every ounce of feeling he had for me. "No, David, please! Just sit down!" But right behind it and then over top of whatever protests he continued to make, the room exploded.

Pa was on his feet, arguing with the mayor, who seemed mighty pleased with my suggestion, almost as though he'd planned it all along to have me go along. I heard voices of agreement with my offer, and others shouting out that it should be an older man, and wasn't it shameful that the only person man enough to face this thing was a boy? Sheriff Fletcher had pulled out his sidearm and was pummeling Master Burke's desk with the handle, shouting for quiet. Callan had given up trying to speak over the chaos, but he was looking straight at me, shaking his head, and then his eyes closed, and he turned away again. I knew I'd hurt him bad, but I wasn't about to let him go off alone with a man like that, a man with death in his eyes.

As the din settled, I heard Mister Hennessy's voice above the crowd, talking to my Pa. "...surely aren't saying you don't trust my agent to keep your son safe, Brock? The boy...no, not a boy, he's proven himself more than that. The young man's not afraid— maybe you'd better cut the apron strings."

Pa was in a murderous rage, and for a moment I honestly thought he was going to start a fight, but he just sat back down, shaking with anger. He couldn't protest much without making one or both of us look to be cowards, but he weren't done yet, not here, nor I suspected when he got me alone. "I trust men I know. I don't know him," he gestured at Delahaye. "And I ain't taking your word for nothing." The words were spat out like tobacco chaw.

I hated that they was talking about me like I wasn't even there. "Pa, I want to do this. For Almond." And for Callan, and it was a sure thing that Pa knew that, but he just tightened his lips and said nothing.

Sheriff Fletcher had reholstered his sidearm. "Don't mean to throw gum in the works, but there's the matter of Callan Landers' probation. David can't make this trip with him without violating it."

Mayor Casteel waved his arm, dismissing the limitation that had made our lives so difficult like it was nothing. "We can surely assume that an agent of the law could stand as chaperone, make certain that nothing untoward occurs. Waive that provision, on a...on a...er...temporary basis."

"I'm not comfortable with that, Mayor, and it doesn't look like Brock Anderson is, either," the sheriff continued, stubborn, and my heart sunk. If anyone could stop this, he could. "What happened to protecting the youth of our town from filth and perversion?"

There was a hissed intake of breath at that. Such plain speech weren't usually heard in the presence of so many, particularly ladies, and it tore at me that he'd say such things about Callan, though I knew he was just quoting the mayor's own words from the hearing back at him.

"Times change, Sheriff. We got to move with them, or we'll be swept away to wherever the townspeople of Crawford have landed."

"And as agent in charge for this area, I have authorization to set aside court decisions for emergencies and I am here doing so. If you don't like it, file a complaint with the circuit judge." Mister Hennessy nodded as if the matter was settled. "David Anderson will act as guide, leading Agent Delahaye on his journey as best he can. Callan Landers has agreed to accompany them, though we must all pray that his services as healer will not be required." He paused, but it was clear the time for talk was done. I'd got my way, though I felt no triumph in it.

Smooth as ice, Mayor Casteel stepped up. "And speaking of prayer, if Pastor Daniels would be so good as to bless the journey?"

The pastor had been sitting in the crowd, not contributing anything at all. I remembered how Pa had said he was in favor of us cutting and running, and I wondered how sincere his blessing would be. He beckoned me forward, and then gestured to Callan, who come reluctantly; neither of us believed in the Almighty, after all, but we come up to kneel at the front of the schoolroom, doing what was expected of us. And at least I could be next to him here, could feel the warmth of his body near mine; I had no illusions we'd have time alone on this trip—it weren't a holiday nor a walk in the garden. We'd have to be on our guard every minute, for surely Delahaye had come here not to kill the dragons, but to kill Callan, and now maybe me as well.

I closed my eyes as Pastor Daniels begun his words, leaning as near to Callan as I dared, then was thrown off-balance as George Delahaye, without a word, pushed himself between us, bowing his head in prayer.

Chapter 19

I lost track of Callan almost straight off, as Healer Findlay pulled him off to the side and started whispering in his ear, but my Lord, he looked done in. Pa tried to hustle me out of the schoolhouse the minute the last 'amen' echoed up to the rafters, but we kept getting sidetracked by men wishing me luck and giving advice, and praising Pa for the job he'd done raising me up so that I'd take such a risk for others. I accepted the compliments as best I could, considering that the only reason I was doing any of this was to see Callan was safe. Pa just nodded at the men and pushed me up the aisle, but somehow Mister Hennessy had got ahead of us and was standing at the door to the outside waiting, smiling like he'd won the Harvest Fair prize.

"David, Agent Delahaye wants to leave at first light tomorrow. I know that doesn't give you much time to prepare, but—"

"That's hardly reasonable, Hennessy," Pa protested. "The boy just come off a long hunt, needs time to pack, spend some time with his Grandmam—she's ailing, not like to last long."

"No, it's fine." I didn't want to put it off, though I got a nervous twinge thinking of Grandmam, not like to last long.

"Fine, fine." Hennessy clapped me on the back, and it was all I could do to keep from flinching. I must have been getting better at dissembling, else the sputtering torchlight hid my face, for nobody seemed to notice my distaste. "Well, good luck to you, young man. The fate of this town is in your hands."

"And ain't that just a fine thing?" Pa muttered, leading me away. "Near a thousand troops at Fort Eustis down to the south, a full Guard unit at Richmond and Washington is maybe twenty days hard walk, and the fate of our town's left to two boys."

"And a professional killer." Mister Zack come out of the shadows. "I spoke to Nate just now; he thinks he's seen that man Delahaye before, in Richmond. He's hunted all right, but mostly two legged prey, I think."

Pa offered Mister Zack a swig from the flask he had in his pocket. I was amazed as always to see the man use his stump and his good hand to pull the stopper and drink deep, then cap it again without spilling a drop. "Hell, Zack, that's not news. You can tell from his eyes and the way he holds himself. I guess they figure a man can kill another man, he should have the stomach to kill a dragon."

"It's not the stomach I worry about, it's the skill. And the firepower," Zack replied. It was funny, I wasn't even worried about the dragons—I didn't figure we'd get within ten miles of them. The only worry in my mind was whether I could take Delahaye before he killed Callan or me. Oh, I'd killed my share of game and of stock, but to kill a man, and I suffered no illusions that anything less would do, that was a hard thing to ruminate on.

"'Spect there's guns that will do it. A man like that would know." Pa seemed calm enough about it all. You might think, not knowing him, that it was a good thing, but I knew he was just waiting till we was alone. "Good seeing you, Zack. Don't be a stranger—you know you're welcome up home any time." Pa shook hands with Mister Zack, then started up the road. "Come on, David."

Mister Zack put his good arm out to stop me. "Hang on, David. I'm glad your father has such confidence, but honestly, I don't trust Hennessy or the R&A, and I don't like the looks of that Delahaye. My guess is if you stripped him bare, you'd find at least one criminal brand."

"You think he's not really with the government?" I hadn't considered that.

"Oh, no. He's government all right, but the two aren't necessarily mutually exclusive. Do you have a gun?"

I shook my head. "Pa's promised me a rifle for my eighteenth birthday, but that ain't for a year."

"Rifle won't do it. Needs to be something you can hide." He shook his head. "I almost came down here armed tonight. Something in my head told me to, but I ignored it, more's the pity. If you can lay hands on a firearm before tomorrow, then for God's sake do it. Or at least take a good knife."

"David!" Pa was almost to the end of the road.

"Coming!" The crowds was dispersing around me, torches being carried off or put out. "Thank you, Mister Zack."

"Best of luck to you, son. You'll be in my prayers." He sighed and turned away to where his horse was tied to the bar outside the school, and I hurried after Pa.

I was expecting my whole world to explode into angry words and recriminations the minute we was past the town limits, but Pa said nothing, and I followed after him, noting the straight set of his back, struggling to match the grueling pace he set going up the mountain. When we was in sight of the barn, he stopped cold, and I almost run into his back.

He didn't turn to look at me. "David, I know damn well why you've done this fool thing; don't for one minute think I don't see right through you. I ought to forbid it, and I could and nobody could gainsay me, for I'm your father and you're still a child in the law."

"If you'd wanted to forbid it, you should have done it back in town, Pa. It's too late now."

"It ain't. Never in all my days have I shied away from doing the right thing because of what people would think, and I ain't about to start now."

I don't know whether it was me getting older, or the influence of Callan on my thinking, but I knew then that Pa had made his mistake and that I was going to win. "Neither am I. It's the right thing for me to help Mister Delahaye find those dragons. Nobody knows the northern hills like me, except maybe you, Pa, and you know it for a fact. If folks, you included, don't like the idea that I'm going to be with Callan, well, that's just too damn bad, and I ain't ordering my life to soothe filthy-minded gossips. You got to trust me, Pa, else what have we got between us?"

He turned around. Wasn't much light from the heavens, but it was enough to see that Pa had water in his eyes. "I do trust you, son. But I see you growing up, becoming someone I don't know no more. It's the way of the world, but it hurts something awful sometimes."

It surely did. "Being a child was a lot easier, Pa."

"But you can't stay a child. I know that. All right, you go on in the barn and make sure Jerzy did the chores proper, give me time to tell your Mam what's happened and get her calmed down so's she don't do those dragons a favor and take your head off for you."

I knew there weren't any problem with the way Jerzy did the chores; he'd been doing them for years, and would likely be doing them long after me and Benny C and even the girls was off on our own, but I wasn't in any hurry to go in and face Mam, so I played with the barn fire a bit, groomed Lightning till she looked fit for the fair, and spoke to each and every ewe and lamb in the barn. The sheep were mighty indignant; they knew good and well it was past time for them to be pastured out, but we'd brought them home the day Almond died, and hadn't the heart to take them back. I figured Pa would sell that land if he got the chance.

Finally, thinking on how I was supposed to be back in town at dawn, I figured I'd better brave the lion in her den. But as I pulled the latch-string and opened the door, the house was quiet. There was a single lamp burning on the table, and a field pack had been prepared for me with trail food, water containers, and blankets, including my favorite from Before. Beside the pack, Benny C had left my knife tucked into its leather sheath, handle polished to a high gloss. I pulled it out and the ripples of the blade glittered in the lamp's flame.

"Gram." I turned to see Grandmam sitting by the fire, wrapped up in about four blankets, but still shivering. "Benny C calls it Gram."

"After Siegfried's sword. He listens to your tales, Grandmam, just like I do." I sat down at her feet, looking up at her. Pa had said she was doing poorly, and I could tell he was right, even in this poor light. Her skin was like the thinnest old leather I'd ever seen, and her eyes seemed cloudy, like there was fog covering the pupils. But she still smiled down at me like she always had, like I was the most important person in the whole world to her.

"And now I hear you're off to make a tale of your own. Going off to fight dragons, like Siegfried himself."

"Not so much fight them, Grandmam. Just leading someone to them." If there was any fighting, I figured it wouldn't be between me and the dragons.

"With that nice young healer, too. And didn't your Mam have some choice words to say about that. Surprised you didn't hear her clear out in the barn."

So was I. She reached down and stroked my head. "You love that boy, don't you?"

"He's my friend, Grandmam—"

"Don't be prevaricating with me, young man. Folks think when you're old you forget what forces bring two people together, but you surely don't. Not one bit." She looked stern. "You love that boy, don't you?"

I nodded. "But don't tell Mam, please, or Pa."

"Wasn't thinking of it, though I expect your Pa already knows. He sees most things that others miss—that's probably why he's such a good hunter. There's nothing to be ashamed of in loving someone, chickadee. And he loves you right back, doesn't he?"

"Yes." We was quiet for a while, just watching the dying fire, as I rested my head on her lap. Pa's soft snores floated out of the back bedroom and from the loft, Benny C muttered in his sleep. I let the familiar sounds and smells tether me to my home, to my past. I closed my eyes, trying to trap the moment so I could carry it with me tomorrow, and after. If there was an after.

Standing, brushing the soot from my knees, I stretched, thinking it must be gone midnight. "I guess I'd better try to get some sleep."

"Siegfried..." she said, and her eyes seemed a bit unfocused, like maybe the lucid time was passing and she was heading into confusion again.

"Let me help you to bed." I eased her out of the rocker, keeping the blankets close around her and half-carried her down to her room, tucking her into the bed as she'd done to me when I was a child.

"Siegfried used a sword," she repeated. Then she shook herself all over, like a dog does when it's all wet.

"Yes, he used Gram to kill Fafnir. I remember."

"But only because he had nothing better." She pointed to a wooden box on her dressing table. "Get that for me."

The box was old, and heavy for its size; her hands shook as she laid it down on the blanket. "Siegfried used a sword; it was all he had. But I want you to come to a better end than he did." She opened the box, and took out a gleaming pistol.

I turned it over and over in my hands. It was black, but a sort of grey-black, with a shiny barrel and textured handle. It looked dangerous. I know all guns is dangerous, but Pa's rifle was known, it was comfortable to me; I'd spent my entire life with it, and knew what it could do and what it couldn't. This gun was a mystery.

"That belonged to my husband, and he kept it in excellent repair and loaded at all times. I never knew why I held onto it, kept thinking I should give it to your father, but now I know why. I want you to have it. To keep you safe."

I kissed her forehead and pulled the blankets up around her neck, then tucked the gun in the waistband of my trousers. At last, something was finally going our way.

I didn't sleep that night, though I dutifully tried, lying still in the bed with Benny C snoring and stirring beside me. We was leaving from the livery stable, and I planned to get there early in hopes that Callan would do the same and we could have a few precious private moments before Mister Delahaye showed up and this thing begun.

So the minute I felt the shift in the night that signaled the change from dark to day, I slipped out of bed. It weren't raining, but there was a moisture in the air that didn't bode well. I shouldered my pack, closed the door of the cabin behind me, trying not to think that I might never open it again, and by the light of the waning moon made my way down the mountain. The sun was barely starting to peek over the eastern rise when I got to the General, and a lamp was burning in the stable out back. Callan was there.

"I was hoping you'd be here early," I said, not quite daring to touch him. He sat on a bale of hay, resting his head in his hands, and he didn't look up when I spoke. "We need to talk, to plan what to do. I don't figure he'll give us much time alone once we're moving."

Still nothing—it was as if he was stone. "I don't know if he's really planning on trying to kill the dragons, or if that was just idle talk, to cover his real plans. What do you think?" An uneasy feeling, even more than the fear over the journey, began to bubble up in my gut. "Callan? Please, don't be angry. I can't bear it if you don't speak to me."

Finally he looked up, though I wished he hadn't, for his face was naked rage. Exploding off the bale to use his advantage of height for the first time, he practically shouted at me. "You promised! Damn you, David, you promised me!"

And so I had. But he had to understand, he just had to. "I couldn't keep that promise. I wasn't about to let you go off on your own with that man; if he gets you alone, he'll kill you!"

He turned away, clenching his fists. "And now he'll kill both of us. Couldn't you have trusted me? Did you honestly think I was actually going on this insane expedition?"

Now it was me speechless. "What...what do you mean? I saw the way you looked, like the world was ending. Like you was facing death. The way you talked, the things you said..."

"I told you last night that there wasn't time for me to explain. That's why I made you promise. Because I couldn't tell you then that I was going to run." The words dropped in the silence of the stable like stones in a pool. The horses in the back of the stable was getting restless; dawn was in their bones, and our time was short.

"Run? You mean leave town?"

"Yes. That's why I looked like that, why I was so sad. Because I knew I probably wouldn't see you again, and I could hardly stand the thought of it, but it was the only thing I could think to do." He relaxed a bit, the anger ebbing away as he looked at me. "Jeannie says I take on a lot of guilt that I don't own, and she's probably right, but David, there was no way I was going to offer myself up as a sacrifice so the R&A could cover its tracks. Jeannie had given me money, and was even willing to deliver a letter to you after I'd gone, explaining."

I sank onto the hay bale. I'd ruined it all. Callan was right. I hadn't trusted him, had treated him like a child who needed my protection, and in doing so, I'd probably killed us both. "Oh, God. I'm so sorry. You can still go." But the sun was rising and Delahaye was likely on his way. "Take one of the horses and go now!" I got up and grabbed his arm, trying to pull him towards the horses, but he caught me in a tight embrace, pouring what was left of his anger into the strength of his arms.

"No, it's too late. I won't leave you now. We're both in this till the end, but I want you to swear to me on whatever you hold sacred that if I tell you to do something while we're on this journey that you'll do it, no questions asked." The embrace ended as he took both my hands.

"I swear it on our love, Callan. I'll obey." I couldn't have crossed my fingers if I'd wanted to. Using my own judgment had been a disaster. It was like I had said to Pa: if we hadn't trust between us, we had nothing.

"I'll hold you to that. I can't blame you for going back on your word—you thought you were doing the right thing. And I can't stay angry with you, though I've tried; I spent all night working myself up to face you over this. But yes, from here on out till we're back safe in town, you obey."

"Guess I know which of us is the wife, then," I joked sort of feebly, but he took it as a peace offering, as I'd hoped, and kissed me, drinking deep of what I offered, and as his body molded against mine and pressed the gun into my hip, I felt him pull back.

"What's that?"

I lifted my jacket to show it. "My Grandmam gave it to me. Don't know if it will kill a dragon, but..."

He nodded. "It would kill a man."

Chapter 20

There weren't much to say after that. By my foolhardiness and lack of trust, I'd brought down trouble on the both of us, and I could only hope that Grandmam's gun could get us out of it. I tried to imagine myself squeezing that trigger, sending a man to his death, but I couldn't fathom it. I guessed when the time came, I'd just have to do it, not think on it, and save any doubts and recriminations for later, the way grown-ups seem to. It was a sure bet that Delahaye wouldn't let scruples stand in his way; I couldn't neither.

"He's here," Callan said, looking beyond me, out the stable door to where Mister Delahaye was striding across the yard. He had a large, fancy-looking pack strapped to his back; the metal frame with things rolled up and attached to it gave the impression of a lopsided tortoise. I'd have said from the look of it that it was a thing from Before, but as he got closer, I saw the metal weren't at all rusted or damaged, and the cloth parts had no holes nor rot. It was new. Something from the government, or from the cities. I was beginning to see that our world, outside of these hills, wasn't near so primitive as I'd always believed.

He didn't smile, just fixed me with those narrow eyes. "You ready?"

"Yes, sir."

His lips was thin like twigs, and when he smiled, it was a snake's smile. Cunning. Deadly. "Well, boy, I hear you're the one who knows these hills, so I'm counting on you to steer us right." He'd ignored Callan completely so far.

"I don't know about that. But I've got to tell you, I been all over these hills in every season save winter and I've never seen hide nor hair of any sort of nest big enough for dragons."

Delahaye held out his hand for my pack. "Just need to check that you're well supplied." Glad that the gun was safe in my jacket, I handed it over. "No, boy. No nest. Read your folklore, read your Tolkien. Dragons are creatures of rock and fire. It's in a cave that we'll find their lair. There are caves up on the north slopes, yes?"

He gave me back my pack, then without speaking a word to him, took Callan's and began rifling through it. "Hmm. Standard healing supplies, it looks like, some painkilling drugs...hope we won't be needing those. Yes. This will do." He shoved it back at Callan and then shrugged off his own pack and took out a folded-up map, an old one with the U.S.G.S. seal on it. Pre-Ice.

"Look here," he pointed to a series of swirls and circles so faded I could barely make them out. "Caves. You know this area?"

I had seen the openings to some little caverns up in the northern mountains, though I hadn't never gone inside. Tight spaces aren't something I fancy as a general rule. "I can't read your map, as I ain't been schooled to it, but I know where there's caves." I glanced at Callan, who was looking out the window, back towards Healer Findlay's place. I didn't like how Delahaye acted like he didn't exist.

"Well, then, saddle up, boy. Saddle up." He slung his pack onto his back and I caught sight of a rifle strapped to it—it weren't nothing special, not even as good as Mister Zack's, leastwise as far as I could tell.

"Mister...Agent...Sir, I don't mean to be rude," I started, not even sure if I should ask, but remembering what Callan had said back in Crawford, that we was puppets in a show. I was playing a part: the young native guide. And the guide would ask about that gun. "But that rifle ain't going to make a dent in the hides of them dragons."

He looked me up and down coldly. "You leave that to me. I assure you, I have sufficient firepower to do the job."

Callan turned back from the window, calm and cool. He was playing a part, too, I reckoned. "Don't you think we ought to know how you're planning on killing the dragons? In case something happens to you?"

If he'd taken the time to size me up, he did no such thing with Callan. Flat eyes blinked twice, and I realized he weren't a snake. He was a gun, grey and hard and cold. "Don't be worrying about what's going to happen to me." Worry about yourself—I could hear his unspoken words. He turned back to me, and the gun man gave way to the more genial Delahaye that I saw was as much a mask as any I'd seen Callan put on. Was that a thing of city people, or were all adults like that, hiding their true faces? "Lead on, MacDuff."

"It's 'Lay on, MacDuff,'" Callan muttered under his breath, but Delahaye turned his back to him, and I led us out of the stable and along the north road. The sun was up in full now, but it was still early, and the ground lay rich with frosty dew. It hadn't got down to freezing the night before, but it likely wouldn't get too warm today; I could feel it. Callan had come up to walk beside me, and Delahaye was behind some, taking no steps to keep us apart.

"Who's MacDuff?" I asked him.

"It's from Shakespeare. Like the sonnet I sent you, d'you remember?" We was close, but not touching, for I didn't figure Delahaye would stand for that.

"Course I remember; I still got it folded up in my pocket. First thing you gave me." I felt behind me for the familiar square of paper pressing into my back pocket.

Callan pulled something out of the pocket of his greatcoat. My gloves. "I still have the first thing you gave me, too." He slipped them on. I didn't think it cold enough to warrant wool gloves, personally, but Callan always felt the cold more. And so must Mister Delahaye, for he wore warm woolen gloves and a long scarf tossed over his shoulder. I wondered where he was from; surely not Richmond, which was north of us, nor Washington, where everything was sheet ice seven months out of twelve. Those folk would think this a fair summer day.

I set us a hard pace, figuring Mister Delahaye was older and city bred, and might tire easily, giving us an edge, but I was mistaken in that. We were following the old paved road, winding up the mountain toward the turnoff for Crawford, and as soon as Delahaye cottoned on to the route, he easily caught up to us.

"How long do we stay on this road?" He weren't even winded.

"About two hours' hard walk," I said. "There's a sign reads 'Crawford' at the turnoff. It's a Before sign, but you can still make it out—it's been painted up a couple times by the Crawford folk." Who wouldn't be painting it again. I shivered.

"Fine. Let's pick up the pace a bit. I want to get to your caves by nightfall, catch the dragons early in the morning."

If I was recollecting proper, the only caves big enough to house dragons was near to the summit, and I'd normally take two days to make the summit, longer if it rained, which it was threatening, I thought, glancing at the western sky. "Unless you're figuring to run uphill like a mountain cat, that ain't going to happen." It was odd, me talking so bold to this man who by rights should scare me half out of my wits, but I felt like it weren't really me, weren't David speaking so. And anyways, I'd have been shamed to show fear in front of Callan, who had been so brave.

"Well, we can try, can't we?" He shrugged his pack higher up on his shoulders and set out ahead of us.

"We could run," I suggested as he pulled out of hearing range.

Callan shook his head. "He's not that far ahead, and I'll bet he doesn't let the distance get any greater than it is right now. This is his show, David. He's calling the shots, and we're going to have to play it his way."

The incline was getting steeper, and my leg muscles were already twinging. It had been a long winter, and though I was fitter than I'd been that horrible day I'd carried Almond home, I was still weaker than I cared to be. "We're well out of town," I said, frowning. "Why don't he just shoot us now?"

"And do what with our bodies?" I didn't know how Callan stayed so calm, talking on such things as what would happen to our remains once we was murdered. "He couldn't just leave them here; too much chance we'd be found. And burial is hard work. Besides, do you see a shovel anywhere on that pack of his?"

No, I didn't. "So what do you figure, then? He'll do it up the mountain where nobody'd ever find us?" A picture of my Mam the way she'd looked when Almond died, diminished and broken, crossed the front of my mind. I couldn't put her through such a thing again. "Oh, God, Callan. What are we going to do?"

For just an instant, his arm slid around my waist as we walked and he gave me a squeeze. "I don't know, love. Just stay alert, okay? I'm trying to think of something. And keep that gun out of his sight."

He hadn't needed to tell me that. The gun in my jacket, the knife strapped to my belt, that was all we had. Unless... "You got any poison in your pack? We could slip it in his water."

"Nothing that would act fast enough to keep him from taking us with him."

Delahaye had slowed, and Callan allowed himself to drift away from me as we pushed on up the hill, quiet now, for the man was staying within earshot. My mind was working harder than my body, trying to puzzle out what we could do, how we could break free. But even if we did, where could we go? Back to Moline, where folk believed the R&A was trying to help them and we was heroes for facing the dragons? We had no proof of our story, and Delahaye would go back to town and spread all manner of lies about us. We could go away, south maybe, save that we had no money, no supplies to speak of, and spring or not, men died of exposure in these hills all the time.

The sun was at its height, though we never did see it direct, for blue-grey clouds covered the sky as far west as the eye could see. I knew those clouds; I'd spent endless days gazing at them out the cabin window in the cold months. Those were snow clouds.

"It's fixing to snow if the temperature should drop," I commented. "Hope Pa gets the crops covered, else we could lose the whole harvest."

"I wouldn't worry about that," Delahaye called back at me. "I studied the Weather Service reports for the next three weeks, and there's no snow predicted."

I snorted, thinking on the folly of a man a hundred miles away sitting in a government office thinking he could know our weather. You couldn't know the weather in these parts unless you felt it in your bones.

"He can believe what he likes," I said to Callan, soft voiced. "But when the sun goes down tonight, we'll see snow. Hope you've got warm gear." It weren't likely that Delahaye was going to let us sleep together as we had on the Ridges. If we'd been alone on this journey, it would have been near heaven, even with the dragons at the end of it.

Callan didn't answer, just kept on trudging up the hill. We'd passed the Crawford turnoff some time ago and were heading straight up the mountain, following the last of the road, an old gravel trail. The incline was mighty steep here, and I couldn't imagine how the motored vehicles they'd had Before could ever have managed it. Horses couldn't, not easily anyway, though a good sturdy pony or mule might have.

The road was cut directly into the side of the rock, hugging the side of the mountain and winding around, climbing always up and up, till the back of my legs ached with the strain. Callan looked bad; he wasn't near as much an outdoorsman as me, and even Delahaye had slowed.

"Much more?" he asked, as though saying a full sentence would have taxed him too much.

"Not much more road." I pointed up ahead where a rockslide had collapsed the side of the mountain, blocking the road completely. "From here we go overland."

I was powerful hungry. We'd eaten a sort of lunch on the move, just bread and jerked meat, and of course we'd been drinking water from what skins and flasks as we had, but I could stand to sit down and rest, and Callan was pale and breathing hard.

"Any chance of stopping soon?"

Delahaye looked at the sky, which was now so overcast you couldn't barely tell it was still daylight. "Hmm. Looks to be later than I figured." He pulled a fancy timepiece out of his pocket and checked it, then frowned. "Only just after four. No. Can't stop for at least another two hours, three if we can make it." Without another word he slipped his watch into his pocket, squared off his pack again and left the road, moving with purpose through the tall pines.

I offered Callan a drink of water. "You okay?"

"Yes, I think so." His eyes followed Delahaye, who was almost out of sight, his green-brown coat blending into the forest. "You notice he's not waiting for you to guide him?"

I hadn't, but Callan was right. Delahaye knew where he was going; all that about needing me to guide him and asking questions on times and distances was part of the play-acting. "That's not good, is it?"

"No." Callan had dropped his pack for a moment, now he took it up again, wincing at the strain on his shoulders. "I was counting on your knowledge of the land to be our one advantage."

"Boys!" Delahaye called without turning around, and we started up the slope. The ground was spongy, treacherous with slippery pine straw and rotting leaves and who knew what else, and the wind had picked up and now had a definite edge to it. At least the trees blocked the worst of that; the road had been completely exposed. I tried to remember if there was any good camp sites on this side of the slope. No shelters like the shepherd's house, not even lean-tos. Nobody came up here, save for hunters, and not even them often. This weren't ever a welcoming place, even before the dragons had come.

We scrambled over fallen timbers and rock outcroppings, making our way up towards the summit. Delahaye weren't even making a pretense of consulting me about direction no more, and though it might have been just him assuming that up is up, I didn't think so. The whole mountain felt wrong to me; and it finally came to me why. There was no sign of animal life at all. No early birds trying to set out nests, no tracks in any of the dried mud we passed, no droppings, and no fresh holes in the ground where small creatures had burrowed. There was old holes a-plenty, though. I heard a sharp cry from behind me, and turned to see Callan on the ground.

He was up before I could get to him, but I could tell he was done. "You twist your ankle?"

"Nothing serious, I just wasn't paying attention."

"We got to stop." I scouted around a bit. There was a clearing to our left where a bunch of trees had fallen, giving a wind block, and leaving plenty of firewood. "Mister Delahaye!"

He turned back to look at us, and I suddenly remembered a day when I was about ten years old and I came upon Charlie Harris, one of Elmer's gang, torturing a squirrel he'd trapped. Charlie had looked at the squirrel the exact same way Delahaye was looking at us: as though we was vermin, fit for nothing but to exterminate. I'd hit Charlie over the head with a big old log, then put the squirrel out of his misery. Didn't think a log would do me much good this time.

"What?"

"We need to stop." I didn't make it a question. "That clearing looks to be a good campsite." I took Callan's pack from him, half-expecting him to protest, but he didn't, just gave a tight smile and followed me over to the fallen logs where he collapsed down on the cold ground.

"Thanks," he whispered, as Delahaye was coming down to join us. "I couldn't have gone much more."

"Me either." My legs felt like jelly, all shaky and weak. I didn't sit, though—there was chores needed doing, and if I sat, I wouldn't likely rise again for hours.

Delahaye didn't drop his own pack, just reached around and pulled the rifle off it. My chest seized up as the gleaming barrel came round to point between us. Was this it, then? I felt for the lump of the gun in my jacket, thinking of how quick I could get it out and fire.

But he shouldered his firearm. "I'll go look for some game. Don't know about you, but I could use some fresh meat." Then he trudged away into the forest before I could tell him I was pretty sure there wasn't any game to be had. Not that he'd have listened to me anyways.

I gave Callan what remained of my water, then set to laying a fire from the fallen branches. "Your ankle okay?" It might be we'd need to run. In fact, if I hadn't known that Callan was beyond it, I'd have suggested making a break right then. I couldn't believe Delahaye had just gone off and left us alone.

"I think so. I'll wrap it here in a minute. David, you're not near as tired as I am, do you think you could get away?"

"I'm not leaving you," I said shortly, and moved close so that our thighs was touching. Even through the cloth, it was enough. He sighed and sort of leaned against me, and as the fire caught and the tiny warmth began to build, I put my arm around him, and we just stayed like that for a time, not speaking, not thinking even, just being.

We heard Delahaye coming back, far too soon, but at least we had warning enough to separate, and when he come upon us, Callan was slicing bread and I was setting up two makeshift tents from oilskin blankets and rope strung between trees.

I looked up from my work as Mister Delahaye climbed over the logs that formed the edge of our campsite. "You got a tent you want me to rig, sir?"

"No. I'll manage my own things." He handed over a sad excuse for a rabbit. "Best I could find. The game in this country is horrible. I don't know why you stay."

"Because it's home." But he was right, it had been bad lately, since the dragons come. I took the rabbit to Callan. "Can you handle this? I want to get some water." There was a stream about five hundred yards east, if I was remembering rightly.

"No." Delahaye was brusque. "Nobody leaves camp. I have water enough to manage for tonight."

"It ain't far," I protested. "And it's still light enough to see." Just barely, but I reckoned I could make it.

"Wouldn't want my guide to go astray." His tone was light, but I could sense steel behind it. "Besides, I've set up a warning system around the perimeter of the camp; if anything's out there, we'll know it."

And anyone trying to leave would set off whatever alarms he'd done up as well— bells and noisemakers and the like, I supposed. So much for making a break for freedom in the night.

Callan had the rabbit cleaned and dressed by the time Delahaye got water boiling, and we made a sort of thin stew, tasteless and horrid, but I was too tired and hungry to care. Night had fallen completely, and the wind was howling up the mountain. Callan had pulled one of his blankets around him and was using the metal bowl as a hand warmer. It wouldn't have been so cold back home, but we was just north enough and just high enough to make it seem like the end of winter, not the start of spring. I slipped one of my spare blankets into Callan's tent, then sat down and forced myself to eat another bowl of the stew.

In the dim light of the fire, I watched Delahaye sit down in front of his pack and unstrap what looked to be a roll of shiny green-colored fabric with thin sticks wrapped up in it. The sticks opened out to make long poles, and I worked out that it was a tent of sorts, but like none I'd ever seen before.

"I want an early start tomorrow," he said without looking at us, and he slung his pack into the tent, then crawled after it and pulled the zipper closed.

"He's going to freeze in that thing," I commented to Callan. "It ain't even as thick as a good linen sheet."

Callan put his bowl down and got up slow, wincing as his muscles cramped up. "It doesn't need to be. I believe that's a four-season tent, probably rated for everything but the worst winter storms."

Like the pack, I knew they'd made that sort of thing Before, but not now. "But Callan, it's new. There's no way that's a hundred years old."

"No, it's not. I guess working for the government has its benefits." He lowered his voice. "It might be cold resistant, but it's not soundproof. We should just go to bed, try to sleep. There's nothing else we can do."

Tired as I was, I really didn't think I could sleep, but he was right. No sense borrowing trouble or worrying over what you can't set to rights. Making sure Delahaye's door was shut tight, I leaned forward and kissed Callan lightly on the lips, and he responded hungrily. It was far more nourishing than the watery stew; I clung to him till desire threatened to overtake common sense and we reluctantly broke it off. Callan turned away without speaking and crawled into the tent I'd rigged for him.

I understood; it weren't like speech would do any good. Anything we needed to say to each other we'd already said. I built up the fire as best I could, hoping it would last the night, then took refuge in my own tent. I didn't undress, nor even take off my shoes, just in case the chance to flee somehow presented itself. My legs was aching from the climb and I'd swear the hard ground was as soft to me as that feather tick mattress had been, but I couldn't sleep. My nerves was jangling like a jaw harp, my mind racing from one place to another.

I'd been lying there fighting for sleep for what seemed like hours—though it was likely only minutes—when I heard Callan's voice in the darkness. "David, are you awake?"

"Yeah." I listened to see if there was sound coming from across the fire where Mister Delahaye had set his fancy tent, but all was quiet.

"Come here."

"Not sure that's a good idea." I was pretty certain it was a real bad idea, but it was surely what I wanted to do, so I sat up, listening.

"He's going to kill us or we're going to kill him, either way it doesn't matter a damn what we do tonight. I'm not spending what might be my last night on earth anywhere but in your arms. Come here." Something in the way Callan spoke those last words, low and kind of growly, flooded heat through my body, and I couldn't do nothing save obey, clambering out of my tent, dragging blankets across the clearing to slip in beside him.

I'd known Callan hesitant, nervous as he'd been on the Ridges; tender and gentle and patient that night on the feather bed; but I'd never seen him like this. There was no patience nor hesitance now, just questing hands and an eager mouth, drawing pleasure from me as you'd draw poison from a wound. His mouth moved over every part of my body, kisses falling like fierce rain, strong healer's hands ripping clothing aside as though it was paper. I'd known that Callan had been with other men, and not just Taylor Mills, but I'd known it the same way I knew my book learning, in my mind only. Now I knew it as fact, felt it down to the marrow of my bones, for he used skill that could only have been learned from experience to hold me on the edge of pleasure till I was sobbing in frustration and delight.

I didn't give a care about Delahaye next to us in his paper-thin tent nor the dragons nor the town, nothing mattered but that moment, and Callan, and what we did together in that makeshift tent with the snow beginning to fall around us. Then his mouth closed over me and mine over him while the covers enclosed us in our own private country, and my world exploded as we clung to one another, shaking, shuddering, riding out the sensation that overtook us.

After, he held me like a child in his mother's arms, and I felt so safe and warm and full of comfort that I figured a few moments there would be all right. Oh, I'd go back to my own tent, just not yet. But I'd forgotten how tired I was, done in by the journey and the constant worry about what Delahaye was like to do, and within minutes, sleep had hold of me.

I came awake abruptly, aware that I weren't at all where I should have been. I sat up and peeked out of the back of the tent to see the first rays of a red dawn reflecting off a light dusting of snow that covered the ground. I kissed Callan on the cheek, trying not to wake him, pulled my clothes around me, and slid out of the little tent. With luck, I could get back to my own bedroll without Delahaye being any the wiser.

But luck weren't with me, not at all. Mister Delahaye was sitting at the fire, his rifle pointed straight at me.

Chapter 21

"I can explain." My fingers fumbled with my buttons, trying to restore myself to some dignity while fishing about for a lie that might be believed. "It weren't Callan's fault, I swear it. The oilcloth on my tent must have been worn—it leaked, and the snow fell in and I needed to get out of the cold and..."

Callan's hand closed over my arm; my babbling must have woke him. "Never mind, David. What's done is done."

Mister Delahaye was sitting on an old fallen log with his feet out towards the fire, crossed over each other, like he didn't have a care in the world. His hair and his clothes, the same ones he'd wore the day before, looked as perfect as if he'd never slept. "And it doesn't matter a whit to me, anyway. It's convenient, having you together. It makes this easier."

"Please," Callan said. "Let David go. He doesn't know anything."

"Doesn't know anything about what?" His voice was mocking.

"Can we just have an end to all these games? Stop all this playacting and just have it all out in the open?" Callan was shaking all over.

Delahaye gestured with the gun, motioning us forward to sit opposite him on another snow-covered log. It was still cold, the sun barely penetrating through the iron grey morning. "If you like. I regret the necessity of what I have to do here, you know. I have nothing against either of you. I don't even care about your personal habits. You boys would be amazed at how many politicians back in Washington share your...preferences. The senior Senator from Georgia, for example, has a taste for little boys. Everybody knows it, nobody bats an eye." Delahaye snorted. "He has power and influence. You, unfortunately, don't."

"David doesn't know anything," Callan repeated, and his hand clenched tight on my wrist, warning me to silence.

Delahaye looked at me, blinking coldly. "That's certainly believable; he doesn't look like he's smart enough to know up from down or his left from his right. But it's irrelevant. You know things, things you shouldn't know, and because of that, you're a threat, albeit a minor one, to a plan that has been in place since well before you were born. And I can't take the chance that some queer's pillow talk will ruin that. So you both have to die."

As simple as that, the words couldn't be taken back. Callan was wrong; spoken words were as real and permanent as writing.

"Just do it, then," Callan said, weary calm in his voice.

"I wish I could," Delahaye said, and I'd swear he meant it. "But I'm not quite finished with you—did you forget that I have a mission? There are dragons menacing your town."

"I thought you wanted us out. I thought the dragons was your doing." He sort of arched his brow, and I hurried to correct myself. "Not you, personally, the R&A. The government." It made no sense. I'd figured killing the dragons was just a story, just a way to get rid of Callan and me without getting the town in an uproar.

"I want? I don't want anything, except to do my job. The dragons are one means to our end, a rather stupid means when it comes down to it, and now they've got quite inconvenient. I was brought here to handle that inconvenience. You're going to help me, just like we agreed back at your town meeting." He smiled at me, that cold snake's smile again. "And so much for 'David doesn't know anything.'"

Callan breathed in hard, but it didn't matter; not no more. "I ain't taking you anywhere."

"That's fine. I don't need you to. Your presence is more a matter of sending a message. A boy consumed, a mangled body returned to a grieving community; every action serves our purpose."

"My mam, she don't deserve this."

He seemed to be thinking on it, maybe remembering his own mother, for surely even he had one. "True enough. I suppose I need only return one body to the town; his will do. As far as I know, nobody much will mourn him." He jerked his thumb at Callan who didn't seem at all surprised by any of this.

"So they're real?" Callan asked, ignoring the insult.

"Callan, I've seen them; we've all seen them."

"No, I mean, are they mechanical? That would explain why bullets haven't had any effect, why they've stopped working as you want—they've broken down."

Delahaye nodded as though he'd just remembered something. "Ah yes. You're from Florida—you must have seen what's left of the Disney Animatronics. They were quite remarkable, weren't they? A very perspicacious theory, though quite wrong. The dragons are organic—they live, and they will very soon die." He rose and stretched. "Time to go, boys."

I glanced sideways at Callan and he nodded back at me then spoke what both of us was thinking. "Why should we cooperate? You're going to kill us anyway—why should we march up that frozen hill just so we can die there instead of here?"

Narrow eyes went to slits. "There's dying and then there's dying." He looked Callan straight in the eye; I was so proud of him when he didn't look away. I couldn't have faced down those snake-eyes. "You don't cooperate with me, and I'll see it takes you five days to die, and what they bury of you won't fill a slop bucket."

Callan let go my hand and stood up. "I'm not afraid of pain."

Delahaye slung his rifle on his shoulder and took out a wicked long knife that made Gram look like what you'd use to butter your bread with, and I stood up, too, trying to ready myself for whatever might come. We'd go out fighting, at least. "Maybe not for yourself." His free hand shot out and I felt a cruel grip on my throat, a cold blade against my cheek. I froze, knowing for the first time the panic and terror the game snared in our traplines must feel. A searing pain bit into my cheek, and I smelled iron as blood ran down my face. It was all I could do to hold still, keep from crying out—and more than Callan could do, it seemed.

"Stop! I'll...we'll go with you. Just please, don't."

He let me go, and I fell to the ground, my hands reaching out into the snow to break my fall. I stayed on hands and knees for a time, watching the bright crimson falling from my face to stain the snow. Callan reached down to help me up.

"I'm all right. Let me get my pack." The only hope we had was the gun in my jacket.

"Looking for this?" Delahaye held up the black pistol and I closed my eyes. It was over. I had a belt knife, Callan even less. We would go to the summit, and the dragons would come and kill us, doing the R&A's dirty work again, then Delahaye would finish them and take Callan's battered body home. Delahaye would be a hero, we'd be mourned for a time, and then the clearing of the town would go on. There'd be no storybook ending here.

He made us leave our packs; he said we'd no need for them, and he was likely right, for what use is foodstuffs and blankets and medicines to walking corpses? We'd pushed mighty hard the day before, and were within three hours of the summit. Three hours to live. I recalled how Almond had screamed when those talons had ripped her open.

Maybe he'd shoot us first. I could hope. Delahaye tried to set the same grueling pace as before, but with the snow-slick ground and the way we was forced to travel, with him having to stay behind us to keep watch, we slowed almost to a crawl.

We didn't talk nor look to each other over those first two hours. We couldn't plot an escape with Delahaye so close, and I'd be damned if I'd say my farewells with him listening in. Anyway, Callan knew how I felt. He was looking down mostly, judging his footfalls and I could tell his ankle was still tender.

And the ground was slick; snow-slick and pinestraw-slick. Callan lost his footing more than once, catching himself with his bare hands, for his gloves, my gloves that I'd given him, were back with our packs in the little clearing. The third time I helped him up to his feet, I saw something terrifying lurking behind his eyes: a resolve that put me in mind of my Pa. I didn't know what he had in his head, but I knew I wasn't going to like it.

We'd got about five paces ahead of Delahaye, and Callan looked down again and gave a small cough to catch my attention. I followed the line of his sight ahead of us to a small log, about the size of a child's arm, half-buried in the snow. He stepped over it, then called back to Delahaye, "If you expect me to continue, I need some water."

Delahaye reached around his pack to try to get to the skin just as he hit the log; his foot slid out from under him as he cursed aloud; even with the traction of his good boots, he half-stumbled to his knees. Callan flung himself back down the hill, tackling Delahaye and forcing him to the ground, screaming, "Run! David, RUN!"

I wish I could say that I stayed with Callan, grappling with Delahaye for the rifle. But I didn't. May God forgive me, for I know I'll never forgive myself, as soon as Callan's words resounded over the silent hillside, I scampered like a rabbit running from a fox. I didn't think, didn't even hesitate, nor try to come to Callan's aid. I saw wheaten hair slamming back against the snow and Delahaye's black ponytail falling across Callan's face as I flashed passed them, my legs going pell-mell down the slope, sliding and slipping and falling and getting back up again, running like the coward I was, sprinting so fast that I thought my legs was going to collapse under me.

Down the rise the hill dropped abruptly away, and I went tumbling down a rough cliff, and landed hard on my back, wincing as the wind got knocked clean out of me. The jolt of it brought me back to my senses. What had I done? I had to go back, had to help Callan or he was doomed. I was struggling to my feet when I heard distant shouting and then two shots rang out, angry blasts echoing in the silence of the morning, then a scream of pain, and a crow called out and took flight above me, leaving silence behind.

I knew in my heart that it had been Delahaye who had pulled the trigger, and in my mind's eye, clear as ice, I could see Callan laying in the snow, blood pooling around him as his eyes stared up, vacant just like Almond's.

The sobs came then, when I was alone and couldn't be shamed by them—as though my flight weren't enough to be ashamed of—wracking spasms of grief such as I'd never known, not even when Almond died, for more than that, this was truly my fault. I lay there in the cold till all the snow had melted under my body and my clothes was drenched with snow and tears and the blood that oozed from the cut on my cheek. None of it mattered. Nothing mattered. I'd run like a coward, and Callan was likely dead because of it. I wondered if Delahaye would come looking for me. I hoped so, for I surely wanted to die.

But there were no footsteps crunching in the snow, no shadows looming over the cliff above me, and so after a while, I pulled myself up and looked around. I'd never been in this place before; I'd run down and to the west, not straight down as we'd come. The cliff I'd tumbled down was a sheer drop, though not high, only about ten or fifteen feet, and I stood on a flat, narrow surface that looked for all the world like a road. But there shouldn't be any roads here. It was wrong, out of its proper place.

And what did it matter, when my world was destroyed, if this flat place was a sheep path or a dirt road or a twelve lane highway like they'd had Before? But habit run strong and I was curious, so I knelt back down, digging with a stick into a century's accumulation of rotten straw and debris, probing through layers upon layers till my stick hit something that wouldn't give way. I dug with my bare cold hands then, making a hole big enough that I could see through to the cracked concrete beneath. It was a road. A road on a mountaintop, a road that went nowhere. A mystery. I turned to tell it to Callan and then the awful loss struck me again, knocking my heart into my throat, and I caught hold of my breath to keep back the tears.

Callan was dead. The sun was coming out, burning the fog away. That was wrong. I wished it would rain. It ought to rain; the heavens ought to weep even if I couldn't no more, for the tears in me was freezing to ice as anger began to fill me up, pushing the grief aside. Anger at myself, at Delahaye, and at God, if he even existed. Something Pastor Daniels had said at Almond's burying come to mind; something I had barely heard, but which now kept playing over and over in my head the way Almond used to sing the same line of a song till it was like to drive you mad. A time to be born and a time to die, a time to kill and a time to heal.

A time to die. Grandmam's stories talked a lot about fate. Those old heroes were forever trying to avoid their fates, but they always seemed to get tripped up and end up bringing on the very thing they was running from. I didn't believe in fate. A man made his own fate, but it surely felt as though we had been led down a path with only one destination; like everything that had happened to us, all our choices, had led me here.

I didn't really believe in God neither, but there was wisdom in those words from the Writ. If this was the time to die, then it wouldn't be just Callan who'd be laid in the ground. I unsheathed my knife, still strapped to my belt, for Delahaye hadn't seen it as a threat. He weren't worried that a farm boy with a blade could harm him. I intended for that to be the last mistake he ever made.

I was trusting that Delahaye would still make for the summit. The dragons weren't acting as they should; they was a danger to the government's plan, and Delahaye was supposed to take care of them. He struck me as a man who'd take a job serious, letting nothing stop him till it was done. I hadn't seen sign of the dragons since we'd set out, but had no doubt that if Delahaye wanted them, he'd find a way to bring them. He was that kind of man—determined. But not so determined as I.

So I walked along the old road, which curled up the mountain in a slow coil, a gentle slope suited for wagons or for old time cars. I'd never heard that there was houses or cabins on this slope; the summit was bald and rounded with an old metal tower on it, something Pa said used to run electric wires Before—maybe the road had something to do with that. I supposed people must have had to come up to work on the tower. I hoped it led to the summit, at least, for there weren't no way I could go back the way I'd come. Scaling fifteen feet of cliff with neither tools nor ropes was far beyond me.

It weren't as cold as it had been the day before, but I sorely missed my jacket and the warm, dry clothes in my pack. I was like to freeze to death being exposed like this, but that didn't matter. Nothing mattered but getting to Delahaye. I had no doubts now that I'd be able to end his life. He weren't a human being. He was a monster as sure as those dragons were. I'd plunge my knife into his chest or his back, or slit his throat the way Pa would kill an ailing ewe, and think no more on it than that.

And then see to laying Callan to rest proper. Not in the town; they didn't deserve him there, and he wouldn't have cared about consecrated ground anyways. We'd consecrated a bit of ground together last night, and that would be where I'd lay him, if I could manage it. I would dig the hole with my bare hands if I had to, dig till my fingers bled before I'd leave him out to be ravaged by beasts.

The thought of it, of that familiar and beloved body which had brought me so much joy, now cold and pale and stiff, it came over me like snow falling off a bluff, an avalanche that sent me reeling against the cliff wall, seeking support from the earth. But even the earth failed me, and I went falling through a loose weave of branches, hitting the ground again. Recessed back in the cliff side, half hidden by branches and roots, was an opening. It was of good size, big enough for a man to walk upright with room to spare. The branches ringing it were broken as though someone or something had passed through recently. I'd found the lair.

No. Think, David. I could hear Callan's voice in my mind. Big enough for a man to walk upright, but I'd been close to the dragons, and they were larger than any man. This entrance had been used recently, but not by anything so large as a dragon. Some hibernating animal, most like a raccoon or skunk, or possibly a bear—though rare, they weren't unknown in these parts. Knife in hand, I started forward. I had no way to make light, but I'd have a look round the opening, because you never knew what you might find.

I ripped the branches and roots away with my bare hands, for I feared to dull the blade of my knife when I most needed it sharp. The ropy vines bit into my hands, for they was rooted deep into the side of the cliff, but in the end they gave way, and I stood looking into the hole in the mountain. It was pitch dark, as you'd expect a cave would be; there was nothing of interest nor value to me, and I was turning to go when I happened to take note of the shape of the opening. It was arched.

Now, I don't much care for caves nor tight places, and steer clear of them whenever I can, but I know a few things about rock and how it crumbles, and as I felt along the edge of the opening, it was clear that this hole had been cut for a purpose. Hewn by men with tools, not weathered away by time. If I only had a light—there might be something of value in this Before place, maybe another weapon, even. But I had no match, nor even my flint and steel, and I run my hands along the smooth-cut ridge of rock just inside the opening, thinking on how far in I'd be able to go before the light failed completely, when my hand closed over something unnatural.

A switch. We had light switches in our home—it had been wired when it was built Before, and nobody'd ever bothered to take them out, so I knew what I was feeling. Somehow, impossible though it seemed, there had been electric light up here once. Just as I used to play with the switches back home, I flipped this one, just to hear the dull click, like firing an empty rifle. But as this switch clicked, the tunnel come to life, glowing with faded yellow light.

Light to me is sunlight, soft and hazy, seen through clouds and fog; or firelight, candlelight, or lamp light, flickering and smoky. I had to put my head down right near the candle to be able to read by it—it didn't push the darkness away as if it was an enemy the way this Before light did. The tunnel was lit up clear past where it turned and seemed to head upwards, past the limit of my sight. This was important. I might well be risking missing Delahaye on the summit, but this could be the key to all of it. Callan wouldn't want me to put revenge over figuring it all out.

So I followed the lights, which was stuck up onto the ceiling by some unknown means. They wasn't as bright as I'd have thought they'd be. Grandmam talks about how electric light used to turn night to the brightest day, and this, though brighter than anything I'd seen before, weren't near that. But it was enough to make the cavern more like a room and take the edge off the clutching fear I always felt when enclosed, surrounded and buried by tons of rock crushing above me. The tunnel stayed the proper height for a man, not snaking down the way natural tunnels sometimes did, and I followed it, turning and twisting and rising upward in the mountain till it dead-ended against a grey metal door with a small glass window set at eye level. A tiny square covered with numbers was set to the left of the door. I tried the knob, figuring it had to be locked, but it turned easy enough and the door opened silently.

That set my nerves on edge. Doors ain't supposed to open silent—they creak and rasp and squeak. And when they shut behind you they ain't supposed to clang like the gong of a church bell, leaving you trapped in a rocky tomb with buried bits of the past. And there was bits of the past all over that room. The light here was brighter, so bright it hurt my eyes, making me squint from the pain of it. Barrels and boxes and furnishings crammed the little room, and opposite me I could see another door, this one half open. Thick grey dust covered every square inch of the surfaces. I turned in a circle, taking it all in the way a child takes in the wonders that greet him under the Christmas tree.

The echo from the door had faded, giving voice to a low hum coming from a large box of metal with pipes leading up the ceiling and through the stone walls of the cavern. It looked like nothing so much as a big old stove, but as I brushed the dust away, I saw nothing that could have been burners, just a flat surface with a whole lot of buttons and switches and glass-covered numbers. Words was marked on the side of it, but they'd faded over time. I tried to make them out. T, then some spaces, then L A, then more spaces and ARKIX. Arkix? That weren't any sort of word I'd ever heard.

Callan would surely have known. Oh God, he'd have loved this place, with its false light and dusty machines from Before still running, still working somehow to do whatever they did, though the men who'd made them was dust themselves. Papers scattered about, too, old and yellowing but still readable. I could picture how he would have been, sitting cross-legged on the floor, his hair falling in his face as he studied the papers.

That wouldn't never happen. I couldn't unravel this tangle without Callan, and there was nothing here I could use. No gun, no knife, not even a shovel I could use to lay my dearest friend to rest. This mystery place from before the Ice was of no use nor value to me. Likely whatever had been in these caverns had been a small animal looking for shelter. I'd swear nothing human had touched these ruins since the cold came over these hills.

It was time to go, past time, so I retraced my steps over the dusty floor and tried the doorknob. It didn't move. Stupid—I'd got myself locked in. Though I didn't much care right then about my life, whether it ended on that mountain or not, I cared mightily about taking Delahaye with me, so it was a good thing that other door was open.

I started up the passageway which was now lit but dimly, winding my way up and up till I realized that the light I was using to travel by weren't coming from above me no more, but from ahead: daylight. The cavern opened up into a larger cave, and this one was natural; all craggy rocks and jagged edges, dank, musty, and sort of animal scented. Like something had been making this its home for a long time.

And it was pretty clear what that something was. The ring of mottled eggs half-buried in the pine straw, each bigger than a man's head, bigger than a small child even, left me no doubt. This time I'd found the lair for true.

Chapter 22

I smashed those eggs, ground them down to powder beneath my boots, killing what lay in them without a second thought, as I'd exterminate vermin that preyed on our stock, for that's what they were. Vermin in the making, brought down on us by those we trusted. With eggs this near to hatching, the grown dragons wouldn't likely be far from their lair for long, so I worked quickly, and when it was done, I crept towards the large opening where the sun streamed in, keeping to the rough walls of the cavern for safety.

The sun hung high, burning off the last of the fog, and melting away the snow of the night before. It was going on noon, I'd say, or just after, and as I looked around, trying to get a fix on where I was, another shot rang out, followed by a fearsome roar, then the earth shook as though a great tree had been felled. I scrambled up the hill in the direction of the sound, climbing and running and half-pulling myself along, hanging on to vines and branches till I come up on a row of sickly pines, part of a ring around the summit of the mountain.

One of the dragons lay dead in the clearing, and Delahaye stood with a funny-looking rifle in his hand, facing towards the dead dragon and away from me. About twenty paces beyond that was the electric tower, and tied to it, like bait tied to a fishing line, was Callan's body. My blood turned to ice, seeing his head loll forward, and the blood that even from this distance I could see covered his shoulder and chest. Somewhere in the heart of me, I'd held hope that he lived, that the shots I'd heard earlier had gone wide or had wounded him only, but nobody could be that still; surely nobody could lose so much blood and still be among the living. Every dream I'd had, every thing I had wanted in my whole life was tied to that tower, dead.

Nothing mattered no more, just revenging myself on the man who'd done it, and he was there, within my sights. I could have thrown that knife right into his back; I'd practiced that with Benny C on slow summer afternoons and knew I could find my mark well enough. But this couldn't be done from a distance, by an unknown knife in the back. He had to know who'd killed him, and why. I started forward, slow and careful, trying to keep my footfalls quiet when I noticed something off to the corner of my eye.

Delahaye had dropped his pack there, and lying atop his pack, cast aside as though it was rubbish, was Grandmam's pistol. I took it up gratefully.

I can only think that Delahaye must have been lost in thought, planning how he'd do in the other dragon, or thinking on what he'd tell them in the town, for I snuck up on him and shoved the gun into his ribs before he had so much as a chance to cock that fancy rifle.

"Drop it and turn around." The rifle fell from his hands and he slowly circled round, hands outstretched.

"I was wondering if you'd turn up." He seemed almost pleased to see me.

"I see you got one."

He nodded towards the rifle he'd tossed away. "Longwood Fifty Calibre Collapsible Sniper rifle, telescopic sight, last model they made before the Ice—pristine condition."

"This'll do me just fine," I pointed the pistol at him. "Wouldn't do a thing to the dragon, but it surely will blow your brains clean out of your head."

Above us the sun winked out, then in again. I risked a glance to see the other dragon circling, but Delahaye just kept staring at me. "Don't you think you have more important things to worry about, boy?"

"I don't care about the dragon, don't care if it kills me so long as you go first." He was doing what I would have done, stalling, trying to work out a way to get round me.

"Not the dragon, boy. Your boyfriend. Who by the by, makes damn fine bait. Aren't you worried about what that thing's going to do to him while you're wasting time making small talk with me?"

"If I got a choice between saving Callan's body and seeing you die, that ain't no choice." I cocked the gun. It wasn't like anything I'd ever shot before, but I figured I'd work it out. Aim and shoot, same as a rifle.

"Stupid farm boy—can't tell dead from alive."

"Is that the best tale you can come up with? You ain't going to save your sorry skin with lies." But a flicker of hope kindled in me, and I had to fight to keep from looking to where Callan was tied. That was what he wanted—the minute I looked away, he'd be on me. But inside, I was praying in secret, making promises and bargains to God, for in that moment, I'd have believed in God or the devil or Norse Odin if they'd bring Callan back to me.

"Fool. Dragons aren't carrion eaters. He'd have been no use to me dead."

This time I couldn't help myself, I looked, and I don't know whether it was a trick of the light or the wind, which was stirring the grasses and lifting Callan's hair from his face, but as I was watching, I saw Callan move—just slightly, but enough to feed that flame of hope. But the dragon must have seen it, too, must have been able to sense life even from so high up, the way hawks can feel their prey's movement.

There was no time. But if I left Delahaye alive, he'd pick up that rifle or make for his pack, where he likely had other weapons, and if Callan weren't dead, he surely soon would be, and me right along with him. Holding my breath, I aimed straight between his eyes, his unblinking eyes that looked like they hadn't a care in the world, braced myself for the recoil, and squeezed the trigger.

Click. I squeezed again. Click. And again. Empty. Useless. Delahaye began to laugh like a cruel old bird, a crow's mocking cackle, and the dragon was circling lower and lower.

"NO!" I screamed at the dragon, at Delahaye, at myself, running faster than I'd ever run in my life towards Callan, useless pistol thrown aside, knife out, thinking I could cut him free, maybe pull him into the woven metal of the tower where he might be safe. Delahaye made no move to stop me, and I didn't even bother to look at whether he picked up his rifle again.

My knife tore through the ropes and he fell into my arms. He was alive, oh, he was alive. Blood caked his hair and clothes, and there was a strip of fabric cutting deep into his right arm, and above it a sick mess of shredded cloth and skin and horror. But he was alive.

"Callan, please, please. Wake up, please." I shook him gently as the sky above us changed from blue to dragon-green.

He groaned, and I brushed his hair off his face, so horribly pale. The ground shook as the dragon landed between us and Delahaye, but making for us; the weaker prey was always what drew the predator. Dragons wasn't any different from foxes nor wolves in that when it came to that.

Callan's eyes was fluttering; he was starting to wake, but I hadn't time for that. He weren't going to be able to even try to run. It fell to me. I stood up with my knife in my hand, moving forward to stand between Callan and the monster.

It was a fearsome thing close on. Whether this was the one Benny C had wounded or not, it must have learned from that, for its wings was back and up, out of my reach. Its long and scaly neck held a head like every child's worst nightmare, eyes glowing red, cruel teeth bared as it stared down at us. Then the head went back, the neck seemed to flare out, and I knew that it was going to flame, and that would be the end of us.

I ran then, praying that it would follow me and not fall upon Callan as an easy target. I could hear its footfalls behind me, and I dodged and wove around the top of that mountain, drawing the beast away from Callan. There was heat behind me, and the acrid smell of smoke and burning grasses clogged my senses. This was bad; even if the dragon didn't kill me, it was like to set the woods aflame.

I was tiring, and fast running out of places to run; there weren't no way I could wear it down, or hope that it would lose interest in the chase. I had to make a stand, but to stop was to risk being incinerated. I had hunted all my life, but now I was prey, not hunter, and none of what I'd learned from my Pa could help me now.

Vulnerable places—the damn thing had to have them, other than the wings. The underbelly perhaps, but I couldn't get to that, or the eyes, which were far out of my reach. At least three small fires was burning now, and the smoke was starting to tickle my throat, and I could hear Delahaye still laughing, and I'd be damned if that man's laugh was the last sound I would hear on this earth.

So without thinking, for thinking would stop me in my tracks, I turned and run straight towards the oncoming dragon, confusing the beast so it froze, startled, neck outstretched, just long enough and just low enough for me to leap onto it like I used to catapult myself onto Lightning's back when we was playing games as children. The sharp scales cut into my already-sore hands, but I hung on like a stubborn tick on a dog while the thing bucked and tossed its head, trying to throw me. I tried to work my knife into the space between the scales, but it weren't no use; I might as well be trying to cut on stone.

Grandmam told me once about rodeos, traveling groups of riders that would come through the towns when she was young, putting on shows, cowboys riding on horses that was mistreated to make them buck. That must have been what this was like, for it was taking all that I had to cling on, arms wrapped tight around the pipe neck, legs locked under me as it threw me side to side. The world was spinning and I knew I couldn't hold on much longer, so, eyes closed, I started to inch my way up the neck. It's a tree, just a big old tree, and I'm climbing it like I done a hundred times before, I told myself, not thinking about the teeth at the end of this particular tree, nor how the tree was swaying like a tornado had grabbed a-hold of it.

At least it had stopped breathing fire, too busy trying to buck me off. As I opened my eyes, I saw we was far too close to Callan for my comfort. I'd reached the top of the neck, and those teeth were like a cruel army of tin soldiers lined up to attack. And that eye, all purpley-red and angry—the one spot I knew for certain my knife could penetrate. My stomach lurched as the thing tossed its head, frantic now, as though it guessed my plan, but I gripped hard with my legs, locking my feet together under its chin, and plunged my knife into that staring eye, in and up into the monster's brain.

It screamed, a horrid piercing sound, and the snake-neck snapped back hard. I lost grip, went flying through the air, and landed, rocks smashing against ribs. I lay breathless, unable to move, hoping the thing was dead. All was quiet, save for the crackling of the fires. I'd killed the monster.

"Well done."

No. I'd killed one of the monsters.

I rolled over onto my back to see Delahaye pointing his big rifle at me. "Get up. Someone who'd do as you've done should die on his feet."

I felt like every bone in my body was bruised and battered, but I stood, because he was right—a man shouldn't die flat on his back, and I knew this time it was well and truly over. No more miracles. I didn't even have my knife—Gram had done its part to slay Fafnir and now would lay forever in the rotting body of the beast.

"Please. Will you tell me what this is all about?" Mam believed in heaven, in pie in the sky where you sit at God's right hand and watch the doings of the folk on earth. I didn't believe in none of that. This was all I'd ever have. And I wanted to know, not to die on this hilltop and not even know why.

"You want to know what it's all about? It's about the end of the world, boy. The end of the world." He aimed the rifle dead at my chest. "Though yours is ending earlier and with a bit more finality than most, I'm afraid."

I closed my eyes then, not wanting to see it coming, but instead of the sound of shot and the blossom of pain I expected, I heard a beloved voice, distorted with pain and exhaustion. "Not so early as yours."

I opened my eyes. Callan reached around Delahaye, moving faster than I'd have thought possible, slashing my knife across the side of his throat; blood spurted in a short arc as Delahaye turned. The rifle exploded, the bullet sliced the air to my right, and Delahaye staggered and fell. Callan dropped the knife, collapsed atop him, and lay motionless.

The next few minutes was a blur; it was as if the weariness that had gripped me was flung off like a blanket on an August night. I somehow managed to stomp out the fires, carry Callan to a sheltered spot near where Delahaye had left his pack, and get him covered with a warm blanket, for he was shivering something fierce, though the afternoon was turning almost unpleasantly warm. Shock, I guessed, remembering what Mam had taught me about healing. Losing blood made you cold.

And he'd lost a powerful lot of blood, it seemed. I didn't think skin on a living person could even be that pale, and now that I could look close at him, I saw that the mess on his upper arm was where a bullet had hit him, though the band that constricted the arm seemed to have stopped the bleeding. My healing knowledge ended at helping sheep give birth and treating small cuts and burns. For this, a trained healer was needed.

"Callan?" I held up his head and poured some water into his mouth. I took his left hand, squeezing gently. "I need you to tell me what to do. Please wake up, please!"

"David?" Eyes fluttered and opened this time, but they seemed odd, pupils unfixed, like he couldn't see clear. Then the pain must have hit him, and he had my hand in a death-grip. "Oh, God!"

"What can I do?" I remembered he'd had me give some drug to Taylor Mills that had stopped the pain of the lashes; surely it would work as well here. "What can I give you?"

"In my bag...back at the clearing..." Now sweat was breaking out on his face, and he was pushing the blanket away. Oh, dear God, I was helpless. It was worse than being hurt myself.

"Let me see if Delahaye has anything in his pack. Hang on, Callan, it'll be all right." That was what Mam had always said to us when we was sick or feverish, when we broke bones in falls or burned ourselves in the fire, and she'd always been right, but now I wondered how she'd known. Maybe she hadn't, and had just been making up gentle lies to comfort us, like I was doing now.

Delahaye's pack had water and food and some papers, blankets, and that fancy tent, but the only medicine was a small white bottle labeled 'aspirin' in crude handwriting. "Aspirin? Will that help?"

He'd pulled the blanket back around him and was shivering again. "Better than nothing—a bit like killing a dragon with a knife," he said, smiling weakly at me and taking the pills. "You did...well."

Not well enough. "You killed the real monster."

"No. The real monster's still out there. In Washington." He'd pulled himself together some. I didn't know how he managed it; how he'd pried that knife from where I'd left it and got himself across that hilltop to save me in this condition.

"You saved my life."

"And you saved mine." After I'd put it in jeopardy in the first place, but I didn't say that, just squeezed his hand again.

"Should I take that thing off your arm?"

"No. Leave it. Messing with a tourniquet is dangerous; Jeannie can do it if I make it back."

If. "No, not if. When." But the shadows was lengthening, and I didn't see Callan as getting strong enough to walk down that mountain, leastwise not without the drugs in his pack to dull the pain. And it was nearly two days' journey even at full strength. "We should get started, I guess. Can you walk?"

"Not yet. Give me twenty minutes or so to rest, get the aspirin working, assuming it'll do any good at all."

I covered him up with another blanket I found in the pack and pillowed his head with some of Delahaye's clothes. I'd take that pack down with us—his tent was better than oilcloth on rope, and it was a sight easier to manage than my own backpack, and would hold more, too, so Callan wouldn't have to carry nothing. I could take it all.

He'd dropped off into a fitful sleep, so I stood up and surveyed the clearing, or what had been a clearing. Now it was a boneyard, the two hulking dragon carcasses making it seem like the elephant's graveyard in the story my Grandmam used to tell about the young lion who become king. Common decency would have me bury Delahaye, who lay face down in the dirt midway between his two dragons, but he didn't deserve it, and I hadn't the energy to spare. Let all three monsters lie there and rot—I'd never come back to this mountain again.

I did pick up my knife and clean it, then walked around the dragon I'd killed, sort of learning it by heart, for with luck, I'd never see the like again. Even dead on the ground, it was a frightening thing, made even more fearsome by the thought that men had bred it and used it to terrorize and terrify whole towns full of people to do their bidding. Thinking of it like that, it was as much a tool as my knife, really. I bent down to touch the long snout, cold and still, and something glinting silver on its ear caught my eye.

The beast had tiny ears that hardly looked like they'd even work. It must have felt vibrations from the ground like a snake instead of hearing. But the green triangles, set back against the side of the head, was large enough to hold a small piece of metal, one I'd seen many times before on sheep and goats—it was an R&A tag. My proof. My knife had one more job to do, and it did it quickly, slicing through the cartilage of the ear, for the tag alone wouldn't prove nothing. I wrapped the severed ear in a shirt of Delahaye's and stowed it in the pack, then bent to try and wake Callan again.

He come awake at the lightest touch, and it was clear that the aspirin hadn't done much good. "We better go," I said, trying to keep my voice soft and soothing like Mam's. "Let me help you up."

He nodded, and I got him on his feet, slid the pack on my shoulders, and let him lean against me as we started down the trail. It was late in the afternoon; we had two good hours of daylight, maybe three if we was lucky. If we'd both been fit, it would have been enough to take us back to our campsite easily, but I was half-carrying

Callan already, and we'd only gone about thirty minutes when he slid to the ground, breathless.

"Can't walk anymore. Sorry."

"We can't stay here. It's too exposed, and it's going to turn cold." And he needed what was in his healer's bag. There wasn't nothing for it. I bent down and lifted him up in my arms, giving thanks that I outweighed him by a good bit.

"You can't...too far." But his eyes was closed and he wrapped his left arm around my neck for support.

"That's my worry." Now I wasn't wasting breath and energy on talk; nor on thought, beyond that of putting one foot in front of the other.

I won't say much about that journey down. The journey of that Dante fellow into hell couldn't have been worse than my trip down that mountain. My arms ached, muscles spasming out of control and my legs quickly became dead weight, almost refusing to do my will. We stopped a couple times, once when I had to bind Callan's right arm against his body to stop the jostling that was causing him so much pain, and a few times for water, and after each, starting back again was an act of sheer will. It was harder even than killing the dragon—that had been desperation, and had happened so fast that I hadn't time to think.

Here I had plenty of time to think, for talking was beyond us both. And my thoughts was dark and disturbing, full of my own betrayal and how it had led us to this, of the temptation—and oh, it was a mighty one when my arms numbed and icicles of pain was shooting through them—to put Callan down, to give it up. But I couldn't leave him there exposed on the mountain, and I wasn't ready to lay down and die with him, so it was one foot after the other, plodding and slow while the sun sunk lower and lower in the west until I was surrounded by dark with only the moon to guide me.

When we reached that clearing, my body was screaming in protest, and I was starving, for I hadn't eaten the entire day. I lay Callan down in a bed of pine straw, too tired even to get out a blanket to cover him, and half-crawled to where Delahaye had left our packs. I rummaged through Callan's, trying to recognize the drug he'd given Taylor Mills. Hoping I'd picked the right thing and wasn't about to poison him, I dosed him as you would an animal, forcing the medicine down a semi-conscious throat.

I found a round of cheese in Callan's pack and wolfed it down selfishly, hardly even tasting it, then put up Delahaye's tent and dragged Callan inside, bringing all the blankets along as I climbed in after. I hoped the tent was as good as Callan had said, for without a fire, we might die if the weather turned cold again. The blankets made a fine nest, and I curled up against Callan, utterly and completely exhausted.

"Thank you," he whispered. I hadn't known he was awake. He didn't owe me thanks. It was the least I could do, considering it had been all my fault in the first place, from beginning to end, but I kept quiet, and curled up tighter against his body. We was both trembling, from cold and exhaustion both.

"Hope I gave you the right drug. It was hard to see."

"Mmm. Yes, I think so. Lovely stuff, works like magic." He giggled lightly, and it seemed like he was drunk. "Completely wreaks havoc with your inhibitions, though. Kiss me."

My breath caught in my throat, and I propped myself up so I was looking down at him, then slowly bent and kissed him, just a gentle brush of lips against lips then I pulled away. "You rest, okay? We've got a long day ahead of us."

"You can't do that again, David. Carry me like you did, I mean. I know I'm not likely going to make it down the mountain; you'll have to leave me. Just stay with me now, okay?"

"I ain't going to leave you, I swear it."

His breathing was slowing, like a wind-up toy running down. "Best thing...ever happened to me was the day I met you."

Best thing? Because of me he'd been arrested and lashed and branded, had been shunned by half the town and then dragged up here on this horrid journey and shot, and now I was trying to use him for my own pleasure like he was a toy. I sat upright, disgusted beyond words with myself. This weren't how I was raised, to treat a friend in such a way, let alone one I claimed to love. I didn't even truly know what love was. Callan had fallen asleep, and I knew I couldn't stay there, couldn't trust myself not to hurt him further.

And he was right. I couldn't carry him no more, not all the way home—it would take days, and though I had the will, I hadn't the strength for it. I left the tent, shivering as the night air hit me. Callan had been right about the tent's warmth, like he was right about most things. But he couldn't help me now. I had to decide what to do, what was best—not just for me, but for him, and for the town, too, which needed to know what was happening as soon as possible.

I built a fire without thinking and sat before it, using the poor light to look at the papers in Delahaye's pack. I didn't understand much of them, but they made it clear that the R&A was involved in what was happening. The grown folk in town would know what to do with them, would understand them. If I could get down the mountain, that is. I had no chance carrying two plus the pack.

Oh, I knew what had to be done, but I didn't want to do it. I could go quick on my own, running mostly, flying down the mountain as I had as a child, when it was all a game. I could take what we'd found to the town and send back men with a stretcher who could make sure Callan got to Healer Findlay in time to save his life. He deserved at least that much from me. I'd done him so much wrong, after all. Surely I could manage one thing right. And then I could leave him alone, let him find some peace, as Pa had said, and as Callan himself had said he wanted when we met up on the road to Crawford.

I scrambled through Delahaye's pack, found a pencil, and scrawled a note to Callan, hoping he'd find it the next day, then set the remaining food and most of the water along with the bottle of pills within his reach.

I could see him in the firelight, sleeping more peaceful under drugs than he had the times I'd seen him sleep natural. All the troubles and pain was gone, and I understood then why some men turned to whiskey to forget. I stroked the matted hair, whispering, "I love you," then kissed his forehead, tasting the salt there. It was a kiss goodbye, and though I knew he would not remember, I would.

Chapter 23

What had taken us ten hours to travel on the journey up and would have taken me three days or more if I'd had to carry Callan, I managed in about five hours. I still don't know how I done it without breaking both my legs, for I flew down that mountain at breakneck speed, falling head over heels more than once, but always picking myself up and moving on, keeping a slower pace before dawn, then picking it up as the sun rose. It was looking to be a second dry day, and I was powerful glad for that.

I had to force my thoughts away from Callan waking alone in that tent, had to hope he'd find my note and be well enough to read it, so he'd know that I hadn't truly abandoned him. As I had when I was carrying Callan, I forced my thoughts on my feet and my task, and finally, going on noon, I stumbled down the last of the road to the General, where we'd left from two days before.

Ben, Joe Haig's man, was in front of the shop setting out barrels of something, so he saw me first. "David?"

I couldn't catch my breath enough to even gasp out his name, but sank forward onto the steps of the store, not even able to ease the pack from my back.

"Mister Haig, come quick! It's David Anderson, and he's covered in blood!"

A blanket was laid round my shoulders, though it weren't cold at all, and then Healer Findlay, hair all frizzled round her face like she'd been asleep, was peering down at me. "David? Are you injured?"

I shook my head, trying to clear my mind. "No, ma'am. Blood's not mine. It's Callan's. Mister Delahaye shot him, and I thought he was dead, but he ain't and then we started to come home till he couldn't walk no more and I had to leave him there in the Before tent." I knew I must have sounded crazy. "You got to go back for him!"

Healer Findlay straightened up, taming her hair into a bun. "Joe, get me five men and six horses, and fetch the litter I've got in my storage shed."

Joe Haig just stood there staring. "You say Mister Delahaye shot him? By accident? Did the gun misfire?"

"No sir. I'll tell you the whole of it, I promise, I'll tell everybody, but please, just go save Callan, he's hurt bad and I had to leave him all alone."

Mister Haig went off quick to do Healer Findlay's bidding as she helped me up, my leg muscles screaming in protest, and led me over to a chair on the porch. "Are you sure you're not hurt? Do you want to lie down?"

"No, ma'am. I'm just tired. Carried Callan from the summit for about four hours yesterday, then run the rest of the way today. I'll be all right."

She stared at me. "You...carried...David, you're remarkable, you know that, don't you?"

Remarkable. Not the word I'd have used considering the results of my bad choices over the past months, but I flushed at the praise anyways. "It weren't so bad, except that Delahaye's pack kept slipping and..." I remembered what was in the pack. "The pack!" I'd left it back on the steps, and it was all the proof we had.

She fetched it, and I held it tight. "There's so much I got to tell you—the R&A set the dragons on us, Delahaye tried to kill us both, but Callan saved me, and—"

I stopped short. The mayor, with Mister Hennessy at his side, was bustling down the street along with Sheriff Fletcher. The word had spread; folks was congregating around the General, and all eyes was on me.

"I wish I could stay with you till your father gets here." I wished she could, too. I was more afraid of telling my tale to the whole town with Mister Hennessy standing there listening than I'd been of the dragons.

"I'll stay with David, Jeannie. You go on and bring your assistant home." Relief flooded over me—it was Mister Zack Tyree. If I couldn't have Pa with me, then he was the next best one. Nobody'd cross Mister Zack, nor try to make me do anything I didn't want to do when I was under his protection.

"Much obliged to you, Zack." Then she bent close to my head, so nobody else could hear. "I don't know what all this is about, but if you want to see Callan when I get him home, you just come round the back and I'll see to it."

I nodded, but I knew I wouldn't. Maybe in time, for Mam said that time healed all wounds, but not yet.

I clutched the pack in front of me like a shield as the mayor climbed up onto the porch. "What's this nonsense I hear about Mister Delahaye trying to kill you?"

Taking a deep breath, I looked Mayor Casteel straight in the eye and saw for the first time how weak he was. "Yes sir. The Reintroduction and Agriculture Department is behind the dragons. And I can prove it."

I dug in the pack and took out the severed ear with its silver tag and handed it up to Mister Zack, who examined it and nodded.

"It's an R&A ident tag, sure enough." He held it up so the crowd could get a look.

"That proves nothing! The boy probably got it off a sheep or goat, put it on that ear after Delahaye killed the dragon."

Someone from the crowd spoke up. "Mayor, you know we can't take those tags off and on. Takes a special tool."

"Then it's counterfeit! Made up to look like an R&A tag." But he was sweating harder, and looking to Mister Hennessy to back him up.

Smooth as ice, that man was. "Well, Mister Mayor, the fact of the matter is that the dragons were bred by the R&A, in an experiment gone wrong." Before the mutterings could spread, he continued. "That's why we sent one of our own to exterminate them, which he has apparently done with great success." Then he turned to look at me. "And where is Agent Delahaye, young man?"

I stared right back at him, all my fear vanishing like fog when the sun come out. Funny how killing a dragon and facing the worst fears of your life makes little men like Hennessy a lot less scary. "He's dead, up on the mountain. I cut his throat because he tried to kill us to keep us from talking." That was a lie, but Callan weren't in any position to face questioning. And I would have killed him; I'd certainly held murder in my heart.

Now the murmur became a roar, and the mayor was leading the pack. "Sheriff, I want him arrested for murder!"

"I got papers, too, papers that prove what I'm saying."

Mayor Casteel and Mister Hennessy exchanged glances. "I think I should take custody of those papers, young man." The mayor stepped forward.

"I'm giving them over to my Pa. Not nobody else." Even Mister Zack, I couldn't be completely sure of. But Pa, him I could trust with my life.

Mister Hennessy reached out to take the pack from me. "Don't be ridiculous. Those papers should be turned over to the proper authorities, and that is His Honor, the Mayor, not some hayseed farmer."

Mister Zack was in front of me so quick I didn't even see him move. "If David says he wants to wait for his father, then we'll wait. I don't reckon it will be very long."

The mayor was losing control and he knew it. "Sheriff, I told you to arrest that boy, now goddamn it, arrest him, and confiscate anything he's got. Now!"

Sheriff Fletcher just folded his arms on his chest. "I 'spect we can wait for Brock. David isn't going nowhere."

Mayor Casteel scanned the crowd. "Fine. You won't do your sworn duty, I'm deputizing Elmer. Get up here, boy, and take that pack!"

Elmer pushed through the crowd, spoiling for a fight as always. I'd never been scared of him, but now, after Delahaye, after the dragons, he was less than nothing.

"Elmer, you lay a finger on me, and I swear it'll be the last thing you ever do." I didn't shout nor even make my voice sound threatening, but something in the way I spoke must have shook him, for he backed off, waiting. "We're waiting for my Pa. When he gets here, I'll give him the papers, and he can give them to you, Mayor, or to you, Sheriff, or to whoever he thinks should have them. But till then, they're staying right here with me."

I sat back down then, and out of the corner of my eye I saw the party of horses heading up the north road. They'd bring Callan home and he could get on with his life. I hoped Callan didn't do anything foolish like confess—feeling against him in the town had been pretty high before we left. He wouldn't likely be treated as I would.

Mister Zack had been right—it didn't take Pa long to get to town. He must have set off soon as he heard I was back, and he was on Lightning, who for once seemed to be living up to her name. The crowd parted for him like the Red Sea for old Moses in the scriptures and I stood up to meet him. "Pa," I started to explain, but he grabbed hold of me and crushed me into a hug, the first time such a thing had happened since I was very small.

"Oh God, David, I thought we'd lost you for sure," he whispered in my ear. Being so close, I realized how small he'd got, or was it how big I was now?

I pulled away and rummaged in the pack. "Pa, these papers prove the R&A brung the dragons here to try and drive us off our land."

Now things moved quick, and moved out of my hands as well, with Pa skimming through the papers, then sharing them with Mister Zack and Sheriff Fletcher while the Mayor stood and sweated. I was so tired, deep-down bone weary, it was beyond me to follow any of it then, so I just leaned against the porch rail while the fate of the town swirled around me. I was about to sink down onto the porch, not caring how it looked, only caring about sleep, when I saw from the corner of my eye that Hennessy was edging away. Pa was deep in talk with the sheriff, and Mister Zack was nowhere to be seen, but I saw Mister Curtis Henslow, who'd took Callan's side at the Grand Jury, standing at the bottom of the stairs.

"Mister Henslow, sir, it looks like Mister Hennessy is making a run for it," I said.

Almost as one, the crowd turned and looked at him, and I was taken back to a talk I'd had with Callan once, about the burning of the libraries and what mobs was capable of. I wouldn't have wanted to be in Mister Hennessy's shoes then.

Sheriff Fletcher took him by the arm. "Mister Hennessy, sir, I'm going to have Aaron take you back to your house and watch out for you till we get this all sorted out." I could tell Mister Hennessy didn't like that much, but he looked at the ring of men around him and then at Mayor Casteel, who surely wouldn't have been any help at all if it came to a fight, and let himself be led away.

The buzz of voices started up again then, and the world sort of seemed to fade, with a ringing in my ears that grew louder and louder till it was a roar, like how I imagined waves on an ocean must be. I would have liked to have gone to an ocean some day. With Callan. I closed my eyes, thinking of what it would be like, on a beach from a picture, walking beside him under a sun that truly warmed. I could almost feel it—

"David?" I jerked my head up and realized I'd been sleeping on my feet.

"Sorry, Pa."

Pa took hold of my arm. "I'm taking my boy up home. His Mam will want to see him, and he's been through enough."

I'd done what I could. Callan was in good hands, and I couldn't fight it anymore; I let myself be mostly dragged up into Lightning's saddle. Pa took the reins to lead us away. "Sheriff, I'll leave the papers David brung in your hands."

"I really think that I would be the more logical..." Mayor Casteel's voice dropped off as he heard the mutinous rumblings of the men surrounding him.

"I'll take them out to Nate Clemmons' place, Brock, if that's acceptable to you. He's better fit to make sense of it all than I am. I expect we'll need another meeting, and we might need to question David some."

Pa started to answer, but I spoke over him. I wasn't a child to be spoke for, not even when I was so tired my bones felt like they was about to melt into pudding. "That'd be fine, Sheriff. Just send word, and I'll be at your service."

Pa gave me a look, but didn't say nothing, just tugged on Lightning's reins, leading me away.

I think I slept for a night and a day and another night, and would have slept into the following day, if not for the fierce hunger that woke me. I dreamed, I think, but have no recollection of the meat of the dreams, just flashing images of Callan and the dragon, a sense of being tossed off the neck of the beast into Callan's arms. Some of the dreams was real personal, and I hoped I didn't cry out in my sleep, but couldn't be bothered to care too much. Let them all know how I felt about Callan—it was over now anyway.

Mam made me stay in bed for the morning and fed me up good with bacon and eggs and hotcakes, and the girls planted themselves one on either side of my bed like they was afraid I'd vanish again, and even Benny C stayed close.

"Pa's gone down to town again," he explained. "He been down there yesterday and today, left me to do all the chores...not that I mind," he said, sort of shy. "Did you really kill a dragon with your knife?"

"Yes." I thought about what else that knife had done. I should have left it on the mountain top, for now every time I used it or saw it, I'd remember it stained with Delahaye's blood. "But I don't want to talk about it now, okay?"

"Grandmam's not left her bed since you left. She ain't eating neither."

That didn't sound good. I dislodged Delia from my right side. "I need to get up. You girls clear on out of here."

They scampered down the ladder, and Benny C was moving to follow when he stopped. "David, I heard something else. I heard you killed a man. That true?"

I nodded, thinking Callan must not have given lie to my words. "Don't want to talk about that, neither." Then it occurred to me that Pa and Mam wouldn't have told Benny C such a thing. "Who'd you hear that from?"

"Down at school—there's been a powerful lot of gossip about all this. You wouldn't believe it." He moved past the little dormer window, and I saw that he had a big old shiner on his left eye.

"You been fighting?"

He colored red. "Mam already wore me out for it. But there's a couple boys on the yard saying you was a liar and...other stuff, so I had to fight them."

I could imagine what the 'other stuff' must have been. "Thank you, Benny C. I ain't always been the best brother to you, but you surely have to me. Listen, did any of the talk in the schoolyard happen to say whether they got Callan back safe?"

"Yeah. I heard they brung him home early morning, alive, but hurt. Don't know anything more than that." He looked down to his feet. "I could take a message if you want."

"No. I just wanted to know he was okay." Benny C went on down the stairs. Callan was all right. Hurt, but alive, and Healer Findlay would heal him up just fine. He'd be able to get shut of this town, away from all the pain he'd had here, most of which had come from me. But the thought of him leaving without me twisted like a knife in my gut, and it was all I could do to keep from calling after Benny C and changing my mind.

Grandmam was asleep when I come downstairs, so I set beside her for a good long while, just stroking her hand, the skin so dry and papery you could almost see through to her bones. She was shrunken and sunk in on herself, hardly looking at all like a living person. If I hadn't seen the rise and fall of her chest and felt the warmth in her tiny hand, I'd have thought her dead already.

Mam came in behind me and rested her hand on my shoulder. "It won't be long now, David. I'm glad you're back, that you came back before...before the end. She wanted to see you—I think it's part of what's kept her going."

"Where's Pa?" I felt odd, like I'd lost several days—which I had, when I came to think on it—and I was running to catch up.

"Down in town again. They've been over those papers six ways to Sunday, trying to make sense of it all. You surely stirred up a hornet's nest, son."

"It weren't my fault!" Grandmam moved restlessly in her sleep as my voice rose, so I dropped to a whisper. "All I done was brung them home; it was Delahaye and the R&A that wrote them. Would you have rather have kept on in ignorance?"

"No, of course not," she said, but in her eyes I seen the true answer of her heart. Not for me. I couldn't live in a make-believe world.

Mam went back to the kitchen and I kept on stroking Grandmam's hand, talking soft to her, just nonsense really, about memories of times we'd had. I'd been talking for about ten minutes or so when I felt her hand squeeze mine.

"Grandmam?"

Her eyes opened and she smiled. "David. I knew you'd come home. Did you do it, boy? Did you slay Fafnir and take his hoard?"

I remembered the things in that cave, things I hadn't told to Pa nor any of the men in town. I supposed those machines would be Fafnir's hoard, though I couldn't see that they was worth much. Real gold would have been better. "I killed the dragon, Grandmam."

"With my Patrick's gun." She smiled again, and I hadn't the heart to tell her what had really happened, so I just squeezed her hand.

"You rest, Grandmam, rest and get strong again. I'll tell you all about it when you're better."

Her breathing was all raspy, like a saw going through rough wood. "I was waiting for you, David. Now you're here, I'm just fine."

"That's good. You just wait, we'll be sitting out on the porch shelling peas together again in no time." Long lazy afternoons when the wind dropped enough to let the sun warm us up, she in her rocker and me on the wooden boards of the porch—that was summer to me.

"Not this year, lovey. To everything, there's a season, and my season for pea-shelling is over and done."

"No, Grandmam, don't talk that way." My voice sounded all gruff, like I had something caught down my throat.

"Don't you be silly, boy. It's my time, and I'm glad of it. Now go look in that box the gun came in."

The decorated box was still sitting on her dressing table where I'd left it, empty now. "There ain't...isn't anything here."

"Rip up the lining." When I hesitated, she tried to sit up. "I'll do it myself, then."

"No. Lay down and rest." I ripped up the red velvet lining, and underneath, just slightly smaller than the box itself, was another box. I picked it up, remembering then that the first time I picked up the chest I'd thought it heavy for its size.

"Open it." She was waiting, watching me, and I lifted the lid to see the dull glint of gold. Coins, lots of them—a pirate's treasure trove. And not just dollars, but five dollar pieces, and ten and twenty, and coins I didn't even recognize.

"Grandmam—"

"Hush. They're for you. For you and your young man, so you can make a good start in a better place than this. I started saving when I was first married, been collecting it ever since from odds and ends here and there. It's yours."

"I can't take this." I didn't care if it was unmanly—tears was spilling out of my eyes and I made no move to stop them. "It's too much."

"You take it, David, or I'll come back and haunt you, you hear me?" She smiled, though, a sort of weak smile, like she knew she'd won and I'd do her will. "You be happy. That's all I want."

Happy. She intended it for Callan and me together, but with this, I could pay Callan's debt to Healer Findlay, take care of his bond so he could go free from Moline, and maybe find some happiness for himself. "Thank you, Grandmam. I love you so much." I kissed her forehead, tears splashing down on her hot, dry skin.

"Go on with you, David. Send your mother in—I need to make peace with her. She's been a good daughter to me. And a good mother to you—better than either of us deserved, I expect."

I took the box and walked out of that room, knowing I'd never see her alive again.

Chapter 24

Grandmam died that night, quiet, in her sleep. We buried her near Almond with mostly just family present at the gravesite. Reverend Daniels didn't come to speak words over her, because he was in the midst of packing up and leaving town. A good third to half the townfolk was fixing to leave. Mayor Casteel, who'd pleaded ignorance (a claim that Mister Zack said was the most believable thing he'd ever heard from the mayor's mouth), was urging everybody to pick up and go, head for Richmond to meet with our Assemblyman and from there to parts unknown, presumably wherever they'd resettled Crawford.

The Reverend, who wasn't so concerned about all the politics of it, said it was clear that God was abandoning Moline, which again prompted Mister Zack to quip that the only persons abandoning Moline at that time was Mayor Casteel and Master Burke, neither of whom were particularly God-like. Mister Zack was like that sometimes, full of dry humor. And we needed all the humor we could lay hands on.

So like I said, we buried Grandmam and I planted some seeds from a shriveled old apple on her grave, hoping it would grow into a fine shade tree some day that we would be around to see, and then we went back up the mountain and life went on. It didn't matter that folk was leaving, or that my heart was breaking in two with every breath as I was missing Callan so much, the crops still had to be tended and the stock managed, and schooling for Benny C and the girls went on like normal, though once Master Burke left, school was called till they found a new Master.

I went down into town twice in those first two weeks, both times to speak to the sheriff, or the mayor before he left, and other important townsfolk. Mister Hennessy was still being held in his home, and wasn't being allowed to leave with the others, and that was mostly Pa's doing—he wanted somebody on hand to answer for the R&A's crimes. I supposed they was questioning Callan as well as me, but I never saw him, which was a mercy, for my resolve wouldn't have survived being in his presence—it was hard enough just keeping my dreams under control.

After a while things settled down, normal life going on like it always did, even after a loss. I'd learned that when Almond died, though now it was a double loss, with Grandmam dead and Callan as good as dead to me. I hungered for word of him, though where before I'd found cause to go into town to see him, now I shrunk from it, even when Mam had need of errands run or Pa would be going anyways, I stayed home just for fear of what I'd do should I truly be confronted with Callan in the General or on the street.

Then one morning, about a month after we'd come back from the mountain, Healer Findlay came to the house.

I'd seen her since my return: once when I'd been questioned, and at Grandmam's burying, but both of those times she'd hung back and not spoke to me at all. I'd thought nothing of it, figuring she was busy, or didn't want to intrude on family grief in the case of the funeral, but this time it was pretty clear to me that she wanted nothing more to do with me than she had to, giving me only a nod in greeting before speaking warmly to Mam, then asking Benny C to take her up to the tanning shed to speak to Pa.

The last words she'd spoke to me had been warm enough, so I could only think that Callan was angry with me for not coming down to see him and had let it slip to Healer Findlay. It weighed on my heart that he was angry, but I knew he'd move past it in time. I had to keep to my resolve, and in truth, I would have been embarrassed to face him after all this time. I'd said once that he deserved better than Taylor Mills. Well, he deserved better than me, too.

But because I just had to know, I hung about the barn making work for myself, waiting for Healer Findlay to come down. It was about an hour later when she come striding down the path with a troubled look on her face. She went straight by me as if I weren't even there and started to untie her horse.

"Healer Findlay?"

"Yes, David?" She didn't even look up from messing with the reins.

"Can I ask you something?"

"I'm in a bit of a hurry." She started to lead the horse out of the shelter of our barn.

"It won't take long, ma'am." I followed her out, wishing she'd look at me, just once. "I was wondering if you could tell me...I wanted to know how Callan's doing."

She rounded on me with such fury in her eyes that I instantly regretted wishing she'd look at me. I'd known the healer my entire life, and hadn't never seen her look at anybody, not anybody, as she looked at me then. "If you really cared at all, David Anderson, you'd have come down to see for yourself!"

"I can't, just can't. I..." I didn't know how to make her see without giving the private details of our lives. "Please. Just tell me if he's okay."

She softened a bit, relaxing against her horse. "He's doing as well as can be expected. Honestly, David, what on earth has possessed you to abandon him like this now when he needs you most?"

When he needs you most. That didn't sound good. "What are you talking about? He's all right, isn't he?"

She looped the reins around a post and took me by the arm, led me off to one of the barn benches. "Are you telling me that you don't know anything? I find that fairly hard to believe, as it's not exactly been a secret. Your father certainly has known."

Tell me! I wanted to scream, but I kept calm. "He's said nothing to me of Callan at all. Last I heard was from Benny C who said he'd been brought home alive. I know it looks bad, me staying away, but I truly thought it was for the best—I ain't good for him at all. Won't you please tell me what's happened?"

"The tourniquet that man put on was tighter than it had to be and on longer than it should have been. And the bullet was nasty, one of the exploding type that I didn't even think they made anymore. It shattered the bone beyond my ability to repair." She was staring down at her hands, as though angry at them for failing her. I surely understood that.

"So he's got to be sent to Richmond, then? They've still got proper hospitals there, don't they?"

Healer Findlay took my hand and squeezed it. "No, David. There's nothing that can be done to save his arm."

It hit me like a blow. Oh dear God. I stood up quick, turning away so she wouldn't see what her news done to me. "You mean..." I couldn't say it. To say it would be to make it real.

"It's his arm or his life, David. And right now, he's choosing to lose his life." She stood, too, grabbed me by the shoulder, and whirled me round. "And that's your fault!" Her grip was strong, digging into my shoulders—healer's hands, strong hands. Like Callan's. My stomach roiled. "He won't speak of it to me, won't even mention your name, but I can tell how your betrayal," she spat the word, "how it's eating at him, rotting him from the inside the way the gangrene is destroying his arm."

"I never meant..." I pulled away and went back to the bench, my head in my hands. Even in trying to do right, I'd done wrong. There just wasn't any end to this nightmare.

"I think you'd better tell me what it is that's kept you away. I thought you were friends; was worried, in fact, that you were closer friends than most in this town would be willing to accept."

"We were." And I knew I had to tell her, so it all spilled out in a big ugly rush, how I'd run like a coward on that mountain and how it was my fault Delahaye had shot Callan, how if he lost his arm, oh God, it was my fault, all my fault, and didn't she see that I couldn't face him, that he was better off with me out of his life?

"No, I can't see that at all," she said when I'd finished, barely holding the tears back as I told it all for the first time. "He told you to run. He chose to make the greatest sacrifice one person can make for another, and he chose to make it for you. I don't have much use for what my daddy used to call 'disorganized' religion, but sometimes the Scripture gets it right. 'Greater love hath no man than this; that he lay down his life for his friend.' You did as he wanted. There's nothing to be ashamed of in that."

"I guess; but I don't deserve that, not at all."

"Nobody deserves the love they get, David." She put her arm around me. "Not one of us. But Callan deserves to live, and he won't do that if he thinks you don't care."

I nodded. I had to see him. It was simple as that, and yet more complicated than I could fathom. And something else was nagging at my mind. My Pa had known; he'd known that Callan was bad hurt, he surely knew what he'd meant to me, and he'd said nothing. Anger was beginning to burn like fire deep inside me. "I'll come today. I've got something needs doing here first, and then I'll come straight away."

She stood up again, taking hold of the horse's reins. "You'd better. I'm not exaggerating when I say if the surgery's not done in the next day or so, it will be too late."

I watched her ride down the trail, then set my shoulders straight and walked up the dirt path to the tanning shed. Pa was sitting outside on a workbench, scraping the hide of some animal one of us had taken in the trap. He looked up when I come near, and something in my eyes must have told him this wasn't to be an easy talk, for he put his knife down and waited.

"Why didn't you tell me?"

"I'm guessing Jeannie told you about Callan Landers, then."

"I shouldn't have had to hear it from her, Pa. You knew. And you knew Callan was my friend. I had a right to know too."

He picked up the knife and started in scraping again. "I didn't figure there was anything to be gained from telling you, son. You ain't a healer or nothing that could make a difference."

"I'm his friend. I could have been beside him."

"No, you couldn't have. By law, he's to keep away from you, and it's high time that was properly enforced. We've been far too—"

"No!" My fists was clenched, and I swear I'd have hit him without a second thought. "That law's wrong! Let me tell you how it's going to be, Pa. I'm going to town to see Callan. And you're coming along to go to Sheriff Fletcher or whoever you need to see to get that goddamn probation lifted so that Callan can have his life back again, and I can see him when I want." That was if he even had a life to have back, but I wasn't going to think on that. "We've sacrificed enough."

The knife was down again, clattering dully to the ground. "David—"

"No. I've had enough of it. I love him, Pa." The words hung in the air between us, and I waited for him to speak, but he just kept quiet. "It ain't Callan's fault, ain't nothing he done to me—it ain't nothing except me being who I am, who I've always been. Always will be."

"The law—"

"The same law that set dragons on us, killed Almond, and tried to run us off our homes? Those folk in Richmond and in Washington, they're no better at knowing what's right than I am. Pa, you taught me to think for myself, to be a man and do what's right by my own lights, and I've tried my best to do that all through this thing. It ain't always worked out the way I planned it, but I wouldn't take back one minute of the time I've had with Callan."

"I don't approve, son." He sounded more sorry than angry, but I wasn't going to soften.

"I'm right sorry for that, but I'm not a child. I've earned the right to make my own choices. Now you going to see to that probation? They're only concerned with him being near me because you are."

"What if I say no?"

"Then when Callan is well, I'll take him away from here, and none of you'll see me again. This is my home, and I love you and Mam and the rest, but my life and future's with Callan, no matter what the cost of that."

I turned and left him then, hoping he'd follow me, but even if he didn't, I had to go, for Callan and for me, too. And I'd not got beyond the first turn in the road when I heard the sound of footsteps behind me, so I slowed and Pa sped up, and we was walking side by side, two men together, going to town.

We didn't speak at all on the walk down, and he turned off at the sheriff's office just as I'd hoped, while I kept on till I got to the Healer's house. Healer Findlay come to the door in answer to my knock, and she nodded and smiled when she saw me. "I hoped you'd come. Come on in."

I started up the stairs towards the tiny bedroom Callan had shown me a lifetime ago.

"No, David. I've had my own bed brought down into the parlor—it's the warmest room in the house, and he's so cold these days."

"He's always cold. The weather here don't suit him." I stood outside the parlor door, hand on the knob, like balancing on the edge of a great cliff, afraid to take the step that would send me plummeting over it for good.

Healer Findlay gave me a push. "Go on with you. I'll be in the office, if you have need of me."

The parlor was where we'd sat drinking hot cocoa and talking of Huckleberry Finn. But now the center of the room was taken up by a big double bed, and Callan lay in it, sleeping with a heavy quilt drawn up over him. There was a smell in the room I knew—I'd smelled it that morning at the tanning shed: the stench of death and rot.

I let go of the door and it swung shut with a slight click, loud enough in the silence to sound like a gunshot. Callan come awake immediately, turned towards the sound, and saw me standing there. He looked bad—there weren't no other word for it; just like you'd expect a man to look who had spent a month in bed, dying slowly. His face gave away nothing of what he thought on seeing me there.

"David," he said, his voice all wonderment and surprise.

"I..." It was as if we was strangers, and I didn't know what to say. What could I say, when I'd brung all this on him? Then in a rush, just like with Healer Findlay earlier, it all come out. "I'm so sorry, Callan, I'm sorry! It should have been me. I should have fought him, not you! I should have stayed, should have fought him for you. I shouldn't have left you!"

One handed, he pushed himself up and patted the left side of the bed. "I promise, David. The very next crazed government agent who tries to kill us, you get to fight." He gave a weak sort of smile, and I flew across the room, burying myself into his shoulder like a child.

"I left you." My words was muffled by his good shoulder. I couldn't bring myself to look on the other one, not yet. "How can you even stand to be near me after the shameful way I acted?"

"Oh, David." I felt his hand in my hair, so wonderful, how could I have thought of giving this up for all time? "I told you to go. I meant it."

"But Healer Findlay says...she says you're going to have to...that she's got to..." I didn't dare say it. Saying it would make it real. "And that's my fault. I don't expect you can understand, but I can't forgive myself, I just can't."

I felt him exhale, and we just rested together quiet for a while.

"My father was a doctor." He must have sensed my confusion. "Just listen, you'll see where I'm going. A real doctor, not a medic or a healer or even a nurse, trained at one of the last real medical schools left from Before. He was much older than my mother, and they loved each other very much. He died when I was quite young, and I don't remember him at all."

"But I grew up knowing what he was, how respected he was, and I wanted to be like him. More than I wanted anything in the entire world. I learned to read so I could study his textbooks, used to have Gray's Anatomy as my bedtime reading. My mother worked in the medical library at a hospital, used to bring home books for me to study, and by the time I was twenty and through college, I'd probably read them all." His voice sounded sort of stale and harsh, like he hadn't used it much recently, or like he'd been screaming a lot. I didn't want to think of that.

"There are still proper medical schools, though they're not what they once were. One in California, one in Louisiana, and the most prestigious of all, in Washington, DC. I expect it was at least partly my father's name and reputation that did it, though I certainly had a good academic record, but for whatever the reason, I was accepted to the DC school, and the day that letter came was the best day of my life. Until I met you." His fingers played gently in my hair. "Mother had been given permission to come with me, as of course you need permission to live in Washington, and she was going to find work and keep house for me while I studied, and then we'd come back home to Florida and I'd be the doctor I'd always dreamed of being, or at least as close to it as I could get. So we sold most everything we had, save for our clothes and our books, bought an old wagon and a horse, and started north."

His arm tightened around me. "I don't know exactly where we were—somewhere north of Atlanta, I think—and I remember it was the first time I'd really felt cold, though it was June, and you would have probably thought of it as a hot summer night. We'd camped near a stream between two large stands of trees, had built a fire, fixed some dinner, and were just about to bed down for the night when we heard them. There were five of them, men, all drunk and looking for a good time, I guess. Mother and I tried to dampen the fire so they wouldn't know we were there, but it was burning too well and they were getting closer, so Mother had me take the horse to the furthest stand of trees while she hid in the nearer."

Oh, this story wasn't going to end well, I just knew it. "Well, they ransacked the wagon, looking for valuables. Found most of our money, some jewelry of Mother's, our food. Then they decided the fire wasn't quite big enough to suit them, and they started throwing the books on. Those books were all I had left of my father. The only connection between the man I wanted to be and the boy I was, and I was such a boy then, so stupid. You wouldn't think it, would you, that I could be so stupid?"

I shook my head, not wanting to say anything that might stop him. "I started shouting at them to stop it, to leave our things alone. Well, you can imagine how that went over. They stood there ringing the fire like wild animals with me as their prey. I should be dead."

"She saved you, didn't she?"

"Yes. She ran out of the trees without a second thought, screaming at me to run, and oh, David, I ran. I didn't hesitate, just ran for the trees and the river and safety, figuring they'd follow for sure and that we were both dead. But they didn't follow. Men like that, a pretty young woman—and she was young, in her mid-forties, and looked much younger—I expect you can guess what happened next."

I didn't want to hear it, wanted to stopper my ears with my hands, but Callan had lived it, so the least I could do was hear it.

"I heard her screaming—horrid, piercing screams, with the men's voices laughing, they were laughing as they...and then the screams died away to these awful gurgling moans, and I forced myself to go back. She'd...they'd..."

"I know. You don't have to say." The fire; I remembered how he'd blanched at the body of the tiny girl in Crawford. "Try not to think about it. You did what she wanted." As I had done with him.

"I couldn't even bury her. I hadn't tools for it. I did the best I could to leave her in some dignity, then started north, remembering that she had a brother in Charlottesville, like I've told you, and I was ashamed to go home, after what I'd done. It's been almost two years, but I hear her screaming, I see what they left of her every night in my dreams. Every night save the ones I've spent with you."

"You were young, it weren't your fault."

"I was nearly twenty-two. Not a child, and certainly old enough to know better. And I hadn't been able to forgive myself, could not face that she'd done what she did out of love for me, and that for her, it was the right thing to do. Not until that moment on the mountain when I saw the log on the ground and knew I could get you away safely. It was like a light came on and I understood my mother, finally knew what love was really all about. So please, David, please believe me that I do understand how you feel, but I'd do it all again in a heartbeat, even knowing the cost."

The cost. I sat up and pulled back the quilt, and he didn't stop me, just lay quiet with his eyes closed while I looked on what Delahaye had left of his arm. "You're going to let Healer Findlay do what she has to do." It weren't a question.

"Yes," he whispered. "Now that you're here."

"Good." I kissed his forehead and his lips, then bent and kissed the fingers of his right hand, all black and swollen. "Does it hurt?"

"Yes. Though the drug you gave me up on the mountain helps; Jeannie gave me some about an hour before you came."

"That's good. But it ain't going to get better, that's what she tells me."

Even wasted and pale, he was so beautiful I could hardly breathe.

"She's right."

"Then let's have it done."

Chapter 25

Healer Findlay was waiting for me in her examination room, turning pages in a big old book one after the other. I tried not to look at the stark white sheets over the examining table, nor the wicked collection of knives and saws she had laid out in neat rows beside it, but of course I couldn't keep my eyes away.

"He's ready," I said, and she nodded.

"I thought so. You go on back and stay with him. I have a few things to see to first."

So I sat beside Callan, stroking his arm, touching his hair, calming him like I would an injured creature. It seemed that Healer Findlay must have had a good bit to arrange, for the minutes stretched on and the shadows lengthened across the room and still she didn't come. Callan's drugs must have started wearing off, for he commenced in to twitching some, and his eyes, which had been unfocused and relaxed, grew tighter, staring off to some point on the wall.

"You okay?"

His breathing was light, shallow panting. "No. Not really."

I cast about for something to say that wouldn't be a reminder of what was coming. His hand gripped mine hard enough to make me wince. "Callan, you're hurting. Can I get you something?"

He shook his head. "Not time yet. That drug's addictive. The last thing I need on top of everything else is an expensive drug habit." He laughed harshly. "Jeannie's spent a small fortune on me; I'll owe her for the rest of my life."

I thought of the money Grandmam had given me. Perhaps that could go to paying Healer Findlay back, though I suspected she wouldn't take pay. "Don't you worry about that none, love." The pet name seemed odd on my tongue, but hearing it seemed to lighten Callan a bit. "My Grandmam, she gave me money before she died, and it's for us, enough to pay for whatever you'd need, or for us to leave here, make a new start somewhere else if that's what you want."

"Jeannie told me...I'm sorry about your grandmother." The words were more halting gasps than anything. "Didn't know her well, but she seemed a remarkable woman."

"I miss her." And I surely did; every day I looked to her familiar seat by the fire and wondered where she was. "She wanted us to be happy, knew we belonged together, I guess." That made me remember something. "Callan, if it's okay with you, I'd like to wear that ring again. I told my Pa everything; ain't no reason to hide no more."

"In the trunk, bottom left corner, wrapped up." There was a smallish trunk standing at the foot of the bed. I took out the ring, marveling again at its weight and beauty. I was about to slide it back on my finger when his good hand caught hold of my wrist.

"Don't feel...obligated. Things have changed since you made those promises. I won't hold you to them."

I slid the ring home. "Don't be silly. You think this," I said, stroking his ruined arm, "changes anything?" But I remembered Callan's hands on me, touching and teasing and pleasuring. I saw his hands working like lightning, trying to save Almond. It changed nothing. And everything. "Mister Zack Tyree's got one arm, and you couldn't ever tell it from knowing him—it'll be the same with you. You'll see."

The door opened, and Healer Findlay come in, followed by Joe Haig and Ben from the General, and my Pa.

Boldly keeping hold of Callan's hand, I stood up. What was Pa doing here? Surely he weren't about to make trouble now of all times?

"Callan," Healer Findlay's voice was soft, soothing. "I'm so glad you're going to let me go ahead with this. But you know I've been concerned about my ability to do the surgery properly—my muscles aren't what they used to be."

He nodded, and all remaining traces of color was drained out of his face. It was as if the white sheets had leached it all out of him.

"So I've asked Brock Anderson here to do the actual cutting, and he has agreed." I glanced at Pa, but his face gave nothing away, like always. "I've got complete confidence in him. He's got lots of experience in..."

"Butchering," Callan said quietly. "It's fine, Jeannie. You know I trust you." Then he turned to Pa. "And you as well, sir. Thank you."

Pa pursed up his lips. "I'm still not convinced you didn't corrupt my boy—"

"Pa!" I reddened, and Joe Haig looked down to his feet. "I swear he never—"

"If you'd let me finish, David. What I was going to say was though I'm not convinced he didn't corrupt you, he's done good for this town, and I'm pleased to be able to help."

"And when it's over, sweet, I've arranged for you to go and stay with Zack Tyree for a while. I figure he's the best one to be able to help you learn to cope."

"See," I said, still keeping hold of Callan's hand. "I told you how good Mister Zack is, and he's patient, too—he breaks horses, so he's got to be. It'll be all right." Let it be all right.

Callan didn't reply; he was looking at Joe Haig and the other men. "I'm guessing you don't have chloroform, and they're here to hold me down?"

Healer Findlay was quick to reassure him. "No, love, you'll be under, but I'm not confident in the strength of the anesthetic. They're here just in case. I doubt they'll have to do anything other than get in the way."

Callan nodded, then slowly stood up, leaning on me as we walked into the examination room. Healer Findlay and Pa was washing up good, and the other men stood awkwardly round the back of the room.

I helped Callan onto the table, wondering if I dared to kiss him in front of all these people.

"Go on outside, David. There's no point in you being here."

Healer Findlay laid a hand on my shoulder. "He's right. You don't belong here now."

The others didn't matter, not even her—it was like we was alone. "No. I'm not going nowhere. I run out on you twice, ain't never going to do it again. I'm right where I belong." My throat was almost closed up tight and I took gentle hold of his bad hand. "Can you feel that?"

He nodded.

"Then hang on to it. I want the last thing you feel to be my hand in yours."

Healer Findlay come over then and helped him to lie down; she had to wipe away tears first, and she kissed me on the cheek before putting a cloth over Callan's face. Then I smelled something sweet, and slowly felt his hand relax in mine. Pa came forward then, and reluctantly, I let go and backed away to the corner of the room.

The long minutes ticked by while my pa and Healer Findlay worked with silent urgency over Callan, and the sharp scent of blood mixed with the sickly odor of the chloroform to turn my stomach inside out. There was so much blood, splashing into the silver basin, staining the old mat placed on the floor. I didn't know how a body could live losing so much blood.

Things was moving along, with Healer Findlay doing the first part of it all, till Pa picked up the bone saw and commenced to work, and then the chloroform wore off. I won't say nothing more about what happened then. That's Callan's story to tell should he ever choose to. I still wake at night, hearing him screaming in my dreams, probably always will, but I can't speak of it. It's funny how I can talk all about the congress of our bodies, but not this. I guess pain is more private than sex when it comes down to it.

But Healer Findlay was right there with more chloroform, and Joe Haig and his men done their part, though I noticed they was awful green looking, and when it was over and the healer was taking the last stitches, they got themselves outside fast as rabbits. I stayed to the last, though, and carried Callan back to the bed as I'd carried him down the mountain, seeing him safe and comfortable as he could be while he slept his unnatural sleep. Then I figured it was wrong to leave Healer Findlay to clean up by herself—she loved Callan too, and it must have been mighty hard on her, doing what she done, so I went back to the examination room.

The sight and smell of blood was bad, but I mastered my gorge and was ready to help her mop it all up when I turned round and saw what looked like nothing but a joint of mutton gone bad sitting on a counter, and I knew of course what it was. I've heard tell that when you die, every moment in your life flashes before your eyes. That happened to me there in that room—every single instance Callan had ever touched me with that hand came flooding back as the room grew hot and shrunk in on itself. My ears begun to ring and my stomach churned and I knew I was going to be sick, so I fled the room and the house and found myself on the ground, clinging tight to handfuls of grass and gulping in cold air like it was water.

I'd just got a-hold of myself and was starting to breathe more normal when an insect started up a strange buzzing sound, and it was the exact sound the saw had made going through the bone, the same grinding, cracking, horrible din, and I retched into the grass, voiding everything I'd eaten in days, sobbing at the shame of it.

There were hands on my shoulders, and I sat up to see Pa kneeling beside me. "Easy, son. Be easy."

"I'm sorry—"

"You've got nothing to apologize for. Older men than you would lose their suppers, seeing what you've seen today. If it makes you feel better, Joe Haig's round back puking into a bush, and he didn't have no feelings for your Callan one way or another."

I sat back on the grass. It was a fine summer day, a bit warmer than usual for early June. My Callan. "Pa, I want—"

He cut me off, then sat down beside me and stared off down the street, not looking at me at all. "When you have a child, when you first hold your baby in your arms, you dream dreams for him, David. You think about his first steps and his first day of schooling and the day when he'll marry, become a father himself. But you never know, when you're raising him up, if you're doing right by him or not, if he'll soar or fall, not till he stretches his wings and flies by himself."

"I know you're disappointed, but—"

"David, quit interrupting me, and for God's sake don't put words in my mouth. This has been a hard year for all of us, you most of all. You stood up against some pretty powerful people armed with nothing but your own certainty that what you was doing was right, and that's a hard thing even for a grown man to do, but you done it without a second thought. I watched you today, listened to what you said, thinking of you not as my son, but as a man, and I was proud of the man you've become. What you said to your friend today, that wasn't corruption nor evil. It's love as true and pure as that between your Mam and me. I don't understand it and I really don't like it, but I have no choice but to accept it."

I remembered how Pa had voted against Callan with the Grand Jury because he couldn't face a truth and lie to himself. "Then you'll speak to the sheriff?"

"I already have, son. Your Mam isn't going to like it one bit, and you've picked yourself a hard row to hoe, but I won't stand in your way. But for God's sake, try to be discreet. The law may be wrong, but it's still the law."

"Yes, sir." I had won. The victory had come at a high price, but Pa had always said nothing worthwhile come easy, and I guess he was right on that.

"On another matter, I ran into Zack Tyree at the sheriff's office. He needs a man to help him break some horses this summer, wanted to know if you'd be interested in the job. You'd have to stay at his place. He said he'd train you in what you'd need to know."

Callan was going to be staying with Mister Zack, too, and Pa knew it. I could hardly believe what I was hearing. "Won't you need me at home?"

"Benny C can do your work—it's about time that boy started pulling his weight. And it's time you was out on your own."

"Pa, Callan's going to be staying with Mister Zack while he recovers."

"I was listening to Jeannie, thank you, David. I don't have to tell you that I expect you not to abuse Zack's hospitality nor behave in any untoward way in his house." He looked at me stern, but my heart was singing.

"No sir, you can be sure I won't. Thank you." I gave him a rough hug, and we sat quiet for a while, soaking in the sunlight, just like the grass was doing. It surely was a glorious and terrible day.

The front door to the house opened, and Healer Findlay stepped out. "David? He's awake and calling for you."

I was up and through the door before the last words was out of her mouth, flying down the hall to the parlor, pushing the door open to see Callan laying still, covered by the sheet. It was odd how it fell away on his right side to nothing; it made him look not quite like a real person, more like a doll that'd been broken. But he smiled when he saw me, a sort of drowsy, woozy smile.

"You okay? In any pain?"

"No, not just yet. I don't know what she's given me, but it's surely strong. And we're alone, so please, please, kiss me."

I brushed my lips against his, feeling the stubbly cheek. I supposed learning to shave left-handed was going to be a challenge—I wondered if he'd grow out a beard instead, and how he'd look with it, all soft golden hair against his face. "I got news," I said, settling myself beside him, careful not to jostle or bang him around. "I'm going to be staying with Mister Zack too—we'll be together."

"That's not smart, the sheriff won't like it."

"Pa's fixed that. He's...well, I guess you'd say he's come around."

He turned a bit onto his left side to face me slightly, but he winced as he did it and went straight back flat again. "You don't have to do that. You know that, right?"

I kissed him again. "Want to. Want to be there with you, to help you."

His left hand reached out to where the other one should have been. "Guess I'm going to need it. It's so funny—I can feel it. They talk in the medical books about phantom pain in amputees, how you feel the limb that isn't there. Well, I've got phantom pleasure, I think. I can still feel your hand holding mine. The pressure of your fingers and the way they closed over mine, the pad of your thumb stroking my palm." His voice caught. "And it's going to go away, I know it will fade, I'll forget what it's like, what it felt like to hold you."

Gently I held him, so helpless to do anything but soothe and listen.

"Oh God, I was going to be strong, but I haven't any strength left, not one bit. You must think I'm so weak."

"Weak? You're the strongest man I've ever known. But I'll be your strength—your right arm too, if you'll have it."

We cried then, together, until both of us had fallen asleep. And I defy any man to berate or chide either of us for it—if for everything there's a season, this was the proper season for tears.

I woke maybe an hour later to find Callan resting his head on my shoulder, still fast asleep. I dislodged myself, straightened his covers, and kissed his forehead, which felt sort of fevery-hot. It was early evening, and I should have been hungry, but I couldn't imagine ever eating again. There weren't any sign of Healer Findlay in the house, so I went out onto the porch. The sun was getting ready to go down in a glorious burst of color with a sky tinged to show that storm clouds was coming in. Well, we'd had a good two days clear—that was better than average.

"David." Mister Zack was sitting on the porch, smoking a pipe, his feet on the porch rail.

"Hey, Mister Zack." I sat down beside him. "Pa told me you offered me a job—thank you, sir."

He passed me the pipe, and though I declined, the gesture stirred something in me. That was the sort of thing one man did for another. "It's no favor. I've hard work needs done—you'll more than earn your keep."

"I'd hope so." There was still a few people out on the streets, but some of the houses was dark and shuttered where the folk had left town. "Mister Zack, is Callan going to be all right?"

"First of all, David, it's just Zack. I consider the men who work for me my friends and equals. And I suppose he will. Jeannie and your father did a good job, there oughtn't to be any complications."

"No, sir. Not like that. Not physically, but inside. I figure if anyone would know, you would."

"That depends mostly on him, and you'd know him better than I to say. It's a different situation than me, David. I don't have any recollection of myself as other than I am now. He'll never forget what it is to have two hands; the loss will always be there, and he'll likely never feel quite right again. He's lost his life's work, and that's something that goes hard with a man—"

"What do you mean?" That didn't make sense—Callan still knew everything he'd ever known about healing and medicine.

"A healer needs two good arms, David." He pulled a flask out of his jacket and drank, then passed it to me as well. I took it and drank, gasping as the harsh whiskey hit my empty stomach.

"So you don't think he'll...be okay?"

"Didn't say that. I said it was up to him. And to you. I can tell you from experience that he's going to wish he'd died on that table more often than he's going to be grateful he's alive during the first few months. Every little thing he tries to do from walking to writing to eating is going to feel wrong and awkward, and he'll lash out at whoever's closest to him, and I suspect that's going to be you." He handed me back the flask, but I waved it away.

"Smart of you. No answers in a bottle."

The sun was getting ready to sink behind the mountains in a great rush, and I stifled a yawn. "Sorry, Mi...Zack. It's been a long day."

"I hear that. Long week, long month. Long year. But in answer to your question, yes. I think he's going to be all right, because I've watched you for a long while, David

Anderson, and you don't give up on anything that matters to you, and clearly that young man matters."

It seemed a good opening to discuss that very thing. "We're going to be in your house, so I'm thinking you need to know—"

"What goes on behind closed doors is private. You'll have a room, so will he. Whether either of you stays where I put you is your own affair."

"Ain't you worried about the law?"

"The law? Look around you at this town. Mayor's gone, most of city council's gone. The preacher's gone, along with most of his flock. The school's closed, probably for good unless they can find a Master. There's Bill Fletcher trying to hold things together, and if you think he's got time to worry about your personal life, you're deluding yourself."

"That was what I would have thought. What I don't get, ain't never got, is why the law ever cared. It don't seem like such a thing hurts anyone, so why on earth go to the bother of making it illegal?"

While I spoke, the door opened behind us and Healer Findlay come out and took a seat in her rocker. "Because, David, some people aren't happy unless they're telling others how to live their lives."

Mister Zack sighed and stretched. "You can say that again. Don't know how well you know your history, but this country was founded on two different and pretty much opposite ideas. One was that God or some supernatural being is guiding our destiny and controlling our ways, and our job as human beings is to find out his will and do his bidding. The other idea, well, that was that folks had come over to these shores to be free, and a man could do pretty much whatever he wanted, so long as he didn't harm anybody else. For an awful long time, those ideas sort of coexisted peacefully, but then things started to get ugly in the Twenty-first Century, back when your grandmam and my own grandfather were young, and for a while, it looked like we were headed for a civil war, not based on race or geography like the first one, but based on ideas. We avoided that, or maybe postponed it, because the Ice came, but I'm not sure that we're not moving in that direction again. If not in my lifetime, maybe in yours."

I thought on that. It certainly explained a lot. "So the Ice was a good thing, in a way?"

"A convenient thing, anyway—which, let me tell you, has fueled the fires of conspiracy theories ever since." He chuckled. "My uncle used to say he figured some whacko religious group found a way to harness the weather, brought the Ice so people would turn to God. Tragedy and disaster seems to do that for some folk. I always thought he was off his rocker, but in a world where the government sends dragons to burn law-abiding people out of their homes, anything's possible." He pocketed his flask. "I'd better head home. David, I expect I'll see you tomorrow—we still need to work out the details of the job." He nodded to Healer Findlay. "Jeannie." Then he disappeared into the dark.

I stood up, thinking how dark it would be on the path home. "Guess I'd better be getting on home too."

"Stay put. I'll make you up a bed in Callan's room." Healer Findlay rose as well.

"That's good of you, Healer. But my folks will be worried, I reckon."

"Just Jeannie, David. I'd say it's more than time for that. And your father knew you wouldn't be home tonight. I told him I'd see to you."

I didn't know what it was had changed, whether it was me killing the dragon or the man, or something else entirely, but I'd crossed a line I'd been dancing over the edge of for a long time, wanting so desperately to be a man, and taken seriously by grown folks. And now I was. And though I was flattered and pleased and wouldn't go back to my childhood for nothing, it struck me as I followed her into the house that I'd given up something precious as well.

Chapter 26

Healer Findlay, Mister Zack, Pa, and I worked out that I'd stay in town to help see to Callan while he recovered, and then move on to Mister Zack's place to start my job soon as he was strong enough to be moved. Every morning I'd get up thinking I'd go up home to see my folks and get my things, but then Callan would have need of me, so I'd put it off. Oh, he never asked me to stay, but I could see how hard it was those first few days, specially as Healer Findlay was cutting off the pain drugs quick rather than slow. So I read aloud and talked to Callan, or just held him as he worked through the pain. I spent the time he was sleeping doing chores for Healer Findlay. Fixing loose hinges, nailing on shingles, doing the sorts of things that a man generally does around a place, though I was surprised by how handy she was with tools.

"I have to be," she explained, holding a board in place for me as I patched a hole in her shed. "I've never had a husband nor even an assistant till Callan came along, and though I dearly love that boy, I'm not sure he knows which end of a hammer to take hold of."

"Got pretty good with an axe last winter, though." I stepped back and pretended to look at my handiwork, but was seeing Callan's strong arms wielding the axe on our woodpile. He'd tried to feed himself for the first time earlier that day, hadn't been able to cut his meat nor butter his bread without help. He'd made a joke about it, but I'd been driven nearly to tears. I slammed the hammer hard against the nail again and again and again.

I felt a hand on my shoulder and dropped the hammer to the ground, breathing hard. "Easy, David. I know this is hard on you. I expect it's every bit as hard for you to watch him struggle as it is for him to do it. Harder, maybe."

"It's just not..." I stopped, not wanting to sound like a whiny child.

"Fair?" Jeannie finished for me. "No, it's not. Not at all. You know, you've been by his side or doing something for me practically every waking moment for the past two weeks. Why don't you go on up home today, see your family?"

"Callan might need me."

"I can see to whatever he might need today, sweet. He'll understand. And David, part of Callan's healing has got to be learning to do for himself. You won't always be there."

"I will," I said stubbornly.

"You know, I do believe you just might. But get on up home for the afternoon anyway. Things in this town are just in a terrible state—don't waste any time you might have with people who love you."

Truth be told, I was hungering to see Pa and Benny C and the girls, but was fair nervous about Mam. She wasn't likely to embrace my new life with open arms, and I didn't relish the idea of having the door of my home slammed in my face, or having my sisters kept away for fear I'd 'corrupt' them. Oh, I knew my Mam loved me, but whether her love was stronger than her fear, that I weren't sure of.

There weren't any way that I'd just leave without speaking to Callan, not after what we'd been through, so I stopped into the parlor and stroked his hair softly till he woke. "Hey," I said. "If it's okay with you, I'd like to go up and see my folks today. I'll be back by nightfall."

"Of course it's okay. I'm not going anywhere, love."

"If you need me—"

"David." He pulled himself up to sit. "Don't use me as an excuse. If you don't want to go, then don't."

I sat cross legged on the bed. Jeannie's bed was mighty fine—as good and soft as the feather mattress back in Crawford. "It ain't that I don't want to go; I'm just scared, I guess."

"You fought dragons, silly. What's so scary about home?"

"My mam."

He laughed a little, and gave me a weak push off the bed. "Go on, go on with you. Beard the lioness in her den."

So I left him with a stack of books that I doubted he'd strength enough to read, borrowed Jeannie's horse, and rode up home. I took more pleasure in my solitude than

I'd expected to—I was used to being in the woods off by myself, and all the time spent in town surrounded by people was wearing on me more than a bit.

Not that I minded Callan, for being with him was like being with part of myself, nor even Jeannie really, but when I went out into the town, I could feel eyes on me, could hear hissed voices saying words I couldn't help hearing. Truly, I would have stayed locked behind doors had it been left to me, but Jeannie seemed determined to push me out into the world at least once a day, and I supposed she was right. It didn't do no good to hide from trouble; it always come looking for you. So I went out with my head held high and pretended I didn't hear nor see, and I guess it must have been working, for I was getting used to it.

That method weren't likely to work on my family, though—they wouldn't allow me to glide on by them with a nod and a word. I tied up the horse outside the barn, hearing the sounds of work from within. Pa and Benny C was rebuilding the sheep folds, Benny C holding the boards while Pa hammered them in place. He stopped midstroke when he seen me.

"David." He took my hand and shook it the way he would Mister Zack's or any proper grown-up's. "Good to see you, son."

"You too, Pa."

Benny C was just standing there with his mouth hung open. "Greet your brother proper, Benny C."

"Hey," he finally managed.

"Hey. You look good—been working outside?" He looked as though he'd filled out some, even in the past five days. Benny C was on the edge of manhood, and I hadn't even noticed it.

He nodded. Pa was stowing away the tools. "You have time to stay for a bite to eat?"

"Yes, sir. I've missed Mam's cooking something fierce."

"See that you tell her that." Pa led me into the cabin, and it was just so foreign and strange. As though I was a guest, not kin at all. Even the sound of my boots on the porch seemed wrong.

Mam was sitting at the table, reading lessons with Delia and Ruby, likely trying to keep them up so when they got a schoolmaster, they wouldn't be so far behind. They looked up when we come in, and the girls both dropped their books and flung their arms around me, nearly knocking me to the floor

"Easy, easy," I protested, but I was smiling big, and they knew it. "I ain't going nowhere right now."

"But you are going back?" Mam was trembling a bit. Even in the poor light of the cabin I could see it.

"Yes. I start work with Mister Zack in a week—seems like it makes more sense for me to stay with C—"

"Well, you're here now. I'll make you some dinner." She whirled around to the stove and started banging pans. I strayed over to the fireplace, to the spot where Grandmam had always sat. Her chair was still there. I supposed they hadn't the heart to move it. I stroked the worn back of the rocker.

"Ruby's in Grandmam's room now," Delia said. "And Benny C and me have our own rooms too—just like rich folk!"

"That's fine, Delia." I started to say she'd become a fine lady living so rich, and end up catching a town husband, but figured that weren't what Mam needed to hear. One child had left her through death, another grown up to a future she despised—she wasn't like to welcome the thought that the others would leave in their turn. So I just smiled at my sister and gathered up what things was mine from my room.

Mam called us to the table and put a plate down, but not in my usual place, instead at the spot reserved for guests. I weren't to be allowed to feel at home at all. My eyes met Pa's and he shook his head. So I sat quiet and ate with relish, and that weren't pretended, for the fresh peas was perfect and the fish she fried up melted in my mouth. "This sure is the finest food I've had in a week, Mam. Thank you."

"So there's something we got that ain't better in town?" She was scrubbing at a pot in the sink, not looking up at me at all. "Thought maybe living an immoral lifestyle would make you hanker for caviar and champagne instead of honest food."

"Mam..." My brother and sisters was staring at me, waiting. I wondered what Pa and Mam had told them about me, about Callan.

Pa cleared his throat. "Benny C, get on back to the barn and start in on the next stall. Girls, why don't you go—"

"No," Mam said. "Let them stay. Let them hear how their brother is sunk down in depravity, abandoning everything we brought him up to be." Her eyes was brimming over with tears, though she was blinking them away fast as they appeared. I figured she'd been stewing over this and rehearsing the confrontation in her head again and again, probably since the very day I'd gone down to town.

"May-Marie, I don't think—"

"No, Pa. Let them stay." I clenched my fists, digging my nails into my palms to try to force myself to stay calm. "Mam, you brought me up to be true to myself and to do right by people. You brought me up to stand up to anybody, high or low, if my cause was just. I remember when I was four or five years old, you stood up at the summer Circuit and spoke out for Anise Walters. I was too young to even know what adultery was, but I saw even then how the whole town was lining up to condemn her on her husband's word, and you was the lone voice saying otherwise."

"But Anise weren't guilty of her crime. Butch Walters just wanted to set her aside so he could marry a woman who could give him children. It was wrong."

"And it's just as wrong for folk who don't even know Callan nor me to tell us how to live when we ain't hurting nobody. You did the best job with me you could do; it ain't your fault that I took a different road than you wanted for me. Nobody made me like this. And even if Callan were to die today," I swallowed hard, "I'd still be drawn to men, not to women."

I felt their eyes on me, and just like I did in the town, I fixed my stare on something else and kept on going. "I love you, Mam. You raised me right; now you got to let me live my life as I see fit."

"If I'd raised you right, you'd do right." She turned away from me.

I started towards her, thinking a touch might move her where words had failed, but Pa shook his head slightly, so I stopped, nodded to him and the girls, and walked out of the cabin with my head high.

I'd got the horse untied and was getting set to mount when I heard Benny C calling my name.

"What you need, Benny C?"

"You forgot this." He was holding my knife. I took it, turning it over in my hands and seeing it plunging into the dragon's wing and eye, across Delahaye's throat. I considered giving it to him, for he truly loved it and it was filled up with memories I'd just as soon forget. But I thanked him and strapped it to my belt, for it was filled up with memories I'd best not forget, really.

"Will I see you again?" He sounded like a little lost boy.

I swung onto the horse. "Hell, yes. You'll be back to school soon and in town every day. And besides, I got to come to your nuptials with Daisy, right?"

"Aww, you..." But he weren't mad, not really. It was teasing like we used to do, and with that as the last thing between us, I started back down the hill.

Jeannie was waiting for me in her barn when I got back. "Glad you're back, David. It's been a long afternoon. He's trying to practice writing, and I think it's just a bit too soon for that." She sighed. "And I was talking to Sheriff Fletcher. It seems there's going to be a meeting at the schoolhouse next Saturday evening."

"Another meeting?" Seemed to me we'd congregated more in that schoolhouse in the past year than the rest of my life put together.

"Yes. We need to elect a new mayor, for one thing, and figure out what's to be done about schooling for the children. And Bill Fletcher's concerned that we're being isolated."

"Isolated?" I was starting to get the horse out of his tack, but she stopped me.

"I've got to ride down south to see a patient. Just feed and water him, if you wouldn't mind." She followed me as I led the horse around to the water trough. "Bill says we haven't heard anything from outside since before you came back. No R&A agents, and no post riders. None. The mail's piled up at the schoolhouse, waiting. It's not good. And..." She hesitated, chewing on her bottom lip.

"What?"

"A traveling tinker told Bill that there's some sort of oversized vultures raiding flocks to the east."

Dragons. "They're dead! I swear it, and I smashed every last egg."

"Every egg in that nest, maybe. This thing, whatever it is, goes far beyond this one town, I think." She gave me a hug. "Don't fret over it—you've done more than your share already. But anyway, Bill wanted to make sure both you and Callan would be there."

The sheriff wanting to see us didn't fill me up with hope. "Are we in trouble?"

She laughed. "Not a bit of it. I think he wants to publicly thank you for what you did. You're heroes, you silly boy."

I was a hero. I hadn't never thought of it like that. Heroes in stories never seemed to have the fears and doubts that filled me up all the time.

"I'll be gone all tonight, probably won't be back till tomorrow afternoon." Jeannie heaved her packs onto the saddle. "You can handle changing Callan's dressings, can't you?"

I nodded. "Yes ma'am. Don't you worry about nothing here. We'll be fine by ourselves."

By ourselves. Alone in a house for a whole night. And Callan was doing better, physically at least. I felt all hot and tight thinking on it, watching Jeannie ride away south. There was rain moving in. I hoped she'd get where she was going before it hit.

Callan was sitting up with yellowed sheets of paper from an old notebook torn and tattered around him, and a pencil clenched in his left hand. His expression was tight and tense as he tried to force the hand to move in unfamiliar ways. He was so intent on his task that he didn't even hear me come in.

The pencil lead snapped under the pressure. "God damn it!" I cleared my throat, and he saw me. "I'm sorry. It's just so...I mean, look at this!" He'd been trying to write his name, but it was barely legible. "I know they used to joke about doctors' handwriting, but this is ridiculous." He struggled one-handed to crumple the paper and toss it against the wall, but it wouldn't ball tight and just fluttered to the ground like a dead leaf. I started to pick up the pieces of paper.

"I can't even make an angry gesture properly anymore," Callan sighed. "Never mind that, come and tell me how your trip home went."

Home. It weren't that any more. But that was my burden, not Callan's. "It was about like I figured. Mam's mad at me, but she'll come around." I hoped. "And I got my stuff, figure I can use your old room till we move on to Mister Zack's."

He slid over, giving me an invitation I didn't dare accept. "This bed is more than big enough for both of us. There's drawer space in the dresser for you."

"I didn't want to presume. Seems sort of rude, us being...together in Jeannie's bed."

"She wouldn't mind, I know it. And anyway, she's not here today. She told me as soon as you came back she was off till tomorrow. We're alone, David." Callan was breathing sort of shallow, and I knew the cause, for I felt it, too, like a wire connecting us, drawing us tighter and tighter together.

"It's not nighttime," I said, but it was a form protest, and I was already moving towards the bed, pulling off my overshirt.

"Lock the door, then." Callan was fighting with the buttons on his pajama top. "I need this, need you. Please."

It was so strange to be in bed with the light streaming through the windows, but the strangeness was soon swallowed up by kisses and feather-light touches. My fingers pushed his aside and teased him out of his pajamas, tracing over his body so lightly it was a wonder he could feel it at all, so feared of hurting him I was.

But he was feeling it—his reaction left me no doubt of that, nor any doubt that he wanted as much as me. It had been so long, all that time when I'd lay on the floor barely five feet away from Callan, aching to be touched, and not daring to touch myself for fear the sound would disturb him; I could hardly hold myself back now that we was finally together.

He might not have been able to write with his left hand, but there was plenty of things he could manage with it just fine, and his mouth had lost none of its skill, though there was a few awkward moments. It's funny how you never think about how much you use your hands, even in things that ain't got nothing to do with hands at all. But we laughed through them; figured ways around the things that mattered, and ignored the things that didn't; and I honestly think that it meant more to him when he brought me to a climax that had my toes curling and my whole body shuddering against him than when he climaxed himself, for it showed him that he was still whole in the ways that really mattered.

We held each other after, lazing in the bed all that afternoon, giving pleasure as it suited us, napping when we was tired. Mostly we just found comfort in each others' bodies—not only sexually, but through touch, so that when hunger finally drove us from bed, I think there was no part of his body that I had not caressed, nor he mine.

Rain had begun spitting against the windows, and I could feel the temperature dropping. If I was at home—my old home—I'd be out covering the crops right now. Jeannie didn't keep a vegetable patch, and I suspected Mister Zack had people to do that for him. I wondered if that part of my life was over; I hoped not. I liked the feel of dirt in my hands and things growing up under my nurture.

"Penny for your thoughts?" I was curled up against Callan's left side, skin to skin save for the bandage that stretched across his torso.

"Just thinking about the rain. And how hungry I am."

"I think I'll get up for dinner tonight. It's time." Callan sat up, and I saw his bandages had come loose.

"Let me change those for you."

I got the dressing and a bowl of clean warm water from the stove and started unwrapping the bandages while he sat on the edge of the bed, pale in the falling shadows. I'd watched Jeannie do it, but hadn't realized how the cotton gauze of the bandages would stick to the wound, how slow and careful I'd have to be to avoid causing him pain. The cloth tangled in the black thread of the stitches and he winced.

"Sorry. It's harder than it looks."

"No, it's all right. You have a deft touch with this—we'll make a healer of you yet." Callan was smiling, and I knew he didn't mean it, but something occurred to me that just might solve at least one of his problems.

"I could, if you wanted. I said I'd be your hands, and I could, you know, really be your hands. You could tell me what to do, and I'd do it. Then you could still be a healer."

I'd got all the cotton free, so I let the wound breathe while I lit some lamps.

"David, I can't ask you to give up any more for me than you already have. I'm in your debt more than I can ever hope to repay."

I was holding a match when he spoke that last, and I held onto it, staring into the flame as it burned down nearly to singe my fingers. "You don't have to repay me. I love you, and people who love each other do for each other as I've done for you and you for me. It ain't a burden nor hardship. The hardship's leaving off doing for you and letting you manage on your own, truth be told."

I started to lave the stump with the warm water, pressing the sponge against the raw scar that took the place of his right arm.

"But if you're talking of payment, there is some thing you could do for me. Teach me."

"Teach you?"

This was something that had been turning over and over in my mind since we was up the mountain. "Yes, educate me proper. Tell me what I should read and help me to understand it, so I can be learned like you. I want to understand the things you understand, know what you know."

"About medicine?"

"No, that's not what I mean." There was ointment I was to rub into the wound; I warmed it in my palm and started to massage it gently onto Callan. He didn't flinch nor seem to mind me touching this scar. That was good. "The day of your surgery, Mister Zack was telling me about the people who founded this country, and the ideas they had. I'd never heard none of that—all we got in school was fairy tales about brave pilgrims at Valley Forge eating shoe leather till the kind Indians taught them to plant corn."

Callan giggled. "It wasn't quite like that. Surely even in Moline they have better history books than that."

"Not many. But I want to know the true stories—what they thought, and why they thought it."

Callan lifted his left arm out of the way as I wound the clean bandages round. "Political philosophy then."

"And science, so I can understand how things used to be Before. So maybe next time I come across into an old-time machine that's still running, I can make sense of it."

"Machine?" Callan turned, curious, and I remembered I'd never got a chance to tell him about it.

So I told him about the machine; how I'd found it in the tunnel, about the papers around it that I hadn't time to read, the lights that was still burning after a hundred years, all of it. By the time I finished, the rain was rattling the windows, and I was glad I'd laid a fire in the parlor chimney that morning, for we'd need it that night. "Do you think it's important? To the R&A, I mean?"

"Considering the dragons were guarding the entrance to the cave it was in, I'd say yes, it very likely is."

Chapter 27

The days after that moved fast. Clocks and calendars are the biggest liars since Pinocchio—they make it seem like time passes steady with ticks and tocks and one day following another at the same speed, but it ain't true. Time drags when there's something coming that you're eager for, and speeds by when it's coming up on something you dread. And I was surely dreading that town meeting. It was well and good for Jeannie to say the sheriff wanted to thank us; maybe he did. But there was other folk left in town who might not believe what the good we did outweighed what we were.

Jeannie peeked into the kitchen as Callan and me was finishing our dinner. "You boys about ready? We're going to be late if we don't get a move on."

My heart plummeted. The meeting meant facing the whole town, including my Mam, who would surely come down to this meeting if only to have a say on what happened to the school. Jeannie disappeared to get her jacket, and I noticed how pale Callan looked.

"You sure you're up to this? Nobody'd dare say a thing against you if you pled your injury and stayed home."

He run his hand through his hair like he did when he was nervous. Of all the things I'd seen him do that now was different, that gesture somehow struck deepest. The left side of his head was always unkempt and disheveled and the right untouched. It made him seem out of balance, somehow, even more than the loss of the arm did.

"No, I have to face them sometime. Now's as good as any other day. I've killed a man, after all. I'm surprised they haven't come to question me about it, really."

An uncomfortable silence fell. "Um, well...they probably would have, except that I told them I done it."

"You what?" Jeannie was putting out lamps and the house was getting dark around us. "Why on earth would you lie about something like that?"

"You'd been through enough. And I was afraid they'd come down hard on you, being a convicted felon and all." It was a darn good thing I'd had those papers to prove my own story about it being self defense. Mayor Casteel would have been first in line to put the noose around my neck otherwise.

"Well, we have to tell them the truth. Immediately."

I shook my head so hard my brain was rattling. "No. No, we do not. I done what you asked on that mountain and ran when you said it, now you do what I say."

"But—" I could tell he weren't happy with me having the name of a killer, but that weren't the point and I was going to be firm.

"No."

"All right," he said, quiet, and picked up a pullover sweater, trying to get it on one-handed. Without speaking, I took hold of it and adjusted it around him, feeling the soft wool fall into place over his body, wishing we could just go back to the bedroom and forget all of it.

"Later," he said in answer to my unspoken words, and on the promise of that, I figured somehow we'd get through what was coming.

Jeannie'd been right and we was late. She'd gone on ahead of us and saved seats—near the front, of course. So when we walked into that schoolhouse a hundred pairs of eyes turned as one and stared back at us. Sheriff Fletcher was at the podium where normally Master Burke or the mayor would have been, and I gave Callan's hand a final squeeze and, head held high like I'd learned to do when eyes was on me, I started down the aisle to where Jeannie was. And as we passed the first row of chairs, my heart near stopped, for, almost as if they'd worked it out ahead, the entire row of people, farmers and storekeeps and woodsmen, stood, and then the row after, and the next and the next, each standing up as we passed, a silent forest of men and women paying their respects.

My face was beet-red and I was pretty sure Callan was on the edge of crying from the way his breath was catching, but I didn't dare to look at him. Instead, I looked at the sheriff to see if I should sit.

"The people of this town owe you boys a debt we will never be able to repay. You have our thanks," he said, so quiet that it was like he was speaking to us alone, and then we sat, and I could hear the rustling of jackets and chairs and voices as the rest of them sat, too, and no more was said on it. But I stopped worrying that we was about to be hauled off to jail.

Sheriff Fletcher rapped the butt of his gun against the worn old podium. "Let's come to order. We've got a lot to do, so I won't waste any time. You all know, I expect, that it appears the government has their eyes on our land—David Anderson brought the proof of that back down the mountain a month or so ago. What you might not know is that since that time we haven't heard hide nor hair from the outside world." The sheriff continued to tell the tale we'd already heard from Jeannie, explaining about the absence of the R&A agents and post riders while I sat and tried to look out of the corner of my eye for my folks.

"Third row from the back on the left," Callan whispered, and I looked at him, questioning. "Your parents. Saw them when we came in." I smiled and squeezed his hand again, though I let go of it right away. There weren't no point in pushing our luck.

The sheriff was finishing up. "...clear that we're in for a world of trouble, and lots of folk have already made the choice to leave. If any of the rest of you are of the same mind, you got my blessing—I don't want to hold anybody here against their will, but I'd ask you to leave now, not vote on the things we got coming up if you're not sticking around to see them through."

He waited, but nobody moved. "We ain't going nowhere!" A voice from the back of the room shouted out. "Get on with it, Bill!"

"All right, all right. Just had to make the offer. So we need a mayor, as I've got my hands full just being sheriff. So I'll take nominations and then we can vote. And in the open, too. There's been too many secrets in this town already."

There was a stir at that, for the secret ballot was almost like a sacred rite, but I figured nobody'd pitch too much of a fuss. Everybody wanted normal again, and normal meant a proper mayor and council making our decisions. "I nominate Mister Clemmons." I didn't recognize the voice.

Mister Nate got up. "I'm honored, of course, but I'm still serving out my term as State Senator, and feel that my best work for this town will be done in Richmond, not here."

"Right, Nate declines the nomination." Sheriff Fletcher was determined to keep us moving. "Any other?"

"I nominate Zack Tyree." I wasn't sure, but thought that was Gary Stovall, who kept pigs down in the south of the county. It seemed to me, looking round, that most of those who'd stayed was country folk. So many of the town families had gone.

"What about it, Zack? You willing to serve?"

Mister Zack was down about half a row from Jeannie, so I couldn't see him proper even after he stood up. "I suppose so. Not exactly my life's ambition, but somebody's got to do it."

"Fine. So we've got one. Anybody else?" It was quiet for a long while. "Come on, people, what kind of election are we going to have with one candidate?" Jeannie raised her hand. "Not that I don't think Zack would be a fine mayor, but I nominate Brock Anderson."

You could have knocked me over with a snowball. Mayors and sheriffs and council and that sort of thing was always town folk. It had been unusual enough when Pa got picked for the Grand Jury, but this was unheard of. The world was being set on its end. Again.

But Sheriff Fletcher weren't fazed at all. "Right. Brock, you willing to stand?"

"Suppose so, though I can't for the life of me figure out why anybody'd want me. I ain't been to college nor even traveled much beyond this county." Pa was coming up front to stand near Mister Zack while he spoke.

"Because with you a person knows where they stand," Jeannie explained. "We need someone who's going to speak on the level with us. Not that Zack wouldn't," she hurried to say. "But—"

"Oh, quit your prevaricating, Jeannie," Zack smiled. "I'm not offended. Too bad we can't both be mayor, really."

"Do y'all want to make speeches?" Sheriff Fletcher asked, and Pa turned pale and Mister Zack said, "Hell, no," real loud. "They all know us, let's just get on with it."

"All right. Every citizen over sixteen's got the right to vote in this election." Sheriff Fletcher looked down at me and nodded, making sure I knew he meant me as well. "So when I call the vote, we'll divide the hall. Left side of me for Zack Tyree, right side for Brock Anderson. Vote."

The room started to fill up with buzzing voices and the sounds of chairs and benches scraping over the wood floor of the schoolroom. I weren't sure what to do. It hadn't occurred to me that I was going to be given adult privileges and rights.

"David?" Callan nudged me. "Are you going to vote, or just sit there?"

My Pa, mayor. I couldn't fathom such a thing. It would change his life, and Mam's and everybody's back home. I'd be the mayor's son. Better than Elmer, who'd after all been just a nephew. And Pa would be a good leader, surely. But then I remembered how he wasn't much for speech-making, and how impatient he got with government men, and wondered if maybe Mister Zack wouldn't be best after all. Callan laid his hand on my shoulder. "Just follow what you know to be right. Neither your father nor Mister Tyree will hold your vote against you."

Guess that fear was the reason for secret ballot. Callan went off; I didn't see in which direction, for I got up myself and headed over to Mister Zack's side of the room.

When I turned around to look, I saw that both sides seemed about even, and that Callan was standing on my Pa's side. I wouldn't have figured that, not at all.

The vote was counted right quick, and though it was close, Mister Zack edged out Pa by a couple of votes. The two candidates had been confabulating in the corner most of the time the vote had been going on, and now Mister Zack came up to the podium. "So am I mayor? Don't I have to swear on a Bible?"

Sheriff Fletcher whipped a big old book out from behind Master Burke's desk. "Put your right hand on the Bible and er...er..." The usual thing was to put your left in the air, but Mister Zack hadn't a left hand, so the sheriff just sort of scratched his head. "Aw, never mind. You swear to uphold the laws of this town and see us through this crisis, treat everyone fair and square and not keep secrets?"

"I do," Mister Zack said solemnly, and then looked down at the book and started laughing. "You want me to make my oath again, Bill? You just swore me in on Webster's Unabridged."

"The Bible and God and preachers haven't done us much good—maybe the dictionary will do us a sight better. The meeting's yours, Mister Mayor." The sheriff stepped out of the way.

"Right. Everybody take your seats, then." While Mister Zack waited for the room to right itself, I sat back down next to Callan.

"First order of business is deciding what to do," Mister Zack was saying. "There is no doubt in my mind that before winter sets in, the R&A, the government, maybe even the army is going to come in here and try to clear us out. The way I see it, we have two choices. We can go peacefully to wherever they want to send us, or we can stay and fight."

"If we meant to go, Zack, I think we would have gone already, like Casteel and Burke and them." Pa's voice was mild, but I knew him well enough to know there was something behind it. Fear? I couldn't imagine such a thing.

"But fight the army? That's more than I bargained for." I didn't know who that was, but it started things rolling and the debate raged. Go or stay, fight or run, send the young children somewhere away, try to see if other towns was threatened and might join with us. Then after what seemed like hours, Burke the Digger stood up.

"We ain't going to settle this tonight, Zack. Sorry—Mister Mayor, I mean."

"Zack's fine, like always. And you're right. We won't settle anything tonight. And we've got other things to talk about, so just keep it in your mind—we'll be visiting this subject again. I think Brock's right, if any of us was going to run, we'd have done it already. We're here for the long haul, and the army isn't likely to be marching over the hills as we sit here."

The room got real still, and I wondered if the rest of them was doing as I was and hearing boots on pavement, hundreds and hundreds of men, marching in lockstep towards us. Thunder rumbled low in the distance, and I moved closer to Callan and dared to lay my head on his shoulder. That was a mistake.

"Mister Mayor," a woman's voice from behind us cut through the silence. "I don't know quite whether this is the proper place and time…"

"We're all friends and neighbors here, Vandy, say your piece." Vandy Weaver was Perkin's wife, a good friend of my Mam's.

"I don't mean to be ungrateful or nothing, but I can't just sit here in the presence of blatant immorality." My head come off Callan's shoulder like it was fire. Oh, I should have known it was too good to be true.

She stood up and come round to face us, though her round face looked more sorrowful than condemning. "I do appreciate what you two done for the town, and I'm sorry for the loss of your arm," she nodded to Callan, "but I just ain't comfortable with the taint of corruption I'm seeing."

Before me or Callan or even Mister Zack could respond, Nate Clemmons rose and bowed to her, sweeping his hat from his silvery hair.

"Miss Vandy, you're right. There is immorality, and there is surely corruption in our midst." He glanced over at us. My heart was pounding out of my chest. There weren't no way we could get out of this room, no way for me to get Callan to safety if it turned ugly. Then Mister Clemmons' lips twitched slightly, like he was trying not to smile. "But it isn't coming from these two young men. It's coming from Washington, and from Richmond—from people we entrusted with our money and our lives and our homes. I must tell you that I have spent forty-odd years in government service, and never in my life have I seen the likes of this—this criminal cover-up, this blatant attempt at theft and murder by our own elected and appointed officials, and it troubles me more than I can say."

Mister Clemmons always had been powerful good at speechmaking—I remembered that from when he was mayor. He put his hat back on. "But what these two do or don't do, that doesn't matter a damn. If they're hurting anybody, it's only themselves. We used to be better than this—when I was a boy, before all these damn-fool decency laws, a man used to be able to live his life as he saw fit, and whatever moral choices he made were between him and God. And that's as it should be. We've likely got an army on the way, half the town's run off, I'm not convinced we won't see more dragons or worse, and our young people are growing up in ignorance. The last thing we need to worry about is what folks do behind their closed doors." He emphasized those last words and stared straight at me, and I nodded. No more public shows of affection. I understood.

"And about that," Mam spoke up from the back. "What about the school? I got three young people at home, and they need proper teaching."

All over the room there was echoes of the same. Folk tended to have large families, particularly farm people, and few of the grown folk was educated enough to teach their own beyond basic letters and words and numbers. To say nothing of the time it took—time nobody had during this brief but busy season when everything was growing.

The sheriff come forward and rapped on the big desk with the butt of his pistol again. "Settle down, let His Honor speak."

"Picking a new schoolmaster was next on my list. Any volunteers?" Nobody raised their hand, which didn't surprise me none—weren't hardly anybody qualified. "Fine, then I'll take nominations. May-Marie, you spoke first, you got any suggestions?"

"Yes, actually I do, thank you, Zack. I think Callan Landers should do it."

You could have heard a snowflake hit the ground. Mam wasn't shy about sharing her opinion, so I reckoned every single person in that room knew good and well what she thought of Callan and me together. I couldn't believe my ears. She'd trust Callan with children, with Benny C and the other boys?

"Er...um..." Mister Zack traded looks with the sheriff. "While there's no denying he's qualified, there's laws that preclude persons convicted of...um...certain types of offenses from being teachers."

"Laws made by the same people who are trying to do us out of our land?" It was so odd, hearing my own arguments coming back from Mam's lips. "He's clearly not able to heal no more, and it ain't likely he's going to get up to anything untoward in a classroom with thirty children."

"But May-Marie," Vandy Weaver protested, "there's young boys in that class."

"Oh, pshaw, Vandy. Did you ever worry about Jeroboam Burke with the young girls? Needs must when the devil drives. You don't like Callan Landers, you give me a different choice, then."

Through this all, Callan was sitting still as a statue, and I didn't dare glance at him. I didn't know what had caused Mam's change of mind or heart, but I was glad of it. It might be that I could manage to have both parts of my family after all.

Vandy shook her head. "On your own heads be it. I ain't got children in any case."

"Any of the rest of you with children got anything to say?" Mister Zack asked the crowd, but there was silence. Once Mam pointed it out, it really was the only choice that made sense. No able-bodied person could be spared in this season, especially with half the town gone, and in any case, none was as learned as Callan.

"All right, then. You want the job?"

Callan nodded. "But I can't write too well yet."

"We'll work on that, and we haven't got a lot of paper anyway, nor are we likely to be getting more. Penmanship is not a skill I particularly care if they learn. Teach them to read and figure and the facts of our history, and for God's sake teach them to think for themselves. Can you do that?"

"Yes, sir." And Callan squared his shoulders and sat straighter, the old confidence and competence I'd so admired in him coming back. A man needs a purpose in life, and Mam had given Callan this gift, had given him his life back in a way that I couldn't never do, no matter how much help I gave him.

"Right." Mister Zack stretched. "I know it's getting late, but we got one more piece of unfinished business. Sheriff?" He nodded to Sheriff Fletcher who went into Master Burke's, no, Callan's office now, and came out leading Mister Hennessy, walking like he was too tired to put one foot before the other, hands manacled.

Mister Hennessy saw the crowd staring at him and began to shout. "You have no right to hold me! I demand you release me and restore all government property taken from my murdered colleague to me at once!"

"The way I see it, in this country the government works for us. So if it's government property, it's ours." Mister Zack was grim like I'd never seen him before. "And we have the right to protect and defend our town." He turned to face the crowd. "We've been questioning this man since David and Callan came back from the mountains. At this point, we think he's told us all he's going to."

I noticed he didn't say 'he's told us all he knows' and I also saw how Hennessy flinched at the word 'questioning.' It wouldn't have surprised me to find there'd been more than sweet talk and promises used.

"So the question is what to do with him. Brock Anderson wants him hanged for the murder of his girl and of Lorna Massie." The Massies had left with Pastor Daniels, and who could blame them, really? "Sheriff thinks we should hold him indefinitely, keep him as a bargaining chip for when they come for us."

That made a lot of sense to me, assuming that Mister Hennessy was anybody the bigwigs in the R&A would care about. It got quiet while folks was contemplating what to do.

The chair beside me scraped on the floor, and Callan stood up. I'd never dreamed his voice could be so cold. "I say give him twenty stout strokes of the lash and then drive him from this town with only the clothes on his back to make his way in the world as best he may. And may God have mercy on his soul." The words of the sentence echoed in the room as they had that day the circuit judge spoke them. I weren't surprised that Callan remembered them word-perfect.

Mister Zack paused for a moment, looked at Callan, looked at Hennessey, then back at Callan. He nodded. "You got more right than most to say. Done." The sheriff brung his pistol down again, and Hennessy commenced in to shouting and threatening, but nobody was listening. Sheriff Fletcher nodded to Aaron, who come and took the prisoner out, still protesting all the way.

"I'd say he ought to consider himself lucky my Pa didn't have his way," I commented to Callan as the meeting was breaking up. "It's summer; he'll survive."

Callan nodded, but he looked troubled. "You understand why...I mean, it isn't really like me to seek revenge, but it was as though something broke inside me, David, and I just had to see justice done."

"It's all right. You done the right thing." We walked together down the aisle and out into the night. It was misting a little—not real rain, just wet air, really. "And we got better things to fret over than the likes of him. You're going to be schoolmaster. I can't think of nobody better. You've sure taught me plenty."

Now in the dark, I could take his hand, and I was glad for once that we didn't have big old electric streetlights like Before. "Not quite the same subjects I'll be teaching the children, I expect." I could hear the laugh in his voice, and it was like the warm cocoa flooding through my body had been, all creamy bubbling joy. It had been too long since I'd heard Callan laugh. "I owe your mother a huge debt for that. I couldn't have faced my life without some kind of work."

And I couldn't face my life without you in it, I thought, but I didn't say it. I didn't need to. Callan had taught me that what was written would last, but sometimes words just got in the way. I gave his hand a squeeze, and he squeezed back, and that said everything that needed saying. Trouble was coming, sure as winter brings storms, but we'd get through it together.

The rain wasn't letting up, and I could smell the downpour that was just about ready to drench us. "Guess we'd better make a run for it," I said. The trees was lashing back and forth in the wind, like whips. "You up for it?" Callan wasn't near back to full strength, but he was getting there; every day he was getting closer to being...maybe not the man he had been, but the man he was going to be. Someone new, just like I wasn't the boy I'd been a year ago. "Can you run?"

A bolt of lightning split the sky and lit up a dazzling smile. "Better than run, love. I can fly."

And so I grabbed a-hold of his arm, and together we sprinted off home, into the oncoming storm.

About the Author

R. W. Day once had an obsessive teaching career that she has since abandoned for library work. In addition to writing fantastical and mythic tales, she is involved in the Society for Creative Anachronism. She resides in southern Virginia. This is her first novel.

Also from Lethe Press

Vintage: A Ghost Story
Steve Berman

In a small town, a lonely teen walking along a highway one autumn evening meets the boy of his dreams, a boy who happens to have died decades ago and haunts the road. Awkward crushes, both bitter and sweet, lead him to face not only the ghost but youthful dreams and childish fears. With its cast of offbeat friends, antiques and Ouija boards, Vintage offers readers a memorable blend of dark humor, chills and love that is not your typical teen romance.

A finalist for the Andre Norton Award for Best Young Adult Novel.

Available from local booksellers nationwide, the usual internet sites, and www.lethepressbooks.com

Printed in the United Kingdom by
Lightning Source UK Ltd., Milton Keynes
138620UK00001B/302/P